Owlstones

a tale

Owlstones

a tale

Philip Solem

Owlstones: a tale

Copyright © 2015 Philip Solem. All rights reserved. No part of this book may be reproduced or re-transmitted in any form or by any means without the written permission of the author.

Original edition read serially on KAXE Radio, Grand Rapids, Minnesota, USA in 1988.

Second edition, 2015, revised and published in Riberas del Pilar, Chapala, Jalisco, Mexico and Bovey, Minnesota, USA

ISBN: 978-1511544382

Library of Congress Control Number: 2015907366
CreateSpace Independent Publishing Platform, North Charleston, SC

dedicated to Jacqueline

with love

Caminante, no hay camino,

se hace camino al andar.

--Antonio Machado

CONTENTS

1	Shipwrecks and Other Happenings.......	1
2	Ever a Place So Lovely............................	3
3	In the Judges' Rooms.............................	23
4	Crossing the Border................................	35
5	Behind a Waterfall..................................	43
6	'n Burning Graute...................................	57
7	The March..	72
8	Strange Visitors......................................	82
9	Change of Plans.....................................	93
10	Ravenna Rosealice................................	105
11	Tea for Two...	116
12	Through a Hole in the Wall.................	126
13	Wasoo..	138
14	Wails and Sighs.....................................	148
15	The Watching...	156
16	Meeting...	167
17	Kgopuk by the Fire................................	180
18	Looking for Trouble..............................	193
19	The Sick Lagers.....................................	203
20	Report to Korcha...................................	216

21	Mablic Prison	226
22	Welcome the Dane Recruits	235
23	Snowstorms	242
24	At the Front	258
24	The Final Struggle	270
26	The Battle of Cloverfield	287
27	Journey to the Sea	297
28	Quiet Waters	313
29	The Fall of Brighthome	324
30	Hite's Dogs	357

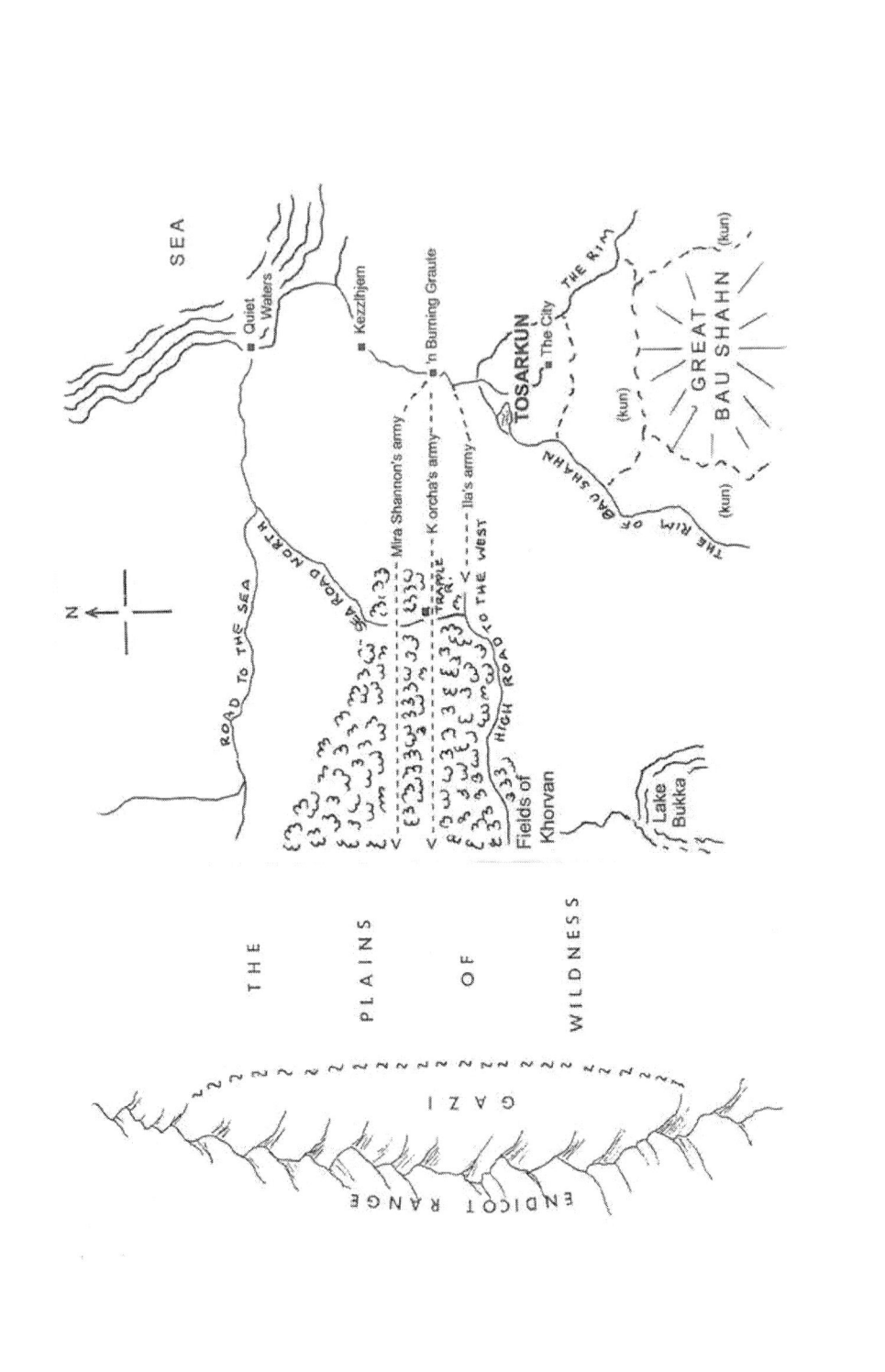

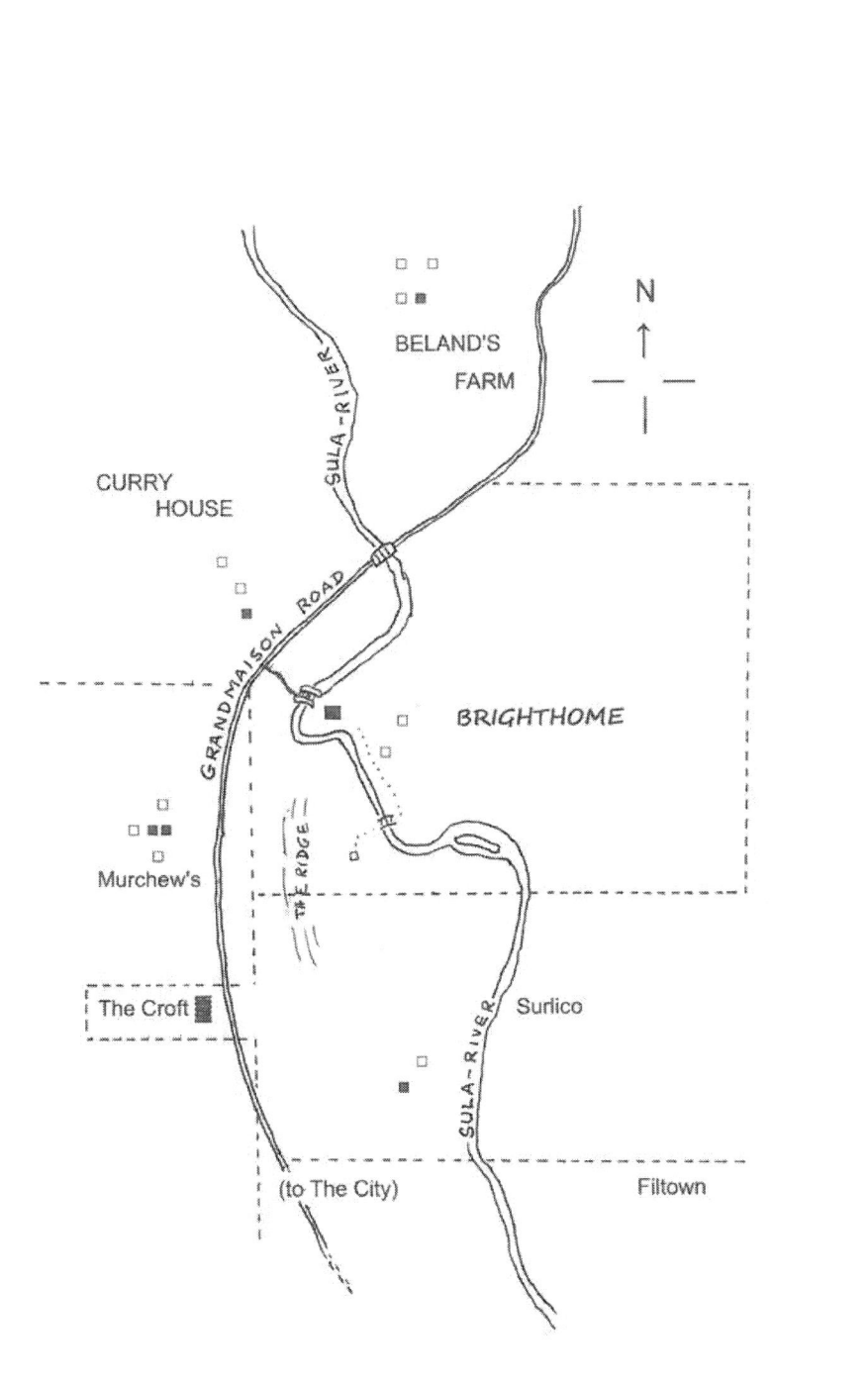

ONE

Shipwrecks and Other Happenings

This tale starts with Nome Ogrodni, who went on many journeys and had many adventures. I could set out right away telling some of them, but my problem is where to begin. It is not so easy to say, "I'll begin at the beginning...," because, you know, there are no beginnings in this life, no real beginnings. We are always in-between, in the midst of something that has been going on.

I can tell some things about Nome, such as who he was, when he lived, and where; but it is not so easy to fit him into our history and our world, because his is a story of what might have been. Surely most of us have reflected on how random and coincidental life seems: "If she had just missed that train...." And so on. How different *everything* might have been, if something, anything, had gone differently! How lives, families, history itself would have taken another course.

Take my great-grandmother, Margaret O'Shea, for example. She came from Ireland when she was sixteen years old, traveling with her aunt and two cousins. Headed for the port of Mobile, they were shipwrecked in a storm. The captain tried to force her to enter a lifeboat as the ship was foundering, but she kicked and screamed and would not get in. She wanted to stick with her aunt and cousins from whom she was being separated. He gave up, leaving her to her foolishness, and tended to other passengers. The lifeboat, by which he had insisted she save herself, disappeared in the storm that day; and all the people in it were drowned. Had she obeyed the captain, who would have married my great-grandfather, who was a Confederate soldier? Would some other woman have borne children with him, instead of being the wife of some other soldier, whose life and offspring would then have been significantly different from what they actually were? In the ripple-effect, would not the very course of The War Between the States been altered in measurable ways? And, from there on, what more? It gets very complicated very quickly. For certain, I would not be here to tell the stories of Nome Ogrodni.

If somewhere back in history, one little event was undone, one meeting had not taken place, everything might have been different; and, in time, people like Nome Ogrodni and Ravenna Rosealice really would have lived; and places like Brighthome and Tosarkun really would have been on our maps. Some things, of course, would be here, no matter how events took place, like owlstones and wythies and other things far more powerful and mysterious—though we call them by different names.

This is a story of how it might have happened. I will begin with that evening when Nome was sitting on The Ridge above Brighthome, ready to play the sun down. What happened there changed his life more sharply than many other things that happened earlier and launched him on his journeys and adventures.

TWO

Ever a Place So Lovely

On summer evenings, after a day of work, Nome Ogrodni would sometimes climb through the woods above his small house to the top of The Ridge, a spine of hill which rose from the forests and fields of Brighthome. There he would watch the western sky and play the sun down on a reed pipe. Sunsets were often spectacular from this spot where the land dropped sharply into a narrow valley and then rose quickly to form a parallel ridge. Along that farther crest ran the Grandmaison Road. This was the main highway from The City in the south, running northward, out past Brighthome and the other rural holdings, past Tamrasset Lake, off beyond the borders of his birth-country, Tosarkun.

Nome had a favorite spot on the high point of The Ridge, a log on which he could sit and lean against the flat of a boulder. Perched there in grasshopperly fashion, heels tucked under and knees shooting out at angles, he would hold the wooden pipe loosely and squint into the fading glory slipping helplessly into some enormous throat at the edge of the earth. He would feel coolness rising up the slopes of the ridge and listen for the breathing, panting, twitching, watchful beings that nestled and rustled about him, ready for sleep.

This was a tall, lanky young man, whose farmworker arms would dangle like cables when he rose from that log with the fluid grace of a good body. His face was narrow and bony, set off by a wave of thick brown hair and dark eyebrows. Below these began a knotty, white scar, which cut savagely from left cheekbone, across the corner of his mouth, to the cleft of his chin. It was the trace of a boyhood game of chieftains and churls, which a group of children had been playing at Aunt Gratchie's Silos the day after school had let out for summer vacation. Beland, one of the boys, had fallen into a rage at the others because he was being forced to be a churl when he felt it was not his turn. Nome had just stepped forward, with the thought of calming Beland by offering to take his place, when he took, instead, a blow from the blade of a hoe the furious boy had swung round his head like a windmill. As Nome grew to manhood, the scar seemed to increase and twist; but the strength of his personality continued to come through his eyes, clear, dark-brown, constant.

The pipe which he held, waiting for the sun to drop a bit more, also came from his childhood. It was a tube of blond, fibrous wood, daintily carved with swirls about the fingerholes and barrel. His grandfather, Manley, had given it to him years ago, saying that it had been carved by his own father, Toohy Ogrodni, before Brighthome ever existed as one of the holdings in Tosarkun. Great-grandfather Toohy had been a legendary pioneer in the region, a fighter of fierce enemies, founder of the Ogrodni ancestral holding, which he named "Brighthome." He was a fashioner of things great, like the magnificent house at the bend of the river, and things small, like this playflute. Nome carried it about in the breast pocket of his work apron. He could not play well, but made his own unrepeatable tunes. Whenever he attempted a standard song, something well known, say, "Washerwoman's Dog" or "Kellybrook, My Home," he skittered and fumbled so badly it was a chore. Playing the sun down, however, he favored long, slow, honeyed notes: goodbye...goodbye...thank you. Come again...again.

There was no traffic along the Grandmaison Road now, of course. From this spot, Nome could look up and down its length for a mile or more. When dusk came, all life seemed to abandon it; and the neighbors of the holdings would be at home with their suppers, their animals, their families. Upriver, at The City, that dismal and dangerous place four-hours ride to the south, the tall gates would be clanging shut for the night. Here in the country, people avoided this official road whenever they could, even during the day. At this late hour, they would certainly use only the backroads and familiar footpaths. There would be no movement on the Grandmaison Road until morning.

Rustling and movement in the grasses hushed; birdsound ceased. In hovering stillness, light upon The Ridge began to change. Trees, bushes, rocks warmed to pale amber, then softened to a golden glow. The sun touched the tip of the tallest pine, almost out of sight at the world's edge. Nome raised the nib to his lips...then paused...and drew it away without a sound.

There was a suggestion of movement on the road. No...yes, a small movement creeping into sight on the left, just coming into view. He held still, watched; and it became clear. A steady movement, now more clearly horse and rider at a good clip. "I wonder if someone's in trouble," he murmured, "someone going for help?" Half-blinded by the half-sun sinking toward darkness, he momentarily recognized the figure: a Tosarman! The horse, the silhouette of flapping greatcoat and distinctive cap-peak. Unusual, very unusual, thought Nome. I've never seen one this late. Riding fast from The City; no doubt on Tosar business to the guarded border crossing into the wild Outlands. Poor fellow has another four-hour ride ahead of him. He's driving that horse too hard. Oh well.

The sun was gone. Nome sat thinking a bit, then slipped the pipe into its pocket without playing a note. He rose and turned to feel for the path to his own little house down below. He thought no more about it.

As we all do, un-gifted as we are at discerning the small events which will change our futures in great ways. In Nome's case: He would never pipe the sun down from this spot again. He would be eating supper in his own cozy house for the last time, sleeping in his bed there for the last night. Without wanting it, he would leave home, become a traveler on the open road, which is no road at all. Without intending it—impossible to imagine—he would profoundly change the fate of his native country. Good thing he knew none of this, for he slept well that night.

....

Tosarkun was a new entity, more a semi-autonomous territory than a nation. When Nome was born there, this state had been in existence fewer than a dozen years. It had been the creation of Lop ge Dol, a hereditary overlord, who also ruled nine similar territories, each also called a *kun*. He ruled from his capital in Great Bau Shahn, which was not one of the *kun* but an independent nation in its own right. Bau Shahn was a powerful hegemon, the beating heart and center of these ten vassal states, packed around it like a hedge. Lop ge Dol did not see this as empire but as fortress. Like his father, Lop ge Liu, and their Lop ancestors for generations, he had no aspirations to absorb and conquer. Bau Shahn's primary value was stasis and continuity, enforced with iron rigor and the awesome efficiency of its Green Troops. Where the Green Troops initially came from, no one seemed to know; for none of them had been drafted from the ten *kun* of the realm. They were used only to maintain order, never for conquest. All that was known was that they were soldiers of Bau Shahn, highly trained, deadly when used. It was said they had never lost a fight. That Lop ge Dol had recently, and with great reluctance, departed from policy in using the Green Troops to conquer and absorb the Tosars on its borders and clamp them to itself as a new *kun* was a rare exception. Such expansion of territory had not been initiated in the previous hundred years.

What prompted it had been seeded three generations back by developments well outside The Rim, which is what Bau Shahn called the outward-facing boundaries of the *kun*. Back, in fact, to the time of Toohy Ogrodni, Nome's great-grandfather. At that time, the Ogrodnis were unorganized freeholders in the Outlands. They clustered just south of Tamrasset Lake with other families and tribal units for economic and protective support and tended to be farmers and crafters. It was then that the Tosars first appeared, coming out of the northeast, a marauding tribe, which roamed the Outlands and lived by preying on pioneering families and undefended settlements. Toohy Ogrodni was building the little house—where his great-grandson, Nome, would one day live—and was just marking out the edges of the holding he called "Brighthome." What would eventually become "The City," capital of Tosarkun, was then only a scruffy village called "Dur" at a fork in the Sula River, just north of Bau Shahn's Rim.

Toohy was an Outlander, of course, and no subject of Bau Shahn. However, he and some of his neighbors had been recruited with pay by its agents to serve as lookouts. A time came when they began to make urgent reports on a large nomadic tribe of people gathering along the northern shores of Tamrasset Lake. What was alarming about them was not only their numbers but their violence. Wherever they had passed, they had left behind smoldering villages and farmsteads, trampled crops, bellowing animals, and blackened corpses. They seemed intent on moving farther south, which would bring them directly over Brighthome, Murchew, Beland's Farm, and dozens of other new holdings. Toohy and the other lookouts tried to rouse the agents of Bau Shahn who employed them and begged that Green Troops be sent out to intercept this advancing horde. Their lookout pay was doubled. They were urged to stay alert and keep their reports coming. But no offer was made to defend them. They came to understand that the policy of Bau Shahn was entirely defensive and that the Green Troops would not engage in matters beyond The Rim.

The Outlanders were on their own. Toohy and his neighbors joined together to resist the enemy, whom they were now calling "the Tosars," after the name of the leading clan family. The freeholders were farmers, not soldiers; but desperation sharpened their wits. By trial and error, they developed what the Tosars eventually called "bandit fighting." As the first ravaging Tosar probes moved south, Outland settlers struck from ambush, moved in circles about the invaders, attacked their rear, and always kept to the woods. They began to organize the settlers all around and taught them to become mobile and evasive and even to withhold or destroy their goods rather than let them fall into the hands of the raiders. They entertained no hope of defeating this experienced enemy but only strove to annoy and tire them, so that this area of plunder might come to cost them dearly and appear not worth their trouble. Perhaps, thought Toohy and his comrades, the Tosars could be aggravated into moving elsewhere, to other unfortunate lands.

It worked, but not in the way planned. Bandit fighting did not tire the Tosars, it enraged them. They surged south in a furious rampage, burning and destroying all they came across. Through Brighthome they passed, and spared Toohy's little house in the woods only because he had disguised all pathways to it. Heavy rains put out forest fires the Tosars tried to set. They raged right up to The Rim itself. That was a mistake. Without warning, the Green Troops of Bau Shahn were upon them, striking viciously from the front and tearing their flanks. The Tosars tried to pull into a circle and make a stand; but, within a day, they were fleeing in panicky, screaming retreat. The Green Troops could have finished them there or pursued them deep into the Outlands; but, instead, they opened an escape corridor on the north and let them run. Such was the defensive style and policy of Bau Shahn.

The Tosars did not go away. Gradually, they gathered again in pain and dismay, far to the north of Tamrasset Lake, in an area of murky bog and forestland. What held them to this area was something that Toohy Ogrodni and the other bandit fighters could not have known about: an internal power struggle within the horde itself. "Tosar" was the name of only one of the families that made up the tribe. A warlord called "The Tosar" ruled all the families: the Obratch, the Klutar, the Zgobrata, and others who had no strong blood relationship to this ruling family. Squabbles, rivalries, disputes among clan leaders, often ending in bloodshed, were common. After the defeat by the Green Troops, a showdown took place. The entire tribe's numbers had been reduced by a third. Most of the families wanted to move on to new territory, where they could continue to raid without resistance. The Tosar overruled them and refused to be driven off. He held them all to that spot. Four clan chiefs died in the ensuing dogfighting before the whole tribe settled into sulking submission. At first, they tried to go on living from raiding; but all human presence had withdrawn from them. For the next generation, they turned to some more honest forms of livelihood. They were not very good at this; and revenge continued to burn in the memories of the Tosar family.

For the freeholders of the Outlands along the Sula River, there was peace. Toohy Ogrodni lived in the little house in the woods with his new wife and his son while he completed Brighthome Manor, the magnificent house full of windows, embraced by a bend in the river. It was the next generation, Nome's grandfather, Manley, with his sisters and brothers and their children all living there, who made the house a wonder to behold. They were glass makers and wood carvers, artists and designers. They added a broad, pillared porch around the entire lower story. The windows were filled with real crystal glass, some etched, some colored. There was light everywhere. The beams, trusses, lintels, handrails were all carved with flourishes, animal forms, flowers and leaves, wise sayings, and occasional jokes—a girl's mischievous face peeping around a pillar, a dog about to lick the face of a sleeping boy. Even the edges of tables were carved, the backs and armrests and rungs of chairs. How these people loved to carve!

Manley's son, Baron, was born here; and the house began to empty, as aunts and uncles moved out to marry into the families of other holdings or establish new holdings of their own. Baron's interests were different from those of his artistically gifted family. He loved the storytelling that took place around fireplaces and supper tables, mostly stories of the old days of Grandfather Toohy and his companions during the Tosar Wars. He loved to play chieftains and churls as a boy; and, as he grew toward manhood, he joined the defense squad that met and trained at The Croft. He did not carve wood, but he spent much time working wood and metal into useful shapes with heft and sharpness that could be thrown or sent flying. Yet there was a soft side to Baron. He loved Rena. Loved her with all his heart. His mother had died; his father, Manley, was dying now. When that was over, he would be holding-master, and he wanted, more than anything, to bring Rena into Brighthome.

That would have to wait. News was arriving, with alarming frequency, of raids on holdings not far to the north of the lake. The Tosars were moving—slowly, cautiously. Baron Ogrodni was the first to rouse the neighborhood and to organize immediate preparations for resistance. He and many of the young men and women of his age had been studying and drilling in the strategies of bandit fighting for years, anticipating this moment. Baron left Brighthome with many of his neighbors to live a wandering life in the woods, weeks before the Tosars reached the northern shore of Tamrasset Lake. For three years they struggled with this angry enemy, delaying and obstructing them without ever engaging in direct battle.

History repeated. Eventually, maddened at swatting these bandit-fighting flies, The Tosar ordered a two-day lightning-strike on all holdings south of the lake. The order was this: spare all property for Tosar use after victory, but extinguish all resisting human life. The bandit fighters had been expecting something like this and had advance notice of its timing. Tosars lunged south and swarmed the holdings all along the eastern shores of Tamrasset Lake and beyond. Their two-day assault took only a single day; for the only life found in the holdings were animals in their stalls, coops, and corrals. The population had evacuated. Furiously, they bore upriver to the worthless village of Dur and put it to the torch, then raged on over the southern holdings. Lop ge

Dol, the Nur of Bau Shahn, did not allow them to reach The Rim. This great sleeping dog rose up, seized the yapping dog by the neck, and shook! Green Troops were upon them from all sides; and, this time, they were not allowed to flee. Holding the Tosars down with one hand, Lop ge Dol reached out his other and drew The Rim around them. He drew it around the smoldering village of Dur, around Brighthome and all the other lovely holdings of the countryside, around Tamrasset Lake, and called this new land "Tosarkun." By that same formula which bound the other *kun* of this realm, Lop ge Dol tamed the wild and reckless Tosar, now captive and afraid.

The first thing Bau Shahn did was create a diarchy, with two powers-at-odds in rule. The Tosar was confirmed in authority as autocrat of the land. However, his old nemesis, the Obratch family, was established as locus of Judges, whose agreements were required for all acts of governing. This tension was then triangulated by a rescript granting a single-generation amnesty to their enemies, the former freehold Outlanders—specifically naming the bandit-fighting leaders, such as Ogrodni, Fann, Potoftok, Murchew, Beland, and others.

Bau Shahn realized that the Tosars and Obratch knew nothing about governing, so it used the occupying presence of the Green Troops to teach them. The Tosars were put to work building city walls, a high, stone Keep from which they would rule, and streets for The City, where Dur had stood. They were also forced to build Judges' Rooms, a two-story blockish quadrangle with spiky ornamental towers at each corner. This domain of the Obratch was located on a long, narrow island within the city walls where the Sula River forked and then rejoined to flow on northward. The commanders of the Green Troops schooled them both in the meaning of law, order, and the purposes of governance. Anyone appointed to a Judge position had to be literate or to become so. Tosars and Judges were drilled on what Bau Shahn allowed and did not allow. The freeholders were left alone; but, first, they were informed who their new masters were and what could be expected from them. This education in civilization took a long time—several years of occupation by the Green Troops. It was the taming of a wild group, the making of a *kun*.

So now the Tosars, who favored brutality, were in charge; yet they needed the agreement of the Obratch to govern. Only once, after the

Green Troops were withdrawn, did each side test the delicate arrangement by trying to eliminate the other. The Tosar, first, issued some decrees without the seal of the Judges, dissolved the Court, and ordered a halt to the finishing of Judges' Rooms. No one reported any disturbance at Tosar's Keep that night. In fact, it was said to have been a quiet night. However, in the morning, residents of The City were staring open-mouthed at the corpse of The Tosar himself twirling upside-down in the breeze from the archway at the entrance to the Keep. Before a new Tosar could be designated, the Judges issued edicts on their own authority, declaring the *kun* divided into two administrative districts, one governed by the Obratch. Again, it was said to have been a quiet night in Judges' Rooms. In the morning the three High Judges seemed to have been misplaced. They were never found.

After that, Tosarkun found its way toward becoming a peaceful and orderly country. That is not to say a pleasant one; for its diarchial rule was harsh and fear-inspired. People who lived in the northern holdings, not far from The Rim, were less bothered by Tosar Guards, as long as they avoided the Grandmaison Road. Seldom did the graycoats enter these holdings along that Road. People who lived in or near The City appeared to cower and sulk and were frequently subjected to arbitrary harassment. The Tosar held absolute power over the life or death of any subject; but exercising it could not be arbitrary, and required full cooperation from the Judges.

....

When the sun rose the next morning, it promised beautiful weather. Nome stepped from the front door of his little house and took deep breaths of the cool air. Pushing shut the bottom of the half-door behind him to keep the goat out, he strolled among the circle of flowering fruit trees that ringed his yard. Three sheep were munching among wildflowers. He whistled a vague tune, but couldn't quite catch a melody. At the far end of the yard, he turned to look back at the solid little house to see if there was anything needing repair or upkeep. Over a hundred years old, he thought, square beams, stucco and half-timber, odd-shaped windows, friendly chimney poking from the roof.

He walked back across the open yard, ready for breakfast, his favorite meal of the day. He liked it, especially, because it was a slow time before work, a quiet time; and today he would enjoy taking extra care in preparing golden-fried eggs, wheatcakes, plumsauce and a smoking mug of khavla. He would eat at his kitchen table alongside the open window, looking out at the early flowers on this spring morning. Today was a holiday, no fieldwork today.

He might have gone up to the big house and eaten with his parents; but he relished this time alone and would go up there to join them for the after-breakfast later. Baron, his father, had declared a holiday for the family and for their holding-helper families who lived in three cottages off near the far edges of the fields. No farmwork today for any of the men and women of Brighthome; no school for the children. Only rest and feasting; and, later, the regular Croft meeting with other holdings-folk and more food and songs and play.

His father, usually so silent, had come to him at lunch-break several weeks ago, flapping a letter, talkative and childlike with glee. Two old friends had written that they would be traveling across the Outlands in the vicinity of Tosarkun soon and wanted to stop by and spend a few days visiting their former comrade-in-arms, Baron Ogrodni. They had already received a written permit to enter the *kun*.

"A holiday!" Baron had shouted. "A holiday for everyone when they come! *Those two!* How did they *ever* manage that?"

Fa seldom talked about the past; but the day the letter came, he talked with fervor about Burton and Mardek, who had been "like brothers" to him. Nome had snatched at the opportunity and tried to pry the rest of the story out of his father, to no avail. All he got was a wink and an invitation to spend the day at the house with them when Burton and Mardek arrived.

"Let the fieldwork go for a day, Nome," he had said with shining eyes. "I'll see that your mother cooks a chicken dinner, the best you've ever tasted. It'll be worth your while to come!"

....

A broad path led from Nome's little house to the Grandmaison Road, but he seldom went that way. He always preferred the narrower path through the woods, crossing the river, into the open fields around the house of Baron and Rena Ogrodni, where he had grown up. He walked slowly this morning, feeling the pleasant weight of breakfast and the gentle brush of sunlight falling in patches through the new oak and basswood leaves. This path was lovely in all seasons—in autumn, like a walk in cool fire, in winter, clean and still with a quilt of snow on the ground and white light through black trees. Now, in late spring, all life was returning. He stopped on the wooden footbridge, which crossed the Sula River, and watched the swift, swollen current from The City pass under him and onward, toward more northern holdings and Tamrasset Lake .

"Was there ever a place so lovely?" he said aloud. "Brighthome. Well-named." Turning about where he stood, he gestured with an open hand, sweeping his arm toward the woods, bowed, and smiled.

Thinking about his boyhood days spent around this river, he continued walking and soon came to the open fields, where the big house came into view. It had been built on a gentle rise, hugged close by a wide bend in the river, and surrounded across both banks by a random orchard. It, too, was built of half-timber and stucco; but Brighthome stood apart from all other holding-houses in the prodigality of its window glass and the extravagance of an encircling porch. A dozen chimneys sprouted from the tile roof, clearly a house of many rooms and warm hearths.

As Nome walked through the ring of fruit trees toward the house, he was surprised to see no one sitting on the porch. They must have finished breakfast by now, he thought. On such a beautiful morning, they should be outside. He had imagined himself approaching—three old men sitting about on rockers, laughing, talking about old times, smoking pipes. He had pictured Mo standing at the railing, smiling and waving, as he came to them through the apple trees, his father rising stiffly and coming forward to take him by the arm to meet his old friends, who would rise, politely remove their pipes, and bow and nod with smiling faces....

All was still. For a moment, he wondered if the guests had arrived late last night and, tired from their travels, were still sleeping. What if they had not arrived at all! The top half of the front door was open wide, so he knew his parents were up and about.

He walked up onto the porch, leaned over the bottom door, and called, "Mo! Fa! Hello! It's me!"

A moment of silence, then his mother came around the corner into the entry hall with light, quick steps, obviously glad to see him. But, even as she moved her wrinkled face toward him, in the second before she kissed him over the half-door, he knew that there was trouble.

"Didn't Fa's friends come?"

"Oh, yes," she said brightly, "they're here. Come on in. We've just finished breakfast and are sitting around talking. Come on."

"Wait, Mo," he insisted, catching her hand, as she turned to go back where she had come from. "What's wrong? Has something happened?"

She let herself be stopped but stayed looking away, holding the pose for a moment like a mannequin in long, soft, flowered dress, her snowy hair braided into a crown around a single, high, lacquered comb. Then she wilted. Slowly turning back, she looked at him for a long moment and let him see her sadness.

"Yes, Nome. We've had some news."

"What news?"

"Please, not here. I don't want to tell you here. Come in with your Fa. I want to be with him. We will tell you in there."

"Is he all right?" asked Nome with a sudden stab of fear.

"He's fine. There's nothing wrong with him. Come on." She tugged at his hand.

They entered a dining room with floor-to-ceiling windows looking out on the prettiest part of the orchard. A round polished table was strewn with the ruins of breakfast; and three old men sat hunched together there, leaning on their elbows, talking in subdued tones. One of them looked up, then rose. Baron Ogrodni's crinkled face had been shadowed in troubled conversation as Nome and his mother entered; but now he came forward smiling to kiss his son. His white, windblown hair floated about as he moved. He had not dressed for the occasion, as Rena had, but wore his usual long leather work apron. He took Nome by the arm to meet his friends.

Burton and Mardek rose and bowed, nodded and smiled, as they each took one of his hands. He nodded, bowed, and smiled in return. Burton was a short man, who stood erect as though raising himself higher. He had a full head of reddish hair that showed only flecks of gray; but his sagging jowls and the orange blotches on the backs of his hands showed him to be Baron's age. His lively eyes were full of good humor; his handclasp was steel-hard, in the manner of an old man demonstrating his grip. His companion was very different. Mardek was a wheezing, bald fellow with an ungainly stoop. He reminded Nome of an old farm dog, endlessly friendly, wagging and humble. His handclasp was a series of short, affectionate squeezes. In Nome's mind, their brown and gray shirts and pants marked them as Outlanders, of what country he had no idea.

When all were seated, Baron began to talk with eagerness about his friends' arrival, about his son, about Nome's little house across the river. Mo brought a fresh pitcher of khavla and another plate of date cakes to add to the other plate of breads, tarts, and biscuits. The two guests looked at her reproachfully and leaned away from the table holding their sides. Nome accepted a mug of khavla, but kept his eyes on his father. He had never seen him so animated and talkative. He glanced with awe at these smiling, nodding visitors, mysterious with age, who were such welcome and enlivening influence in their home. Could it be that these two had brought some terrible news? It certainly did not seem so. He looked at his mother, who sat in a stately pose with hands folded on the table, her polite smile saying nothing.

After a few moments she interrupted. "Nome knows there is trouble, Baron. I only told him we have had some news."

The old man looked surprised. Then he continued in the same lively manner, "Yes, we have had news, Nome, and bad news it is. Although not the worst of news by any means. I've seen and heard worse news than this, by far, in my days; and so have these two, for certain." He laughed and looked at his friends, who grinned and swayed in their chairs, looking down at their laps, and rubbing their knees.

"But it is *hard* news!" Rena insisted irritably. "Very sad news for all of us. About Brighthome. Don't make light of it, Baron!"

"Oh, yes, it is bad news," said Baron agreeably. "I won't deny that. I don't like hearing it and I don't like telling it."

"Well, what is it?" cried Nome. "Do you men bring information from the Outlands...?"

Burton and Mardek sat back with surprise.

"Oh no, not them!" his father said quickly. "They've had nothing to do with it. This news came last night by messenger about an hour after they arrived. They were just getting settled...."

The blood went from Nome's face. "The Tosar's horseman!" he

whispered.

"Why yes," his mother said. "How did you know? Did you see him?"

"I did. On the Grandmaison Road. At sundown."

"That was he," said his father. "Well, now, he came right here, spoke not a word, handed us a paper and was off."

"Here, let me tell it!" broke in his mother. "You'll get only the short version from your father, as you well know. It was remarkable the way it happened."

She told the details. The sudden clatter of horse's hooves on the wooden bridge as they had just come onto the porch at dusk in order to bring the travel packs in. How a Tosar Guard burst into the yard and reined up hard, sat looking down at each of them, one after the other, slowly, not a word. How he reached into his greatcoat...and she screamed at what she took to be a weapon...but it was a piece of paper! which he trust toward Baron, recognizing him at once. How he wheeled the horse about and was gone.

For a while they all sat silent. Rena nervously cleared her throat and offered more khavla, more datecakes? None of the men responded.

"Yes, now there's something else," Baron said at length. Some of his breezy manner had gone. "He went on to at least two other places last night, Curry House and Beland's Farm. Your friend, Curry, came running over here early this morning to tell us. So I told him to get word to as many of the holdings as he can that we've got to have a full council at the Croft tonight. Instead of the party we thought we were going to have. Time is very short now. We have to get everyone together to discuss *this.*"

He pushed toward Nome an unfolded paper, which had been lying at the center of the table amid the breakfast dishes. Nome hesitated. His father nodded toward the paper, then, "It says we are going to lose Brighthome. The Tosars mean to have it."

Nome slowly took up the thick paper. At the top of the page stood the emblem of Tosar's Keep, a two-towered stronghold above the horizontal image of a falx, the long-handled, straightened scythe-blade with a downward-curving point, carried by every Tosarman. At the bottom of the page was the confirming seal of the Judges. Between them was a neat block of text:

"AN EXECUTIVE ACT by the Tosars, unanimous and uniform in their agreement. Affirmed and ordered by The Tosar. Decreed and published in this document and duly recorded in exact copy by the Registrar Clerk at Tosar's Keep this twenty-second day of Munden of the year Three Hundred Forty-second of the Period Second of Great Bau Shahn.

"*It is noted that* one Baron Ogrodni, currently habitant in Tosarkun, did, from the ninth day of Meeden of the year Three Hundred and Six until the fifteenth day of Ronden of the year Three Hundred and Nine, offer real and heinous offense to the Tosars and did commit a series of treasonous and seditious acts and did urge, aid, abet, counsel and instruct others to commit treasonous and seditious acts against their dignity, right, claim and purpose, as detailed, noted, described and documented in Ledgers of Criminal Offenses, Number 162, Ac3 at Tosar's Keep.

"*It is noted that* said offenses by Baron Ogrodni were committed before the year Three Hundred and Ten, in which year the Tosars were confirmed in Authority and Sovereignty over the territory of Tosarkun by Rescript of the Nur of Bau Shahn, Lop ge Dol.

"*It is noted that* said Baron Ogrodni was granted Amnesty for his real, heinous, seditious, treasonous and unseemly offenses in said Rescript.

"*It is noted that* said Amnesty has expired, the statutory period of generational thirty years limitation from the granting thereof having been completed.

"*It is decided that,* in justice and mercy, a penalty be levied upon Baron Ogrodni and upon all that immediately belong to him to the intent that his holding, denoted by private usage 'Brighthome,' staked and recorded in Ledgers of Plats, Properties, and Holdings, Number 14 Nz4, at Tosar's Keep, be forfeit and devolve to the possession of the Tosars, or an equivalent currency amount to be rendered forthwith or in keeping with a schedule to be fixed at Judges' Rooms.

"*Ratified, approved, sealed and confirmed.*"

Then followed the Judges' Seal, a sun radiant, with intricate words and images upon its face, pressed into the texture of the paper, overlapping a generous daub of red sealing wax.

Nome looked up dumbfounded and glanced from face to face. They waited for him to speak.

He tossed the paper onto the table and gestured helplessly toward it.

Burton spoke. "Of course. You have questions and objections. As did we." He leaned back in his chair. "The four of us have had a chance to talk about this all evening and to sleep on it. We've been talking of nothing else all through this glorious breakfast. But now we need a fresh pair of eyes. What are your first impressions, Nome?"

"Well, I...I don't know where to begin! I mean...this is terrible!"

"Yes. It is terrible," said his mother, pursing her lips.

"And I don't understand...," he seized the document again with both hands and scanned. "I understand it says we lose Brighthome to the Tosars.... But then it says...let's see...it says this is going to happen right away...and then, down here, it says it may not happen right away...something about a schedule.... Doesn't make...and then here, Fa, it says you were given amnesty for going against the Tosars in the old days, and then you have lost...*lost?*...this amnesty? What is that about? I mean, how can you lose am.....? It just doesn't..."

"No, it doesn't make sense," said Burton. "Not common sense. But it makes law. You must try to find out what sense it makes not to you but to the Tosars and to the Judges. Because what they mean by it will happen."

"Isn't there anything we can do?" pleaded Nome. "Where would we go?"

Baron scowled. "What kind of talk is that! You've just read this scrap of paper and already you are wanting to give up?"

Nome looked at his father in bewilderment and fear. Like a scolded schoolboy, he squinted at the paper again to see what he had missed.

"Well," he began cautiously, "It says, Fa, that you committed a series of offenses...."

"That I did," agreed his father in a lighter tone; and his friends laughed aloud.

"...and that the offenses took place before the Tosars came to power. But how could that be treason? Or sedition? This was all still Outlands, right? Anyway...."

"Here!" His mother sharply slapped the table in annoyance, looking sternly at the men. "We have no *time* for this! It is pointless and unkind to make him grope along in this fashion when we have had all night and morning to worry ourselves with the meaning of this edict. Nome, a glance at the document says it all: Tosar's Keep at the top, Judges' Seal at the bottom. Their everlasting power-squabble throughout the words in-between. Tosars say, 'Time to get revenge on Ogrodni. We seize his holding, take his home, and drive his family out.' Judges say, 'Remember who rules this country! Not *just* the Tosar family; the Obratch co-rule.' The Obratch, as Judges, control the wording and assert their authority by a challenge: 'Maybe you get Brighthome now...maybe we make you wait a bit.' Whom do they make look silly in this document? The Tosars, with their talk of retroactive treason, expired amnesty, and their stipulation that the seizure of Brighthome can happen in three different ways: Tosars might get the holding immediately...or the *cash value* of the holding immediately...or the cash value paid on some kind of *schedule*...to be established at Judges' Rooms, naturally."

"So, if I am following this," said Nome, "there might be some leeway for us in this last part about 'equivalent currency' and 'schedule to be fixed...' What could that mean?"

"That is the part," said his father, "we are *least* clear about. We are not sure what that means. Equivalent currency *might* mean full cash value. Pay them the cash value of Brighthome, whatever that might be, and we can keep it. Buy Brighthome from them, maybe? (He chuckled.) 'Forthwith' sounds like 'pay right now.' 'Schedule'....mmm....I don't know. Sounds like 'in a while...later.' I just don't know."

"You think there is any hope for us in all this, Fa?"

"No," said his mother.

"I wouldn't be so quick to say that, Rena," he answered quietly.

His mother went on, "We have different ideas about this among us. Baron is more hopeful than I that we can do something with the Judges' garble. I know he has more experience than I in dealing with these...these.... But in this case, with the intention being so clear, and the same thing happening to our neighbors...I just can't see it."

"I'm not suggesting," said Baron, "that the Judges are fair and reasonable or that we can appeal to their sense of justice. But I have been thinking that there may be some opening for us in the political tension this document indicates. Or seems to, anyway. The Tosars are wanting to seize several holdings, as we heard from Curry this morning. The Judges have certainly worded these documents to make it complicated for them. Curry showed me the one they got last night; it's nearly the same thing. I wonder what is going on down there. Maybe we can look for a tiny crack in the masonry...sometimes, if you find such a crack...just enough to get the tip of your pocket knife in...."

Mardek winked at Burton and grinned.

"Why do you think the Tosars want Brighthome and the other holdings?" asked Nome. "And why now?"

Mardek spoke up again. "We have lots of theories about that. And, if they are not enough for you, sir, I am sure we could invite in a few of the neighbors for some more. But, the short of it is that we don't know. No one knows much about the plans and purposes of Tosar's Keep."

"And it doesn't really matter," added Burton. "What is real for you, my friends, is that the document is here on your table. The plans of the Tosars won't be discerned by a closer reading of this paper. Did you notice that their laughable thirty-year statute of limitations on amnesty actually was up two years ago? Why did they not act then? Who knows?"

"I am not so sure it doesn't matter," Baron objected. "I agree that we don't know why the Tosars want these holdings now. But their intentions may matter in the outcome, and perhaps we can learn something about them when Nome goes to talk to the Judges today."

"What?" his son shouted at him. The others gaped at him.

"Oh yes," he said matter-of-factly. "You were asking aways back what we could do about this terrible news. Well, of course, my boy, *that* was the real question. What can we do? We could whimper, fight, run, wait, burn Brighthome to keep it from them. But it seems to me that the place to begin would be the Judges' obscure invitation to talk with them about 'equivalent currency' and 'schedule.' You put your finger right on it, Nome. If Brighthome is to be your future, it seems to me you should go down there and see if they will talk to you about a 'schedule of currency.'"

"But they can't mean that," said Burton, astonished at the suggestion. "They can't be serious about letting you foil the Tosars in any effective way!"

"You wouldn't think so," answered Baron thoughtfully. "But we don't know what is going on, and we need information...and we need time. And we need both *quickly*! That's why I said Nome should go today."

"But, Fa! Why me? How would I know how to talk to Judges, how to find them, get admitted? I've only been in The City a few times in my whole life! The *Judges*! I should think if anyone is to go it would be *you*! This is all about *you*!"

"Good," he answered. "You're right, there are other options. I could go. Or your mother, or Curry or Beland. Let's talk about that now."

They did. The discussion was short. It was clear that, despite his show of reasonableness, the show was mostly ironic. He had been all over this in his mind and had decided that a visit to the Judges' Rooms by Nome was the action needed.

Tired and worried, the others finally yielded to his intuition, his experience, his stubbornness, or whatever it was that lay behind his argument...and his decision.

They got up from the table, stretching their limbs. It had been a long after-breakfast; and everyone needed to move about, get some relief, go out for air. Burton and Mardek were craving to light their pipes on the front porch. Nome followed them on his way to the barn to saddle the horse. Rena and Baron cleared the dishes.

Nome lingered on the porch with the two old men, who were now blissfully pulling on their pipes.

"One thing in there surprised me, my man," said Burton, squinting sideways at Nome through the smoke.

"Only one?" he laughed. "What was it?"

" Do you not know your father's quarrel with the Tosars? Has he never talked about the old days?"

"Almost never. My parents, like everyone around here, have raised us to know it is not safe to be talking about the old days before Tosarkun. And of course, it was not allowed at school. You know my father, how silent he can be, anyway. Why? Is there something you can tell me, Burton?"

"And your Mother?"

"Mo doesn't like to talk about those days. She just doesn't. She's told me a bit about Fa, when they met, and then when they had to wait for years. But not much. And she, especially, does not like us talking about it. Frightens her. Can you tell me anything?"

The old man looked down at the planks and smoked for a moment.

"Well, I suppose not," he said, as though thinking to himself. "Old Baron was never much of a talker. I thought, perhaps with his family....but then, I guess a man is what he is. I guess we saw that in there," said Burton looking sharply up at Nome.

"Tell me," said Mardek to Nome, "have you never heard the ballad called *The Stewart's Tale?*"

"Why, yes," said Nome, taken aback at the sudden lurch in the conversation. "Everyone knows it. I've sung it often as a boy with the other boys. Sometimes at the Croft the women and men sing it. Although, we are told to be caref..."

"And what about *Ride Again, Woldman, Ride?*" Mardek peered at him intently.

"Yes. That one, too."

The two men looked at him in silence. Solemnly, Burton removed the pipe from his mouth.

"They are about your father," he said quietly.

Nome stood as though struck. His face went white, and he gaped at them.

"Now go on your errand, man," said Burton, taking him by the arm and turning him away from the house. Nome's lips began to form silent words, but Burton cut him off.

"Not now. Time is everything to you now. We have done wrong to detain you with further conversation."

"But...."

"Not now. Another time. Be on your way, you have an important work. Go!"

Nome began to walk toward the line of fruit trees. He slowed and looked back...and heard:

"Another time. Go!"

THREE

In the Judges' Rooms

It was a good four-hour ride up the Grandmaison Road to The City, but Nome would have to make it more quickly to avoid being shut in when the gates closed for the night at sundown. He had been to The City several times, but had never spent a night there; and the thought of doing so now was chilling. His father had come to him at the barn while he was saddling his horse, Chalky, and instructed him, to the best of his own ability, on how to pass the main city gate, find his way to Judges' Rooms, request entry and directions, what courtesies (if they could be called that) he should employ in addressing anyone there. Baron himself had never been inside Judges' Rooms, but he had often talked to others who had been. He directed Nome not to keep the confiscation document they had received on his person as he traveled; for he would undoubtedly be meeting Tosar Guards on his way to The City; and it would not be surprising for them to stop him and order him to show his papers. It would not do for them to be handed this one. Nome tucked it into a slit in the saddle leather. Baron reminded him of the proper behavior when meeting Guards on the Road. Finally, he urged Nome to leave The City before sundown, no matter the status of his efforts, and report to him at the Croft that evening as soon as he could get there.

Riding Chalky along this well-maintained road, past sunny farm fields, just planted, through dark evergreen tunnels, would have been pleasant under a different circumstance. There was an occasional inn and a few village rest places; but these were sad-looking places, worn, clearly not prosperous. He met very few other travelers, only those with oxcarts or horse wagons pulling manure, equipment, or covered goods for barter. He worked to keep his mind on maintaining Chalky at a quick, even pace; for his anxious mind wanted to strain forward in fear toward the Judges, and his bewildered mind wanted to work backward to understand what he had just learned about his father.

Here came a platoon of Tosar Guards, four abreast, two behind, all graycoats. Each of the front four carried a sheathed falx hanging from his belt and two more falces strapped on either side of the saddle horn. Only the two behind had longbows across their backs and had quivers, instead of falces, strapped on either side of their saddles. Nome appropriately reined Chalky to a stop, dismounted, and stood in the tall grass at the side of the road, eyes to the ground, holding his horse. The platoon slowly passed by. He had no idea whether they had even looked at him.

He went on and reached the city gates by early afternoon. Not bothering to eat anything, he passed through the high city walls by the main gate, after answering to the Guards posted there. He could see the Keep ahead, rising darkly over the rooftops of buildings before him; so he moved toward the left, and eastward, through a warren of twisting streets. His only instructions had been to thread his way until he came to the Sula River and then to follow the river streets upstream to the bridge crossing to the islet on which Judges' Rooms stood. This he did, until he found himself in an open square before the main portal of a brown, blockish, two-story building with tiny windows and spiky towers at each corner. He was surprised to find three corrals where petitioners could leave horses for a fee, and to be told that the first two he approached were full. At the third, however, Chalky was let in, secured, watered, and fed. Nome paid the fee and said he would return well before sundown. It worried him to think that Judges' Rooms might be so busy and that he had arrived so late.

Once inside, there was no way to know where to go. The cramped entrance lobby opened onto a maze of stairways and hallways with little signage and no information panels. There were, however, many people coming and going. A few appeared to be officials in brown uniform— high collar, black belt, black boots—carrying sheaves of paper, walking quickly, with serious faces to discourage interruption. The others were ordinary people like himself, some with children in tow, city folk, country folk, moving slowly and uncertainly, whispering, scanning for letters or numbers on door plates. Nome tried to ask the brisk officials where he might get information but was ignored. Once or twice, someone simply pointed and kept moving. What was striking was how silent this very large, honeycombed, building was. There were only the sounds of people moving, papers shuffled.

He randomly chose a hallway and walked down, then a flight of stairs and walked up. Here the hall was wider and seemed more important, so he began asking questions of anyone in brown uniform.

"Excuse me sir?" he said at a doorway. "I've received this notice from the Keep? About our holding? And it says...."

"Not here. Try References. Down th' hall, a right."

A few moments later: "Excuse me, please. I have this paper from Tosar's Keep? And I'm supposed to..."

"Wrong office. This is References."

"Yes, well, could you tell me...."

"Try Land Rights. Left, down the hall."

"I just came from Land Rights. They told me...."

"Try Conveyance. Right then right again.."

Once again: "Excuse me...."

"There's others ahead of you. Leave your name and take a seat."

He left his name, took a seat, noticed no one else around to be ahead of him, noticed that no one looked at the paper where he had left his name, waited some more, got up, left. He wandered on, filled out some forms, was told to go home and return the next day with certain missing information, was sent to other offices to fill out more forms. He was looking at the crown of a man's head and watching the pen scurry inches below the man's nose. Suddenly, Nome banged his fist down on the desk and saw the pen stab a wound across the page.

"I've been called here by the Judges!" he shouted at the top of the man's head.

It jarred something loose. The clerk actually darted a glance at him, then scuttled around the desk, seized the Tosar's document from Nome's hand, and led him down the hall, down a stairway, down another hall, around a corner to a room marked "Judges' Hearing" and knocked. They waited a long time. The door opened; and the man, who had led him there, silently handed in the Tosar's document, then backed away and disappeared the way they had come. Nome stepped into a small waiting room with benches along the wall and only a few people waiting. They were keeping as much space between one another as possible. He picked a spot on the emptiest part of the bench and sat.

For the next two hours, he watched people disappear, as names were called by clerks leaning through a door opposite. There were no windows here; and there had been none in the halls he had wandered; so Nome had no idea how far along the day had advanced. He consoled himself with the thought that this was the time of year when days were longest and sundown came latest; but he had not seen the sun, or even a shadow, since he had left Chalky outside in the square. Suddenly "Ogrodni!" was screeched by an old man standing in the doorway, clutching a sheaf of papers to his chest like a pain.

Nome had been picturing a courtroom with rows of benches facing a raised Judge's bench and side tables for clerks and counsel. As he passed through the doorway, he became weak. It was a large office. Opposite, three High Judges sat at a massive conference table. Angling away from each end of it were long, plain work-tables, seating ten Minor Judges, five on either side. There were no windows to the room. There was no ornament, no fabric. The room was silent, except for the scratching of pen-points and rustling of paper. No one looked at him. The clerk who had led him in had abandoned him standing at the middle of the room. Nome realized, with a hollow, sinking feeling, that he did not have the document anymore.

Eventually, the High Judge in the middle slowly adjusted her shapeless brown robe, took up a paper, and peered past it at Nome with an expression of distaste. It was the first time anyone in the room had looked at him, but suddenly all eyes were on him. The High Judge's face was sharp and ashen, with purple sags beneath her eyes. She looked ill and angry. The other faces about her were expressionless. As she slowly spoke, her lips seemed to stick together.

"Ogrodni, Nome. We have your appeal concerning this matter of holdings named Ogrodni, Curry, and Beland."

Nome was bewildered. Earlier, he had filled out a form entitled "Appeal," but nowhere had he mentioned Curry House or Beland's Farm.

"Yes, Your Hon...Your Lord...Ye-yes..."

"You have received notice concerning the surrender of these properties?"

"Yes."

"Well?" There was a long silence. She glared at him with malice.

"Uhh...there was mention in the notice we received about other terms...."

"You wish to pay the equivalent currency of these properties?"

"I...uhh...." He was finding it hard to breathe.

"Do you take us for cashiers?" she raised her voice without a glint of humor.

Nome was sinking. Across his mind floated an image of himself slumping to the floor and scuttling backward out the door. He wanted to bow his head and slide into helplessness, but he knew that the moment for which he had come was before him. Taking a long, slow breath, he straightened his back and carefully looked from face to face, beginning at one end of the row of Judges and sweeping across to the other. The High Judge's face was beginning to twitch with impatience at the delay. When he spoke, Nome's voice was lower and steady.

"I am sorry, I do not know how to address you. I have not been told. Your Honor? Is that the correct form of address? We do not wish to surrender our holding, and we do not have money for the cash value at present. I do not know what the cash value of Brighthome would be now, but I am sure it would be very high. And I know even less about the value of the other holdings you mentioned."

The stony expressions on all sides gave no encouragement. He continued.

"A document was handed to us last night. I believe you have it there, Your Honor. It mentions some alternatives. I have come to ask for these."

"What are you talking about?" she snapped.

"I don't have the wording exactly in mind, Ma'am...Your Honor (excuse me). You have the paper there before you, I believe? The part about 'a schedule of payment to be established at Judges' Rooms.' I have come to ask about that."

She continued to stare at him as though she waited for more...as though this were the stupidest thing she had ever heard.

Then she turned abruptly and began whispering to the Judge on her right. The Judge on her left leaned across to join them. Again Nome found himself ignored. The whispering continued, spreading to the Judges at the side tables and to clerks and pages who were called forward and sent from the room to fetch papers. He felt relief and used these moments to pull together his thoughts and prepare an argument. This was unnecessary. As quickly as it began, the commotion stopped, and attention was back on Nome. The High Judge raised a sheet of paper before her face and pronounced:

"We have decided that the immediate foreclosure execution upon properties denoted 'Ogrodni, Curry and Beland' be deferred, on condition that the currency equivalent be rendered to the Tosars at Tosar's Keep, in accumulating increments, in amounts and upon a schedule to be set forth herewith, the initial amount to be rendered at Tosar's Keep one day from the proclamation of this decision. It is further decided that the foreclosure of the holdings of Gamgame, Surlico, Filtown, and Surd shall not be deferred but shall stand in effect forthwith."

On and on she read for a full five minutes, from a document obviously prepared ahead of time. Nome could not absorb the details, but he understood the main points. Brighthome, Curry House, and Beland's Farm were safe as long as substantial payments were made on time. The first payment on these three was due tomorrow, and it was a shock to hear the amount required. A schedule of future due-dates for that same amount was set out at "hundred-day" intervals. But the most crippling specification was this: The current owners of the three holdings were prohibited from using the assets of the holdings to raise the monies to be paid at the end of each hundred-day. They could sell neither parcels of the land nor farm equipment nor its produce to raise these monies. They could not sell animals or buildings. To do so, it was stipulated, would be to use up the Tosar's eventual property and assets and lower its value in order to pay their own debt to the Tosars. It was a schedule designed for the gradual impoverishment and collapse of the debtors.

Nome was dismissed. As the ancient clerk led him out, another handed him the original Tosar's order and the new three rescripts from Judges' Rooms with instructions to deliver two of them to Curry House and Beland's Farm. No mention was made of Gamgame, Surlico, Filtown, and Surd; and for that he was grateful.

....

The sun was setting when he rode past the forlorn holding of Surd. Only at Surlico was there any sign of activity, a wagon loaded with furniture and household goods. Nome did not stop. Fa had told him to get to the Croft as soon as he could, but his heart was not into driving

Chalky hard. He was awash with uncertainty and dread. For a while, his trip had seemed successful; but that was a mirage. The cash he or Fa would have to deliver at Tosar's Keep tomorrow would take all the ready money they had at Brighthome. They might even have to borrow from neighbors, without knowing how they would be able to repay. They would not be able to keep the holding-helper families who worked the fields and lived in the three cottages. They were effectively in a financial lock-down, not allowed to work their holdings. The prospects for Curry House and Beland's Farm were probably even worse.

The Croft came into view, that roomy wood-frame community hall used by the neighboring freeholders for meetings, entertainment, weddings, and dinners. It was night; but the windows glowed, and the shapes of mules and horses tied at the porch railings were visible. He led Chalky to join them, tied him; then, with a heavy heart, let himself in the front door.

"Here he is!" someone called out. The hall smelled stuffy. Some thirty people sat in a ragged circle, interrupting a weary discussion. Babies and small children were sleeping on blankets in the corners. Older girls and boys hung around the kitchen serving window near the food and drink. Several men jumped from their chairs and came forward to meet him. "What did you find out, Nome?"

He accepted the chair-space made for him in the circle and looked about at the waiting faces: Curry and his mother, Fa, Mo, Burton, Mardek, Beland and his younger brothers and sisters, other men and women from nearby holdings. He felt a clutch of pain at the sight of Patoftok from Gamgame, Murchew's daughter, newly married and living at Surlico, Paley and Brill from Filtown. Silently he slipped the leather pouch strap from his shoulder and took out the rescripts from Judges' Rooms. He unfolded these on his knees, wishing there were a way to avoid speaking at all. He began to tell about his day in The City. He read the Brighthome rescript aloud and explained that those for Curry House and Beland's Farm were almost identical, except for the money amounts. He said he had no rescripts for the other four holdings.

"That is it. I don't know if there is any hopeful news here at all. It gives three of our holdings up north a little more time. It definitely gives no good news for those of you upriver."

Seeing his embarrassment, Murchew's daughter spoke from across the circle: "Don't worry, Nome, we already know. Those of us at

Surlico, Gamgame, Filtown and Surd got notices last night, too. From the same Tosarman. We knew last night that our holdings were gone. Our notices were blunt and short, not like the one you got."

"What are you going to do?" he asked.

"That's what we have been talking about here all afternoon." She looked at the black windows and added, "...and all evening. It's not all worked out yet; we were waiting to hear what you had to say. But most of us can go to relatives or will be taken by neighbors on the other holdings. Branny and I, of course, will go back to the Murchew holding, and I think my folks there will be willing to take in some of Branny's folks...I have to talk to them yet about it."

Someone else said, "We're trying to make sure no one has to go to the towns in the south or to live in The City."

"Your news is a great relief to me, Nome," said his mother. "You were right to send him, Baron, I have to give you credit. I am sure we can get together enough money for the first payment tomorrow; but what you have told us, Nome, still doesn't say what the Tosars are up to...why three of us were given leeway and four others will lose their homes outright."

"*Leeway?*" Beland barked. He was scowling darkly and leaning forward with his large hands planted heavily on his thighs. "What '*leeway*' you talking about, Rena? They're just playing with us! They're making us *pay them* for taking our homes away from us!"

"Well, it *is* leeway," insisted Rena, "or a little extra time or whatever you want to call it. Months, at least; you heard what Nome said."

"Yeh, I heard him; and I heard him say we can't work anymore to raise the money to *pay* 'em. But we still have to *pay* 'em. We're finished." He thumped back against his chair and folded his thick arms across his chest. "I ain't paying 'em. Not a shugget! I ain't paying 'em tomorrow or anytime to take the Farm!"

Curry, sitting next to him, raised his hand uncertainly as though requesting to speak. He was nearly Nome's age but looked much younger with carrot hair, blue eyes, and a face full of freckles. He had an eager-to-please manner when he said, "Nome, you're mother says we can't figure out what the Tosars are up to, and that's right. We were hoping you could tell us. We don't know why they are taking holdings along the river...it must have to do with that and...."

Another man interrupted, "And you didn't learn nothing else up there? About what are they going to do with this land, or if this is just the first step...or....?"

"No," Nome answered, "I was just happy to get in and out of there the same day. Nobody was in an explaining mood up there. I was just going to ask you the same questions."

"Well," said Curry, "that's what we have been talking about all afternoon."

"And?"

"And...well...," Curry laughed weakly and looked around for support.

"And *nothing*," grunted Beland. "Face it. There's nothing we can do."

Nome slowly searched the faces around him and saw they had nothing to give. Beland's was clouded, his eyes on the floor. Curry gave a twitchy smile, embarrassed. Mo looked to him with intense hopefulness. Fa watched him, looking like he was about to speak. But he didn't. Burton and Mardek leaned back in their chairs, observing. Nome was aware, in the silence, that his hand cradled his elbow on his lap while the other hand was at the side of his face, at its habit of stroking the scar which ran from his cheek to his chin, absent-mindedly feeling the smooth gristle of tissue against the prickle of whisker stub on either side of it.

"All right, " he said. "All right, I know what we have to do."

There was indefinable tensing in the circle. Beland's scowl remained, but his dark eyes flicked up. Nome looked steadily across at Beland and Curry.

"You two and me. There is something we can do."

Curry's hands went down and took hold of the sides of the chair seat. Beland stiffened his legs against the floor, and his chair skittered back a notch, as he continued to regard Nome sternly from under a furrowed brow.

Nome had been between these two in more ways than age. Curry, quick-witted, enthusiastic, idealistic, was a year younger and had always looked up to Nome and talked things over with him. As boys they had explored the dangerous Outlands in fantasy and adventured there in play. After his father's death, Curry had taken over the holding and helped his mother run it. He continued to spend much time down the road and across the river at Brighthome with his best friend. Beland was two years older than Nome. Nowadays, he came through the back path to Brighthome mostly to talk over farming problems with Nome and his father. He was stocky and strong, a hard worker, but unimaginative, dark, and suspicious. Nome had been one of Beland's few friends, even when they were boys. When he was nineteen, Beland's parents both died of flu within the same week. All at once, he was left with responsibility for the Farm and for his younger brothers and sisters. Nome watched him grow more fearful and uncertain. Later, Beland married; but his wife came to live with him at the Farm only for a short while and then went away. Whether they were still married or where she had gone, Nome had no idea. Beland would not talk about it.

"What have you got in mind?" asked Curry.

"We have to leave," Nome answered. "We have to go out of Tosarkun into the Outlands to find work, send money back. They have cut us off from working here. We have to find a way to keep making the payments."

Silence...then a beginning of murmur and muttering around the circle.

"But for how long?" cried Curry's mother.

"I don't know, Magda. I don't know how long. I can only think about what we can do for now, and it is clear from the Judges' decision I read you that we are all frozen out of working our holdings. We are not even allowed to barter or trade our property or our produce. We have to go where we *can* work. Now, if we can each come up with enough for tomorrow's payment...."

There was an eruption of babble around the circle, with nodding and head-shaking and glances back and forth at the three young men in question. Beland sat up straight and looked around stupidly, then shouted, "Wait! Listen!"

Suddenly, quiet in the hall. He huffed, as though offended, "Whuh...whuh...whell, what kind of work? You talking about the *Outlands?* Who'd take care of the Farm? How do we know we could find work in the Outlands? It's *wild* out there, wild and *dangerous!* We don't know anything about the lands outside Tosarkun. None of us here have ever been to any of 'em!"

There was a moment's awkward silence, then: "Some of us have."

It was Burton speaking, rising to his feet as though he were about to make a speech. "I realize I may be out of place speaking up, since we are not from here. But I would like to add a word of agreement to what Nome Ogrodni is saying. I think he is right, going to the Outlands is the only way you are going to find enough money to meet the payments. But, Nome, allow me to suggest one change. You would have to find more than just work. I mean, if you plan to go out there and hire out as farmhands, you might as well stay home. You would never make enough money to make the kinds of payments your Judges have stipulated. Let me suggest that you would have to go *to seek your fortune,* as they say in the old tales. A lot of money quickly, a stroke of good fortune is what you would need; and it is what you would have to gamble on. Mardek and I can tell you something about the Outlands. You people don't call them 'wild' for nothing. On the other hand, Beland, with all due respect, they are not as uncivilized as you imagine. At least, parts of them aren't. I can't tell whether or not you would succeed; but it seems to me that, if you set out to seek your fortune, heading off toward the wild places is the way to go about it." He sat down.

Curry looked happy. "What other choice do we have? Remember, Nome, how you and I used to always want to go exploring in the wild Outlands?"

"The *Outlands?*" shouted Beland. "You *want* to go to the Outlands? You're crazy, Curry! If you want to go somewhere to find work, why not go south to some of the other countries of Bau Shahn? At least they might be a little bit like here!"

"Yes, why does it have to be the Outlands?" pleaded Curry's mother. "Wouldn't it be safer to go the other way and stay somewhere else in Bau Shahn? At least we know that any lands under Bau Shahn would be orderly."

"Look how orderly Tosarkun is, Magda," someone else said. "Look where we are now!"

"Orderly," piped up Burton, half-rising to his feet and then sitting again, "but 'orderly' is not the place to go to seek your *fortune!*"

Baron Ogrodni spoke for the first time. " I agree with our visitor from the Outlands. Sometimes the safe way is not the successful way. This may be a reckless scheme, but I think it is the only chance we have. I am grateful to you, Nome, and proud of you, for your willingness to go. I hope Curry and Beland will decide to go with you, because you will need friendship and help. And I think you must get ready to leave at once. Tomorrow."

Several were on their feet, speaking at once. It became four or five meetings, and there were arguments, harangues, and irrelevant anecdotes. Eventually, with shouting and a few shrill whistles, order was restored; and the hall quieted. The discussion continued; but, now that a decision had been made, there was hope and energy. And new problems: Where to go? How to get money back home? Who would care for the holdings? How would money be raised for the first payments due tomorrow? They talked late into the night. Beland was finally persuaded. Brighthome had just enough cash available for the first payment, but Curry House and Beland's Farm were short by half. Neighbors agreed to secretly buy and quickly transfer livestock and implements before the ban could be enforced. Care for the three holdings was arranged among relatives and neighbors. Burton and Mardek made suggestions about how to start and where to go.

Talk began to fragment and die out, and women began to stand up and look about for belongings and infants sleeping on the floor. Men were saying good night and moving toward the door, stuffing pipe bowls. A young child, roused from sleep, sat up and said, "Is it time for the song?"

"The song! The song! We forgot the song!"

The movement reversed, and women, men, boys, girls, sleeping children on shoulders came back into a shaggy, shuffling circle. They stood looking at one another, waiting for someone to start.

Murchew's daughter said, "Nome, before the song, would you play a piece on your pipe? It may be the last time we hear it for a while. We will miss you." She looked from him to Curry, then to Beland. "We will miss you all. Very much."

Nome let his leather pouch slide to the floor and took out the white, carved pipe. As he drew breath for the first note, the memory of a dark horse and rider against a setting sun came to him. He played out the naive melody he would have played then, trilling high first, searching, falling and rising, then floating like a feather to a slow, sweet, final note.

Whisperings of "Thank you" about the circle. Then an old, rusty voice, full of emotion, intoned "The Song of the Croft." All joined, and the stately music swelled to fill the hall.

FOUR

Crossing the Border

It was a fair morning, good weather for traveling. A small crowd had gathered in the yard at Brighthome. Curry and Beland were there, ready for the trip, their horses freighted with saddlebags, bedrolls, sacks, leather squeaking, pots clunking. Folks from their holdings were also there to say goodbye. Nome had made a late start and was harried and hurrying to pack. His mother kept bringing him things she was sure he would need. Relatives and neighbors stood about in small circles, talking quietly, assessing the packing with a critical eye. Every now and then someone would call out with suggestion of a different way to fit something in or tie a hitch. With so much help, Nome was finding it hard to finish. Baron led his own horse from the stable, for he would be riding to The City that morning to make a combined payment on the three holdings at Tosar's Keep.

"You would have done better taking a wagon," he said, looking up from under his horse as he pulled the cinch tight. "That's what I think."

"No," answered Nome between clenched teeth, "we'll manage this way." They were continuing an argument started earlier.

"I'm surprised that you won't listen to experience," said Baron, straightening and looking wrathfully at his son. "I have done a fair amount of traveling in my time, you know. You have done none! Look at all that baggage you have strapped to that horse! It will take you hours every day to pack and unpack. A wagon would provide shelter. You could sleep in it or under it. And it might provide protection you need some day. You'd be thanking me for it."

Nome dashed a bedroll to the ground and glared. "I don't want to keep talking about this! I want some freedom of movement out there. I don't want to be looking after a wagon."

A malicious voice came from the crowd: "You'll move free as a bird, Nome. Chalky'll never make it out to the road!" Laughter rippled through the yard. He looked about with sweaty anger, then stepped back to look at the horse. Chalky appeared to sway and stagger.

"Better start over, Nome," said Curry. "I went through the same thing at my place before coming over here. Come on. We'll help you."

Nome turned his back to his father and furiously began unpacking the load. Beland and Curry lent a hand and put some order into the things he was throwing down. Nome cooled, and the three of them carefully sorted and repacked the animal, pausing frequently to discuss what they would need and what they would have to do without. After a while, Nome looked about for his mother, thinking to give her back several blankets, a robe, and some iron pans and ladles that she had urged him to "slip in" with his gear. He noticed that she had not been hovering about to help him for some time. He inquired about her, but none of the bystanders had seen her around the yard. "Have you looked in the house?" they asked, which was what he was just about to do.

The house sounded hollow and felt empty as he stepped into the hallway. Ducking his head into this room and that, he softly called, "Mo? Mo? Are you here?" He put the blankets and the robe on a long couch in the sitting room and gathered up the pans and ladles to return them to the kitchen.

There he found his mother sitting in the middle of the room on a low stool, with her dog, Chindit, seated before her. She held his head in front of her, cradled in her hands, as though to hold it steady, while she stared into his eyes. Nome stopped at the doorway, taken aback. His first thought was that she had retreated to her kitchen in grief and was seeking consolation from her dog. But neither she nor the dog looked up as he appeared; and he had not done so noiselessly when the pans had clanked in his hands. It was a strange scene: he had never seen a dog endure the fixed gaze of a human without glancing aside. Chindit stayed still and did not pull away or take any notice of the distraction at the doorway. Rena seemed to be humming or muttering very softly and appeared to be studying the dog's face.

"Mo?" he said softly. He wondered if she were crying; but, as she serenely looked up to him, he saw that she was not. "Mo, are you all right?"

"Yes, dear, I'm all right. I was just talking to Chindit a little."

"Mo, I'm sorry, I just can't take these things along. We are repacking from the beginning and have to cut out a lot. Poor Chalky's almost tipping over."

"All right," she said, standing up and pointing to the table for him to put them there. They looked into each-other's faces for several long moments, then she said, "I want Chindit to go with you."

Nome frowned. "Why?"

"I want him to. I do. Take him, Nome."

" But, Mo! He's *your* dog. You love that dog!"

"I love you more, Nome."

He threw up his hands and wrinkled his nose: "I can't take care of a dog! I don't want to take him away from you, Mo. He won't be any help."

"Chindit will take care of himself," she said. "Maybe if you would just feed him when you can...when you have food you can give him.... He won't be a burden to you otherwise. And he won't make Chalky tip over."

Nome laughed and looked at the floor. Then he turned his head and looked at her out of the corner of an eye and said, "All right. But I don't get it." They walked out into the yard. The dog followed.

....

Farewells at the Grandmaison Road were long and tearful. There were many people to hug, and no one knew when the three young men would return. Burton and Mardek had drawn maps of the first part of the Outlands and given them information and suggestions about where to go to seek their fortune. There was, however, no routine communication from the places to which they were going; so Beland, Curry, and Nome were going into the unknown.

Baron, too, was on horseback. For a few steps, father and son rode side by side; then each reached out and took the other's hand; and so they rode on a way farther, holding each other in a fierce grip across the space between them, until Baron pulled away and turned to ride in the opposite direction toward The City. Waving and shouts followed the three until they were hidden from view around a bend.

They rode in silence for half an hour. Each man savored his grief and worry privately and let himself be carried limply on the rolling back of his horse, staring between the animal's ears at the road, blind to the loveliness of the countryside beneath a mellow summer sun. Nome was the first to break from reverie, and he did so with a start. He realized that, all this time, the dog, Chindit, had been happily trotting alongside.

"Houda!" he shouted, in the expression of their district, "did one of you call this dog after us when we left?"

"Not I," said Curry.

"Not I," said Beland. "Rena is going to be angry when she finds him gone."

"Go back!" shouted Curry. "Go on! Get back home, Chindit, back to Rena!" He waved his arms and pressed the horse sideways toward the dog, who glanced up and continued to trot, tongue dancing from a smiling mouth.

"No, wait!" said Nome. "I'd forgotten about him. Are you sure neither of you called this dog? My mother wanted him to come with us. I tried to talk her out of it, but she insisted. Well, here he is. Let him come."

They traveled more easily now, and the mood lifted. They breathed in the warm air of the fields, looked about, straightened their backs in their saddles, and were talking about what lay ahead. In a few hours they would reach the border and have to face the Tosar's Guard. Would they be allowed to pass? Would the papers Nome had been given at Judges' Rooms be honored? Would they be harassed? Fear began to creep about them, like prickly animals, as they imagined the crossing; and, ironically, they longed to be far into the Outlands with the border station at their backs.

Riding north along the road, they noticed that the farmlands and holdings were more poorly tended; and the bog and forestlands appeared wilder and more overgrown. At last, they came to Hite's Farm, which was said to be the last holding before the border. Wilman Hite, a bristly, rude, old bachelor with leather-wrinkled skin and a matted beard down to his stomach, had attended meetings at the Croft on rare occasions. Most of the people of the neighborhood thought him mad. Nome had heard his

Fa speak favorably of the old pioneer and seen him frown darkly whenever jokes were made about old Hite. None of the three travelers had ever been this far north; and they were fascinated at the sight of the plain, rough buildings of Hite's Farm; although none of them had any inclination to drop in for a visit. Dogs came running out into the yard to bark at them, but there was no sign of the old man as they passed. At this point, the road began to descend gradually, then turned toward the east to go around a sprawling tamarack bog. The farm was scarcely out of view, when they saw something on the road far ahead that brought them to a halt.

"Well," said Curry, "want to go back?"

"Yes, I'd like to go back," replied Beland as the three of them squinted down the road. "I think I'd rather go back and ask madman Hite if I could join him in a mug of brew or a few games of dokkers."

"So would I," added Nome, "but here we go." And they nudged their heavy horses forward.

The broad Grandmaison Road appeared to be swallowed by a wide, squat building which lay in its path. As they approached, they saw that the road split and passed on both sides of the border guardhouse. A dozen gray-uniformed Guard stood motionless by the building, heavily armed, watching them approach. When they drew close to the building, the three halted. They looked about for someone to tell them what to do; but the guardsmen remained tense and still, continuing to watch. Nome, Beland, and Curry dismounted and looked about meekly. At length, one guardsman separated himself from the rest and came forward, motioning them off to the side of the road with a gloved hand. Still, no word was spoken. Other guardsmen sauntered forward and began unpacking the horses, dropping the gear to the dust of the road.

An hour passed, with the three young men standing or sitting at the roadside, watching a desultory inspection. Every effort of theirs to speak to a guardsman was cut short by a menacing glare or a hand that curled into a fist. Then they were beckoned into the building and left to stand before a desk at which sat an obese, sweating man in a gray uniform. He irritably questioned them and wrote a good deal on paper. Eventually, he demanded documentation from Judges' Rooms, and the three men eagerly pushed forward the rescripts Nome had brought from The City. The official looked these over disdainfully, as though they were worthless, then scribbled something on each of them and shoved them aside. He leaned back considering the three men before him at length and said:

"Well, yes, you can leave the *kun*. But, of course, you can't take all this." He gestured out the window to where the horses stood surrounded by scattered baggage.

"Can't...take...? Can't take...what...sir?" asked Nome.

"This! This! This!" he shouted, jerking his thumb rapidly toward the window. "Didn't you *read* these papers you gave me?"

They had read them many times, studied them. But to none of them had it occurred that they were taking "livestock" out of Tosarkun. Even Chindit was called "livestock" and denied passage. The larger items of their baggage was declared property of the holdings, whose confiscation was pending; and the fat official heatedly accused them of trying to smuggle animals and goods out of the *kun* before the Tosars could claim them. In the end, they were led outside and turned over to another guardsman who roughly poked through their gear with a boot and sorted out what they could take and what they would have to leave behind. In terror and panic, they scrambled among their things, trying to claw together whatever they could. Nome was especially heartbroken at the realization that he was going to lose Chindit, and was remembering his words to his mother that morning: "I can't take care of a dog!" How bitter that he had been right, and already had let his mother down.

They all assumed that their animals and equipment were being confiscated and were astonished when the guardsman who was sorting through it with his boot asked, "What are you going to do with all this?"

They looked up. Nome said, "Sir?"

"What are you going to do with it? It's getting toward sundown, and we *close* at sundown. You can't leave this clutter on the road and allow these animals to wander about. And if you don't cross today, I would say you don't cross. I don't think the captain will let you try again tomorrow."

Squatting and kneeling in the dust, they looked from one to the other in bewilderment. Suddenly, Curry looked up to the guardsman and said rapidly, "We plan to take them to Farmer Hite, sir. We'll ask him to take care of the animals and see that all this gets back to the proper holdings."

Nome and Beland stared at him in amazement. The guardsman grunted and turned away. They roped their gear haphazardly to the horses and began walking them back up the road along which they had come. The sun was low, indeed, in the western sky; and they hurried along, worrying about what kind of reception they would get from madman Hite. As they came through the gate, Wilman Hite stood in the yard, legs spread and planted like trees, hands on hips. They halted at a respectful distance, three nervous, foot-shuffling men and three horses towering with clutter. Hite broke his stance to whirl and roar at his two bellering hounds. They cut it back to surly, toothy growls.

Nome stepped forward. "Good afternoon, Farmer Hite. Hope we are not troubling you. I am Baron and Rena Ogrodni's son, and...."

"I know you are!" he shrieked, beard jiggling. "Know who you all are! Saw you go by. *Thought* you'd be back. Untie those horses! They look bad! Then come in the house! Got supper for you!"

They nearly wept with relief and hurried about the work, piling useless gear in a neat pile by the barn and keeping their eyes on the sinking sun. Nome went on ahead to explain to Hite that they could not linger. He found the house poor but tidy and the kitchen table neatly set for four, with bowls of food steaming.

"What? Can't stay the night?" shouted the old man indignantly. "Agh! I supposed not. I know them!" Into Nome's mind flashed a sudden, sharp image of his father. "Well, we have to get some food into you men before you cross. The Outlands aren't so bad. I've been there many times, you know. This used to *be* the Outlands! But I think it's the first time for you young men, am I right? Got to have food."

Beland and Curry stepped politely into the kitchen, and all sat down to the meal. Wilman Hite looked as mad as ever; and every word was shouted, as though he were furious. His kindness was without limit. He assured them he would care for the horses and the equipment and return them to their holdings. He jumped up from the meal and disappeared into a shed, where he rummaged about and emerged carrying two backpacks, which he gave them for their journey. They began to get anxious and fearful about the time and gingerly urged him to let them be on their way; but he kept bustling about for ways to be helpful.

Finally, he let them go; and they trotted out the gate at the road, calling back their thanks and waving goodbye. Chindit ran alongside them. Nome tried to make the dog stay with Hite, but he would not go back. In desperation, he called to Curry and Beland to go on ahead and he would catch up.

He knelt on the road and clutched the dog by the head and said firmly, "Chindit, you've got to stay! You *can't* come with me."

Panting, the dog looked away. Then an idea came to him. Nome dug about in his pouch for a paper tablet and pencil. Carefully he wrote a short note to his Fa and Mo, tore off the page, fished about for a bit of thin wire that he carried in a loop. He wired the note to the dog's collar, then said, "Go home, Chindit! Home to Mo! Go to Rena!" The dog turned and trotted away up the Grandmaison Road toward the south. Not once did he glance back.

"Houda! Holy!" muttered Nome; and he went north after his friends, at a full run.

The sun was setting, as the three men came to the guardhouse. Gray-coat guardsmen were putting barriers across the road on both sides of the building. Nome, Curry, and Beland staggered and sprinted, packs swinging wildly and banging their sides. One of the Guard hesitated with the barrier and let them pass, shouting something they did not understand. They stumbled to a walk, sobbing, heaving, panting. Glancing back, they saw the last of the Guard disappear into the building. They were in the Outlands.

FIVE

Behind a Waterfall

The setting sun looked to the three young men like the slipping away of home and happiness and the onset of uncertain darkness. Behind them stood the guardhouse, blocking all hope of return. Ahead, the road plunged into a black spruce forest and disappeared. They walked on in silence for a mile, eager to be out of sight of the Tosar's Guard. The light seemed to be dimming, and they knew they would need to find a place to sleep soon.

Both sides of the road were hemmed close by a tangle of spiny spruce branches and tight undergrowth. There were no clearings in sight, and it seemed impossible to penetrate the forest to get off the road. At length, it grew so dark that they stopped looking for a favorable spot and settled for any higher ground, less likely to be swampy, and pushed their way into a thicket of branches and spikes. There was a great deal of thrashing about and snapping of branches as they tried to clear a spot. They worked in nearly complete darkness, for whatever light remained on the road was gone here in the matted woods. The spruce were close together and the ground rocky and uneven; but, eventually, the furious scratching and grunting and muttering abated; and each man lay on his back listening to the other two breathe.

"Let's get a fire," said Nome.

There was no shortage of dry kindling; and soon a merry flame lighted the strange bedroom in which they sprawled at three awkward angles. They brought food out of their packs and eagerly ate. There was nothing to drink; and the last thing Beland said before they dropped into exhausted sleep was, "I sure wish we had some water."

In the middle of the night, they were all awakened at the same moment by a deafening crack of thunder tearing open the sky. Until then, it had only been rumbling and churning. Rain, which had been channeling for some time along the backward-forward sweep of the needled branches upon the sleeping figures, now became an unyielding torrent. The sky raged and flashed, and water poured as though under pressure. The men screamed and flailed in panic and confusion, as though they had been surprised in sleep by an enemy ambush. They called out to one another "The tent! The tent!" Curry, who carried the tent in his pack, scrambled in the darkness with fastenings. Nome and Beland clambered over to Curry's spot and squeezed alongside him. There was no possibility of erecting the tent in this cramped and cluttered space, so they grasped about for the front flap and drew it over the three of them together like a sack. It did no good. By the time they stopped rolling and tugging and sliding, the cloth of the tent had become just one more soaked layer of covering; and they found that they were lying in a pool of water on the ground, inches deep. So fierce was the downpour, that water had nowhere to run off. Finally, they gave up all efforts to resist and lay huddled together, waiting for misery to end.

They waited for hours. This was not the usual summer thunderstorm, which strikes hard and passes quickly. It was a floodstorm, which would be remembered for years and talked about by people sitting about over khavla and telling one another tales of tragedies. At this moment, roads were being washed away, houses flooded, barn foundations undermined.

Nome, Curry, and Beland clung to one another in numbed grief. They did not try to speak above the roaring of the storm. They were dazed and trembling with cold. From time to time the sounds of "Holy, oh, Holy!" were muttered like a sob in the darkness.

Leaden dawn arrived slowly, and the storm yielded to a monotonous drizzle. They dragged their packs and the tent out of the tangle of forest onto the road. Then occurred their first major dispute.

"I'm going back," said Beland.

"Back?" the other two said together. "You can't go back!" Nome insisted. "What is there to go back to?"

"Home, you fool! Home!" Beland screamed. His angry child's face was wet with rain and tears. "I can't stand this!"

"But, Beland," pleaded Curry, "you're losing your home. That's why we've come. If you go back, you won't have any home to go to."

"I don't care! I don't care! I can't stand this!" He sunk to his knees in the mud of the road and shook.

Curry looked at Nome through the rain. "What do we do now?"

"I don't know," said Nome. He looked down at the pathetic bundle at their feet. "I don't know."

"Perhaps we have to let him go back, Nome," said Curry.

"That's right!" shouted Beland, voice muffled by his hands in front of his face, "You two go on without me. You'll do fine. You don't need me! I'm going back."

Nome jerked his head up as though he had heard something. He felt a rising anger with Beland and yet a strange affection for him. He had been startled by the man's unguarded revelation of jealousy.

"We can't let him go, Curry," said Nome. "We need him."

"Nome, we don't need *this!*" cried Curry. "Get up, Beland! Pull yourself together!" His face was flushed, his voice furious. "What's the matter with you? You let a little rain stop you, and you blubber like a kid!"

"Stop it, Curry" commanded Nome.

Curry swore and pulled back his leg, looking as if he were about to kick Beland; but he stamped hard on the mud instead, pivoted, and strolled a few feet away in disgust. Nome said, "I don't know what to do." Then he squatted down beside Beland and placed his hand on the man's humped, sodden back.

"Beland, I want to go back, too. But it is far. We can't get out of this rain by going back. It is too far. We have to find something closer, someplace where we can get dry. A house, a barn, a shed. Underneath a bridge, anywhere. We can build a fire, dry our things. There's got to be something up ahead. Something in the next hour. You'll see."

"I want to go home, Nomo," Beland whimpered. "I'm cold." He had used the nickname of their childhood. Nome had not heard himself called that for years.

"Come on. I want to go home, too. Come on, we've got to keep going. Get up, Beland. You and Curry and I." He put his hand under Beland's arm and gently lifted. "Come on."

Slowly, Beland struggled to his feet, bent to pick up his pack, and began to trudge forward on the road. Curry looked at them in surprise, then stuffed the tent into his pack, with fierce, jerky movements, and stomped up the road ahead of them.

"Curry, wait up," called Nome.

But Curry would not wait up. He was very angry.

They walked on in this sullen formation, one ahead, two close behind, for several hours. Nome pondered what was happening to them. He sensed that Curry was angrier with him than with Beland; and he felt a smoldering resentment at being caught in their jealousies. He had thought hardship would draw them together...brothers. Dreams and fantasies.

The rain stopped, but the skies remained leaden. They rested to eat and emptied out the packs to see if anything was dry. Nothing was. Their lightweight toasted nuts and grains were not much affected by the dampness, and exhaustion made them ravenous and ready to eat anything. They sat together at the side of the road avoiding what had happened between them, speaking little. Nome worried. How little they had talked to each other ever since they had set out yesterday morning. He himself did not know what to say to either of them.

"Where are we going, anyway?" Beland suddenly asked in an offhand manner. "Does anybody know?"

"Why, we're heading north and east to some of the towns Burton and Mardek told us about," said Nome. "Remember? They drew this little map to get us started."

"I don't know how to read maps," Beland said giving it no more than a glance. "Have never needed to. What are we going to do in these towns?"

"Beland!" said Curry sharply, "Are you going to start pulling your weight or not? Are we going to have to do the thinking for you? You know as much as we do about where we are, where we're going, what we're going to do when we get there! We figure it out as we go, that's all we can do."

Beland frowned darkly, but looked down and rummaged about in his food bag, looking for dried apple, and made no reply. Nome spread the limp, smudged map out on top of his damp pack for them to see.

"I don't know how far up the road we are here, but we have not come to this bridge crossing a river...the Gaffling River, it says...and then aways up beyond that...see, here off to the north and east...is 'n Burning Graute. Funny name. Burton pronounced it 'in Burning Grau-teh.' He suggested we go there and ask around for someone called 'Korcha Rabon.' Here, he wrote that on the back. But he said we needed to do that carefully because this man could be both helpful or dangerous. Anyway, Mardek told me that, if we don't turn up any way to make money there, we should go on farther north here...here to Kezzlhjem...Kezzel-he-yem. It's hard to tell how far distances are because Burton said none of this was to scale."

"What's that mean?" asked Beland.

"Means that the map shows the positions of places but not accurately how far between them. So that from 'n Burning Graute to Kezzlhjem could be twice as far as it looks here. Or half as far."

Beland grunted.

"And what'd Burton mean about this dangerous man we are supposed to look for?" asked Curry.

"Korcha Rabon," said Nome. "Burton said we should ask about his whereabouts as soon as we begin to get near 'n Burning Graute. He may not be there anymore. And he said if we ever meet Korcha Rabon we should be as honest as possible...tell him everything about our situation and see if we can join up with him in hopes of making a lot of money fast."

"Well, who is he?" asked Beland. " I don't see why we want to try and find some dangerous man and ask to join him. Sounds like a criminal to me."

"I really don't know who he is. I'm just telling you what Burton and Mardek said. There wasn't a lot of time for them to explain. You're right, the way they referred to this Rabon made him sound like a sort of bandit-chief; but not like the old Tosars. Mardek said he had been camping in the neighborhood of 'n Burning Graute for several years trying to pull together an army to go back off west...way far west somewhere...to right some old family wrong, reclaim some heritage that had been taken from him, or something. The thing is, there is a lot of money involved. Money along the way and all we would need when we get there...if we get there. At least, that was what Burton and Mardek insinuated when Fa and I were talking with them. This was about the only clear suggestion they had. Although, they couldn't guarantee that Rabon would be still around...maybe he's already set off out west, they didn't know. If that doesn't work out, they said we could move on to Kezzlhjem where there is a local prince or lord and we might find employment there in his service."

"That sounds safer to me," said Beland. "Let's skip this Burning Graut and go right on to ask for a decent job at the other place."

"You really want to skip the first town, Beland?" asked Nome mischievously. "I thought you were wet and cold."

"Don't remind me," Beland grinned. As much as wet and cold, he was feeling lonely. Still prisoner of his habitual pessimism, and embarrassed by the memory of his tantrum, he was looking for ways to join the campfire of friendship. Full of regret, he was looking for openings to prove to them that he would be cooperative and brave.

"Well," said Nome, "I think we should take things as they come. We are in a pretty desperate situation, with the likely loss of our homes to the Tosars and the ruin of our families."

"I agree," added Curry. "We have to try everything. I think we will all feel better once we get somewhere to dry our clothes and packs and have a warm meal."

"I think so, too," said Beland. "Maybe we should get moving." He stood up.

They walked along in better spirits, talking lightly about things they noticed on the way. Their clothes weighed heavily upon their shoulders, and their feet squished in their boots with every step. The mournful sky continued to threaten rain. After a long time, the spruce forest crowding the road ended; and patches of meadow appeared. There were still no signs of homes or farms, but this land must have been settled at one period. Nome became excited when they came upon a narrow, rutted road running off toward the west, because he was sure this must be the side-road indicated on Burton's map by a short pencil-flick off to the side. If so, they were not far from the bridge crossing the Gaffling River. He wondered how Burton would have remembered such a poor, ill-kept side-road in such a nondescript landscape. Perhaps it was more significant than it looked and was a main link with the west Outlands. He had noticed that the Grandmaison Road appeared to have ended at the Tosarkun border; and the rough continuation they were on now appeared to have no name. Once they passed the bridge, it might still be a long walk to the town. How they missed having horses!

Curry had just made the comment that it was surprising that they had not met a single traveler since crossing the border, when they saw the figures of two men standing on the road far ahead. They did not appear to be approaching; rather, working on something. A moment later, two more men came into view, farther on.

"If they are friendly," said Nome, "we may be able to get help with a place to stay tonight or information about where we can go to dry out. And we will find out how far it is to 'n Burning Graute."

"And if they're not friendly?" asked Beland.

"Let's wait and see," said Curry. "At least they're not Tosarmen, we know that."

"You sure Tosarmen don't come this far?"

"No," said Nome. "They don't go beyond the border. I've always heard that. We are about to meet our first Outlanders. Relax, remember that Burton and Mardek are Outlanders, too."

As they approached the working men, they began to hear a rushing sound, far off and muffled, but growing to rumbling as they went forward. All at once they stopped and squinted ahead, no longer watching the men, but straining to see the bridge. There was no bridge. Their road came to a ragged end above a frenzied, thundering brown-and-white torrent. The workmen, wet and mud-covered, bedraggled with fatigue, stood staring at them. Two were at the road-end by the splintered fragments of bridge-footings, and the other two were on the far side of the chasm, cut off, forever it seemed, by the murderous spume of the stream. Heavy timbers were piled near them, and a long rope ran from the remnant of a footing on the far bank out into the middle of the river downstream, where it whipped and tossed aimlessly in the current. As the three travelers came forward, one of the workmen on the near side threw down his shovel; and the other came toward them quickly, waving his arms in front of his face shouting for them to go back.

"But we cannot go back," Nome called to him. "We are from Tosarkun and the Guard will not allow us to re-enter."

"Then you must go off to the west along that road back there! You cannot go this way! The bridge is down!"

"Yes, we see that. How far are we from 'n Burning Graute?"

"No, no!" the man insisted. "The bridge is down! You cannot go that way. In two or three days, perhaps. But now you must go back!"

"Is there no other way?" Nome pressed. They now stood face to face with him. "How did you get here and those other men on the other side?"

The man, who seemed more frightened than angry, wagged his head, waved his hands in front of his face and stamped one foot. "No, no, there is no other way! Two or three days, maybe, but now you must go back!"

"But tell me," said Nome, "how you got across. Either you or those men must have...."

"You see that rope there in the current, don't you?" the man turned and thrust a stubby finger toward the water. "That's how. He and I came across on that. But there was another one of us, and the river got him! We couldn't find him! Do you want to go the same way he did, if it is so necessary to get across? Now, please, go back! We have work to do! We must hurry!"

Nome, Curry and Beland looked at one another, and Curry flicked his head for them to move apart a bit for a discussion. "Let's see your map, Nome," he said. The three of them huddled about the dirty paper while the workman stood watching helplessly. "Here," said Curry, "how about this?" He traced with his finger the road by which they had come to the river, then left the road and followed the river to the north around a bend and directly to 'n Burning Graute. "If we walk through the brush and keep to the riverbank, we won't have to cross at all and will come to the town, which looks like it is built on both sides of the river."

"It's a possibility," mused Nome. "It looks like that would double or triple the distance to the town. It probably means we would spend another night in the woods. But I don't see any other way of doing it, do you, Beland?"

Beland had taken a step backward and smothered an exclamation. He stared at the paper with black, glistening eyes, raised a hand and pressed a thick finger hard against his lips, then slowly shook his head.

Nome stepped back to the workman, who stood as though he were guarding access to the river, and pointed north. "What about following the riverbank? Couldn't we follow the river and eventually get to 'n Burning Graute?"

At that, the man exploded into such a cascade of protests and flailing of arms that Nome turned back to his friends and said, "Come on, there's no use talking to him anymore. Let's go. They can't stop us." The three travelers stepped from the road and waded through the low brush toward the river. Followed by the shouts and pleas of all four workmen on both sides of the stream, they forged ahead and quickly disappeared into the woods. Beland glanced back several times, deeply worried. It seemed to him that they had taken the course that the workmen had most wanted to prevent.

Back at the bridge site, there was a hurried, shouting conference among the men on both sides of the river. Then the excitable man, who had spoken to the three, carefully slipped into the brush and followed them, keeping his distance. On the other side, one of the workmen hurried away up the road toward the town at a trot. The remaining two returned to their work.

The trek along the river was slow and arduous, for there was no hint of a path. At times, they had to move deep into the woods to go around places where the swollen river had spilled over the banks and flooded the forest. On their left was the constant noise of the water's rush, and many trees had been torn from the bank and lay overthrown like corpses with their leafy heads half in the furious watery course. They painfully pushed through bushes, stumbled over roots and hidden rocks, clambered over fallen trees. Nome remembered how he had wished for a horse, and wondered now what he would have done with one at this point. What about the wagon Fa had insisted he take!

After several hours, they threw themselves down on a high, grassy lip of the bank and had supper. They thought it was supper...they still had no idea how much daylight was left to them. They studied the sky with concern and saw that rain would be falling on them again soon. It was very clear that they would spend another night in the open, for they had not yet reached the point where the river bent sharply to the east; and that point was only half-way to the town, according to the map. They agreed to begin watching for shelter—a leaning boulder, a thick nest of trees where the ground was flat and open, or a gouge in the bank where overhanging turf would make a roof. There would be no question of starting a fire. If only they could cover their heads!

They pushed on for a while, and Curry was arguing in favor of stopping at a spot where a large rock outcrop offered meager cover. The terrain had begun to change a little, the ground slowly rising away from the river; and Beland favored looking farther for better protection in case of another downpour. Suddenly, Nome halted and held out an arm.

"Shh! Listen."

"What?"

"Listen. Doesn't it sound like the noise of the river is louder?"

"I don't hear anything. The steady noise of the river has numbed my hearing."

"No, but listen. There's something else. A deeper rumbling or roaring sound...like thunder."

"Oh, no! Not thunder!"

"No, it's not thunder. Too constant for that."

"I think I hear it now."

"What do you think it is?"

They pushed forward, distracted from their discomfort and worry. Curiosity drove them on, and they struggled through the undergrowth, pushing whipping branches away from their faces and eyes. Now all of them heard the sound, unmistakable and growing louder as they went forward.

"A waterfall," said Nome. "It has to be a waterfall. Or some tremendous rapids."

"Let's go see it!" said Curry.

With new energy they pressed on, scanning the tangle of trees ahead for the first glimpse of tumbling water. It seemed that they would have to come upon it at any moment, the roar was so loud; but they kept thrashing forward and, still, the sound grew louder.

"Wouldn't that be something!" shouted Curry.

"What?"

"I have heard that sometimes there are caves behind waterfalls. I have never seen one...waterfall, I mean; but I've heard about it. Remember, Nome, one night old Murchew was talking about some cave behind a waterfall he'd found? Remember that night he was telling that story at the Croft?"

"Yes, but you can never be sure about what old Murchew says...."

"I know, but I have heard of it other times. Haven't you? Wouldn't that be *something?*"

A few moments later they could feel it. The air chilled, and they seemed to be breathing an invisible mist. The roar was deafening now, and they had to shout to one another to be heard. Then it stood before them: a slow, tumbling giant, amber, white, and brown. For minutes they forgot themselves and stared at this wonder of power and dignity. Never had they seen anything like it. Suddenly Curry darted off to the side, paused to look harder, and ran along the bank for a closer look.

Beland and Nome could not hear a word of his shouting but saw his frantic beckoning and ran to join him.

Curry cupped his hands and shouted, "There...behind the falls! Look! Isn't that an opening?"

It was. An arching, black dent in the rock wall stood exposed by the overload of floodwater, which thrust the falls out away from the rock face. They clambered down the muddy bank and shakily picked their way forward along an oily ledge, clutching the stony wall with fingernails. They swooned with vertigo, as all their senses were swallowed in thunderous wet whiteness and speed. Only by not looking down, or back, or out into the killer curtain of water, and by inching forward, with their attention fixed on arriving, did all three men come to the safe shelf behind the waterfall.

They threw themselves down to rest. It was obvious that this would be no place to spend the night, wet and deafening as it was. Beland recovered first and began to explore the back wall. He turned to nudge and tug at his companions, his voice no use. At the far end of the shelf, half-hidden, almost tucked into the smooth limestone, he had found a low opening. They crawled into it a short way, feeling all surfaces carefully and dragging their packs behind them. The narrow passage seemed to open out into a cave—they could not be sure, because of the utter darkness. As though someone had shut a door, the roar of the the waterfall had been cut to background noise. They sat in the dark a long time; but their eyes did not adjust; and each of them could sense, rather than see, that the cave rose and spread out deep into the rock. A draft of cold air, sucked from that darkness, steadily brushed past them toward the waterfall opening.

Now they were able to talk to one another and agreed that this would be a good place to spend the night. The rock floor was dry; the sound was tolerable; they had a roof. But safe? They needed to know more about these strange lodgings; so each man, on hands and knees, began to feel about, pawing and tapping the walls and floor. They spread out away from one another and roped themselves together with constant talk.

"Wood!" cried Nome. "Shavings! There's a whole stack of it here! Wait, stay where you are. I'm going to see if I can do anything with this."

They listened to him scratching flint on steel for a long time, and occasionally saw a sharp spark flick in the dark. Suddenly, there was a bright glow, and Nome's face appeared like a half-moon, bent over a bright glow on the floor. The vision faltered and died, then bloomed into the strong, clear dance of a fire. They all gave yelps of joy, and Curry and Beland scuttled forward, while Nome carefully added kindling.

An hour later, they lay naked near the fire, while their clothing steamed on shaky ricks of firewood propped together. Their packs and food pouches lay open and spread out. Nome was twisting a tight knot of shavings into the forked end of a stick of wood.

"I am going to explore back in this cave," he said, lighting the torch. "There is a regular air current coming in from somewhere. Has to be another opening."

He was gone for what seemed like a long time. Just when Curry and Beland had begun to worry that they should not have let him go alone, a tottering light appeared in the passageway where he had disappeared; and, a moment later, Nome stepped back through the opening—fully clothed. His raised hand held a stubby rag-head torch, from which rolled sooty waves of oil smoke.

After their cries of astonishment, he said, "We're camped on someone's doorstep. There is another room back there stacked with stores and supplies. I am not sure if anyone is actually living there, but there sure is a lot of weapons and equipment."

"What about another opening?" asked Curry.

"I didn't find any. All I could see is that the draft seemed to be pulled down from a narrow split in the ceiling. Nothing big enough for a person to go through."

"What kind of equipment?" asked Beland.

"Come on, and see for yourselves. Come as you are. As you can see, there are dry clothes back there. Lots of them. I didn't search the place thoroughly."

They followed him, stooping low at first, gradually able to stand upright, as the roof of the passageway lifted. They entered a large, domed room stacked with crates and shelving in orderly rows. Part of the walls of the room were smooth from eons of working by subterranean water; the rest of the walls and the floor showed the chiseled scrapes and grooves of more hasty work. What was most in evidence, stacked on open racks, were weapons: axes, bows, lances, shields, maces, and longtubes for firing pellets. There were many weighty, sealed barrels stacked around the walls of the cave. Each was marked with the crudely painted word: "firedust." At the center of the room were the rows of crates containing clothing, boots, packs, tents, and a variety of items, of which these men were in great need, at the moment.

They lighted a few more torches, taken from a stack by the entrance, and began to explore. Each wandered alone among the aisles, probing and inspecting. Curry and Beland dressed themselves with clothes from the same chest Nome had opened on his first trip into the room. Curry was moving along an aisle of similar chests and paused to inspect one quaintly constructed. It was far more solid than the clothing crates, bound in steel bands and held firmly shut by some peculiar circular fastenings. He hefted it by the steel hand-grip on one side and found that it appeared to be bolted to the floor somehow. Curiosity welled up, and he set himself to solving the problem of the chest, while his companions roamed about the room like market shoppers. After several minutes of tinkering, he discovered a way of making the circular clasps unscrew. Clasps popped free; he lifted the lid, and stepped back with a cry.

"Here we are, friends," he said in a dreamy voice. "This is what we have come for."

Nome and Beland came to his side and gaped. The left side was stacked to the brim with plates of silver, each the size of a small book; the right side was tightly packed with tidy stacks of gold coin.

"Houda," murmured Nome. "Whose can this be?"

"Judging from all these weapons," said Curry, "I would say this belongs to someone who accumulated this by force."

"Someone?" said Beland. "Looks like a lot of someones to me. This is equipment for a small army."

"Bandits?" wondered Nome.

"It doesn't fit my picture of bandits," said Curry. "Everything is so neat. Look at the way that money and that plate is stacked in there. That does not come from some highway raid."

"You would think there would be a guard around that much money," mused Beland. "If I had all that, I would not stash it off in a cave in the woods, where anybody could stumble on it the way we have."

"Well, the question for us now is what do we do about this," said Nome. "This is the answer to all our hopes, all at once. There is enough money here to buy and sell Brighthome, Beland's Farm, and Curry House three times over. But it isn't ours."

"But, Nome," argued Curry, "it can't be honest money...hidden away like this, surrounded by all these weapons, like Beland says."

"Right, but are you saying we can just take it for ourselves and go home?"

"Well...I don't know.... I am sure tempted. What about you, Beland?"

He chewed his lip and looked stupidly at the open chest. "Sure, I'm tempted, too, but...but...I'm also scared. I know I wouldn't let something like this lay around without checking on it. And, even if we did decide to take it, how would we get it out of here? Can you imagine hauling all this...even part of it...even piece by piece...past that waterfall?"

Curry ran his fingers through his red hair and sat against a crate behind him. "Listen to us. Look at us. We are desperate for money. Our homes and families are utterly depending on our coming up with a lot of it. We set out to seek our fortune; and, in a day or two, we find our fortune; and all it has cost us is a day and a night of uncomfortable weather. Now, here we are standing around wondering if we should *take* our fortune. This robbers' gold. This bandits' loot."

"But we don't know," insisted Nome. "We don't know for sure whose this is or how it got here. At least I agree with you about this, Curry...it seems like we have come directly to a fortune. And, whether we take it now or take more time to find out whose place this is, I think we are at the source. I'm not sure we can call ourselves rich men yet."

"But...." Beland was about to voice his rising fear. However, he was spared this. Another voice interrupted, one none of them had heard before.

"Put your hands out away from your bodies! Spread your legs wide where you stand! If you resist, you will be killed at once."

From the gloom of the shadows, where the light of their torches would not reach, they saw the glint of steel and heard the soft shuffling of feet. Open-mouthed, they obeyed and glanced wildly about. There was a moment's silence; then a man slowly strolled into the circle of light, holding a sword pointed, chest-high.

SIX

'n Burning Graute

"What's the condition of the tents?"

"Tents are all right, sir. Eighteen collapsed during the worst of it, but they're being repaired quite easily."

"Equipment?"

"That's the worst, sir. Five barrels of firedust ruined."

"Five *barrels*?"

"Yes, sir. Perhaps some of it can be dried and used as low-grade explosive, but it's no good in tubes anymore."

"Who was responsible for it?"

"Several people, sir. Ultimately, Quartermaster Kuranska."

"Have all of them before the court by evening. No cover-ups! No mercy for Kuranska. (Five barrels!)"

"Yes, sir."

"Roads?"

"Washed out and impassable in eleven places. Only five of those eleven critical to our purposes. There are crews on them now, and all roads should be back in use in three days. Four houses collapsed into the roads or the river. Seven others just teetering over gaping washouts."

"Any of them our people?"

"Two. Ubraka and Dro families."

"Double the road crews. Have them done by tomorrow evening. Take care of Ubraka and Dro."

"Yes, sir. The families have already relocated."

"Any of our people lost?"

"Yes, sir. Two here and one trying to repair the south bridge on the Gaffling."

"Oh yes, the bridge is out down there, I heard that. You should have mentioned it. I need to eat something. Have Bima bring down my lunch, and tell Ila I would like to talk to him while I eat. No one else...for the next hour. Anything else to report?"

"Yes, sir. I'm sorry, I should have mentioned it sooner. Three strangers were captured inside the caverns. They were alone, we ascertained that. Appear to have just stumbled upon it by chance. Dealing with them has delayed the road and bridge work, sir."

"Don't excuse yourself! I hate that! Just report. How could anyone 'just stumble' on the caverns? Where were the guards?"

"At their posts. Apparently these three men got behind the waterfall."

"Are you *serious*?"

"Conditions were unusual, sir. The thrust of the falls was far out from the rock facing because of the swollen river. The opening behind was clearly visible from the bank."

"*My* failure. I should have assigned guards to the falls. How much did they see? Where are these intruders now?"

"They saw nearly everything, sir. They are in the jail and have been under constant interrogation since they were brought in last night."

"All right. Have Bima bring lunch. Dismissed."

The room in which this conversation took place had been storage for a cavernous forge and ironworks shop on the other side of the wall. A massive sliding door connecting the two areas had been sealed; but steady, muffled clanking and hammering continued to come through it from the other side, where twenty to thirty people were at work. The storage room, turned military headquarters, was square, empty space, without ceiling, rising to the steel girders and steep roof sheeting. Pale light came through three small windows; and the only furnishings were a heavy conference table, ringed with chairs, a desk planted at the center, where the commander had sat, and, off in the darkest corner, a field cot, precisely made up. One wall was papered with sheets of detailed, hand-drawn maps.

Korcha Rabon had ridden in from Kezzlhjem that morning and still wore mud-splattered clothes, the drab brown uniform he never varied.

He was a small, intense man of middle age, with sunken cheeks and burning eyes. Today, as usual, he seemed exhausted; but he was constantly alert with quick, brittle glances. His staff said he seldom slept more than three hours a night. In conversation, his voice was smooth, quiet, pleasant to listen to and reassuring. In public speeches, it rang sharp and clear. Korcha Rabon was celibate, abstemious, single-minded. When driven to rage, he grew rigid and silent, and his decisions were ruthless. He suffered from severe headaches. In his home-country of Gazi, he had worked as a tailor. What he really understood was war.

He lay down on the cot and massaged his face with long, slender fingers. Then he lay still until the door opened and an old woman brought in a tray of food. He rose, straightened the blankets on the cot, and sat at the desk.

"Thank you, Bima," he said.

The woman withdrew. Korcha looked at the meal: a slice of bread, two chunks of pickled fish, a slice of cheese, several sprigs of raw greens. A cup of tea. His brother, Ila Rabon, a very different man, entered and pulled up a chair to sit opposite. Ila was tall, heavy-bodied, with bushy hair and full mutton-chop whiskers. He, too, wore the drab brown uniform. He was noticeably older than his brother, whom he now studied in silence, waiting to be addressed. Korcha was eating slowly, eyes down, lost in thought.

At length, he looked up. "Have you seen these new prisoners, Ila?"

"Yes, I've looked in on them from time to time during the interrogation. I just came from there now. They are pretty broken down. It didn't take much."

"What do you think?" asked Korcha, squinting intently and chewing slowly.

"Three hapless fellows. I believe them. I think they just wandered into our supply rooms, incredible as that sounds. The problem now is what to do with them."

"What do you think we should do with them?"

"Shoot them. We can't let them go now, after what they know."

Korcha's look returned to his plate, and his slow chewing came to a stop. For several minutes he held this posture in silence. Ila waited, used to these scenes. Eventually, he began shifting in his chair, then drew a pipe and tobacco pouch out of his bulky pocket and started to stuff the bowl."

"Would you please not smoke just now," said Korcha quietly. Ila glanced up, offended. Then he shrugged and shoved the pipe and pouch back into the pocket and folded his hands in his lap. "They are not our enemy," Korcha continued thoughtfully. "I don't like shooting people who are not our enemy. Unless they might be spies?"

"No, I don't think they are spies. They are naive young men who are out looking for adventure and trying to get rich quick. For a moment in the caverns they thought they had done it. If we let them go, there is every chance that they would become useful to our enemies. If you don't want to execute them, Korcha, at least you have to imprison them permanently."

"Yes, that would be best. But I don't think we can count on the town council here to maintain them in prison indefinitely after we have left. And I don't want to divert our funds to maintain three fools in jail, especially after losing five barrels of dust. Did you know about that?"

"Yes," said Ila, smoothing back his whiskers with thick hands. "Kuranska was drunk. They nearly washed into the river. He's finished."

"We will have to replace that dust. That will cost us more than we have just now, won't it?"

"It will."

"But it will not delay The Day of the March. We stay on schedule, storms, floods, spies, fools, no matter what," said Korcha, pushing his plate away. "Now, as to the three fools, I won't shoot them or jail them or let them go free. Perhaps we can use them."

"How?" frowned Ila. "You mean keep them with us? How could we trust them? They are not our people."

"We would have to watch them closely and put them to work. We could use the extra help now. Maybe we can think of them as three extra workers that the Greatsada has sent to us to help prepare for The Return. And, as to whether we will be able to trust them, I don't know. I want to interview them."

....

Nome, Beland, and Curry sprawled on the stone floor of a cell in dreamless sleep. They had been through fourteen hours of interrogation, during which they had been questioned, badgered, threatened, and occasionally beaten. Clothes and belongings had been taken away. Like the half-dozen petty thieves and murderers with whom they shared jail in the town of 'n Burning Graute, they were dressed only in dirty green ponchos.

The jailer, who had rolled them in here just three hours before, was now at the iron door rattling his stick against the grating and calling loudly for them to wake up and come with him. "More questioning!" he shouted. "Here, you other prisoners! Give those three a few kicks to wake them up!"

This was done. Nome, Beland, and Curry staggered to their feet, wild-eyed and bewildered, clutching the ponchos around themselves to cover their nakedness, muttering, "Holy! Oh, Holy! Houda!" They were led down a hallway, around several corners, and into a plain, white room with stucco walls. There were no bars, no windows; but the thick walls were punctured at intervals with fist-sized holes that let in air and light. The jailer motioned for them to line up on a bench. Sitting on a chair facing them, writing on a pad, not looking up, was a man in brown uniform. He had a very serious face. The jailer assured him he would be just in the next room and received a slight nod of dismissal.

"Your names?" the man asked crisply, ready to write down every word.

It began all over again. They had been through this all night. Slumping forward, elbows on knees, or leaning against one another on the hard bench, they told their names, where they were from, why they were traveling. They told about the Tosars and the holdings, about the Croft meeting and Judges' Rooms. They repeated their story of being caught in the storm, their desperation to find shelter, the meeting with the workmen at the bridge and their effort to get to a town called 'n Burning Graute. The waterfall, the caves, the storeroom, their arrest. During the night, they had been separated and made to tell it again and again in greater detail. They had been asked about names and places and events they had never heard of.

This new interrogator was somewhat different. He sat stiffly before them and listened. He did not shout at them or berate them. Sometimes, he appeared to forget to write and scrutinized their haggard, unshaven faces. When they pleaded for their freedom and promised that they would get out of the area and cause no one further trouble, he did not order them to stick to answering the questions, but studied them and simply asked a new question. He dwelt on different matters, too, spending less time on how they found the waterfall, showing more interest in their opinions and attitudes.

There came a moment in the process when the interrogator became so involved in an interchange with Nome that he absentmindedly let the writing pad drop to his lap, so that what was on it lay in full view. Curry stared at it. The page was a lacework of scribbles and doodling. Only "Burton Mardek" could be read, traced over repeatedly, and embroidered with curls and strokes and shading. The man sensed the change in Curry, realized what had happened, and snapped the pad up before himself again. Then he stood, holding the pad clasped behind his back, and addressed them.

"All right. That is enough. You will be allowed to live. You will join us as camp hands—what we call 'handlers'—and you will move when we move. You will be given what you need to live; and, if you are loyal and do your work well, you will receive some pay. If you try to leave us, you will be killed without question. When we are once again a free people in Gazi, you also will be free to stay or go your way. But that may be a long time yet."

The three men sat stunned, looking up with bleary eyes.

"Who are you?" Nome managed to ask.

"I am your commander. I am Korcha Rabon." He pivoted and walked from the room.

....

I have one desire—
to rescue my people from the tyranny of strangers
who have disgraced and dishonored them,
to restore freedom and peace to the mountains and valleys.
With my own hands I want to bind their wounds, wash the blood from their clothing,
rebuild their houses, sweep the rubble from their streets.
I want to see the holy fire once more in the house of the Greatsada.
Then I can go. Gazi restored will not need another tailor.
          —from the journal of Korcha Rabon

Nome, Curry, and Beland were set to work in the misk quarries. Every morning, they were shaken out of sleepsacks in the tent they shared with eight soldiers of the Rabon army. After a stout breakfast in the field with the troops, they were marched off under guard to a spot several miles from the town, where a quarter of a hill had been cut away, and where nearly a hundred people crawled about the gash like ants. They were assigned, most days, to the crushing sheds, hammering and rolling the soft rock into powder.

Misk was something completely new to them. In fact, it had been discovered only a few years earlier by a woman from a nearby village and was hardly known outside the area of 'n Burning Graute. This woman was a potter and had been experimenting with new glaze techniques. She had mixed certain chemical solutions with the chalky scrapings of rock, which she had found clinging to the roots of a tree uprooted in a windstorm. The result was no glaze but a type of clay that made pots which would not shatter. She named it "misk" and knew that she would soon be rich from the making of unbreakable pottery that was smooth, pearly white, and very easy to work. Burrowing into the hillside, where the first rock had been found, she uncovered an unlimited supply. Crushed to a powder and mixed with a solution, it made a thick paste which could be molded, shaped, and smoothed until it set up, within an hour, to the hardness of rock. In time, she saw other applications for misk and began making tool handles, wagon wheels, even furniture.

The town council of 'n Burning Graute became very interested in her discovery and began to work with her. By the time Nome and his companions arrived, misk was everywhere. Buildings were made of it, footbridges, statuary, implements. The cell where Korcha had interviewed them had been made of it. This wonder-material had limitations. Although nearly steel-hard, as a tool or weapon it would not take an edge. As pottery, it would not accept glaze, but it could be painted. Its indestructibility might have been a problem for, once made, how could it be unmade? It was almost impossible to cut or break down. However, the ingenious potter who had discovered misk discovered its unmaking. Knowing the properties of chemicals and compounds, she experimented further and intuited her way toward the invention of a clear liquid which would slowly dissolve hardened misk back to a paste.

A new industry grew up around 'n Burning Graute. Those who worked the material were called miskwrights. Sample diggings in the hills around the first quarry showed the supply of this rock to be endless, but the chemicals for forming and cutting misk were rare and quite costly. Formulas were kept secret, and only certain screened and selected miskwrights were allowed to develop the chemical products.

So Nome, Beland, and Curry found themselves breaking rock from early morning until late in the evening. They emerged from the sheds at the end of the day white from head to foot with dust and, before supper, joined the other workers bathing in the Gaffling River. Occasionally, their work assignments were rotated so they would have a chance to be outdoors, picking at the rock face or loading the oxcarts and helping drive the loads of powder into the miskworks at the edge of town. Whatever the job, the labor was hard and long. They and the other workers and soldiers of the Rabon force were fed well.

After lunch each day, they attended a two-hour education session. These were obligatory gatherings for all Rabon people, except for those on guard rotation. They were classes in Gazi history, mixed with ritual and exhortation. Soldiers, handlers, family members, all interrupted their work or training or drilling shortly after noon and gathered in groupings of twenty or thirty. From these instructions, and from conversation with their neighbors, the three Tosarkun newcomers gradually learned the story of these people who called themselves Gazines.

They were refugees from a country far to the west. Their towns, villages, and rich farmland lay cradled in the valleys and low spurs of the Endicot Mountains, a range many hundreds of miles long, so high, and with such treacherous passes, that communication with lands farther to the west scarcely existed. Gazi nestled against the eastern slope of the Endicot Range just beyond the Plains of Wildness, a great barren stretch of wasteland. Its people had been highly cultured and fiercely independent, with a proud military tradition.

The center of life was the old city of Mhaveen and its shrine of The Greatsada. As Nome heard the story told, he thought that The Greatsada was very much like what he had learned to call The Holy. But there were differences. The shrine housed a sacred flame, which was tended day and night and never allowed to die. This fire was the soul of the people of Gazi. It was more than a flag or a symbol; it was their spirit. If the flame went out, it was believed, the Gazines would no longer live as a people. Life, they understood, was this tenuous. All of their beliefs and traditions had come from the Plains of Wildness, where apparitions had occurred long ago to certain men and women who had gone there. Apparitions had continued down through the years, feeding belief and devotion. The fire itself was said to have come from nothing and nowhere in the searing heat of the Plains.

The present generation of refugees were scarcely more than children, when Gazi was invaded from the north. A great horde, known as the Momicks, came sliding along the Endicot Range with the inevitability of a glacier, taking country after country. Their home was Moma, a spreading empire far to the west, on the other side of the highest peaks. They must have found a pass up north, out of range of anything known to anyone in Gazi. Until the Gazine outposts first gave alarm about the approach of an enormous army, the very existence of Moma was unknown on this side of the mountains. Gazi's initial resistance was fierce and desperate, but it was overcome in a few days. The sacred flame had been taken out of Mhaveen into hiding; but, when it became known that Mommick policy was to subdue, rule, and tax, while allowing their subjects to keep their traditions and way of life, the fire was returned to its shrine.

Occupation was bitter for this once free people; but their fire still burned, and they were alive. However, in the twenty-first year of occupation, a revolution took place in distant Moma, with consequences that rolled out across all the countries in the Mommick empire. This nearly crushed the life out of Gazi. Treachery and assassination had brought a new ruler to power in Moma and, with him, a change of policy toward subject peoples. A new Momick nation was to be created: *One People, One Heart, One Power* was the chant. Regional differences of custom, belief, currency, language, government would give way to doing things as they are done in Moma.

Many factors led to this change of policy. One was that the Mommick empire's eastern edge had advanced to the point where communications and supply beyond the Endicot Range were very difficult for its conquering army. Holding a patchwork of defeated peoples in good discipline, while they kept their old national feelings and folkways, was becoming a serious problem for an army with ambitions to continue moving even farther east. The new policy was to make everyone Mommick. For Gazi this meant that the fire would be put out.

The danes and fohtars of the Mommick troops had occupied Mhaveen from the first days of the conquest, but they had scrupulously avoided entering the shrine of The Greatsada. On the day of repression, a squad of danes marched into the vestibule of the shrine and were stopped there by an armed crowd of Gazines who knew what they were coming for. Mommick reinforcements were called in and the Gazine resisters barricaded themselves within. "Then give them *unholy* fire!" the captain of the fohtars had shouted. And the shrine was put to the torch.

At this, the entire population of Mhaveen rose up, and fighting raged for four days. By the end of a week, there was not a building standing in what was once the capital; and a pall of black smoke lay all across the valley like a brooding presence in the still summer air. A series of repressive measures began to be imposed throughout the whole mountain country, the worst of which were the branding orders.

Every man, woman, and child throughout the empire was to be branded on the left cheek with a delicate design of two down-strokes curving away from each other crossed by a horizontal bar. This was the emblem of Moma and now would be borne by every person, willingly or not, as an ever-visible sign of One People, One Heart, One Power.

The branding began in the town of Burbaki, not far from where Mhaveen had been. Reports of resistance, fomented there by the Rabon family, had been coming to the Mommick leadership even before their attempt on the shrine of Mhaveen. Branding stations were set up throughout Burbaki in eight or ten places, and citizens were ordered to report to them by neighborhood. Because of this arrangement, the Mommick forces were dispersed, vulnerable, and unsuspecting. Before the first face was marked, armed Gazines, who had been waiting, slipped out of houses, shops, and stables and cut their way through the Mommicks. Not one Mommick escaped Burbaki that day; and news of the uprising did not reach the occupation headquarters until the next day, when a search force was sent to find out why those who went out to execute the branding orders had not returned.

In the meantime, the Rabon family, Rilda, the eldest, and her three brothers, Ila, Korcha, and Mehtor, had rallied most of the population of the town and had fled up into the mountains. Under the passionate eloquence of Rilda and the magnetic personality of Korcha, they drew together a following, who lived in caves, learned to survive in the wild, and ambushed the enemy. Rilda had been a seamstress, Korcha a tailor. Mehtor was a police guard and Ila the town factor, responsible for civic monies. None of them had preparation for the dangerous work they took upon themselves. Their resistance would have been without hope or meaning, and they would have had no following, had not word come from high up the mountains: one of those barricaded against the attack on the shrine of Mhaveen had escaped its burning.

He had gone to Rilda Rabon several days before the Burbaki uprising with news that others had escaped with him, taking the shrine's sacred flame into hiding. He told that the flame was still burning somewhere in the mountains; but he refused to say where, fearing betrayal from collaborators, of whom there were many at that time. After talking to Rilda, he had set out from Burbaki, with two trusted friends to confirm the truth of his report. They headed for the mountains to find the cave where others were guarding the holy fire; but, on the way, they were overtaken by Mommick fohtars and killed. With them died the secret of where the flame of Gazi was burning.

"The fire burns" became the watchword of the Rabon rebellion. It spread among the towns and villages throughout Gazi, along with ambush and disruption of all Mommick enterprises. It had a sinister meaning for the Mommicks, who suffered repeated attacks from small squads of darting and retreating fighters and often returned from a chase to find their camps or settlements in flames.

For two years, the resisters continued their campaign under the inspired leadership of Korcha Rabon. They could not drive the enemy from their land, but they had stopped the destruction of the Gazine people. Then, at a moment of hope, when it appeared that some accommodation might be reached with the Mommicks, Korcha and most of his fighters were drawn into a trap, and the rebellion was all but defeated.

Retreat was no disgrace for the Rabon Gazines. It had been a standard maneuver in their strategies. Now, however, it was their only hope. Korcha and Ila had barely escaped with their lives, along with a small band of fighters. Rilda, Mehtor, and hundreds of others had been killed in the entrapment.

Korcha led a desperate flight across the Plains of Wildness, where some strange things happened which were not of the Mommicks' doing. Eventually, they moved into what people of Tosarkun would have called "the Central Outlands" and met a larger group of Gazine refugees, who had escaped by a different route. It was a shaggy, despairing mob that Korcha now struggled to pull together. They were ready to admit defeat and to look for a friendly population with whom they could merge.

Korcha told them that the fire still burned. He held them by the force of his will and personality. Morning and evening, in fields and under forests, he harangued his people in beautiful poetic language, stirring on the vision of a Return. He encouraged a cult of the heroine, Rilda, Mother of the People of Gazi. He found respite and hospitality with the lord of Kezzlhjem, ruler of a small, unorganized principality that included 'n Burning Graute and a number of other towns and villages.

An agreement was reached between the prince and the warrior by which the battle-wise Gazines would provide police protection for the principality, and especially for the miskworks, while they trained a native military force who would eventually be able to do this for themselves. In return, Rabon's forces were given a place to settle, train, gather resources, and prepare for The Day of the March which would begin The Return.

They settled in and around 'n Burning Graute and, across great distance, re-opened secret communication with many Mommick-branded, but still loyal, people in Gazi. Word that the fire of the Greatsada still burned somewhere high in the mountains circulated among the Gazines in the homeland and in exile. Whether the sacred fire was, in fact, still being tended or whether this was wishful thinking, there was no doubt that it still burned in the hearts of these people, returned from the dead, who were preparing to throw themselves once again at the forces of Moma.

Korcha had the whole population with him mobilized for battle. Family units were kept together, most of them dispersed in houses in the town. Some lived in family tents on the field at the edge of town. For single adults there were women's tents and men's tents. There were many children in the camp. Non-warriors cared for one another and for household needs. Nearly all adults trained as warriors, but Korcha had no intention of developing a standing army. The constant training was seen as the implement of a temporary struggle, until they were home and free again. Bringing whole families to the struggle, rather than a professional soldiery, maintained this focus of purpose. Some of the families, especially those who had arrived later and who bore the Mommick brand on their cheeks, were being trained to re-enter Gazi secretly, to settle once again, and to wait as an internal force for the day of The Return.

This style of combat, which relied on the whole population,

operating from their natural settings, sometimes surging forward, sometimes withdrawing and dispersing, rather than on battle formations on the open field, was suitable to the purposes of the Gazines. To Korcha's surprise, he discovered that a similar fighting tradition called "bandit fighting" had existed in these very regions where they were now settled. From songs and stories and discussions with the old people, he was learning all he could about it.

....

While others trained for war, Nome and his friends trained to be handlers, first for the march, then to provide material support when the time came for battle. Their loyalty remained in question, and the fight for Gazi was not their own. Otherwise, they mingled freely about the camp and the quarries with the fighters-in-training.

Each of them had a different attitude toward this situation. Curry was fascinated with the drama of the story and infatuated with Korcha. Beland was terrified. He vacillated between wanting to cling to safety through obedience and wanting to make a reckless dash back to the protection of Bau Shahn. Nome was relieved that they had found service with the dangerous man spoken of by Burton and Mardek, but despondent that, as handlers, they would not be able to send their paltry earnings back to their holdings.

One day—it had been nearly two months since they had left home—Nome, Beland, and Curry sat together, away from the others, during lunch break at the quarries. They were still under light surveillance and had few opportunities to talk openly with one another. Today they sat at the edge of the work area close to the woods.

"It is hard work, but they are treating us well," Nome was saying.

"We are being fed and clothed and given cots to sleep on, if that is what you mean by 'treating us well,'" said Beland. "But I don't see where this is getting us. We are prisoners. Slaves. And we haven't seen any pay this Korcha promised. I don't think we will."

This nettled Curry. "Korcha's a hard man, but he's honorable. Everything we've seen of him, everything we've heard shows that. He knows our needs. He knows we are losing our holdings and are fighting to keep them from the Tosars. That's the kind of thing he understands and respects. These people are doing the same thing with Gazi, only on a bigger scale. He'll come through for us, Beland. Have a little confidence."

"Well, I just don't like it! I don't like being prisoner. I've never been cooped up like this and told when to get up and when to eat and where to go to work and who to talk to. From morning to night. I've often thought I was too hasty leaving the Farm. I wonder if we couldn't have found a way to hang on to our holdings without leaving them. The more I think of it, the more I think it was a dumb thing to do."

"It is hard listening to the two of you," Nome said. "Beland, you see nothing but the dark side of a situation. And, Curry, you sound like being captives of Korcha Rabon is the best thing that ever happened to you."

"It *is*, in a way. No, no, listen to me." Curry held up his hands. "I think I've seen more and learned more about the world these past two months than I have in most of my twenty-four years before this. I have *always* wanted to travel and to see more of the world than Curry House. The Outlands are nothing like what we've been told. They're not wild, fearsome places. Those were children's stories. Think of those old tales, those adventures we used to listen to in the Croft, Nome! We loved to hear them. Remember how we used to play them out? The Battle of Sweetwater, Danny Moor, and all that down at Big Rock and Aunt Gratchie's Silos? We are *in* one of them now, Nome. Beland? Keep your eyes on this Korcha Rabon. He is a remarkable man."

"No doubt about that, Curry. Korcha is remarkable," Nome agreed.

Beland leaned forward with his elbows on his knees. He let a long hack of spit slide to the grass between his feet. "Well, Curry," he said in a low, thoughtful voice, "I played that stuff with some of you back then, too. That was fun. This isn't. I think you are forgetting something. Your mother is back there trying to hang on to Curry House. And Rena and Baron are waiting for Nome to make some money to send to them. And my folks at the Farm are expecting me to save them, too, somehow. It doesn't look to me like we are doing too good. I don't care how remarkable Korcha is. Let him go off to the west and fight whoever he wants and get even more remarkable. But I wish he would let me alone. I don't want to go with him. I want to get back to Tosarkun."

"I know, Beland," Curry said more peaceably. "I know we are not much alike, you and I. I am sorry you cannot be more hopeful about our situation, because I think we are in the right place, hard as it is at times.

Korcha did say, when we first met him in that jail cell with the misk walls that...."

The bushes near them rustled suddenly, and a dog came quickly through them, limping, with a panting grin, ears back and head low, body wiggling with a furiously wagging tail.

Nome jumped up. "Chindit!" he shouted.

The commotion of the dog scurrying from one man to the other, giving high yelps of delight, rubbing up against their scratching and thumping of ribs, Nome's hugging of its head—this commotion drew a ring of curious onlookers who were just getting ready to go back to work on the misk rock.

"It's his mother's dog," Beland and Curry answered them as Nome knelt and joyfully continued to rub and stroke the dog. "No, I don't know how he got here. The last we saw of him was when we were crossing the border of our country. No, that was a couple of months ago! No, I don't know if anyone came with the dog, he just came out of the woods here. No. No, I have no idea."

Nome suddenly hunched over the dog and became intent on something. His hands searched around the neck, along the collar, which seemed unusually thick. He asked to borrow a fine misk-pick from one of his fellow workmen who stood in the crowd, and went to work carefully on the windings of a tight wire that held a slender leather band to the collar. A few moments later, he was unfolding a piece of paper. A surge of grief and happiness swelled in his chest and rose to his throat and his eyes, as he recognized that most familiar handwriting and read: "Our dearest Nome...."

A thick, hairy hand reached down around his shoulder and grasped the edge of the page. Nome indignantly gripped the paper and began to pull away. His eyes followed the hand up the arm until they came to rest on the gray whiskers and flushed face of Ila Rabon. The paper slowly slid from Nome's fingers.

SEVEN

The March

That same day, the date for the march was announced. In seven days, the entire Rabon force of five thousand would gather in the tent fields and begin moving westward, the first stage of the long-awaited Return. 'n Burning Graute became a beehive, as the Gazines stopped their routine work and training and began packing. Local people from the town replaced them in the quarries, and the newly trained native police replaced the Gazine security forces throughout the whole district of Kezzlhjem.

Nome, Beland, and Curry left the miskworks and became handlers. They had an opportunity to see, once again, the place where they had been captured. Joining a crew of a dozen men, they made many trips to the caverns behind the waterfall to extract the precious arms and supplies gathered there over the years in preparation for this week. The loading entrance was high above the falls, back in the woods, away from the river. It had been sealed with a cleverly concealed stone plug in the ground. Five men were needed to move it. The falls were tamer than when Nome and his friends first saw them: its water dropped straight down in powerful dignity, and no opening was visible behind it.

Chindit was caged back at the tent field. Nome himself had been required to build the cage under the instructions and watch of several soldiers. When Ila had intercepted the letter from his parents, Nome, Curry, and Beland had been taken before Korcha. He and Ila had studied the letter a long time over the desk in the room at the back of the ironworks, while the three worried men stood waiting. When they were satisfied that there was no code, no hidden meaning in the words, the letter was returned to Nome. In fact, it confirmed the story the three men had told.

"This, then, is how you will send your money back to your parents?" Korcha had asked.

"Sir?"

"Your dog. Your mother's dog apparently knows the way. This is a trained messenger dog, is it not?"

"Yes, sir. No, sir," flustered Nome. "I mean, yes, Chindit went home after I sent him away; and he found us, somehow, with the letter from my mother. But he's not trained to do this. He's just a farm dog, just my mother's pet. I am as amazed as anyone, sir, that the dog found us here. He must be an incredible tracker!"

"Well, apparently your mother knew the dog would find you," said Ila. "Why else would she attach a letter to the collar?" He turned to his brother. "We could use such a dog, Korcha. A messenger dog? Why not? Here it is already trained. It might not take much to adapt this training to our purposes with the help of this handler here."

"Mmmm. I don't think so, Ila," said Korcha.

"Why not?" Ila argued. "If you are thinking there isn't time, now that we are about to begin the march, I would say that training could go on as we are underway. He might be even more valuable once we get to Gazi and have to communicate through Mommick lines."

"It is a nice idea. But, if I heard the man correctly, he said the dog is not trained to carry messages. I think we are looking at something here other than a smart dog. There is something about the relationship between this man and his mother that goes through the animal. I don't think it is something we will be able to capture and use." He addressed Nome: "You may keep the dog, but he must be either caged or on a leash attached to you. If he is found loose, I will order him destroyed. How is he with children?"

"Children, sir? Uhh...he loves children."

"Uh-huh," said Korcha. "Well, that is the one exception. You may let him free for the children to play with. Especially on the march; the march will not be easy for them. But the dog must always be under supervision by one of you three. Understand?"

"Yes, sir," all three answered at once.

"I want you sending no messages before you are paid. And then you talk to me before you do. Understand?"

"Yes, sir," said Nome. "Excuse me, sir, you mentioned getting paid. I don't mean to sound...ahmm...out of order here...but when would we get paid? There is a deadline we are facing that is coming up pretty soon, and we were hoping that the three of us might put our pay together and try to find a way to send it home and at least make the hundred-day payment on one of the holdings."

"Everyone in the whole company gets allowance based on their needs when we arrive at the cache hole, ten days into the march. You'll get yours then. If you are planning to try the dog, that would be the time to do it. But remember, see me first! Dismissed."

....

The Day of the March was one of the first mild days of early autumn. The sky was clear liquid blue. There was a touch of coolness to the air. The leaves were just beginning to turn color. Tents no longer stood on the tent field; but there were five thousand exultant Gazines milling about, giddy with eagerness for this day, which had for so long been promised. At the center of the field, a large fire had been burning since the middle of the night. The crowds were directed into orderly rows, forming a circular amphitheater around the fire. The contour of the field provided a perfect setting, for it gradually sloped down from all sides to a natural depression where the fire was being tended.

Nome, Curry, and Beland sat at the outer edge of the crowd, on the packed wagons, and listened to the songs, the chanting, and what sounded like memorized choral poetry. They could make nothing of the words, for it rose up as a blended roar of rhythms and cadences. Eventually, Korcha Rabon entered the open space at the center near the fire. He was tiny, hardly to be noticed from where the three handlers sat. But when he spoke, every word rose to them like a shot. He began by talking about the fire burning there before them, a pale reminder of the fire of the Greatsada, which still burned somewhere in the mountains of Gazi. "Look around you," he shouted, "and see that Gazi lives! Look around you and have no doubt that the fire burns!" He talked about the years of exile they had endured together and about the hard work the people had done. He praised them, he thanked them, he honored his brother, Ila, and his martyred sister, Rilda, and brother, Mehtor. He talked about the suffering of their branded people in Gazi, about reports of their precarious welfare, brought to him across the great distance. Finally, he warned, again and again, that what lay ahead would be hard, and for some deadly. He warned about the rigors of the march, the uncertainty of spirits on the Plains of Wildness, the inevitable warfare they would face when they came to their land, crushed by the Mommicks. "...but today!" he concluded, "...today...we are going home!"

A roar went up from the crowd, an unrestrained thunder, which rolled on and on, and gradually settled into a chanting of "...the fire burns!...the fire burns!...the fire burns!..." At length, the frenzy died away; the crowd began to break up; and all five thousand churned and muddled across the field to their assigned places. Horse carts jerked into motion; wagon wheels jolted forward; the march was under way.

The citizens of 'n Burning Graute lined the roads, as this parade passed near the town, and cheered them on, waving, bowing, many in tears. It had been an unusual relationship. The procession slowly wound its way down to the river, along the bank, and crossed the bridge. At that point, over the next hour, it split into three columns, each heading in a different direction.

Already, weeks before they would encounter the enemy, the Gazines were moving into position for the attack. Their separation into three columns, wide apart but linked by close communication, was an essential stage in their strategy. The success of The Return depended on it.

The *southern column* was led by Ila Rabon, taking the main road to cross the south bridge of the Gaffling River (newly rebuilt after the flood, two months earlier) to join the High Road to the West. There were about a thousand of them, mostly families with the very young and the very old, who would follow the easy High Road all the way to Gazi.

The *northern column* of two thousand warriors was led by Commander Mira Shannan. They moved away from 'n Burning Graute in a northwesterly arc that would straighten out and proceed in parallel with Ila's route.

The *central column*, also two thousand strong, was led by Korcha Rabon himself, plunging straight ahead into the woods between the southern and northern forces.

Both routes, Korcha's and Mira Shannan's, took them through dense forest and wild, rocky terrain. They followed old overgrown roads, abandoned for a generation or two. The firmness of a roadbed was needed for the wagons; and local guides, who knew the territory, had been hired to lead the way. The entire route of the northern and central armies had been scouted and marked several times during the year before the march; for it passed through the territory of a hostile forest people before it arrived at the open desert of The Plains of Wildness.

The strategy of the march was to send the smallest band with Ila, out in the open, heavily laden with most of the supplies. It was hoped that the first reports to reach the Mommicks would be about this force, while the other two armies would be approaching out of sight. Korcha's army traveled lightest, pulling many empty wagons. They were to load with arms, money, and supplies at the "cache hole," which had been secretly stocked ahead of time. Eventually, the three armies would come into the open simultaneously at The Plains of Wildness; but there would be no Mommick scouts in that vast, eerie place. The Mommicks would be preparing in southern Gazi only for a force of a thousand, burdened with dependents, and approaching from a single direction.

Nome and his companions traveled with the central company. By day, they worked with the hackers, ranging far ahead of the wagons, cutting trees and clearing brush. Evenings, they helped to make camp, collect firewood, cook, haul water, wash dishes. Nights, they slept on bare ground as soundly as they had ever slept in their lives. Each day's stopping place had been marked ahead of time by scouts; and there were days when Korcha drove the company beyond exhaustion, long past dark, to keep on schedule.

On the ninth day, they entered hill country, and the terrain became rough and cruel. Mercifully, at noon of the tenth, they arrived at the cache hole and settled for a two-and-a-half-day rest. The cache hole was concealed under a rock field that ran down between two hills. It was a maze of tunnels, unguarded, but heavily booby-trapped. After disarming the traps, checking the cache, and ascertaining that all was undisturbed, Korcha announced that the rest of the afternoon and evening was free time, that allowances would be given out after supper, and that the work of emptying the cache hole would begin in the morning.

When they had finished washing dishes and resupplying the campfires for the section to which they had been assigned, Nome and his friends eagerly got in the line leading to the quartermaster's tent. In hushed voices, they talked among themselves about how much they might be given, feeling that they had worked hard enough in the past weeks to be given a good wage and hoping that, when they all put their pay together, it might be enough to ransom at least one of the holdings for another hundred-day. Maybe, they said, folks back home could come up with the balance somehow...maybe neighbors would give something. Despite what Beland had said about slave labor, they were earning a wage—although whatever they were paid, it would be far from making their fortune.

As they stepped to the table, the quartermaster glanced up at them and said, "Ah yes, you three. I have a note here from Korcha about you. You certainly must have done right by him. That's a lot of money." He pushed forward three stacks of coins, the largest to Nome, a shorter to Beland, one slightly shorter to Curry.

"This is our pay?" gasped Nome.

"It is. Take it." the man said, turning to his accounts.

"But...but...."

"Something wrong?" he looked up sharply.

"No, sir, nothing wrong, thank you," Curry said quickly, scraping his stack from the table into his hands. "Thank you very much."

The others did the same and hurriedly backed away from the quartermaster, nodding further thanks. When they stood by themselves, they counted.

"Houda! There is enough here for full next hundred-day payment on all three holdings!" exclaimed Beland.

"May the Holy wrap Korcha 'round!" Curry fervently whispered. "What a man he is. We certainly came to the right place when we came to him."

"He said allowances were given based on need," said Nome, "but I never guessed...."

"I'm sorry for what I said about him," Beland admitted humbly. "He's wrung a cruel amount of sweat out of us, but he sure has paid generously. If we can only get this home to Tosarkun now, we are good for another hundred-day."

"And that's the next problem...and a big one," said Nome more subdued. "How can we get this home? Chindit couldn't carry this weight."

"Oof!" Beland snorted. "I forgot. What a joke! We're rich enough here, but the Farm is a couple of weeks away; and Korcha has a leash around our necks, just like Chindit's."

They were all glum and silent for a moment. Then Beland continued, "Here's what I think the smart thing to do now would be. Hear me out, you might not like this, but here is what I think. We could easily slip away now, just slip off to the side into the woods and head back along the way we came. It's clear and open all the way, and we could travel fast. They would never follow us. They are going in the opposite direction and are thinking of only one thing—keeping on schedule. We know the way. We could be at Tosarkun in a week, handing the payment in at Tosar's Keep in plenty of time."

"Beland, just like you," said Curry in disgust.

"No, Beland," said Nome. "I wouldn't go along with that until we're desperate."

"But we *are* desperate! We have to get this money back! It's too heavy for the dog...and it would be a crazy idea to tie so much money around the neck of a dog...and we are being dragged farther and farther away from home every day! Let's get out of here!"

"Calm down, Beland," Nome ordered. "We have some problems; we are tired out; we are worried about our folks; but we are not desperate. One thing at a time. Our next step is to go and talk with Korcha. That is what he told us to do when we got paid. Remember that?"

Beland was furious, and he was tempted to leave them and go back alone. But he was not brave enough to go against them to that extent. Or to face a week-long hike through the wild Outlands by himself. It was a good thing, too; for he did not realize that Korcha had ordered the watch on the three men intensified, once they received their pay, knowing that this would be a critical test of their trustworthiness. Had they tried to "slip away" that evening, arrows would have brought them down in the woods.

Instead, the three asked to speak to Korcha Rabon. He was in conference in his tent, and they waited restlessly for nearly an hour. When they were finally called in, he was sitting on a camp stool in the tent, hunched forward, clutching his head. They stood tentatively near the door, suddenly fearful and uncertain. He released his head from the pressure of his fingers and lifted it heavily, showing a pinched, ashen face.

"Yesss," he said, "you're here to see me as I told you."

"Yes, sir," said Nome. "Are you all right, sir?"

"Never mind!" he snapped irritably. "Yes. Yes, I'm fine," more softly. "Now," he stood and took a breath and paced back and forth for a moment as though trying to concentrate on the topic. "That dog of yours. Have you decided to send your pay home with him?"

"Well, sir," Nome replied, "we wanted to talk with you about that. We are extremely grateful to you for the amount you have paid us. We can't tell you how surprised and how appreciative we are. I mean, we had no idea, sir...well, anyway, what I want to add...hoping you won't take this as a complaint...is that we still have a big problem. You are suggesting we send the money by the dog, but that amount of coin is far too heavy for him."

"That's no difficulty," said Korcha casually. "Just trade your coin in with the quartermaster for a note of trade."

"Oh, yes si...note of trade?"

"Yes, we still have some reserves registered with the town council of 'n Burning Graute."

"But, excuse me, sir, but we have to send the money to our families in Tosarkun."

"I understand that," said Korcha testily. "You are not familiar with notes of trade, I see. Well, I don't have interest in going into it for you now; but take my word for it, a note of trade from me given to your families and passed on to your Tosars will be accepted as gold and redeemed at 'n Burning Graute. You men have a naive and isolated view of what is going on in the world. There is more commerce between the *kun* of Bau Shahn and the so-called Outlands than you are aware."

Beland impulsively pushed forward and blurted: "But a dog, sir! Putting all that money on a dog who could get killed or lost as easy as anything on the way! Couldn't you let one of us go back, sir, to take the money to our folks and get it safely...."

The rest of the speech stuck in Beland's throat, paralyzed by icy fright, for Korcha had suddenly gone white and rigid, fixing him like a cobra. Then came words at him exhaled in a hiss:

"I...will...not...hes-s-s-itate!"

With a great effort, Nome reached out his arm, put it around Beland's shoulder, and slowly pulled him back behind himself whispering, "I am sorry, sir, I'm sorry." Korcha held his transfixed stance for another moment, then gradually relaxed and turned away.

Long, painful moments passed in silence. Then: "You two men go and bring that dog here. After that, you are dismissed. You stay here."

Korcha had never called any of them by name. Yet, even though his back was to them, they knew immediately what was wanted. Curry and Beland darted out of the tent, and Nome stood still. The commander paced and brooded for a full five minutes, ignoring the man who stood in the tent with him. Curry and Beland hurried back in with Chindit on a leash, handed him over to Nome, and vanished without regret.

"Have a seat," said Korcha pulling a camp chair with arm-rests over to him. Korcha sat down opposite on his own stool and studied Nome's surprised, anxious face. "I am sending you alone with a message for Ila. I want you to leave tomorrow morning. Our scouts will give you detailed instructions about how to find the way to the High Road to the West, where Ila is. It will take you two full days to get to the road, because you will be traveling south...actually south-southwest...cross-country. I will allow you a half-day to find Ila. He should be right at the spot where you come out, or a few miles east or west of it on the road. Then you must get to the Sea Road going north, as fast as you can, and follow it until you arrive at the inn at Trapple Rock. Because you have the road at that point, you will easily be able to get there in a day-and-a-half. We will be there. Ila will send a message for me back with you."

"Could you go over that again, sir? I'm not sure I got all of it...."

"No need to," said Korcha, involuntarily raising both hands to the sides of his head. "The scouts will go over it with you in detail in the morning. Rise early. They will draw you maps. Just understand this: today is the first of the month; you set out on the second; the morning of the fourth you meet Ila; and, by noon, start back north. On the fifth, be at Trapple Rock. My army will rest here for two more days and unload the cache hole. Then we will make a two-day march to Trapple Rock. We will see you there. Ask for the innkeeper. He is a friend."

"Yes, sir, but may I ask...," Nome hesitated; Korcha was pressing both sides of his head forcefully with his fists. "...may I ask why you are sending me? I know you have some doubts about our dependability. Understandably...I mean, we are not from your people."

"Do not have any illusions that I trust you," Korcha answered lowering his arms. "I have learned that, in a struggle like ours, trust is a vain and foolish feeling. My judgment is that you will not betray me or try to escape. For one thing, it is in your interest to stay with us because we have what you need: the money for your payments. Moreover, I have a hostage. No, not your friends, your dog. I want you to write a note to your parents right now—see, there is paper and pen over there. Get them now and write your letter. Then I want you to turn in your coin, and that of your friends, for a note of trade from the quartermaster. You will come back here with it; and I will have read your letter. I will watch you fasten it to the dog's collar. Then I will keep the dog with my section, away from your friends, until I meet you at Trapple Rock. At that time...when I see you again, when you hand me a message from my brother...your dog will run free and hopefully homeward."

"I see, sir. You can count on me, sir. I will do what you order. But, still, I seem like such a strange choice for this job. I don't understand why you are not sending one of your own people, where there is no need of guarantees and the like."

"Well, it's quite simple," replied Korcha. "The errand you are going on is quite dangerous. If someone is killed, I would rather it be you than one of my people. Now write your letter, and keep it brief. I don't want to talk anymore."

EIGHT

Strange Visitors

When Nome had done all that Korcha had ordered, it was dark. The camp was settling down for sleep, but he was not ready. Taking the white wooden pipe from his belongings (it had been returned to him after he had been released from the jail), he moved off to the edge of the camp near the sentries, and not so far away as to arouse suspicion. He sat on a log to think and to play some soft, low tunes. He found that he could not think calmly; but the music soothed him, and he continued to pipe for an hour or so, until a sentry came over and told him he had better get to bed. He carefully felt his way among the sleepers on the ground in his section, trying not to step on anyone or knock anything over. All about, he could hear the sleep-breathing, washing like waves, and the rasp of snores. As he shook out his sleepsack next to the spot where he judged his two friends to be, he heard a whispered:

"Nome."

"Curry?"

"Yeh."

"You still awake?" He continued to straighten his sack, pulled off his boots and pants, then crawled in.

"Where were you so long?" whispered Curry.

"Talking to Korcha. Then I went off over there to think for a while. He's sending me away from here tomorrow...to take a message to Ila down south on the road."

"What?"

"Yes," Nome chuckled, "and he's keeping Chindit hostage till I get back. Isn't that bizarre? Is Beland awake?"

"Wait, what are you telling me? No, I don't think he's awake. Beland?"

"Beland?"

"He's long gone," said Curry. "I'm surprised he can sleep, at all, after the look Korcha gave him. Houda, what a dumb move he made in there! Now, tell me again, what did you say?"

"Well, first Korcha has me write a letter to Fa and Mo, and then go out and get the money from you two, and trade it in for a note of trade; and then he reads my letter over a couple of times, and has me wire the letter and the note to Chindit's collar while he watches. He's a sick man, you know, Curry. He was in agony through all of this, with a headache he was trying to ignore. He looked awful."

"I know. He really looked in pain."

"Anyway, after he has me do all this...or was it before? I don't know, I'm getting mixed up about what happened when. Anyway, he tells me to sit down; and he gets me a chair; and he tells me I am to leave early tomorrow to go cross-country to find Ila on the road, and give him a message, and to bring one back. And I say, 'Why me?' and he says, 'I would rather have you get killed than one of my people.' And he says, 'I'm keeping your dog, with the money, hostage to make sure you come back.' You are all going to push on in another few days, and I am supposed to join you at a certain spot four days from now."

"Houda," was all Curry said for a while.

They were silent, each on his back, staring through black tree boughs at twitching stars.

"What do you think of that?" Nome asked.

Curry did not answer at once. Then he said, "I think you are lucky."

"Lucky!" The word came like a cough.

"Korcha Rabon is a remarkable man," Curry continued in a dreamy voice. "This is a remarkable people, and their cause is right. I envy you, Nome. I would not mind being given your assignment. I would like to do what I could to serve."

"Curry, what...what are we talking about here? Yes, he's quite a man. I respect him, and I am afraid of him. But I don't much care for being sent out where I can be killed! I don't know what the dangers are out there...in a way that makes it worse. I'm like Beland, I keep wondering why we decided to do this in the first place. I'm not going to be any good to Brighthome dead out here in the woods."

"No," said Curry, "the Holy wrap you 'round! But...you know...somehow what we are caught up in here seems so much *bigger* than our worries about Curry House and Brighthome and Beland's Farm. I know we are responsible to our families, and I really do want to follow through for them. And I think we can probably best do that and save our homes by serving Korcha."

"Yes," agreed Nome, "he said again to me tonight something to the effect that we could keep meeting the payments by sticking with him."

"Did he really?" said Curry with admiration.

"Yes, and I think you and he are right, that being with the Gazines is our best hope of saving our homes. But keep in mind, Curry, that what we are going through here is the easy part. After this we are heading into war."

"I have been thinking about that, Nome," he replied evenly, "and I have been thinking that I would rather serve as a soldier than a handler. I would gladly fight for this man...for this people. I wish I had his trust. That is why Beland makes me so mad. At times, I wish I were not associated with Beland."

"Take it easy on Beland, Curry. He's scared. That's all. *I'm* scared."

"I know," said Curry quietly, "I know. Funny, I am not scared. I wonder what the days ahead are going to bring...."

They whispered on this way; but the conversation was becoming loose, disjointed. At one point, Curry was talking slowly, speech slurred, and what he said did not make any sense. He left it unfinished....

"What?" said Nome.

No response. Measured, deep breathing.

Then began Nome's night of terror. He lay listening to the words he had just spoken; and he knew, for the first time, that he might truly die. This may be the last day; and it has already gone, passed into darkness. How long he lay like this, rigid with imaginings, he could not know, as he slid into dreams, murky and slippery: Murchew's daughter gaunt and disappointed, tearing apart a yellow flower, Mardek with a racoon's head, silently giving a resounding command: Go and do not come back! A gagging dog he had never seen with a thick collar choking it, he clumsily trying to work it loose with a misk-pick, jabbing the furry throat, the blood...He awoke from some devouring nightmare he could not remember, rose up from the ground on one elbow and looked about at the tousled, sleeping shapes all about him and thought, 'They are all dead. These are the fallen. I am dead.' He knew he was awake; he could see the sentry fires far off, burning low; but he also knew he was dead. All is lost, he thought. He dropped back to the ground and twisted his face aside in anguish. He shut his eyes; and there was no time; and he saw it coming, the boy whirling the hoe; and it smashed his face into many pieces, which then lay scattered on the ground. "I can't stand this," he cried, "I want to go back!"

....

It was dawn. Nome knew it, though he did not open his eyes. He was aware of awakening, and felt such delicious peace that he was afraid to disturb it. He felt the clammy dampness of his shirt and sleepsack against his skin; and he did not remember the night...but he knew. He did not want to remember. He wanted to feel this cool morning air on his face. He could see the light, dimly now, through closed lids and dared to move languorously and to stretch. Amazing, he felt rested, content. Today he would go on a journey, he thought. Why did that bring him joy? He let his eyelids open and saw the gray-blue sky behind waving green leaves, so many of them, thousands and thousands clustered there, flickering in a light breeze. Again, he inhaled deeply and held his breath to savor it, then let it escape slowly. He could feel the nearness of dried leaves by his face, fallen pine needles matted on the moist ground. He anticipated the smell of wood smoke, campfire smoke, breakfast cooking. He remembered wheatcakes, plumsauce, fresh honey, steamy khavla. Slowly, Nome turned his head sideways, as he lay on his back, and looked to see what was watching him.

Two paces from his face were two beings, one slightly behind the other. At first they seemed to be stones, shin-high; but they were definitely gazing at him with solemn, innocent eyes. Then he saw that they were feathered, at least toward the top; but their eyes dominated, round, unblinking, yellow eyes with large black pupils. Were those wings...or arms...clasped firmly to the sides as though painted? Owls, thought Nome. No, stones painted like owls, put here beside my head by someone. But they moved, or they seemed to move. He did not actually see them move, but he knew within himself that they were alive. For moments, he had no feelings, no questions, no judgments about what was near his cushioned head. He looked at them, and they looked back. And now, one of them blinked. He saw that. And the other one blinked. They are owls, he said to himself, the large eyes, the hooked beak dropping down, the round head of gray feathers. Yet these are stones. They seem to be stones, I am sure of it. What is this? he heard himself begin to ask. What are these? What is happening here? He glanced away for a moment, to see if he were fully awake, and knew he was. There was a sharp clarity about the woods, the sleeping bodies on the ground, the wheels of the wagons beyond. He could feel the brush of the sleepsack on his legs when he moved and the firm ground beneath his back. These beings that were planted there, staring at him with intense presence and interest, were just as real and solid. Nothing dreamlike about them; but he could not decide if they were stones or birds. They will startle and move away when I get up, he thought; and he raised up on one elbow for a better look. They did not budge, but one of them blinked a slick, full blink. "Holy," he whispered; and he felt the first twinge of anxiety in his chest. He sat upright, hoping with the sudden motion to shoo them away; but they only moved slightly and gazed at him with keen interest. "Oh, Holy!" he muttered, now afraid. Will these things fly at me? he wondered; and instinctively he shrank back and scrambled to his feet. But they had turned and were slowly moving away from him with a gentle waddle, comic figures, their feathered backs to him, tottering toward the forest. He whirled this way and that to find someone who was awake, someone else who saw it; but no one was, no one did. When he looked again, they were gone. Did they go around that tree? He cautiously tracked them, but could find no sign of the creatures, no prints or disturbance of the ground.

Then he looked down and realized that he had gone after them with his pants off, so he hurried back to his sack and dressed.

The scout was up early, on Korcha's orders, and helped Nome kindle a small fire for breakfast. The rest of the camp slept on, for this was the first day of rest since the march began. As they ate, the scout described the terrain to Nome, and told him what to look for and what to avoid. On his lap, he spread out a map he had drawn and, with greasy fingers, pointed out landmarks here and there. He told Nome that it should be quite accurate and the distances quite close to scale; although, correctly mapping a trail cross-country was always harder to do. He was a pleasant fellow, and Nome enjoyed the conversation; but the moment came when the scout stood up and pulled a packet from inside his shirt.

"Here, put this string around your neck and tuck this pouch inside your shirt," he said. "It is the message for Ila. I have made up your food supplies over here. You'd better get going."

Nome checked out with the sentries, then plunged into the woods. The going was easy, through high virgin pine with massive trunks and crowns that soared into a cloudless sky. There was little undergrowth with which to wrestle, and the floor of the forest was layered with cones and dry pine needles. The scout had instructed him to keep the sun in front of him and to his left, adjusting gradually throughout the morning as it rose toward noon, so that it would appear less and less to his left and more directly in front of him. In the afternoon he was to reverse the adjustment gradually and keep the sun more and more to his right; and, in this way, he would keep a southerly direction throughout the day.

It was impossible to see the sun, however, in these early morning hours, through the dense cover of trees; so Nome had to estimate the angle of the sun from the cast of light and shadow high in the trees. He knew that, if he maintained a southerly course, he could not miss the High Road, which lay across his path for many miles. It was a beautiful fall day, with just a nip of chill in the air, and Nome was enjoying the walk. He realized that this was the first time he had been alone since he had left Brighthome.

He found himself thinking of those owlstones, puzzling over them. He decided that they must have been some kind of queer animal he had never heard of, some kind of turtle with hard shell...and feathers? No, he chuckled, I don't think so. He remembered, particularly, their watchful eyes and their silly tilt in waddling away. A strange animal, no doubt. He wished he had asked the scout about it. He would have known.

He stopped for lunch on the shore of a little jewel of a lake. He had jumped for joy when he saw it, glistening silver and blue through the trees; for it was marked on his map, and this meant he was on course and on time. After lunch, he played his pipe for a while, then continued his walk, full of energy. By late afternoon he was growing weary; but he took short rest stops and continued over rougher and gradually rising land. The pine forest was behind him now; and he could keep his bearings by the sun which was sinking toward the horizon on his right. When he stopped for supper, it was too dark to travel farther, so he found a level, protected spot and rolled out his sleepsack. A beautiful sunset told him he need not fear rain and could look forward to another fine day.

It was a fresh, clear morning which woke him. However, his breakfast was disturbed by the two strange beings...or two just like the ones he had seen the day before...standing, one slightly behind the other as before, about ten paces away, alongside a huge oak. He ate slowly, chewing sluggishly, his eyes on the creatures, who mildly gazed at him in return. What are those? he thought in alarm. Could they have followed me? Some kind of animal; but they don't move; and they look like rocks painted to resemble owls. But, look, that one just moved. They look heavy. He called out, "Shoo! Shush! Get! Get away!" and flapped his arms. The round eyes changed just a flicker. Amusement? Was that amusement in those animal eyes? Nome jumped to his feet with a shout; but he thought better of rushing at them, even though they were small and in no way looked fierce. He sat down on his log and pondered. He leaned over to pick up a stick of wood to throw at them; but, as he drew back, he knew he should not; so he dropped it. Not knowing what else to do, he prepared to leave; and then he noticed that the owlstones were gone.

He saw no more of them the rest of that day, although he saw deer, hundreds of birds, mice, a fox, and perhaps a lynx. That night he went to sleep worried, for he had not come upon a second lake marked on the map near the High Road. He hoped that he had only veered east or west of it and was still quite close to the road.

The next morning he skipped breakfast, in order to be underway quickly; and, before the sun was far above the horizon, he was overjoyed to find himself stepping out of the brush onto the High Road to the West.

This must be it, he thought. It certainly is broader and better cared for than that little side-road we saw the day after we left Tosarkun, the one we thought was the road to the west. Maybe that was a feeder road. This one is in great condition. Ila's people are fortunate. This reminds me of the Grandmaison Road. Now I have to find Ila.

If Nome had not veered too far east or west on his second day, Ila's army was scheduled to be passing this point within a few hours. Perhaps they have passed already, he thought. It would not be hard to keep schedule and make good time on this road. Wait here? Or go to look for them? Waiting assumes that they are still coming from the east; but, if they have already gone by, then my waiting here would mean their leaving me behind. Obviously, I have to start west to catch up with them.

He started hiking west at a brisk pace. He realized now that, if the army were behind him, he would be keeping a steady gap between himself and them; and they would not meet. I wonder at Korcha's giving me such vague directions for this part. He just said for me to meet them here...but perhaps I have come out at the wrong point. Or, if Ila's army is not on schedule...or ahead of schedule...I am really in trouble. He quickened his pace. They will be around here soon, he thought. I probably will meet travelers that I can ask.

But he did not. He was alone on the road for three worrisome hours. Finally two horsemen approached from the west. Nome hailed them and asked if they had encountered a large crowd of people. They had not.

"How long have you been riding this road?" Nome asked.

"Since yesterday morning."

"Have you passed the turning for the Sea Road to the North?"

"Of course!" they laughed, and rode on.

Then Ila is behind me! he said to himself. He retraced his steps, and the sun passed the mid-point of the sky. Noon: according to Korcha's directions, he should have given the message already and arrived at the Sea Road. Here he was walking *away* from the Sea Road and losing time. "Oh, Holy," he said aloud, "let Ila come along quickly."

The heat of the day was ebbing, as the sun dropped in the sky. He passed the point on the road where he had come out of the woods, and kept walking east, expecting at any moment to see movement on the road, far in the distance. Late in the afternoon, he met another traveler, this time coming from the east. He, too, had no crowd to report. Nome turned and started west again at a trot. He was baffled and panicky. Ila's army seemed to have disappeared, and he himself was now nearly a half-day behind schedule. The only thought that occupied him now was to get to Trapple Rock on time. He would have to face Korcha, with the message undelivered. That would be frightening. But to look for Ila any longer would be worse. To do so would mean that Korcha's army would leave Trapple Rock without him; and Korcha was serious about holding Chindit hostage until Nome's arrival.

Again, he passed the spot where he had come out of the woods. It was now evening. He had been looking since shortly after dawn.

Get to the Sea Road! Nome panted to himself. Get to the Sea Road tonight! Then I will be a half-day behind, and I can try to make up my time tomorrow on the road turning north. He gave me a day-and-a-half on that road. Maybe I can make it in a day.

His side ached, his lungs ached, his legs were going stiff. He ignored his body, looked away from the pain, and kept moving, now walking, now trotting, now walking again. Darkness closed in, and the stars appeared. Still he went on. A brilliant three-quarters moon rose up over the edge of the world behind him. He was numb with his steady, driving motion. There was a low buzz in his head, and he crowded the right side of the road, peering toward the ditch and the bushes for any opening that might be the road north.

Suddenly, there it was, quiet and open, as though it had been there all along. And there was a solid, carved sign at the edge of the ditch, which he could read in the moonlight: "Sea Road-North." He threw himself down at the base of it, heaving and panting, feeling he had been saved from disaster.

"No...more...tonight," he said, "No mo..." With an effort, he dragged himself, like a wounded animal, off into the bushes, slipped out of the pack harness, and slept that way till morning.

At daybreak, he was up again; and, after a quick breakfast, he was on the road again. Korcha cannot blame me for not finding Ila, he told himself, if Ila was not where he was supposed to be. I will return Korcha's message to him unopened. I will tell him what I did and how hard I tried, and I will describe the road and the Sea Road sign to him, so he will know I did what he told me. He will see I did all I could.

Within the first hour, he was having trouble with his legs. They were stiff and especially painful in the knees, but he kept walking at a fast pace, pushing past the pain. Shortly, the discomfort became so strong that he decided to rest for a while by the side of the road. He looked like an old man, lowering himself to the ground under the shade of a tree. When he was motionless, the pain was gone, and he felt blissfully relieved. As he rose to continue on, his knees screamed. He hobbled forward on the road, anxiety rising. A day-and-a-half to make in one day: Korcha was expecting him at Trapple Rock this evening!

For the rest of the morning, he walked on, grimacing and moaning. He tried walking backwards, walking sideways, walking stiff-legged, not bending at the joints, anything he could think of to change the tearing stress on inflamed nerves and tendons. He knew he was losing time, but did not know what to do about it. If only some travelers would come by, someone he could ask for help. But these were dreadfully lonely roads. He wondered at their being so well maintained with so little use.

By mid-afternoon, he knew he was not yet halfway to Trapple Rock; and it was now certain that he would be late. Would they wait? No, of course not. He would have to go after them along the woods road they were opening. Fortunately, the army could not travel as fast as a man could walk; and perhaps, with another night's rest, his legs would recover. But Chindit. What about Chindit and the money? Would Korcha think that Nome had betrayed him and fled? Would he continue to keep the dog with him, thereby reducing chances that Chindit would find the way home on time?

Eventually, he stopped thinking and put all his strength into hypnotic motion. His suffering continued, but he no longer cared. Suddenly, from behind, he heard the sound of hooves on the road. Turning, he saw two horsemen approaching at a brisk trot. I've got to get help, got to get them to stop. I have to ask them, offer them something, what can I offer? What can I promise them? If only one of them would let me ride behind.

As they came up to him, Nome stood at the center of the road and called, waving his arms wildly, pleading for them to stop. They spurred and quickened their pace to a canter and passed him by, looking down with indifference.

"No, no, please!" he cried.

But their backs were to him, and they receded up the road. He stood defeated, arms dangling, looking after them. Then he looked away, and his eye caught something in the grass that gave him a start. The same two owlstones stood there, looking at him. He gave a cry and stumbled backward. I am going mad, he thought. Why are these things plaguing me? Not now! Not now! He glanced back up the road and, for a second time, could scarcely believe his eyes. The horsemen had stopped. One was standing in place and the other had turned and was slowly coming back to him.

"Oh, thank you! Thank you! He's coming back for me. Oh Holy!" And Nome took a step or two to meet the returning horseman. Then he glanced over to the grass again...warily, fearfully...and he saw the two creatures continuing to stare at him with what seemed like new intensity. He looked at the horseman. He looked back at the owlstones. He looked at the horseman, who was now more than halfway back to him. Suddenly, his heart jerked; and he lunged for the side of the road. He dove into the tall grass, past the owlstones, and buried himself in the bushes. Farther away he scurried, now squatting low and hobbling in a zig-zag path, moving into the thickest part of the undergrowth. There, under cover, he lay still, trying to suppress his panting breath and quiet his pounding heart. He heard a sudden burst of hoof beats; and, from his cover, watched the horseman rein up at the spot where he had left the road. The man nudged the horse this way and that, squinting into the woods where Nome was hiding. The man dismounted and took a few steps into the grass, looked about, and returned to the road. He shouted something to his companion. A thin voice called in return. The man made some gestures and shouted back. With one last hard look all about the edge of the woods, he mounted his horse and rode off.

Nome waited a long time, listening. Then he dragged himself from the undergrowth and returned to the road. All was clear. It was near sunset. He walked on.

He slept under the trees that night, not far from the road, knowing he was now officially late for the meeting with Korcha. In the morning, his legs were still bad, but he continued to walk. The day passed slowly, without incident. Mid-afternoon, he limped into the courtyard of the inn at Trapple Rock. The innkeeper, a huge, brawny man, who had to duck his head when passing through doorways, came out to meet him. Not waiting for introductions, Nome quickly asked about Korcha Rabon and the army.

"They left this morning," said the innkeeper. "Come inside. You look like you need some food and rest."

NINE

Change of Plans

"Troutman," said the great man affably. "Imber Troutman is my name."

"Nome Ogrodni." Nome bowed stiffly, nodding and trying to smile as they walked into the building.

"Wait here," said Troutman, indicating one of the dining room tables. "It is a little early for supper for us, but we have just started cooking, and I'll see If I can hurry something up for you."

"No, wait," said Nome, catching him by the sleeve as he was about to go off to the kitchen, "I can't pay. I don't have any money with me. All my belongings are with Korcha's army. It's all right, I have some food left in my pack. I just need to rest up a bit before I go after them."

"Go after them?" said the innkeeper turning back. "Ogrodni, I saw the way you came limping up that road. You'll fall in a heap if you try going anywhere without a hot meal inside you. I've been keeping this inn for thirty-one years, and I've become a fair judge of the condition of a person when they walk or ride through my gates. Don't worry about the pay. You're paid for. You're part of Korcha's army, aren't you? He and his people paid generously when they were here. You're just getting your share a little late." He turned and went off to the kitchen.

Nome continued to look at the door through which he had gone. The man's wavy reddish hair going gray, his gentle freckled face, his bulky frame were a comfort to the weary traveler. He felt welcome and safe. Tenderly, he lowered himself to a bench at the table and waited.

He looked about the room, built of heavy logs, with rough beams straddling the walls and a board ceiling rising up to the center-pole. The dining area was in a kind of porch, off to the side, with windows all about and sunlight streaming in. It reminded him of Brighthome, in a way. The floorboards were rough and heavily traveled, especially near the entryway. At the far end, opposite the dining area, there was a lounge area, where fat, upholstered chairs and a pair of sturdy rockers cozied around a cold fireplace. On the walls hung hides of various large animals, some embroidered about the edges, stretched out like tapestries. Also high on the walls, resting on pegs, were tubes of various shapes and lengths, firetubes that Nome had first seen at 'n Burning Graute. As far as he knew, there were no such weapons in Tosarkun. The Gazines had been stocking them for war; here, apparently, they were for hunting.

A stout, rosy-cheeked woman bustled into the room, steering before her a steaming tray of food. A pretty young woman followed, carrying a pitcher and a giant mug.

"I'm the innkeeper's wife, Mister Ogrodni, this here's my daughter. Imber told me how you were worn out and would be needing something good to eat quickly, so we did the best we could in a short time, I hope you like it. And isn't it a shame that your people have gone on without you! What a shame, what a shame. Now if there is anything we can do for you, Mister Ogrodni, or if there is more of anything here that you would like? I hope you have enough of everything, can we get you something? Well, we will leave you to eat your supper in peace, and then Imber will be back to show you to a room...."

She continued to say a few other things, all without taking a breath or allowing time for Nome to respond or do anything but nod and smile. The daughter said nothing, but nodded and smiled, and then followed her mother back to the kitchen. Nome wished the daughter had said something. He wanted to hear her voice. As he began to eat with relish, he kept glancing up at the kitchen door, hoping the daughter would come back...he imagined her needing to straighten up some things or clean in the lounge area.

But, when the door swung open again, the doorway was filled with Imber Troutman, ducking his head, out of habit, as he passed through. He joined Nome at the table and said:

"How is it, Ogrodni? Getting enough?"

"It is wonderful, Troutman," answered Nome, wiping his mouth and beard-stubble with a napkin. "I don't know how I can thank you and your wife...and your daughter...for this. I feel my strength coming back. Such good food on such short notice. May the Holy be kind to you in return."

"Thank you. Well, we're innkeepers, you know. Have to be ready for people on a moment's notice, you know. We are used to it. Been thirty-one years we been doing this. Although I've never been put to work the way I was when that Rabon crowd came through here. That is a record number for Imber Troutman!"

"Where did they all stay?"

"We have some fields out back, big ones. They put up their tents out there. Some of those that were sick stayed here at the inn. I tried to get Korcha Rabon himself to stay here, but he wouldn't. Had to stay in a tent. We fed a lot of them, though. Yessir, they pulled out early this morning. Good people, but I felt bad about helping them go on to war. I don't believe in that, you know."

"I would appreciate it," said Nome, "if, after a while, you would point out to me the way they went. I'll just let this good supper settle in a bit, then I'll be off after them. Your wife mentioned something about a room, but I've got to be setting out right away to catch up with them. I will be able to track them easily through the cut in the woods they are making."

"Ogrodni," the innkeeper looked at him somberly, "you can't go after them."

"What? Why not?"

"You don't know this territory, do you? Trapple Rock is at the very edge of the Muicmuic lands. Traveling alone onto their lands is certain death. I don't even go there."

"Who are...what are 'mic-mic'?" asked Nome turning pale.

"Muicmuic. Like 'quickquick.' They are a strange people that live in the woods and keep to themselves. Very protective of their woods and almost never come out. Although they come here at times to trade with me. That stew you just ate was made with meat they brought in just last week. I don't do any hunting anymore. I have been dealing with them for twenty-five years now; so I know them pretty well; but I don't speak their language. No one does but them. I don't think they want anyone to learn it. Although, one of the scouts that Rabon had with him seemed to know a fair bit of it...I don't know where he learned it. Anyway, nobody goes into their woods. They don't allow it. And if you tried, Ogrodni, you wouldn't get far."

"But how could our people go through there then if...?"

"Oh, that's different. For one thing, you folks are an army, and the Muicmuic are no fools. They are not about to take on an army; although I suspect they could if they had to. And for another thing, that scout of Rabon's had been here several times before and must have come to some kind of understanding with them. I was sure surprised about that; but he did it. So, what it comes down to, Ogrodni, is that you missed the ferry. They can get through the Muicmuic, but you can't."

"But, couldn't you talk to them...or let them know that I am with the army...get me safe-passage or something? There has to be a way I can catch up with them!"

"I'm afraid not. I trade with them, and they are peaceable with me. In fact, I think they would protect us here at Trapple Rock if someone were to threaten us. But they aren't friends with me. I've tried, but they aren't interested in friendship with outsiders. And I don't go to find them; they come here when *they* are ready."

Nome moaned and put his forehead down on the table top alongside the supper dishes. He was quiet for a moment, then sat up, showing a miserable face, and looked at Troutman.

"Any way I could go around these Muicmuic? Are there many of them?"

"Yes, that's what you will have to do. But, yes, there are a lot of them. Their lands go far up north and down south almost to the High Road to the West. You will have to go back the way you came, if you want to go west looking for your folks."

Nome moaned again and lay his head back down on the table.

"And now, I think I will go and get that room ready for you, Ogrodni," said Troutman compassionately. "No need for you to be going off this evening."

When his host had left him alone, Nome stood up. His knees screeched with pain, but that seemed unimportant now. He was filled with despair. He limped and shuffled about the room aimlessly and drifted over to the fireplace and leaned heavily against the stones. Cut off, he thought, cut off from all we had hoped for. All is lost now, friends, fortune, home, even Chindit, poor dog. He cursed Korcha for his sketchy instructions and his heartlessness, cursed Ila for not being where he was supposed to be on the road, the fool! Himself for wasting crucial time going back and forth when Ila did not show up. This disaster need not have happened!

He pressed his face hard into the rough stone grit to the point of pain...drew a long breath...which began to swell to a sob...tilted his head back, mouth open...and...and his eyes rested on something that halted sighs, sobs, and breath. Tucked halfway behind an oil lamp on the mantelpiece, only a few inches from his face, was a curling piece of birch bark on which a single word had been scratched with a knife point, a word Nome had only heard at home in Tosarkun: "Houda."

Slowly, slowly, he reached up and took it down, stared at it, then turned it over and smoothed out the curl. There was scratched: "Chindit escaped! B."

He felt a rush of joy; and then came sobs, sobs that were waiting to come; and he dropped into the upholstered chair and shook silently. "Tha...thank you! Thank you, Beland," he whispered wetly, "Thank you."

....

That evening there was a sharp chill in the air, and Troutman decided to light a fire in the fireplace. He invited Nome to join him for some conversation and pipesmoking. The two men sat till late, talking of many things. It was a small fire, for not much was needed yet; and the dancing flames threw a bobbing glow on their faces as pipe smoke curled about their heads and rose to the rafters. Nome was feeling very content. Eventually he asked Troutman about the dog.

"Yes, I saw it," he said. "I did not mention it to you earlier, because I had no idea it would be significant for you, Ogrodni. That dog was as calm and cooperative as you would want a pet to be, right up to the last moment. Then, just as they were transferring him from one leash to a longer rope for the journey, away he jumps, and off he runs like a fury. What a clamor and yelling after him there was. But he was out of sight in a minute, down the path they had all come the day before. Never came back. I did not know what to make of it until you just explained it to me a minute ago. Well, Ogrodni, I don't mean any disloyalty to Rabon, but I am glad for you. Glad for you. I see you are feeling better."

"Yes, Troutman, much better, thanks to your kindness and the news that Chindit is on his way home. I really believe he will make it."

"Well, good."

"And now," said Nome, "I am also feeling very tired. I think I will be going to bed."

"Do that, Ogrodni. Sleep late. Stay as long as you like, and rest up before you take to the the road again. I enjoy your company, Ogrodni; and there are no other guests at the inn just now."

Nome stayed for three days, long enough for his legs to recover. Long enough to think through his plans, long enough to eat well and rest, long enough to spend time with the innkeeper's daughter. He woke each morning thinking of her. He talked with her in the garden, where she was cleaning vegetables, and played her some songs on his pipe. He drew her into conversation when she waited on him at mealtime. She was pleasant and friendly; and she obviously enjoyed the attention. But there was something reserved in her manner; and, in the end, she did not encourage him. She was, after all, an innkeeper's daughter, used to the passing flattery of travelers.

When he stood in the gateway, at the end of three days, saying goodbye to the three of them, he suffered with a very different kind of pain from that with which he had walked in. He ached at leaving this place, which had become home. He was not ready to forgo the kindness of Troutman and his wife. He was a little bit in love...and he was leaving. Waving goodbye and setting his face toward the open road reminded him of that lovely summer morning when he had left Brighthome.

The Sea Road North continued past Trapple Rock many days' journey and arrived, presumably, at the sea. However, Nome walked south, in the opposite direction, retracing the way he had come, wondering what the sea would have been like, and if he would ever see it. He had spent most of the past few days trying to make plans; but he still did not have a clear idea of what he should do. There seemed only one realistic possibility: to rush on and try to catch up with Ila's army or to take the High Road all the way to Gazi in hopes of finding Korcha's army there. He had no maps, no idea of how long it would take. And there was a new problem. He had only the food Troutman had packed before he left. It would last three or four days, if he were careful. He had no money. All he could think of was to look for work along the way in exchange for meals and lodging. That would slow him down, but he saw no other way.

He walked at a steady, even pace, not hurrying. He had decided that his leg cramps had come on because he had been rushing for long periods in deep anxiety. Now his trip back down the Sea Road was pleasant, when he could keep his mind off his worries. He only met a few other travelers and guessed that some would be staying at Trapple Rock that night. At times, he played the pipe as he walked, to keep himself company. Again he was feeling lonely and found it difficult not to worry. Mostly, he worried about money and the loss of all opportunity to ransom Brighthome. When he thought of this, he found himself anxiously speeding up to the beat of a thumping voice in his brain: "Got to catch up, got to catch up."

Nome was three-quarters of the way back to the High Road by the time it was too dark to travel. He wished nightfall was not arriving so early at this season. He slept on the ground among the trees, out of sight of the road. Sometime during the night, a large, lumbering shape moved into his campsite, sniffing and snorting about. As it nosed about Nome's head and sleepsack, he held his breath and lay motionless, fearing death. The black shape reared up and lightly clawed the tree from which the food pack had been hung; but it was out of reach, far along a stout branch. Nome could see the huge animal standing on hind legs, with pointed head and nose reaching high, swaying against the luminous night sky like a serpent enchanted. It dropped back to all fours with surprising lightness, turned, and ambled off into the forest.

At daybreak, he was back on the road, grateful for breakfast from his pack. He expected to arrive at the High Road within a few hours. It had been occurring to him that he might turn left, instead of right, and return to 'n Burning Graute to seek employment in the miskworks. Perhaps he might even seek his fortune in Kezzlhjem with the prince there. He would be closer to Tosarkun, and the problem of getting money home would not be so great. This seemed, however, to be a meek solution; and the words he remembered his Fa speaking in the Croft the night before they had left came back to him: "Sometimes the safe way is not the successful way." Nome knew in his heart that, when he reached the High Road, he would turn right and begin to walk west toward the Endicot Mountains.

Other fragments of remembered conversations were bumping about in his mind as he walked. He was hearing again what Curry had said to him, as they lay in the dark, about his desire to bond with the Gazine people and to fight in the service of Korcha Rabon. Could this be something that was drawing Nome onward, too? Perhaps he, too, had fantasies of being a soldier...no, a warrior. Like Curry, he was disgusted at being tied to a never-ending quest for money, a vain grubbing that could go on for the rest of his life. What a life! To fight alongside a brave and desperate people for their existence and their freedom, that was something more noble, something worth doing. Perhaps, when Gazi was one day free, he would be able to return with his friends to Tosarkun to fight for the freedom of their own people. His land would one day be given a new name.

    A recollection of something Troutman had said about the Gazines, that first evening, interrupted these thoughts: "Good people," he had said, "but I felt bad about helping them go on to war. I don't believe in that, you know." Believe in what? wondered Nome. Surely their cause is just. They have to return to fight the Mommicks. "I don't believe in that" kept coming back to him. Troutman had not said more, had not elaborated on this thought. But this simple, pointed statement stuck in Nome's memory like a barb. It led him to think of what the fighting in Gazi would be. He had seen the weapons they would use. He had carried them in his own arms and hands, load after load, during their transfer from the armory in the cavern behind the waterfall to wagons, in preparation for the march. Tubes, firedust, misk shields, all sorts of pointed-piercing, sharp-slashing fashioned steel. The liberation of Gazi would come by hacking and maiming, crushing and killing, blood and exposed, broken bone. These tools would strike people dead. There would be wailing and groans and shrieks, tears and contorted faces. "Oh, Holy!" he muttered, slowing his steps; for he was grievously weighted by these imaginings. "I don't know what I want. I don't know what is right. Oh, Holy, I am sick at heart when I think of this."

    He had stopped walking. He stood stock still, looking ahead. There was the High Road crossing his path, far ahead, almost out of sight. He knew he had, not two, but three options: He could go right or left...or back to Troutman's inn. On his right, at the edge of the road, a slight movement caught his eye, and he looked. There they were again, the two owlstones; but now they were not standing and staring but waddling along the top of a grassy ridge, in a comic fashion, moving intently toward the High Road, occasionally doing a stiff quarter-turn of their bodies to glance at him. He laughed and felt the oppression lift from him. He began walking forward again to keep up with them. They tumbled and waddled along, with considerable speed for such awkward little creatures, and kept twisting to look, as though to see if Nome were following. He waved at them. They kept moving. Side by side the man and the strange owlstones followed the last of the Sea Road; and, at the junction, without hesitation, the owlstones turned sharply to the west and continued to travel alongside the ditch of the High Road. Nome followed.

A short time later they were gone. Nome did not observe their going. Perhaps he had looked away for a moment; and the next they were gone. He walked along the High Road for the rest of the day, occasionally passing travelers or being passed by them, playing his pipe from time to time, looking at the diminishing food in his pack, enjoying the orangey-rose sunset toward which he traveled. He slept in the woods again that night and was not troubled by any animal.

In the morning, while he ate breakfast in the woods, he kept peering about, expecting to see owlstones, and was disappointed when none appeared. But shortly after he began his walk on the road, a delightful surprise overtook him. A conveyance called a sutton, traveling in his direction, passed and then slowed to a stop. It was an enclosed passenger carriage drawn by two brown horses. A well-dressed man with a laughing, friendly face leaned out the open window and asked if he wanted a "hop to." At first Nome did not understand, but then realized that the man was inviting him to ride in the sutton. He stretched to look inside and saw there a woman of flashing beauty and another man. All three were dressed in expensive, elegant clothes; and the interior of the sutton was padded with peach velvet. Nome was acutely aware of his own dusty, travel-stained clothing and looked down to his boots in confusion.

"That's all right! Perfectly all right!" said the man with the laughing face, opening the door. "Hop to!"

So Nome tossed his pack into the compartment and climbed in after it. As the sutton jolted forward, he found himself sharing a seat with the other man, who wore a scowling face, and who, when introductions were made, said only "Pleased," an obvious lie, and then turned his face to look out the window and said nothing more the entire journey. Nome sat opposite the beautiful woman, who smiled at him with pretty eyes. The laughing man carried the conversation with an easy manner.

"To be honest," he said, nodding sideways to the woman, "it is my cousin you may thank for the hop-to, Mister Ogrodni. She's the one who had me call to the driver to stop for you, although I am certainly happy that we did, and am glad that we could be of service to you. It is a long road until the next inn or village. I do think you wouldn't have reached any decent rest stop before nightfall, traveling on foot. Where did you say you were going?"

Nome felt some alarm at having to tell his plans, which were not at all clear to himself. He was immediately aware that he might be giving information detrimental to the Gazines; and, not having time to fabricate a credible story, he talked at some length about his quest for money to save Brighthome, about some of his early adventures, and then candidly explained that there were some things about his future plans or hopes that he was not at liberty to discuss. He only said he was heading for the Endicot Mountains.

His fellow travelers accepted this graciously and made no effort to pry. The woman entered the conversation and chatted with Nome, with great interest, asking him all about his home and his occupation and his family. She seemed very eager to hear his views and opinions of things. It turned out that the three of them were cousins from neighboring estates and were on their way, as they said, to attend a wedding and inspect some family holdings in the west. The laughing man had a gift for words and soon made Nome feel quite special and welcome; although, from time to time, he would make little teasing comments in the direction of the scowling cousin, who only murmured, "Hmmm," and settled more deeply into his frown and looked more intently out the window. Nome soon found himself grinning and winking with the other two at these lighthearted exchanges.

Then the two lively cousins began talking about money; and Nome could only nod or exclaim, "Is that so?" or express admiration; for this was beyond his experience. He was able to talk a bit about the big house at Brighthome, for it was a treasure, with all its craftly carvings and cut-glass windows. But these two were talking of great holdings and investment and sprawling wealth. Nome began to wonder if some opportunity might be developing for him here, something much more promising than a simple ride along the road.

Lunch time! the laughing cousin announced. The beautiful woman drew a large, handsome box from under the seat and began to serve the food. Such a lunch Nome had never seen: cockles and wine! The cockles and the delicate cheese were preserved in an ice pack. Ice, where had it come from? How had these people preserved ice with very little melting inside this padded box-within-a-box? There were light, thin breads, too, and round wafers with designs pressed into them. During the lunch, Nome was startled to feel the woman's foot brush his ankle. He discreetly pulled back, but a moment later felt the sweet pressure of her foot again. A little later she teased him about his appetite and urged him to finish the cockles.

After lunch, sleepiness descended upon them all; and the inside of the sutton grew quiet. Each dozed or napped. Nome drifted away, marveling at his good fortune. When he woke, he began to think of a way to inquire about possibilities for employment, beginning to hope that he might be seeking his fortune in some place other than war-threatened Gazi. He lay back against the soft upholstery, felt the easy sway of the sutton, and admired how broad and smooth this High Road was. He was no longer pulling his ankle away from the woman's foot. Through half-closed eyes he studied her sleeping face.

In time, they were all alert again; and again the conversation continued about money and the things money will buy. Nome was trying to take part, but he found himself distracted by another very incongruous thought. Suddenly, inappropriately, he asked:

"I have heard about the difficulties of The Plains of Wildness. Could you tell me something about how I might get through them?"

"Oh, don't worry about that," said the woman, as though it were the most natural question in the world and she had been expecting it. "We will take you through." She returned, at once, to the discussion with her cousin.

At that moment, Nome turned and looked out the window. He saw two owlstones standing in the grass at the side of the road. Standing, not trotting alongside, rooted and watching him pass. At the sight, he felt a rising terror. He seized both sides of the window frame and jerked himself forward, crying out "Ohhhh," leaned far out and watched the two tiny figures recede. He did not want to leave them behind, desperately wanted them to be following. But now they were out of sight. He slumped back to his seat and wildly looked about at his companions, who were still amiably chatting, as though he had done nothing unusual. He looked from one face to the other and found no recognition. He looked to his left at his uncongenial companion, who was still staring fixedly out the window. Through that window, a signpost came into view that read "Hay" and pointed with an arrow to a rutted, gravel side road.

"Please! Stop the sutton," he broke in. All three looked at him in surprise. Even his seat-mate turned; and, for the first time, the frown was replaced by a puzzled look. "Please," Nome insisted, "I must get off here. That is my road. We just passed it. I have to get off!"

No one was chatting now. No one laughing or smiling. They seemed alarmed and bewildered. Nome leaned out the window again and called to the driver to stop.

"What?" said the woman in a shaky, humorless laugh. She had gone pale. "That road? That goes to Hay!"

"Yes," he answered looking away from them, busying himself with his pack from under the seat, "I must go to Hay. I have a change of plans."

They all gave a sputtering laugh together. "Hay is just a pig village!" exclaimed the man who had worn the laughing face.

"Yes, I have to go there. Or past there. That is my road. I am sorry...I thank you ever so much for the ride...for the hop-to. And for the lunch...."

"No, wait...," they insisted as the sutton rolled to a stop.

But Nome was out the door, dragging his pack after him, continuing to thank them and to bow away. They continued to protest, but he gently, firmly shut the door and stepped toward the back of the sutton.

It stayed there a moment, then began rolling and slowly disappeared down the road into the west.

He watched them go. He did not know who they were or why he had done what he had. He had seen their indignation, hurt, and surprise as he left. Strangely, he did not feel foolish or guilty. He turned and looked eagerly in the grass all about the road, walked back up the road the way they had come, scanning the edges; but he saw nothing. He walked back to the wooden sign, a crude, tilted arrow pointing down a pair of ruts toward the southwest. Bleached and weathered, "Hay" was all it said. As he stepped off the High Road, gravel crunched under his step; and he began to walk. He did not know why he was doing this, but he was at peace.

TEN

Ravenna Rosealice

Catlike, Ravenna Rosealice watched the long trout shadow glide along the bottom of the pool. Watched it hover, twitch, and flick to the side. Watched it stalk the fly, coasting on the surface. She glanced, for an instant, to the fly, a death-trap placed by her low, arching cast, primed with a coiled spring of barbs, cocked for the fishbite. The trout struck, and water exploded! The woman was on her knees, pulling in the string, hand-over-hand, yielding a moment, pulling again. The fish broke water, flipped completely free of the pool, flopping furiously through the air. She drew it in toward the bank, drew it to herself and, with hand poised, judging the right moment, plunged and seized the fish by the eyes between thumb and forefinger. Paralyzed, the trout allowed itself to be raised from the water, inspected, freed from the barb, and dropped into her creel, where it began to thrash once more.

The woman studied her take of fish. Seven, this last one the biggest. It is enough, she decided, and took up the barb on the end of her line to see if it was damaged. She wound the stiff, hair-fine wire into a tight coil and set the trigger, then tapped it; and the barbs flew out in three directions and bobbed like three tiny jacks-in-the-box. She tucked a wisp of brown hair, hanging in her eyes, behind her kerchief and gathered her tackle and fish in order to return to The Huts where she lived.

As she left the river and passed through the undergrowth, seeking the path, Ravenna Rosealice moved with a slender gracefulness, dipping beneath low branches and stepping smoothly over fallen trunks. She was tall and well-tanned, even her bare legs; for, although the women at The Huts wore long skirts, she usually hiked hers up between her legs and tucked the end under her belt to give her freedom of movement in the woods and the fields. The coarse skirt, gathered and girded about her hips, was mild tan; but her airy, short-sleeve blouse was an embroidered cascade of tiny, tight-stitched flowers and looked like one of the fields at high summer. She was a woman of clear beauty, with firm mouth, high cheekbones, and blue eyes that splashed like drops on the surface of water.

After she found the path, it was still a half-hour walk home, most of it in the open; for the woods clung to the river areas and yielded, on higher ground, to endlessly rolling fields. From them, this country took its name, The Fields of Khorvan. At this season the fields were soft buff and matted, but a few weeks earlier they had been surging and waving under the wind like a dark-yellow sea. At other times, they made a patchwork of dark and light and filmy green; and, at others, they were acres of pinks and blues and yellows and whites.

Fields of Khorvan was a settled territory, not quite an organized state. It was secure from attack, situated, as it was, with the fiercely reclusive Muicmuic peoples on its northern boundary, and the desolate Plains of Wildness on the west. Forming a soft buffer around its edges, especially near the High Road to the West, were a few nondescript towns and villages, such as Willow, Stoat, or Marten. The expansive interior of rolling field country was partitioned by large land tracts referred to as "houses." These houses were actually large estates, owned and governed by local lords, living in luxurious manors, surrounded by vassal neighborhoods, villages, and hamlets in feudal arrangements. There were nearly a score of these manors, with names like House of Trabert, House of Hedges, House of Mizelle; and, of course, The House of Ghan. This latter was foremost among them in wealth, prestige, and power; yet it ruled over none of the others; for all houses were independent polities. Ghan, however, was reputed to be oldest and most influential and had been ruled with an iron fist during the last generation by a tyrant, referred to only as Old Ghan. Old Ghan was still alive, but feeble now and addled. His unpredictable son, Mintor, had recently become head of the House, inheriting an implied power, if not to rule, at least to intimidate lesser houses.

There was one exception to this pattern of settlement in The Fields of Khorvan: an area called "The Huts," tucked along the western edge, among mixed field and woodland, not far from the desert. It was different in almost every way. There were no grand houses, no estates, only one-level dwellings favoring rounded shapes, domes and tube-shaped arcades. These were molded with clay over lattice-work and decorated around doors and windows with bright paintings. The place was sometimes called "The Women." Except for three or four men and a number of boys of various ages, only women and girls lived there. They ate almost no animal meat and lived well on fish, fruits, and vegetables. Inside the homes, no square-framed pictures could be found on the walls, of the sort that filled the grand houses of the land, especially the House of Mizelle, with its great art collection. No, here the interior walls, themselves, were the paintings and sculptures, frequently being discussed, displayed to neighbors, amended and done over, a never tiring topic of delight in their society. These women liked to say they brought the outside in and the inside out. When any of the women decided to marry men and form family, they generally moved out to live in similar dwellings, somewhat removed, in a perimeter around "the heart" of The Huts.

Perhaps the most distinctive feature of their culture was the tradition of the starwomen. It had been held among them, for many generations, that a dark, starry sky is a mirror in the heavens of the inner lives of those who tilt their faces up to look there for meaning. Although study of the positions and transit of the stars, and of the mysterious free-wandering of a few special ones, was a popular activity among The Women in general, it had also been held that there are always some unaccountably gifted women among them who could guide others in reading the stars. A few novice starwomen in each generation were selected and trained by elders to develop their gifts for the service of others. They were instructed not to pursue this as a power of prophecy or prediction but rather as guidance to assist individuals in trance into looking into a mirror of their own souls. A starwoman would lead someone outside on a clear night and begin pointing out star pictures. Within minutes, she might have the other person, not only talking about them, but spinning dreamy stories. Stories from the depths, where secrets can disclose, enigmas unknot. The starwoman was always the guide, never the storyteller.

Not surprisingly, this training was sometimes compromised. A mystique had grown up around this phenomenon among outsiders who looked to special starwomen for clairvoyance and spell-working. On occasion, some of them had exploited the gift for money and position and had established themselves in places of influence among the high and powerful houses of the land. The highest of these houses, and by far the most powerful, was The House of Ghan. As long as anyone could recall, a Lady Ghan had always been a starwoman.

Ravenna Rosealice had come to live among The Women when she was eight years old. Her father had grown up in the Endicot Mountains, far to the west, and had come to The Fields of Khorvan on trade. There he had married a woman named Yuna Urlinda and settled with her in one of the perimeter dwellings near The Huts. They had a son, who died while still a child; and then Ravenna was born. When she was only eight, her father was killed in a hunting accident; and her mother never fully recovered from the news of it. Mother and daughter were brought to The Huts to live with her mother's sister, Aunie.

Aunie, too, had lost a husband and two children. The two sisters had responded to their tragedies differently. Yuna became ill and spent most of her days in the cool darkness of her bedroom. She made listless efforts to be cheerful; but she developed rashes and blisters; and each breath seemed an effort. Ravenna and her aunt eventually gave up trying to pull her up from sadness and simply nursed her. Aunie had begun life again among The Women; and she was full of laughter and vigorous work. There was always good food in her hut, woven rugs and fresh flowers, hanging bundles of drying grasses, and bright paintings on the plastered walls. Aunie became mother to Ravenna, who grew to be much like her. From Oba, a blind elder, Aunie had received training to serve as a starwoman; and she, in turn, transmitted the training to Ravenna from the day the child first came to live in her hut.

As years passed, Ravenna grew to become a lovely woman. And now she was crossing the open fields, with her tackle and heavy creel, to take a short-cut, where the river and the woods bent away and then doubled back to the place where The Huts first came into view. She was almost home.

She entered her hut, a graceful round house with several rooms, and leaned in at one of the doorways to say, "I'm back, Mama." A muffled response came from the twilight. She went to the sink and stood beside

Aunie, who was scrubbing dirt off carrots. Ravenna lifted the lid and tilted the creel: "See?"

Aunie drew a breath through puckered lips and shook her head. "You're a wonder, Venna. Where am I going to keep all the fish you bring me?"

"Let's eat this big one for supper. One less to smoke."

"No," said Aunie firmly. "Carrot soup. I've already started."

"Oh, come on." Ravenna gave her an elbow jab. "Fresh trout. Mother loves fish. We haven't had fish for a long time."

"*Ravenna* loves fish," said Aunie, bending to look for a pan and hide a smile. "Winter is coming. We need to put up all we can."

"Those carrots will be a pretty color with this nice, white trout. Mother! Get hungry. Fresh trout for supper!" Ravenna took a slender knife and began to filet the fish, as deftly as if she were arranging flowers.

Aunie was slicing the carrots lengthwise, instead of chopping them into chunks for soup. "You are a wonder," she repeated. "The Leaping Fish is surely your cluster."

"Well, as a matter of fact, I have been spending most of the summer watching that cluster and breathing it every night before I go to bed. It is one of my favorites. Aunie, do you *really* think something like that could affect whether I catch fish or not?"

"Certainly."

"How could it?" She turned toward Aunie, careful to keep her gory hands over the counter. "How could stars affect whether fish bite or not on any given day?"

"Of course they don't tell the fish to bite. But they affect you. You just said so. You are the one watching that cluster. Breathing it in. You've been getting yourself ready, just like I taught you. You're the fisherwoman, no question about that," and she gave the wicker creel a little poke with her knife. They worked side-by-side in silence for a moment. Then she added quietly, "And you are the starwoman."

Ravenna looked up, "What's the matter?"

Aunie put aside the carrots and turned to face Ravenna, hip leaning against the counter. "She was here again today."

"The bent old woman?"

Aunie nodded.

"What did she say? I gave her my answer very clearly."

"She didn't say anything. She didn't want to talk to me. She wanted to talk to the starwoman."

"What *is* this?" Ravenna gave a desperate little laugh. "You're more starwoman than I will ever be. So are some of the other women here. What do they want with me?" She turned to the sink and scrubbed her hands harder than needed.

"Sit down." Aunie lifted the end of her own apron for a towel. They sat together at the table. "Venna, you don't know the seriousness of this. I'm sure you don't. I have been watching you brush this trouble away as though you thought it might *go* away. Now Druska Paba may be coming back today, I wouldn't be surprised. I told her you were out in the woods, so she knew you would be coming back soon. Whether she comes again today or....Venna, I want to take you out to read the stars tonight, will you do that? You have to meet yourself. Forget the Leaping Fish. I have others for you to watch, it will be a clear night. Will you come with me?"

"Yes," quietly, looking into her lap. "I just wish they would leave me alone."

"They will not leave you alone."

"Who is this Druska Paba? Do you know her?"

"I know what she...I know who she is. She is counselor to Count Mintor Ghan, and was to his father before him. Some of the women say she is related to the Ghans, a bastard daughter, perhaps, or someone related, but never accepted into the family because of her deformity. I don't know that I believe any of that, mostly gossip I think. In any case, she has kept a position of influence in The House of Ghan for a long time; and that is not something easily done. I would be interested in getting to know her, if she were not coming here on this unpleasant business."

"Well, I am not available for Count Ghan. I have told her that. And, if she comes back, I will tell her again."

Aunie sighed deeply and looked at her.

"Well, do you blame me!"

"No, of course not," Aunie said softly. "You have no business marrying a man like Mintor Ghan and getting mixed up in that family. It's just that I worry you can't escape it. Like I told you, they won't leave you alone. I know something of this Mintor, too. He is terribly powerful now. But he's not a man...that's the impression I have...more a child in a man's body. I don't know. A boy...and a nasty little one...willful, selfish...."

"Have you met him?"

"Yes, twice, and that was my impression, the second time stronger than the first. It confirmed what I have heard of him."

"Well, as far as I'm concerned...."

"Let me finish. I said he was willful. That is an understatement. He is stubborn and unstable. He has a fierce temper, I hear, and probably no scruples, I'm afraid. Worst of all, Venna, they have the power to force you."

Ravenna looked at her, aghast. "You...*force* me?" She stood up, shaking her head and stepping back, as though it were her aunt who was trying to force her. "No one is going to force me!"

Aunie's eyes filled with tears. "The Good Mother protect you," she whispered. "No, no one is going to take you, Ravenna. I won't let that happen. But I am afraid you will not be able to...stay...with...me." And she broke into sobs.

....

Druska Paba came that evening. Ravenna remained standing during the whole visit and ignored all of Aunie's invitations to sit and join them for some herb tea. The old woman did not appear to be dangerous or the bearer of bad news. On the contrary, bent over nearly double, as she was, leaning upon a stick, peering from under shaggy brows with a doleful look, and constantly working her flaccid lips with a chewing motion, she spoke in pleading tones. Each time she slurped her tea from the cup, drops of it spilled on her coarse, stained smock, where it dropped across her knees. She understood Ravenna's feelings, she said, and did not want to urge her case too hard, but asked that Ravenna listen to some of the advantages of becoming a member of The House of Ghan. She said that Ravenna's mother, Yuna Urlinda, would be most welcome to come with her, and that the two physicians attached to the house would be able to care for her.

"They are superb! The most skilled doctors you will ever find; and one of them is a woman!" she argued. "And you, dear," she nodded to Aunie, "you would be welcome at any time. If you should wish to join your sister at our house to help her and to be closer to your niece, why, that would only be our gain!"

Ravenna insisted on hearing why Count Ghan was so determined to marry her. She did not even know him. Druska Paba wagged her head and winked conspiratorially. She told about how he had often seen Ravenna and asked about her and gone out of his way to wait at places where she might pass. It seems he was a love-smitten man too shy to press his suit directly.

"Don't ever tell him I've told you all this, dear, oh no," and she chuckled and wobbled on the chair with her eyes screwed up tight, and then she winked again. "Oh, he would have my head if he knew I was telling you!" and she had another fit of laughing. "Oh, yes, my dear, you have quite an influence over him. Quite an influence."

Druska Paba got up to leave. Almost incidentally, as though she had nearly forgotten what she had come for, she turned back to Ravenna and said, "He asked me to invite you to come to the house tomorrow. He wants to meet you. It doesn't commit you to anything, dear, he just wants to meet you."

"But I've already told you...."

"He is sending this cab for you mid-morning, this same one I came in," and, ignoring Ravenna's protests, she leaned to look out the front door to say, "I suppose that poor man, who has been waiting there on the cab for me all this time, is getting quite tired and quite impatient. Poor fellow. I've enjoyed this visit with you women so much! You have been so kind to me. I am afraid I lost track of time and have kept that poor man waiting. Well, goodbye. He will be back for you tomorrow. Goodbye!"

Ravenna stood across the room, watching the hobbling figure disappear. Aunie studied her niece closely.

"What a queer, pathetic creature," said Ravenna.

Aunie looked at her quizzically, then said slowly, "That woman is strong as rope."

That night they were under the stars. Ravenna lay flat upon a blanket on the grass, with another thrown over her, for the chill of autumn was on the ground. Aunie sat cross-legged near her head, occasionally speaking to her quietly. Ravenna talked about the stars she recognized, stitched imaginary threads from one to the other, told what they made her think of, rambled on in desultory conversation with her aunt...her friend...and gradually her voice relaxed, and her speaking slowed, and...she traveled and saw. Fear hunched up before her, and she shrank back. She told a sad and beautiful story about a girl who was traveling on the river with her father and mother. The boat came apart. There were so many people there, and she drifted down the river, reaching back and crying out, but her father and mother were not coming, only people, people, and she jumped from what was left of the boat, but she did not fall into the river, she was on the ground...and running...!

How long had she been lying here? She had not been asleep. The story had tumbled out, leading nowhere. The black sky bending over her was cold, dusted, and endlessly remote. Warm hands stroking her hair, warm fingers wiping away the wetness running across her temples to the roots of her hair. She turned her face and clutched the hand and kissed the palm hard.

The two women stiffly climbed to their feet and returned to the warmth of the hut. That night Ravenna climbed into her mother's bed, as carefully as she could, and slept beside the uneven breathing and soft moans.

....

Inside the mansion of Count Ghan, lights were burning brightly in a grand sitting room that sagged with gilt and velvet. Druska Paba perched on a padded, ivory chair watching Mintor Ghan pace back and forth in sloppy agitation, one hand thrust deep into his pants pocket, the other waving and gesturing. He was a plump man, with mussed blond hair, red eyebrows, a puffy face. His coat jacket, apparently a military uniform, had been yanked open at the throat. He was ranting.

"I told you, Druska Paba, that I wanted that woman here. Today. Tonight at the latest! Where is she? 'She declined to come!' Declined to come! Does she think she is going to say 'yes' or 'no' or 'I'll think about it' to me when she is my wife in my house? Is that what she thinks? Why, I'll...."

"Now, Mintor.....," the old woman attempted.

"*Count* Mintor!" he shouted. (This was a bad sign for Druska Paba, whose existence depended on intimacy with the rulers of this house.) "Yes, I am offended! Yes, I demand to be called by my title...because it seems that some people are forgetting who I am! Just who I am!"

"Now, Count Mintor, sit down. Please sit down," she said gently but firmly.

"I will *not* sit down! I sit down when I am tired. When I want to rest from standing. I am not tired!" He paced in silence for a moment thinking of his next outburst. He sat down.

"Now, Mintor," she ventured, "things are going well with the young woman...."

"Yes, that's what we were talking about!" he popped up and began pacing. "I told you to bring her to the house. I did not ask you to invite her. I told you to convey the message that I have selected her to be Lady Ghan. Where is she, Druska Paba? Where is she? Don't tell me that you have failed me."

"Mintor, listen to me for a moment, will you?" she said in exasperation, then choked and had a fit of wheezy coughing. When she recovered, her watery eyes were reproachful. "I have been asking you all along to let me handle this business. This is a woman's work and has to be handled in a woman's way. I know all about these starwomen. And I know *you* fairly well, Mintor. I know you are not going to want a wife who is impudent and independent and doesn't listen to you. These starwomen are like animals in the wild, Mintor. You can't rush up to them and grab them if you want them. They have to be tamed. I am not just getting you a starwoman, I am bringing one into The House of Ghan."

He muttered and continued to pace.

"And it is going quite well, I might add."

"Is it?" he asked, mildly appeased.

"Yes, it is. The woman is delighted that you have chosen her. She can hardly believe that she will be Lady Ghan...but she is frightened. Awed and, sort of...well, sort of holding back...it's a silly thing, but I've seen it often before, a common reaction. That is why this has to be handled carefully. I beg you, Mintor to let me handle this part of it."

"Well, she had better be here tomorrow. I am sending a cab for her tomorrow, did you tell her that?"

"Yes, of course I did. And I think I'd better go along to see that all goes smoothly. I tell you this girl is honored and delighted that you have chosen her, Mintor."

He nodded.

Druska Paba shifted awkwardly in the chair, took the measure of the man, and risked a little further: "If this girl is too timid, Mintor, not the right kind of stuff for a Lady Ghan, it might be best if you let me cultivate someone else. It wouldn't do to have a wife who was so awed and confused by the honor that she could not bear herself with dignity. *That* is my only worry. There are other starwomen at The Huts, you know, some of them quite lovely...."

"Now, Druska Paba," he stopped in front of her wagging his finger, "we have been over this before! I don't want any other one. Are you sure you are not having trouble...?"

"Nonsense, Count Mintor! Everything is going very smoothly, I tell you."

She knew what she had to do. Mintor, stupid though he was, was beginning to have doubts about her. This she could not afford. She would have to deliver this Rosealice woman tied and gagged, yet dignified.

"If you please, Count Mintor," she said, smiling coyly, "let me remind you that I am an old woman...and not strong like you. I need my rest, you understand that, don't you?"

"Yes, go ahead. Go to bed," he said gruffly, still pacing and scowling.

She thanked him, said goodnight, and hobbled off to her room. However, she did not go to bed. She fumbled about in the back of a cupboard among some jars and drew out a packet of white powder, sniffed it, then slipped it into her bag.

ELEVEN

Tea for Two

The next day a horse-drawn cab rolled to a stop on the circular driveway in front of the mansion. Two butlers hurried from the front door and down the white steps to attend the passengers. One opened the door of the cab and, with practiced solicitude, eased Druska Paba to the ground and made sure she was stable on her cane. A moment later the face of Ravenna Rosealice appeared, cautiously looking all about before stepping to descend. She declined the arm of the doorman and shook free when Druska Paba touched her wrist, implying that she needed someone to lean on. With deferential inclinations, the servants stepped back a pace; and the bent, old woman decided to walk on ahead. When they came to the steps leading up to the main door, Ravenna felt a moment of remorse, for her companion was shuffling and pulling herself up one step at a time with obvious discomfort. Ravenna's wariness was great, however, and she did not proffer help. Her eyes darted this way and that, taking in everything around her.

The massive front doors, twice the height of a person, opened into a vaulted hallway in which there were settees and polished tables, and from which doorways led off to the side parlors and waiting rooms. They passed through this entry hallway into a square open courtyard surrounded by the four wings of the house. At the middle stood a stone fountain with a tall spume of water dancing and splashing over a circular garden of mossy rocks and ferns. Around the four sides of the courtyard on the lower level ran a graceful walkway of pillars and arches, an arcade from which doors led off into the many rooms of the ground floor. The upper level was enclosed on three sides, with shuttered windows overlooking the courtyard; but, on the fourth side, a wide marble staircase, beginning at ground level behind the fountain, swept up to a majestic open balcony whose railing ran the entire width of the house.

As Druska Paba led her through the courtyard, around the fountain, and up the hard white steps, Ravenna paused to lean over the marble railing and squint down a shadowed hallway leading from the courtyard to the rear of the house. She had glimpsed a flash of daylight back there as someone came or went through a back door. Servant entrance, she thought. Now that she was in this place, her mind was attentive to all possible ways out.

Near the top of the stairs they had to stop, for Druska Paba was out of breath. Ravenna coolly surveyed the courtyard, the hallways, the doors, the arcade from this height. She had never been in such a building and marveled that anyone would know how to put such a place together. She was impressed, but not charmed, for this was enemy territory. She was also aware of being observed by many eyes from cracks at windows and doorways. They think they're seeing the next Lady Ghan, thought Ravenna irritably.

They walked the length of the balcony and turned left down a long carpeted hallway lined with portraits of unsmiling people. Druska Paba stopped at a set of open doors through which could be seen a magnificently appointed parlor. She turned to Ravenna.

"Be so kind as to wait here, dear," she said, pointing into the room with her cane. "The Count Mintor Ghan will be delayed. Some very urgent matter came up just before the cab was sent for you. He feels very embarrassed at keeping you waiting, and he asked me personally to beg your patience and understanding. It could not be avoided."

Ravenna primly nodded her head, but her mouth was set and hard. She was feeling very uncomfortable and wanted this over as soon as possible.

"I, too, have to leave you for a while," she continued, "but the Count Ghan has asked that Lady Locloude be available to have tea with you while you are waiting. Myla is her name, I am sure she will want you to call her that. She is really a fine and friendly person, Myla. And something else you have in common with her—she was raised among The Women! Only as a child, however. I think she left there when she was seven or eight, something like that. Perhaps you knew each other! Wouldn't that be something to talk about. Here she comes now."

A young woman came down the hall toward them from the opposite direction. She had a light and casual step and a cheerful smile. Druska Paba introduced them; they in turn bowed and nodded. Lady Locloude reached out and gave Ravenna's hand a little squeeze.

Druska Paba secretly gloated over her choice and the arrangements. Things were going very well. It had not been easy to convince Ravenna Rosealice to leave her house and get into the cab that morning. Only after she had astonished the young woman and her aunt by throwing a small tantrum and squealing that she was "sick and tired of doing the Count's courting for him!" and insisted that Ravenna come with her and give her answer in person, did they begin to take her seriously.

"I keep trying to tell him what you have said!" she had burbled in a teary voice, shaking her head back and forth as though exhausted. "But he won't believe me, he thinks I am not trying, and I'm getting into trouble over this whole business! Please. Please don't send me back there alone, or I will just be back here on your doorstep tomorrow! I can't take much more of this."

It had worked. The aunt was startled and alarmed when Ravenna suddenly changed her mind and agreed to go. She, too, was tired of this whole business, she had said, and would give her "No!" to the Count in person. Over Aunie's protests, she had climbed into the cab.

But Druska Paba cared nothing about the aunt at this point and considered her out of the picture. The Rosealice starwoman was in the House of Ghan now, that was enough. Her next achievement would be to keep her there—and to keep her subdued until she was under Mintor's control. Then Mintor would be appeased and satisfied; and he himself would once again gradually slide back under Druska Paba's control. She knew this starwoman would be a hard one to manage, but that morning's victory over her showed it could be done. The old woman was very pleased with herself. She realized, however, that it was time for her to stay out of sight. It was obvious that she annoyed Ravenna. Lady Locloude could be left to charm her while Druska Paba tended to other matters. First, she had to keep Mintor Ghan away a while longer, for it was too early for the starwoman to see what a clod he was. And next, she had to get to the kitchen to help the cook brew the tea. The starwoman had to be put into a more loving mood when she eventually did meet Mintor Ghan.

Druska Paba obsequiously backed out of the doorway, once the two women were standing in the parlor, and drew the double doors shut upon them. Then, slowly, with painful caution, she silently turned the outer key in the lock.

Lady Locloude was as enjoyable a companion as Druska Paba knew she would be. She was simple and informal and insisted on being called Myla. It turned out that she and Ravenna had lived among the Women at the same time for a very short period when they were children, but they could not remember each other. As they chatted, Ravenna's feelings about this visit were growing confused. She had promised herself that she would stand her ground and accept nothing from these people— nothing! She knew she was being wooed and looked for falseness in every word, every polite gesture. But this Myla was someone she could really like. If their lives had been put together in a different way, this might have been a friend. It was clear to Ravenna that Myla was expecting her to be the new Lady Ghan and was already looking forward to a close and longstanding relationship with her. She and her husband, Lord Locloude, were not exactly family relatives of the House of Ghan; but they did live here.

Myla was having difficulty with the conversation. Ravenna was aloof and preoccupied, while making efforts to be polite. A tour of the room might ease the awkwardness, and Myla began to show her the venerable old paintings on the wall, the charts of family trees, imported cut-glass pieces on the tables, the floor-to-ceiling display case in the corner which held a large collection of gold coins behind glass. They strolled in front of the three tall windows, which allowed a view of the courtyard, and paused at the middle one to lean against the back of a long, sumptuously upholstered couch, which was pulled away from the windows, allowing them to be opened inward.

Their attention was drawn across the room to the doors, where there was a jiggling and rattling of the handle. Then a knock, and the door opened hesitantly. A butler carried in a tray with a porcelain tea serving and a plate of delicate biscuits and placed it on the low table before the chairs on that side of the room where they had been sitting earlier. He bowed himself out of the room and shut the door with a lingering rattle of the handle.

Ravenna had been looking at him darkly. She had not come for tea.

She had come to tell Mintor Ghan that her answer was firm and she wanted to be left alone. Why was she here with this chatty woman in this luxuriant place? What did this have to do with her purpose? She renewed her decision to accept nothing from these people. Perhaps it was time to tell this Myla that she insisted on seeing the Count at once...but, here!...she is pouring tea...!

"No, thank you! Please, I...I don't care for any tea," she interrupted.

"Oh," Lady Locloude stopped, surprised, the cup half-filled. "Oh, well...you're sure? A little bit perhaps? Or a biscuit...?" She was confused, never having found herself in this situation. She hurriedly filled her own cup with as much poise as she could manage.

"Thank you," said Ravenna, quietly returning to her chair. "Not just now." Her eyes strayed to the doors. Lady Locloude sipped her tea, uncomfortable with the silence. And she sipped her tea.

Moments passed with no words spoken. Ravenna was framing a respectful way to excuse herself from this tea party in order to go looking for Druska Paba or the Count himself. Then she looked back to the other woman's face and was startled at the change she saw. Lady Locloude sat slightly slumped with her hands holding an empty teacup pressed into her lap, tilted and about to roll off the saucer. Her head was cocked slightly to one side, and she was gazing at Ravenna with a liquid, simpering expression.

"You're such a lovely person," Lady Locloude suddenly said. Her voice was full of honey.

Ravenna looked at her with amazement. "Oh. Thank you," was all she said.

"Will you come to see me again? I love talking to you."

Ravenna said nothing, looked away. When she looked back, the full, gray-blue eyes were still gazing at her lovingly.

"Ahhm...just a moment," said Ravenna, standing up. She crossed to the middle window behind the richly upholstered couch again and looked down into the courtyard. She glanced back at Lady Locloude, who sat in the same position, but whose eyes followed her faithfully. Ravenna walked across to the doors saying, "Just a moment, please..," and placed her hand on the handle. She twisted, stopped in disbelief, jerked hard, then went pale and stiff.

"Greatsada!" she hissed. "Good Mother, help me!"

She strode quickly to the Lady on the couch and began to say something, but the woman merely looked at her with a wan smile. Ravenna whirled and looked all about the room. She ran back to the door and jerked it hard, then stood staring at the panel for a moment. She turned and crossed behind the couch to the middle window and threw open the casements.

At that moment there was a rattling of the door handle, a prolonged jiggling, then the door opened suddenly. A young man stood there, arrested by what he did not expect, as he was about to enter. He looked all about the room, then crossed to the woman sitting alone by the tea setting.

"Myla! Where is she?" he cried.

"Oh, hello, Lanny." Myla said, gazing up at him lovingly, still holding the saucer, although the empty cup had now rolled over onto her lap. "She's over there," pointing languorously toward the opposite wall where the double windows stood open wide.

"What's the matter with you?" he demanded. Then not waiting for an answer, Lord Locloude ran from the room calling, "Count! Count Mintor! Come quickly!"

Almost immediately, Mintor Ghan ran through the door, with Lord Locloude behind, him pointing to the open window. The Count dashed to it, leaned out and looked down, looked along the narrow ledge running just below the window, looked up toward the eaves.

"You, down there!" he shouted into the courtyard, "Where did she go? Did you see her?"

A faint voice of inquiry floated up.

"Did you see anyone? *Here*, coming out this window! Ahh...begone!" He whirled about in disgust. "You," he descended on Myla, "where did she go? *You* saw her!"

Myla smiled sweetly and pointed across the room, "She's over there."

The Count looked at her as though she were a freak. "What's the matter with you?" He looked at Lord Locloude who stood in the center of the room staring helplessly at his wife. "How could you let her get away?" the Count bellowed at Myla. "Why didn't you run to let someone know?"

"I didn't," she answered slowly, utterly at peace. She began to point again, "She's over...."

"Begone!" roared the Count. "Locloude, get moving! Have all

guards block and search the grounds. She can't have gotten far! Check the walls, the gates, the rooftop! Everywhere! Send in Mockroot and Burgiss!" he shouted after the disappearing Locloude. "And Druska Paba, curse her!"

The two guards came running, and the Count ordered one to search the room thoroughly and the other to draft an alert-notice to be posted throughout the entire northern region of the Fields of Khorvan. It was to offer a description and a reward of two thousand kurakhs—no, *three* thousand!—for the capture and return of the fugitive starwoman, Ravenna Rosealice, belonging to The House of Ghan! No time to lose. At once! Move!

As the guard, Mockroot, returned from his examination of the room, shaking his head, the Count ordered him to assemble the rest of the guard not occupied in searching the grounds. They were to organize a search throughout the immediate countryside. One detail was to be sent immediately to The Huts. The woods along the river were to be scoured.

Lady Locloude had just been sent to her room. Druska Paba shuffled in, wagging her head and chewing her lips more vigorously than usual. The Count began to rail at the crooked old woman. When he paused for breath, she pointed out that she had done what he asked, had brought the starwoman to this very spot, had posted one of his closest associates to watch her until he himself would arrive, had even locked the doors so she could not escape.

"I am sorry, Count Ghan," she concluded, "that Lady Locloude has played a questionable role in this matter. You may remember, however, that only last week I reported several rumors...."

"Yes, yes," the Count was brusque, but was gradually seeing things her way again. She talked on, in her businesslike manner, as they walked from the room. He was frowning and nodding. Druska Paba glanced down at the tea serving, as they passed, and noted that both teacups had been used: a little tea left in the cup that would have been Ravenna's. She was baffled.

....

It was well past midnight, and moonlight streamed through the three windows and bleached the carpet of the room. The tea tray had been taken away, the room tidied, the casements of the middle window shut, and all was still and orderly in the silvery dark.

Then the couch moved. It shifted and slid on the carpet, humped up momentarily, and tipped slowly forward. It dropped back again to all four feet with a soft thump and stayed still, as a dark shape rolled away behind it and lay quiet on the carpet. Ravenna breathed slowly, stifling a need to groan, gradually flexing her arms, her legs, her back.

At the last moment, before the doors had been unlocked, she had scrambled under the couch and found that the framework of the piece was uncovered. She had slithered up between the cross-bracing and lain still on the stout wooden grid. At one point, the guard, Mockroot, had raised the skirt of the couch, scanned about, and had even reached in an arm and groped; but Ravenna, suspended just inches above, had been missed. Hearing people coming and going throughout the day, hearing the tea things being gathered and the room straightened, she was never sure whether the room was empty, and had lain as still as she was able until nightfall. Then she had eased her way out of the gridwork and had lain on the carpet under the couch until she knew it was very late and noises in the house had ceased.

She had been allowed a long time to think; and now she had plans. She knew she would no longer be safe in any place familiar to her. She would go into hiding, try to contact her aunt and mother, but not go to The Huts again. There were some friends elsewhere perhaps.

She sat up and continued to massage the stiff and sore places. Peeking around the couch, she could see that the doors of the room stood open. She crawled across the carpet, avoiding patches of moonlight, and silently swung them shut. Then she stood upright, steadying herself on the wall, and went to a table where she had seen a metal letter opener lying beside some books and crystal ware. With the slender blade in hand, she worked her way over to the corner and began chipping and prying about the lock of the tall glass case which held the gold coin collection.

A half-hour later, the case stood open and robbed. Backings and mounts littered the floor and the empty shelves. Ravenna was slipping down the darkened hallway toward the balcony overlooking the courtyard. She came out into the open and dropped to her haunches. The moon was near full, washing the open courtyard in ghostly light. She scuttled across to the top of the staircase and hugged the top railing post. Looking down, she guessed that the wide stairway was exposed to view from every window overlooking the courtyard. However, the thick marble pillars of the railing threw a descending pattern of shadows onto the steps. After a moment to ponder, she hurried to the first of the shadows, curled into its darkness and waited many minutes. Then she carefully lowered herself to the next and waited.

When she was almost to the bottom, in the shadow of the next-to-last pillar, the front door of the house opened and shut. Someone was emerging from the entryway on the far side of the courtyard, moving in her direction. She watched a man carrying a long pole, a spear or pike perhaps, walk directly toward her, passing around the fountain and approaching the steps on her side. Her huddled body was directly in his path, and he was about to trip over her. At the last moment, he side-stepped into the moonlit area and brushed past with a tip-toe tread up the stairs and disappeared beyond the balcony.

Ravenna looked across the courtyard, deliberating. To reach the front door, she would have to cross the entire moon-lighted courtyard. The only other possibility was to duck around the stairway and move toward the back door, which she had glimpsed in the morning. If that proved a dead-end, she would be taking too much time and risk and would have to attempt the front door after all. Probably no doors would be unlocked to her...but, perhaps, from the inside, a bolt, or a bar?

She glided around the bottom railing post and quickly slid along the base of the stairway to the hallway leading toward a back door. Now she was moving into blackness and had to cling to the wall, inching along, tapping and feeling for door frames. Her foot struck an empty metal pail, which sounded with a hollow scrape, nearly tearing her heart out! A minute passed, and she began to breathe again. She edged along more carefully, feeling ahead, tapping with her foot as well as with her fingers. Ahead, she was blind. Behind, she could see the pale light of the moon-washed courtyard. Suddenly, she had a sense that something was blocking the passage. She could see nothing, feel nothing with her hands when she reached out; but there was a sensation of cool flatness blocking off the space ahead. She rested her hand on a door frame on her right and hesitated. She took a breath and prepared to grope forward to touch what stood in the way.

A muffled sound came from just behind her hand, and the door to her right jumped open. A warm body, smelling of sweat, moved in front of her into the passageway. Ravenna stiffened, did not have time to shrink back. With grunts and sleepy breathing, the body turned away from her and stopped. There was a shallow sliding of steel, a grunt and a breath, a tugging on wood; and the door opened to the moonlit back yard, silhouetting the lumpy form of a man in a nightshirt. He stepped through the doorway and off to the side, out of sight; but the door stood open behind him. Ravenna waited, weighing her chance. From outside came a watery hiss, then a steady splatter. Darting through the doorway, she dodged to the left and ran, hearing a startled, "Ayuhh! Wha? Who's 'at? Ayyy!"

She was running along a wall enclosing the backyard, expecting at every moment to hear shouts and alarms and the baying of dogs; but there was only the crashing sound of her breath, the thudding of her feet, an excited jingle of metal in the pouch of skirt, which she clutched with her left hand. The wall met another, turning right. She sprinted along it and came to another corner, again turning right. But there was a gate! She pushed; and, to her relief, it swung open. She ran through and straight into a group of fleshy mounds upon the ground, which jolted and rose up, snorting and bellowing. Startled cows, struggling to their feet.

Running as though in a dream, dreading the chase which was certain to come, she left behind the black heap of the building. None of its windows blinked to light. She ran with the dry grasses brushing her legs. She was in the fields. In the open, running.

TWELVE

Through a Hole in the Wall

Nome Ogrodni sat hunched over a rough table, leaning on his elbows. His head hung above a bowl, from which he was mopping the last streaks of greasy soup with a wad of bread. The corners of the room were nearly in darkness; but shuddering light from a candle stub, shoved into daubs of wax on a saucer, made the faces of the two men sitting opposite glow in a hideous dance. They had finished supper, pushed their dishes aside, and were continuing their empty talk and laughter. Both had been hired hands here on Dumpy's Farm for years. Rodey was a silly constant-talker, who thought himself witty. He regularly amplified this wit with a donkey-bray laugh. Jude, mild and cloudy-eyed, had few thoughts but tried to keep up with his partner's humor by repeating things he had heard others say or that he himself had already said several times.

Nome was the newcomer, hired by Dumpy the evening he had walked into the village of Hay. For three weeks now, he had eaten soup at this table after the chores were finished. These two men were his only meager company. Dumpy himself was old and getting crippled with painful stiffness and swelling of the joints, so that he did little farm work. It was all he could do to walk across the yard to give gruff orders to the hands; and he could no longer stand the jolts and bumps of riding a wagon. His wife kept to the house mostly, except when she was caring for poor Natty, a speechless, crazed old relative, who had been sent to them recently and who lived as a recluse in a shed built against that side of the barn, where Nome had a bed in a portion of the loft.

This unkempt, shabby farmstead was a far cry from Brighthome; but the work was familiar to Nome, and he needed a job. Perhaps he was taking a rest from seeking his fortune. Perhaps he was just exhausted from all that had happened to him. The pay here was paltry and would add up to almost nothing toward a hundred-day payment; but Nome was content for the moment. More truthfully, he was at a standstill, with no plans, no hopes, merely earning his bread and shelter from day to day. Often, he thought of Brighthome and of sitting with Fa and Mo at the long table in the dining room, looking out at the orchard on a sunny morning. But now he was sitting at this table, in a shed on this mucky farm, at the edge of a "pig village," as the fatigue of evening weighed heavily. He sat here with Rodey and Jude.

"So you ain't going wench-hunting with us, hey Nome?" Rodey was saying to him, prodding his wrist with a cup to command his attention. "Nghee-uhh! Nghee-uhh! Nghee-uhh!" He winked to the side at his partner, an unsubtle grimace.

Jude was bobbing, squinty-eyed, in a silent chuckle, as though something very funny had just been said. "Yeh, come on wench-hunting with us, Nome, come on."

Nome looked up and grinned at them through the bread in his teeth and slowly shook his head. He was willing to be the new boy and the butt of their jokes. "You fellows go on without me. I didn't bring hunting equipment with me."

"Ngee-uhh! Ngee-uhh" brayed Rodey louder, "Judey! He doesn't have the right equipment to go wench-hun...wench-hu...ohh-ahh!...the right equipm..." and he doubled up in a tight spasm of laughter and actually rolled off the bench onto the floor.

Jude, too, held his stomach, as though he had just been punched, and rolled off the bench to the floor.

Nome watched them for a moment, grinning with amusement at this display, then stacked the plates and cups of all three on a tray at the end of the table. He rose from the bench and said, "You two go wench-hunting. I'm going to bed." It was just the thing to say, for the hooting and screeching and moaning from the two men on the floor re-doubled as he stepped out under the stars and pulled the door shut behind him.

Wench-hunting. It was all those two had talked about since the three of them had seen the posters tacked up in the village when they had gone in for feed in the afternoon. The runaway starwoman was all anyone was talking about in Hay, especially about the size of the reward. One farmer said these same posters had been up a week earlier down there in the bigger towns; but it had taken all this time, as usual, for news to get to this boggy corner of the Fields of Khorvan. The rumor was that this escaped woman must be carrying some great secret or must have stolen something very valuable for those Ghan people to be putting out such a search for her. The police, who had put up the posters in Hay that morning, had also been questioning people and snooping around; and there were stories coming from southward of searches being made in houses and along the roads.

Three thousand kurakhs, thought Nome. He had made the translation several times in his head: enough for a hundred-day, and more, of payment on Brighthome and the other two holdings, easily. Or for Brighthome alone, nearly two or three hundred-day...almost a year. I could rest, he thought. I could go home. He felt like weeping, and he suddenly felt very tired.

Overhead, The Great Cloud stretched across the night sky, painting it blotchy with stars. He stood in the damp grass of the yard, breathing the close odors of dung and animals and silage, and noticed how the evenings were getting colder. He startled to see a black shadow moving across the yard at a distance, up against the wall of the barn. No...the dogs were not barking...it could not be anything to fear. Of course, it was Natty, creeping back to her shed. She had been up to the house, most likely. Poor old woman, what suffering had she had in her life to make her so bent and silent, scuttling about forever with dirty hair draped across her face, shawl pulled tightly over her, hands gloved against the light? Nome watched her silently slip into her doorway. He went in her direction, entering the barn just beyond her door and groped his way in the dark past the shuffling animals to find the ladder to the loft.

Dumpy would not let him use a candle up here, where there was so much hay and dry wood. He pulled off his boots and his pants in the dark and lay back on the cloth coverlet over the hay. Through the wall, he could hear the occasional muffled noises from the old woman's room, scrape of table legs on the floor, a chair thumping the wall. From below the loft, where he lay, came the patient sounds of cattle bodies shifting and munching. Nome looked up into the darkness, thinking of nothing. Then he was thinking of the three thousand kurakhs and of The House of

Ghan. It reminded him of the prince of Kezzlhjem, to whom they had once thought of going in hopes of entering the service of a great house. He had to get money. Soon he would tell Dumpy...not tomorrow...but maybe in a few days, that he had to leave. He would go south and look for this House of Ghan to see if he could enter service there. He had to go where the money was.

Sleep drifted in like a quieting breeze. But then his eyes were open again. Room noises from the old woman's side. She is restless, he thought. It almost sounded like there were voices. Strange. Someone at her door? Who would be talking? Dumpy's wife, no doubt, come to check on her or something. He thought he heard the door close, but it was hard to tell.

He had felt uncomfortable at the sight of this bent hag when she had first come, especially when Dumpy had told them that she was a little "off her head" and they should just leave her alone and she wouldn't hurt anybody. She had, indeed, kept to herself, scurrying away and keeping as silent as a cat. Normally, he did not give her any thought; but here he was, sleepless and wondering if she were still in her squalid room or if she had gone out again. The silence troubled him.

Without planning to, he reached up to feel for the board near his head that he had found loose when he first moved into the loft. It was a short, gap-filling board along the wall, which he had inspected and had found to be holding in a bank of dirty sawdust that spilled out. So he had pushed it back in place and let it be. Curious, he now pulled it away and listened. Nothing. However, he could feel the slightest draft coming from the wall boards of the attached shed. He hoisted himself forward and leaned carefully close to that gap to see if he could hear anything at all. Nothing.

He had just decided to push the short board back into place when a clear sound from the room beyond his wall stopped him. It was the door of Natty's room scraping open. Instantly, shafts of light shot through slits between the boards into Nome's space. He eased himself up on one elbow with tense caution and pressed his face close until his eyes were at the widest gap between the slats.

There is the hag, were his first thoughts, stooping at her door, looking out, clutching a lantern, speaking to Dumpy's wife. They've been out, just returned. Dirty, black dress dragging in the dirt, shawl wrapped tight around her head, leaning heavy on that cane. Imagine she smells bad. Whispering to Dumpy's wife...so she can talk after all, not dumb. Only those she trusts, the crazy old thing.

Dumpy's wife withdrew, and the door was shut after her. Natty turned, and Nome saw the ash-covered hair straggling like moss across her face. She hobbled forward two steps and set the lantern on the table.

At what happened next, Nome's eyes went wide and his mouth opened. She straightened upright and hooked the cane over the back of a chair. She unwound the shawl and threw back the stringy hair. She tugged off the gloves and threw them on the table. Nome was looking at the stately figure and beautiful face of a young woman. Understanding nothing, he only felt this wordless thought, as she glanced in his direction: Her eyes. Her eyes are like drops of water falling on the surface of a pool from a great height.

All the next morning, Rodey and Jude had great fun accusing Nome of having given them the slip to go wench-hunting after all. Bawling with coarse laughter, they said he must have been up and about all night and hadn't slept a wink, the sly hound! It was true. Nome was bleached with fatigue; and he dragged himself about chores listlessly. He put his head down on his arms at the table for a moment at breakfast. He napped on the grass and skipped eating at lunchtime. Throughout the previous night, he had lain staring up toward the invisible rafters of the barn, and had fallen into a numb, cottony slumber only half-an-hour before Rodey had rattled a stick up and down his ladder rungs to wake him for another work day.

During the next several days, Nome avoided the other farm hands and Dumpy himself, whenever he could get away. Rodey and Jude grew tired of poking at him, because he made no response and seemed absent and irritable. Nome said he was not feeling well and spent nearly all his free time in his loft. Indeed, one day, when Nome said he was too sick to work and needed to stay in bed, Dumpy only cursed mildly and agreed that he looked "like an old beagle."

That day, he had eavesdropped on a conversation which released him from hope and the vision of three thousand kurakhs, released him from ambiguous duty to save his home, and slid him sweetly back into squalor and hopelessness. He had realized, almost at once that first night, that he was spying on the fugitive starwoman, but could not imagine how she came to be here. For several days, he watched her when he was free from work; but her room was still in darkness when he left his loft for chores each morning; and he could only observe her after he returned at nightfall. He watched her move about and keep her small space tidy, watched her sew and read by lantern light, watched her rub ashes and dirt into her hair and arrange it over her face and squat over into her hunchback when she prepared to go out, watched her throw off her disguise when she returned and rinsed her hair with fresh water from a pail and tied it into a horsetail behind her head, watched her slip out of her dirty, black dress and blow out the lantern when she went to bed. Then he listened to her long, slow breathing. He wondered what her voice was like.

Dumpy's wife came to visit the starwoman only during the day, when the farmhands were away at work. Sometimes they would visit up at the house, sometimes for a while in the shed. The day Nome had told Dumpy he was sick and could not work, Dumpy must have neglected to mention this to his wife; for mid-morning she brought a tray of tea and biscuits to the door of the young woman's shed and knocked with the toe of her shoe to be let in. Nome silently joined their morning tea from his perch and, for the first time, heard the young woman speaking. It left him still longing to hear the sound of her voice, for they spoke in whispers. What he learned, however was far more important.

Her name was Ravenna. Dumpy was her uncle by marriage, brother of a man who had married another starwoman, named Aunie. She had lived with some group of women by a river. Whether this brother was still alive or not was unclear from the conversation. There was a discussion of other relatives that was hard to follow. Many names. Some hostile references made to Mintor Ghan. Some laughter. She must have spent days on this very farm as a child. Dumpy's wife asked if she didn't want to get out into the air a bit and to come up to the house in the afternoon; but the starwoman said, no, she had washed her hair clean that morning for the first time in weeks, and she could not stand the thought of heaping dirt and ashes on it again so soon. So, later that afternoon, Dumpy's wife returned for another visit; and they sewed and talked together like dear old friends. Again Nome listened. The name, Aunie, kept coming up, and Ravenna argued that she had to get away for a while soon to see her mother and to be with Aunie again. Dumpy's wife got increasingly agitated about this and argued the danger of going anywhere. She put down her sewing and kept tapping one point on the table to insist on the foolhardiness of traveling back to The Women, where Mintor's guards would be watching like hawks. Ravenna said her disguise had been working wonderfully; and no one had come near her; and she said that it was getting better by the day, because she had not bathed since she came ("don't tell me now that you haven't noticed!"), and that she was going to quit washing her hair even. At that, she impishly bounced up and knelt at the ash drawer of the stove, drew out two handfuls of gray ashes and rubbed them through her hair. Dumpy's wife reached out her foot and gave her a little kick and said she was as stubborn and willful as she was when she was a little girl. Then she picked up her sewing again, laughing and shaking her head, and saying she was not convinced, and was going to tell Dumpy not to let her go.

Nome watched all this, heard all this, and lay awake later that night thinking not of kurakhs but of a woman he had once loved in Tosarkun. He also thought of Troutman's daughter, but could no long remember what she looked like. He thought of that beautiful woman in the sutton...and wondered if she had been real.... And now this woman. What a beautiful name. He slept.

....

Nome stopped spying on the starwoman. He went back to work and stopped being sick. He did his job with grim energy, and Jude and Rodey were a bit afraid of him.

Friday morning, Dumpy worked his way down to the meal shed, wincing every step of the way, and stepping gingerly as though he were barefoot on sharp stones.

"Jude and Nome," he huffed, "you two boys hitch up the team to the long wagon. Not the small one, the long one. And load in them sheep I told you to pen off by the tanks over there. Should be twelve of them. Count them. There better be twelve. Get them to the market at Gree am Slome before noon and get a good price for them. Hear? A good price! Winter coming on, and mutton and wool is up. You boys been down there before, you know how to do it. Jude, you been there lots of times, don't let me down. Nome, you're smart, Jude ain't smart. Keep an eye on him. All right? Rodey, you stay here and do chores."

The three of them yessired their way through this. Dumpy turned to go. Then he leaned back into the meal shed doorway.

"And, Jude and Nome. I'm sending that Natty back. She'll ride along behind with the sheep."

Jude yessired once more.

An hour later, the sheep were jostling against the rails of the long wagon, and the gate of the yard stood open. Dumpy was leaning against the wagon tongue, behind the horses, giving Jude and Nome last minute instructions. Nome watched Dumpy's wife walking quickly from the house to the barn. She stopped at the door of Natty's shed and disappeared. A moment later, Natty emerged, hobbling with her cane and scurried to the wagon. At the rear, she hitched herself up onto the flatbed awkwardly, climbed over the rail, and wiggled in among the bleating sheep.

"Here! You listening?" Dumpy bellowed. "Pay attention! I want you to get this right!"

Nome yessired.

"Never mind about her. She won't be any bother, if you let her alone. She don't talk, and she's a little...," he tapped his forehead, "but she won't be any trouble. Just don't let anybody bother her. She knows where she's getting off. Just let her be. She ain't stupid."

As they drove out onto the road, Jude noticed that Nome's mood had changed. Gone was the dark brooding that had preoccupied him over the past week. He was alert and talkative. Jude took this as a sign that Nome was ready to return to the bawdy banter he and Rodey preferred. As soon as they were clopping and squeaking along toward Gree am Slome, Jude began talking about wench-hunting. To his disappointment, Nome became grave.

"Enough of that talk, Jude. I've heard enough. You've worn that out."

"What's the matter, Nome," Jude persisted. "don't you want to be rich?"

"Not that way. I need money as much as anybody. But I don't want it by selling someone."

"You're right about that, Nome. Sell sheep, that's all right. Ain't it?"

"That's right."

"I sure wish I could find that wench and turn her in, Nome, so I wouldn't have to haul any more sheep. I'd quit Dumpy quick, if I had three thousand in my pocket. You'd see how quick."

"Well, let's talk about something else." Nome shifted uneasily.

"Sure, Nome, I'm agreeable to that," replied Jude. "Know what I have been wondering? I've been wondering why they want to pay so much for this runaway wench. She must be something special. Before I turned her in, I'd like to see her and...."

"I'd like to talk to her, too," Nome broke in quickly, restraining an impulse to glance back. "But I don't like this talk about hunting a woman down for money. Or for anything. I don't like that! I'm getting tired of this talk!"

"You're not getting mad again, are you, Nome?"

"Yes, I am. No. I'm not. Not mad. Just...well, tell me about yourself, Jude. You from around here?"

He was very surprised about a question like this, which he had never been asked. Nome continued to query and, little by little, had him telling about his parents, brothers and sisters, what work he had done before he came to Dumpy's, and so on. Jude was uncomfortable with this attention...but liked it in a way. He wished Rodey were here.

Among the bumping, stumbling sheep, Ravenna Rosealice was watching through the lattice of her matted hair. She kept the shawl pulled tight and averted her head at movement from either man that suggested a glance back in her direction. The lanky man, with the long scar across his cheek and mouth, was the one she was concerned about, the one speaking in her defense. He seemed to turn back to check the sheep from time to time. The other one, at the reins, showed only the back of his skull. She was also feeling confusion about the first man's effort to control the conversation. She wondered about his motivation. Despite this, she could not help the presence of a cautious sense of gratitude, even warmth. For weeks, she had been in hiding, unwashed and in dirty rags, with only Dumpy's wife for company and gentle words. Dumpy himself knew no gentle words; and, besides, he was terrified at the risk he was running. Had she imagined it, that this man up front had been watching her come across the yard toward the wagon? Dumpy had yelled at him for it. She had a feeling this one had not forgotten about dirty old Natty sitting on sheep dung at the back of the wagon. Hold on tight, Ravenna, she told herself. Get ready to run for your life, if you have to.

They rattled along the road for another hour, and Nome gave up interviewing Jude, who in turn was satisfied to leave well-enough alone and drive in silence. Nome tried to doze, leaning his sharp elbows on his knees, but it was hard to keep them there with the jolting and swaying of the wagon. Other roads joined theirs and, with them, other carts and wagons hauling produce and livestock to the market town on the River Slome. Drivers called to each other and traded news; for it had been a long ride, in sleepy autumn sunshine; and they were glad of one-another's company. More than one joked about the black sheep riding at the back of Jude and Nome's load. Nome merrily called out that she was not for sale. Jude took up the joke and repeated it to others with no variation, until Nome managed to distract him once again.

Toward noon, they reached the bridge crossing the Slome, but there was a long line of conveyances backed up and waiting to cross. They pulled into line and stood on the wagon seat, craning to see what was causing the holdup. Police it was, at the bridge. Stopping every cart and wagon and vehicle.

"Oh, Holy!" said Nome.

"What's that?" asked Jude.

"I said Oh, Holy. They are searching everything that crosses."

"It's all right, Nome. They're just looking for that wench. They won't bother us."

"I know they are," he said, and sat back on the seat and stared forward for a long while.

Their wagon rolled forward in stages. Suddenly, Nome stiffened and blurted, "Jude, let's go have a drink at Tove's Keg!"

This was a notorious tavern at the left side of the road, near the bridge. Jude had heard many lurid tales of this place ever since he was a boy. Nome had been regaled with stories of its wild reputation by his partner, Rodey. Police from the town of Gree were routinely posted at the bridge, the usual limit of their jurisdiction, but frequently were called in at the first sign of trouble to squelch brawls. About Tove's Keg lingered the type who are no longer welcome across the bridge in the market town.

Jude paled at the suggestion, "Naw, Nome, your joking me. Ain't you?"

"No, not at all! I got a terrible thirst, and I want to look at this Tove's Keg I've heard so much about! Here, come on! Pull over there in front." And Nome reached for the reins.

Jude saw that he meant it and shrank back. "No, Nome, it's a bad place. We don't want to go in there. Let's wait till we get across the bridge. We'll lose our place in line."

"That's all right, we have time. I want a drink here in this place. I want to see if it's as bad as they say. You're not afraid to go with me, are you, Jude?"

Nome had taken the reins and snapped the horses off to the side, and the wagon rolled toward the front of the tavern. Jude clutched his seat, terrified both of Nome, who was now talking loudly and gesturing, and of the forbidden building they were approaching. He gawked at Nome as though he were mad, but did not dare oppose him. Suddenly, one of the police at the side of a cart a short way ahead thought they were trying to bypass the line and darted forward pointing a finger at them.

Nome jerked the horses to a stop and called, "We're just going over to the Keg for a boot!"

The police officer scowled in distrust, but slowed his advance. "Well, you tie up over there, and I'll get to you later on. But don't think this will put you ahead! You've lost your place now and have to wait till we're through with all these ahead of you."

"That's all right with us, ain't it, Jude!" shouted Nome with gusto. "We're going to the Keg to have us a drink, ain't we, Jude!" Nome suddenly twisted round in his seat and yelled, "We'll even bring a drink out to Natty, won't we? I'll bet Natty would like a brew, although she prob'ly won't say so!" And with that he threw his head back and laughed heartily.

Now they were at the door, and Nome was down on the ground tying the reins to a railing. Jude was timidly climbing down from the wagon, as though he were descending the side of a thousand-foot rock face. Nome swaggered to the back of the wagon bawling, "We'll bring old Natty a brew, won't we? I'll bet it's a long time since old Natty's had a stiff drink!" As he said this, he stretched over the railing and clamped a firm hand on the back of old Natty's neck and playfully tugged her toward him calling, "You'd like a brew, too, wouldn't you, Natty?" She recoiled, but too late. Nome's fierce grip pulled her head forward until it was close to his face. He hissed into the curtain of filthy hair: "There will be a fight. The police will go for it. Then run!" He shoved her away, still bellowing like a drunk. He pulled Jude by the arm into Tove's Keg.

Within a minute, shouts and howls came from the tavern; a stool shattered a window; there were cries for help. Police abandoned their futile search of wagons and carts and surged toward the front door of the Keg, shouting back commands that no one was to move.

No one did. All wagons stayed in place because no one wanted to become a suspect in this feverish hunt. Besides, who would want to give up such good seats at a Tove's Keg brawl? Except for one person, a crippled old crone, who slid down from a wagon and hobbled across the bridge with her cane.

THIRTEEN

Wasoo

Now Nome Ogrodni lay on the top bunk, ceiling a few inches from his face. Not Dumpy's Farm anymore, this was a jail cell he shared with three others. In the bunk below, a man sleeping like a living bellows, sucking in and pushing out a watery, wheezing, drunken snore. In the other bottom bunk lay Jude, finally breathing quietly after moaning and weeping himself to sleep. Above and across from Nome was the shape of a man awake who had risen up on an elbow and greeted them curtly when they were brought in and had then lain back and returned the broad brim of a hat over his eyes, even though there was no light in the cell.

Here he was, the fortune seeker, in jail again, broke, hopeless, having lost all his gear, even the musical pipe which might have lifted his spirits in this dark place. Nome puckered his lips, testing whether he might quietly whistle a mournful tune; but it hurt too much. He lifted a hand to his face and delicately touched the sore places. His eyes were nearly swollen shut, his lip badly puffed. His shoulder pained when he moved his arm. He lay still. He was aware that the man in the top bunk across from him had turned his head and was watching him. He sighed deep and long.

"You and I have the best places," he heard. "I always try to get the top bunk if I can. Air up here is not so good; but, when they sick up, you don't want to be below 'em."

"Mmmm?" Nome turned his head slightly with effort. "Oh...sure." He lay still.

"This is a good place. Good bed. Food's good. Warm. They treat you right in this place. I come here often." Silence. "Not bothering you, am I?"

"Uh? Oh...no, 'ts awright."

"Although this is my last time here for a while. They told me I was abusing their welcome, when I came in, and said next time they'd throw me in the Bludgeon. I know when to back off."

"Uh-huh." Nome was being polite. "What's 'at?"

"What?"

"Buchon."

"The Bludgeon? You don't know about that? It's the real prison, where they throw the criminals. A hole. You don't want to go there! I could get out, but why get in, in the first place?" There was a pause. "What are you here for?"

"Mmmm." Nome wondered that himself. "Oh...fighting. Fighting, I guess." It was painful to form words. "In a public inn. Oww."

"Let's see." The man propped himself up on an elbow again and leaned over the edge of his bunk peering through the dim light at Nome. "Oh, yeh, I see. Pretty badly punched around, hey? You hurt bad? I mean, anything broken?"

"No, I don't think so. Jus' swollen, I think. I'm awright."

"It sounded like you were talking thick, but it didn't strike me you were steeped."

"No, I din't even take a drink. It all happened fast. I don't want to talk about it though," Nome added.

"Most of them in here are pretty steeped when they come in. They're usually not much company till they sleep a good long time. Then they're usually crabby and feeling sorry for themselves when they wake up. Like our neighbor down below you there. What about your partner? This whiny fellow?"

"Jude?" Nome tried to turn his neck and glance down across to the lower bunk. "Aw, I feel bad about that. I got him into this. It's not his fault."

"He was whimpering about losing his sheep. He lose some sheep?"

"I don't know," Nome murmured sadly. "I s'ppose so. I s'ppose we both did. It was a load we were hauling in for the farmer we work for. Sheep are gone, I s'ppose. Horses, wagon, too. Left 'em tied outside the Keg. P'lice took 'em, I think."

"Well!" said the man, "If the police took them, you're all right. You'll get them back when we get out. The police are surprisingly honest here. I told you this was a good place."

Nome wanted to grin, but he muttered "Oww!" instead. He liked this cheerful neighbor and wished he could see his face.

"Here, let's take a look at your face," the neighbor suddenly said, sitting up and sliding out of his bunk to the floor. "I'll get a light."

"There's a light in here?" Nome asked, lifting himself up stiffly.

"No. Out here." The man was now at the cell door, facing the bars. Nome could only see from behind that he had a stocky build and moved briskly. There was some scraping of metal for a few moments, then he made a quick, jabbing motion and there was a thud. The door swung open and the man disappeared. A few seconds later he was back, holding a lantern, clanging the bars to behind him.

He set the lantern on the floor and squatted to scrape flint and steel near a strand of dry wick. A glow rose in the cell. He came forward holding the lantern high to view Nome's face.

And for the first time, Nome saw *his* face. A wave of sandy hair over a high forehead, arching bushy eyebrows, head dipped, offering a friendly, sidelong regard, and a bit of warm smile. The effect was something reassuring, playful, even mischievous. In all, a likable face.

"Let's see."

"Do you have a key?" Nome asked, making no effort to hide his amazement.

"No, that's just something I know how to do. My daddy was a warder. I grew up around locks and keys. Let's see. Oooh, yes. Badly puffed, but I've seen worse in here. Nothing broken? that's good. That old scar on your mouth, did you get that fighting, too?"

Nome started to laugh until pain stopped him. "No. That's from when I was a boy. Well, maybe fighting, not exactly. Another kid hit me with a hoe. I suppose it looks like I am a real fighter? Not really."

"Well, I could tell better if I could see your eyes," said the other lowering the lantern. "I can't see much of them. Kind of squinty like little piglet eyes. I will know you better in a day or two when we get out."

"You think we are getting out in a few days?" Nome asked with respect, for he was already suspecting he was dealing with an experienced person. "Are we likely to get out of here at the same time?"

"Oh, certainly," he answered, lowering the lantern to the floor and finding himself a seat on the edge of Jude's bunk.

Nome slowly lowered himself to the floor and felt about for a piece of the bunk below his, on which the snoring man sprawled. He had to flop a draped arm back across the fellow's chest, which produced a sputtering and blubbering of chewed words and a rolling sideways so that the man now faced the wall. Snores relaxed into whistled breathing. Nome and his neighbor sat facing each other like tramps over a campfire.

"We will get out when we want to," the man continued. "In any case, they won't keep us long. What do they want with fighters and drinkers?"

"And what are you in here for?" asked Nome.

"Dining and dashing."

"What?"

"Having a wonderful meal at The King's Kettle and leaving without paying. They punish you for that, you know, by putting you in a nice warm room here, giving you a bed, and feeding you three times a day. Good food here, too, you'll see. Though not as good as at The King's Kettle, but you can't expect everything. If *you* try it though, make sure you know what town you are in. For example, I wouldn't recommend dining and dashing in Stoat. Although they have some very good eating places there, the jail is awful. Food is terrible and they hit you around. Stay away from Stoat."

"So you try to get into jail on purpose?" asked Nome.

"Only when I have been out of a place to stay for a while and am needing something solid inside of me. Winter is coming on now. Getting cold, have to think of that. Do you have a dog?"

"A dog?" Nome felt thrown off his bearings, just as he had begun to think he was finding them. "Well,...no. I had one, but not with me now...."

"We had a dog, too, now that you mention it. A good dog, like one of the family. People in town said they could see the resemblance. We had a lot of fun together. Daddy taught him to play dockers."

"Dockers!" said Nome, knowing now he was being teased. "You're telling me he was a pretty smart dog."

"Oh, well, not so especially smart. I could beat him most games. He never did get the hang of it. But I like a dog, know why?"

"No. Why?"

"A dog is your best friend because he wags his tail instead of his tongue. Now here am I flapping my tongue, and you are there all sore from being punched around and are probably wanting to get some sleep."

"No, it's all right, I'm fine," said Nome, meaning it. He liked this man. "I'm Nome Ogrodni. What's your name?"

The man grinned as though he thought Nome would never ask. "Happy to be in jail with you, Nome Ogrodni. Wasoo is currently my name."

"Just Wasoo? Wasoo what?" asked Nome.

"If you want me to have a second name, I suppose it would be 'Wasoo,' too. Or 'Wasoo two.' 'Wasoo, Wasoo'...sounds like calling pigs, doesn't it?"

"What do you mean it's your name *currently*?" asked Nome, now amused.

"It's the name I'm wearing. It ain't me. I wear these clothes, but I change them sometimes. I used to live in a pretty stone house with gooseberry bushes around the yard, but I live in this jail now. When I go to a ball at Count Mintor Ghan's mansion, I wear a fine blue suit with a slashing scarlet sash around my middle and shiny black boots. Then I wear some other name, not 'Wasoo,' for sure. When I earn three kurakhs a day hauling horse manure for the municipality of Gree am Slome, I wear brown clothes and scruffy brown boots. And maybe I wear 'Wasoo,' but more likely they know me as Gromber Dinker, the way they did last time. Do you always go by 'Nome Ogrodni'?"

"Well, I guess so," said Nome, never having thought about it. "What did your daddy call you?"

"Daddy? He called me 'Wasoo' mostly, I guess. And I called him 'Daddy,' although my mama didn't call him that. I don't think many other people did either."

There was clanging and rattling in the hallway beyond their cell door, as the warders brought supper.

....

Wasoo was right, the food was not bad. Here it was, two days later, and the four of them were seated on the two lower bunks, spooning vegetable soup into their mouths and looking forward to being released that day. Wasoo worked at cheering Jude up.

"Your boss will get over it, Jude. Why, man, he will just be happy to see you coming in the yard riding that empty wagon and smiling at all the money you'll be bringing back. Just be sure to smile when you ride into the yard. Don't come in, head hanging, for being late, like you are expecting him to kick you around the farmyard."

"It ain't kicking around I'm worried about," sulked Jude. "He's got gimpy legs and couldn't kick over a dog's water dish by accident. But he got a mean temper. And, if I lose them twelve sheep...."

"There you go again, thinking the worst. I tell you, your horses and wagon and sheep are in the hands of the Gree am Slome police; and they are taking good care of them. They'll return them to you, asking if they can be of any further service."

Jude looked at him skeptically. The other two, munching silently, glanced sideways to see if such a story could be given or taken seriously.

"Well...," muttered Jude, "there'd better be twelve. Or I might just as well forget about going back to Dumpy's Farm. You heard him, didn't you, Nome? 'Twelve,' he said, 'count 'em.' He's a hard boss, ain't he, Nome?"

Nome nodded.

"Twelve sheep!" bawled Wasoo, as though he were at wit's end. "Jude! What a gloomy man you are! Maybe there will be thirteen or fourteen in your wagon when you get out."

"What?" Jude reared back. "How could that be? Folks like what hang out at that Keg *steal* sheep. They don't come along and give you a few, add 'em to your load!"

"No, of course not. But from the way you talk, I'm beginning to wonder if you didn't do the usual check to see if any were pregnant before you set out."

The fourth man choked a bit on his soup and had to cough.

"You did check them, didn't you?"

Jude's brow furrowed. He looked intently at the floor. "Well, I counted them...twelve...."

"Counted them? No, no," Wasoo leaned forward toward his difficult pupil. "I know you counted them, but did you check to see if any of them had a lamb on the way?"

"No," he answered meekly.

"No? You let sheep travel when they might be pregnant? And the buyer at market might be getting two for the price of one, and you wouldn't even know it?"

"Well, Dumpy just said count 'em. And me and Nome...."

"I don't want to worry you, Jude; and it will probably turn out all right for you," Wasoo said soothingly. "In fact, my point was that you may come out of this with thirteen or fourteen sheep, if you are lucky. Since you neglected the usual check."

"I see," said Jude, looking puzzled. He was silent for a while, then added, "But what if someone at the Keg stole the whole lot while me and Nome was being hauled away?"

"Jude!" wailed Wasoo, throwing up his hands, "You complain about your good fortune! Here you have a chance of increasing the number of sheep you bring. You get a day or two of complete rest. When was the last time your farmer gave you two full days of rest with a good bed like this?"

"Never," admitted Jude. "He works us seven days a week, don't he Nome?"

Nome nodded, chewing.

"Two days of rest," continued Wasoo, "in a good bed, food served up to you, excellent companions!"

Nome interrupted: "Careful, Wasoo. You'll have this goodhearted fellow following your ways and taking up dining and dashing instead of farming."

But there was no real danger of Jude's being led astray. In fact, Wasoo's attentiveness had reassured him; and, after lunch, he was happily snoozing on his bunk.

When the other man, with whom they had only brief conversation, rolled into his bunk and was snoring, Nome approached Wasoo where he stood looking out the bars of the cell door. In the short time they had been in jail together, Nome felt he had gotten to know him a bit. Even though he was whimsical and unpredictable, Nome felt there was something solid about him. Nome needed someone to trust.

"Wasoo?"

"Hmm?"

"Have you heard of this starwoman they are looking for?"

"Who hasn't?"

"What do you think of it?"

Wasoo was still for a moment, then said, "I think she is a smart woman."

"Smart? Why so?"

"If she is running from Count Mintor Ghan, she is smart."

"Why so? Who is this Count?"

Wasoo turned to him, shoved his hands into his pockets, and leaned back against the bars. He studied Nome for a moment. Then said, "I have been in his house several times. It is really quite a place. The Ghan family is the richest and most powerful in all The Fields of Khorvan. The old count was a nasty fellow. Ruthless, a real bad one. This younger one, Mintor, is not as bad yet, but give him a little time. Right now he's like one of those bellering hounds who is tied up all the time and always making a racket. The whole family's sour. They are superstitious and...and weird. Better to stay away from them. You know, all you have to do is listen around and you hear people talking about that starwoman as though she is crazy to be running away, because she could be rich and famous. They say there must be something wrong with her and that she probably deserves to be caught. On top of it, there is a price on her; and they would be only too happy to turn her in, if they could. That's the talk. I wouldn't like to be in her shoes. She won't be able to last long if she is still in The Fields of Khorvan."

"How do you know so much about this Ghan family?"

"I worked for them once for a few weeks. At other times, I attended their dances and parties and dinners. I have been there in various guises, with other names, on several occasions. I told you, 'Wasoo' is my current name. This," he pointed, "is my current face. No, no, don't laugh, I don't change my face actually. But I do know how to make myself up to look different. If I had my materials with me here, Nome, I could dress up right in this cell so you wouldn't recognize me." He grew serious again. "I learned most about them those two weeks I worked there as a footman. I learned that the real power in that house is a twisted old woman. I don't know what to make of her...but I would be afraid of her, if I had to be there for long."

"But what about the starwoman? Did you ever see her?"

"Starwoman...the one they're after? She was never there when I was. I don't know anything about her. They've always had a starwoman in their family...usually married to the count of the house. But there has been none for several years now. The last one, I think...the last of the old count's wives...died some time ago. She was a pitiful thing, they say. The Ghans are incredibly superstitious on this point. I am surprised they have not moved more forcefully on The Huts and just seized one of the women there. Maybe that's what they did."

"The Huts," blurted Nome. It was an expression he had overheard in the conversations between Dumpy's wife and the young woman in hiding. "What do you know about them?"

Wasoo looked at him shrewdly. "What do *you* know about them?"

"Why, I...well...I heard that expression once...." Then he stopped and looked squarely at his cellmate. "I need to know something, Wasoo. You disapprove of these Ghan people and are cheering for the starwoman they are tracking. But...." Here Nome looked at him more tensely, with his clear, brown eyes wide. "What would you do if...if you knew where she was?"

Wasoo said nothing. He examined Nome's face slowly, sizing him up. Then, for the first time, he looked angry: "I dine and dash. I am loose with the truth at times. I go into the town jail frequently, willingly, deservedly. But I am no bounty hunter. Whoever brings this starwoman in should be paid his three thousand kurakhs and thrown into the Bludgeon!"

"Shhh!" Nome hastened to quiet him and threw a quick glance to the lower bunks where the men were still sleeping. He let out a long, controlled sigh and said, "I have seen her. It is on her account that I am here in jail."

"You have *seen* this starwoman they are talking about?"

"Yes." And Nome told him the story. At the end, he said, "And now I want to follow her. I need your help, Wasoo. I don't know this place."

Wasoo nodded slowly and studied the floor. "Why not let her be? Why would you want to follow her, Nome?"

"I came to know her, in a way. I spent a lot of time beside her. She does not even know I exist, but I have...she is in my mind a lot. I have given up something for her." He stopped and looked away. "No. No, that is not right. I had nothing. But I want to see her again, and I would like to talk with her. Then I would let her be."

"There's not a chance, Nome. Everyone is hunting her. How could you find her again?" asked Wasoo quietly.

"I think she was going to The Huts. She spoke of it to Dumpy's wife, and I think that is why she risked this trip."

"Well, that is not so hard," said Wasoo. "I could take you to The

Huts."

"Would you do that, Wasoo?" asked Nome eagerly.

"Yes, I will," he answered.

....

Later in the afternoon, the four men passed through the jailhouse door into the street. To Jude's delight and relief, the sheep were waiting; and, to Wasoo's chagrin, there were only twelve of them.

"Jude, drive the load to Stoat, since you've missed the market here," advised Wasoo. "Their market day is tomorrow, and I've heard the prices you get are good. But, be sure to be at market there by dawn; and, whatever you do, Jude, don't get yourself thrown into jail again in Stoat! It's a bad jail, not at all friendly like this one."

"I won't be going with you, Jude," said Nome. "I'm traveling on and won't be going back to Dumpy. You'll do fine without me. Better, probably. Tell Dumpy I am very sorry if I have let him down."

"But, Nome," said Jude, alarmed, "day after tomorrow is payday at Dumpy's! You'll miss your pay!"

"You collect my pay, Jude. You keep it for yourself. I'm not going back to collect it. Here is a note to Dumpy saying so. The jailer gave me some paper so I could write this."

Jude took the note reverently, opened it, and stared at the page without comprehension. Then he carefully folded it, tucked it into his jacket pocket, and looked at Nome with awe.

"You keep it, Jude. It's the least I can do. Sorry for getting you in trouble."

"And now!" Wasoo turned to their fourth companion, who lingered near them. "I want to thank you, my friend, for not throwing up and for keeping our cell clean and tidy."

"Huh?" the man snorted, taken aback. "Who said anything about me throwing up?"

"Many of 'em who come in steeped do, you know," said Wasoo breezily. "Makes it unpleasant. I thank you for your thoughtfulness."

"Huh?" the man said again angrily, looking at Wasoo to see if he were being mocked. But he saw looking back only a friendly, open face, so free of guile that he shuffled and muttered: "It was nothing. Don't mention it."

FOURTEEN

Wails and Sighs

The Plains of Wildness is a wide band of rocky desert which appears to flow from the flanks of the Endicot Mountains like dead lava. It forms a barrier cutting all but the most determined communication between the peoples of the east and the west and is not easily crossed. It is a forlorn and blasted place, dusty and rocky, broken by sudden crevices and upheavals.

Ravenna Rosealice had been on The Plains of Wildness for four days. She had not gone very far before being stopped; and now she had been camped for two days on a low ridge, amid a cluster of boulders, from which she could look out but not be seen. No outward obstacle held her to this place. An inner struggle was demanding all her strength of will and left her without energy to move on. She was, in fact, in a trance.

At the end of her second day of travel, after leaving her mother and Aunt Aunie, she had stopped below this ridge, looking for a favorable place to spend the night. The ridge overlooked the way-marker, three piles of stones; and she was glad to know that she had not strayed. Moreover, she was delighted to find palo shrubs for her supper meal. Ravenna had been watchful for ways to extend the scant food provisions in her pack: withered strips of apple, carrot, rutabaga, and pear, beancakes and lentilcakes, dry wheat and barley biscuits, thick hazelnut paste in a separate pouch. Most of the weight was in the swollen water bag. One of the many uncertainties of travel on The Plains was not knowing how long one's food and water would last. There were rare springs and pools of fresh water along the way; but nothing edible was to be found, other than insects and lizards. However, Ravenna recognized the palo shrub at once, as she reached the three stacks of marker stones toward evening. She and Aunie had gathered them often on a barren, rocky area near Stoat. Only the roots were used; the branches and leaves were thrown away. The roots were stripped, mashed, and soaked or boiled. They gave a strong, spicy flavor to soups and stews, and especially to mushroom sauces, and were considered very nutritious. Now Ravenna studied these shrubs carefully, lifting the leaves, looking at the undersides, rubbing the scaly bark with her thumb, pulling one up and stripping the root stock with her fingernail and nibbling. They were palo. The evening before, she had only chewed dry foods. This evening, she decided to lighten the water bag and, not daring to risk a fire, to make a cold soup from the palo root. This she had done.

By nightfall, she was euphoric. The stars ran liquid down the sky. The crescent moon grew to fill the sky and sashayed seductively about, throwing off bursts of color. The hard desert earth became ocean, and she herself walked on the waves. All the voices of the rocks and the dust soared up as an incoherent chorus, thousands of voices, yet each was marvelously distinct and clear. Her experience tumbled on through the night, without time, without reflection. Fortunately, it began to subside just before sunrise, when she became aware of feeling cold. She covered herself under her tent-dress and surrendered to another wave of euphoria. Had she not covered herself, the ascending sun would certainly have done quick damage. Later in the day, her mindlessness dissipated; but she remained in a subdued trance, a suspended watching of the empty desert from the hood tied around her face. Unmoving, she sat on the ground, seeing everything, thinking nothing. This way she passed the day and a second night.

She was aware of great pain in her body, stiffness in her back and hips and legs from pressing down onto the floor of the desert for so many hours without moving, great thirst, a burning sensation in her unblinking eyes. Her pain seemed separate from her; she stood outside it and looked at it with interest. There was no desire to chase it away, to shift or stretch or gulp water. She watched discomfort rise in her body like the sun rising on the sky, glaring and growing hot. Whether she had slept at all would be hard to say. The night had been bitterly cold; but she had been protected from chill, as she was against the day's heat, by the clothing made for her by Aunie before she left.

....

When Aunie had agreed that Ravenna would have to flee from the Fields of Khorvan, if she were to have any hope of safety, they made hasty plans for her to go to Gazi, the only other place in the world where she might find family. This had been her father's homeland, and Ravenna might find there people who would remember him and welcome her. The way there was more hazardous than most, but this would discourage any bounty hunters who might pick up her trail and pursue her. Aunie had hurried among The Women, pleading for someone to accompany her niece; but she had found no one who could or would go onto The Plains of Wildness. Ravenna would have to go alone then, with the Good Mother as her companion, and protected by her own wits and whatever instruction about The Plains she could gather from Oba, her neighbor. Oba was old and blind now, at times confused and often asleep during a conversation. But she knew The Plains better than anyone. She had even made a living for years as a guide for travelers who needed to cross. It was she, in fact, who had helped Ravenna's father cross from Gazi many years ago.

They had gone to Oba's house in the dead of night, the hour when Ravenna felt safest about being out in the open. Oba's blindness made night and day equal, and she slept as often during the day as at night. They were with her until dawn, sitting in the darkness of her house, talking slowly. They were not offered tea, nor a light, but simply sat and listened to the old woman's murmuring and humming and long silences. At first, it was difficult to adjust; but suddenly Ravenna realized that she was totally concentrated on the instruction and taking it in without distraction.

She learned about carrying food, about clothing, about shelter from the sun and from cold nights, about poisonous lizards, and where to look for drinking water. She was told never to build a fire, even when she found dry grasses or withered shrub branches. The smoke, said Oba mysteriously, can be smelled a long way off and may be misunderstood. She asked Oba if there were any maps, and Oba had said no, there were none. She had said nothing then for a long while. At last she began to talk about what she called "stele," which were not stele in the exact meaning of the word, but small piles of rock cairns, which marked the path across The Plains of Wildness.

"It is only a four or five day walk...if you go straight across...to the mountains," she had said in her ponderous, halting manner. "But it would be even shorter...because you would not finish...your walk. Not finish. If you tried to go straight across. No, you must follow the stele...the three piles of stones. They mark the way for you, Venna. Can you walk a straight line? Venna? Can you?"

"Yes, Oba," answered Ravenna in the darkness. "I'm not sure what you mean."

"I mean, can you pick a point far off...like a tall rock sticking up...or the edge of a cliff? Far off? And walk in a straight line toward it...so you don't wander off the line?"

"Yes, Oba."

"I am sure she can do that," Aunie said.

"Good. Because that is what you have to do. The stele are set up like this. One tall stack of flat rocks in the middle. And a short stacks on this side. And a short stack on the other side of it, like this." She was demonstrating on the palm of her hand, and neither Ravenna nor Aunie could see what she was doing. Suddenly, Oba groped for Ravenna's hand and repeated what she said, poking out the positions of the rock markers on her hand. They always stood in threes, the center stack being the pivot and the short stacks the pointers. As she approached, one short stack would line up between herself and the tall center stele. Beyond it, a pace or two, the other shin-high pile of stones might sit to the right or left indicating that a turn was to be taken in that direction. Spaced about an hour's walk apart, these stele traced a meandering trail across The Plains of Wildness, in what appeared to be open wasteland.

"Why?" asked Ravenna.

"Mmm?"

"Why such a wandering trail? Why can't a person go straight across, if it is open and flat?"

"Oh, no, Venna, no. That is a place of spirits, you know. There are places of power which it is best not to go near. You would not see them. I would see them better than you, blind as I am. You would walk right into the houses of living beings which you cannot see and do not know how to respect.

"How do they cross farther north...north of The Fields? There's a great road somewhere up there."

Oba was silent a long time, and they thought she was asleep. Then she said simply, "The same way. Stele." Then she answered a question they had not asked. "I don't know who put the stele there. They are ageless. No one has disturbed them, isn't that amazing? Just piles of rock. Maybe the spirits put them there, I have often wondered."

"Now tell her about the spirits, Oba," said Aunie.

The old woman was still holding Ravenna's hand, pressing and massaging every now and then for emphasis, as she began to speak—her eye-contact in the dark. Although they abound on The Plains, she said, they kept to certain localities and maintained territories, like animals. Most of the spirits were indifferent to people and responded to them no more than do trees or birds. Some seemed curious and hovered about, giving one an eerie feeling, but presenting no danger. There were strong power centers, which must be avoided at all cost. The bends and turns and double-backs in the trail existed to avoid them. Ravenna would have liked to hear more about these, but it was clear that Oba was eager to talk to her about wythies.

"These are the worst. Wythies! You know about them already, don't you. You have told her, haven't you, Aunie?"

Aunie nodded in the dark, and Ravenna said, "Yes, I know about wythies. I have heard a lot about them."

"Well," said Oba, with a sharp shake of her hand, "they are the worst because they will be after you. They are always about, here and there, plaguing us; but, let me tell you, on The Plains of Wildness, they are at home!"

They all knew about wythies, the malevolent gray spirits which wafted at large and clung like moss where they settled.

"Aunie, is that what is plaguing Mother?" Ravenna had asked.

"I am afraid so," Aunie had answered in the darkness.

Oba leaned forward, groping vigorously for Aunie, saying, "No, Aunie, don't even use that word 'afraid' when we are talking about the wythies! We resist them and oppose them, and we cling to the Good Mother. We are *not* afraid. Hear that, Ravenna? Do not be afraid of them. Recognize them, resist them. Especially on The Plains of Wildness."

"But I am running from them," said Ravenna in a husky voice, "running from Mintor Ghan and all the other people he has hired throughout The Fields to come looking for me. To force me! They are in league with the wythies, I am sure of it!"

"Yes," nodded Oba. Ravenna could feel her body bobbing through her hand. "Yes, you are running from them. And you are running into them when you go onto The Plains. It is good to run. I am *glad* you are running, dear. I am proud of you. You know, wythies are a lot like wild animals. Think of that. You don't have to be afraid of a bear. Or hornets. Do you? Unless you get between her and her cubs. Or knock down their nest. See what I mean?" She gave a hoarse laugh in the darkness, pleased with herself. "They are like wild animals. Sure, you are scared if you run into them. But there are things you can do to keep them at bay."

"Except," said Aunie, "that wythies sometimes go after us on their own. They are not like animals in that way."

"You're right about that," said Oba, and she gave her wheezing laugh again. "But you have a good heart, Venna. That is your best protection."

....

This had been some of the conversation that night. And now, here sat Ravenna Rosealice on The Plains of Wildness, not remembering any of this, not thinking anything, in her emptiness, gradually recovering from one of the powers, which had come into her through the palo root. It was not an evil power, but impersonal and strong. Here she had been sitting for two days, protected, not only by her good heart but also by the practical clothing which Aunie had made for her. She was in—and under—a tent-dress. Aunie had begun cutting and stitching from the first moment she knew Ravenna was bound for Gazi. It was a pattern she had from other women, who knew something about travel on that wasteland, and cut from a tough, light fabric that kept out both heat and cold. By nightfall, she had given Ravenna a shoulder-to-ankle loose robe, fitted with a loose hood that could be drawn tight around the face and fixed with a sun-shade. Eight small loops were sewn into the hem. With these, the folds of the dress could be staked out into a wide circle. Her walking stick made a center pole, stuck into the peak of the hood: and she had a tent. She could withdraw completely under the dress and curl around the pole to sleep. Slits in the dress gave ventilation; ties made it tight against the cold of the night. Ravenna had set out with a pack-bag, in which she carried a light sleepsack of the same airy material as the tent-dress. It rolled into a ball the size of two fists. She also carried her food bag, water bag, a second pair of tough reed shoes...and a pouch full of gold and silver from The House of Ghan.

She turned her head now, took her gaze away from the awful empty desert. A woman was sitting on a rock near her, only five paces away. Ravenna did not react. She still had little sense of time or place and only looked her over mildly. The woman appeared young, but of no particular age, and there were streaks of gray in her hair and wrinkles about her eyes. She wore a long black dress, which was dirty and stained with dust, tattered about the hem. Her head was uncovered under the fierce sun, her hair gathered into an untidy bun. Across her lap, she held a knotted walking stick, like Ravenna's, only shorter. No other traveling gear was there. She returned Ravenna's look, as though there was nothing to say. Then she opened her mouth, as though to speak...and closed it again, appearing to think better of it. She looked away, across the flats.

Suddenly, pointing with her chin, she said, "There is water beyond that rise. A half-day walk. Near the next stele." Both women were silent. Then the woman added: "Whatever you do, don't stray off into the canyon leading off to the left. Obey the stele pointing right."

Ravenna nodded. She continued to examine this sudden companion.

"Take these with you," the woman pushed forward, with her foot, the remnant of palo root, which had been tossed aside when the pulp had been put into a marinade for the cold soup. "But they are not for you. They are for others, scraped to shavings and dried in this sun (the woman squinted upward into the yellow sky and Ravenna saw the stringy underside of her jaw for a moment). "They become more powerful. More powerful dried and powdered." The woman looked back to Ravenna. She had dark, compelling eyes, somewhat slanted, very attractive.

"Oba?" asked Ravenna wanly.

"Mmmbaba," answered the woman.

Ravenna frowned slightly.

"You are being followed," the woman said simply. "Two men are following you. From The Fields."

Ravenna lifted her head a fraction, but continued to gaze at her without expression, waiting.

"I will go with you," the woman continued. "You should not go alone." Ravenna did not respond. "You are lonely." Silence. "You should go where you are known." Silence. "You are well known now. That is power."

Ravenna tilted her face just a shade, quizzically.

"Take this," said the woman, pushing the scraps of palo a bit farther forward with the toe of her shoe, "jruska papa chance that you may need it."

"What did you say?" asked Ravenna limply.

"I said, take this, just upon the chance that you may need it."

Ravenna's head dipped into a little nod. She slowly took in breath and let it out in a long, preoccupied sigh. She turned her face back toward the desert and looked down from the ridge upon the three stacks of stones. She shifted position, felt the hardness of the ground, the ache in her body. She looked back toward the woman, but there was no one there.

Stiffly she rose to her feet, carelessly pulling the pegs of the tent-dress loose from the earth at the hem, and staggered on unwilling ankles. She bent and groped about inside her pack bag and found the water bag. Shakily, she uncorked it and raised it to her mouth and sucked hard, three large, warm swallows. She replaced the cork, then the bag, then hunched forward onto her knees and forearms with her face just above the dust. She patted the earth with the flat of her hand, gently at first. Then she slapped down hard with both palms, then caressed the dust beneath her hands and murmured, "Mother. Mother." She continued to pat the ground, then moved on toward a round rock, patting her way, whispering, "Mother, Good Mother."

Light dust was swirling about her, for a stiff little wind had sprung up, unnoticed, while she had been sitting. She listened. She could hear, far off, a hushed, sighing sound and, somewhere in the midst of it, a high, thin keening. Perhaps it was only the wind.

FIFTEEN

The Watching

When Ravenna awoke the next morning from a heavy dreamless sleep, she heard voices nearby. She lay still, eyes wide, looking at the backlighted weave of the tent-dress. Indistinct words, coming through the heated air, were being dropped, without hurry, without feeling. She knew she had not been discovered yet, but listened intently to see if the voices were approaching. At the same time, she began to move her body into position to spring away, inching ever so carefully into a crouching position beneath the tent and pushing her nose out into the open through one of the slits on the side. There was the sound of voices again; and they seemed to come more clearly, now that she could look out onto the sunlit landscape. She saw nothing, but heard a sudden burst of laughter, followed by another laughter which joined it. Men laughing. She continued to move slowly and soundlessly to open the flap of the tent-dress in order to creep out. Then she realized that she could not go forward wearing only her shift; for, if she needed to escape, she would have to be ready, with shoes on her feet and the tent-dress upon her, with the skirt hoisted up between her legs and tucked into a belt. She would not survive long on the desert in her shift.

It seemed a slow, painstaking process for her to pull the pegs on the hem, strap on her shoes, gather her stick and pack bag, all this without making sounds. She could look down from her ridge, between the protecting boulders, and see the stele markers below; but she could not see the people talking, even though their voices came from that same direction. She began to gather some sense of what they were doing and decided that they were breaking camp. When she had almost finished getting herself ready, she suddenly saw them, two men, setting out with packs and walking sticks, crossing in front of the stele, and walking away.

Maybe they are just travelers, she thought; maybe they are not following me. But she did not believe this. At once, she knew what she would do. The way to keep them from following would be to keep them ahead of her. She would be the follower.

There was nothing to hide behind on this open wasteland, in case either of them looked back, so she had to let them get far ahead. Keeping her own line-of-sight toward the next stele marker correct, she also kept the two figures at great distance, barely in view. All through the day, she followed in this way, between the white sun and the pale tan dust, pausing only when the men near the horizon appeared to rest. Periodically, she herself would pause to squat down and touch the earth, saying, "Mother. Mother." She began to talk aloud as she walked, a light, aimless commentary on the heat and the landscape and the cloudlessness of the sky. Soon she was laughing; and her mood lifted and seemed to dance about her head; and she laughed on and on, absurdly amused. Following these two at such a distance seemed a game she was playing, something very funny. It was like a joke she was sharing with the Good Mother. At times, the strangeness of all this came to her; but it seemed wholesome; and she did not feel afraid. So she let her laughing and talking run on; it helped to pass the time.

When at last the sun dropped behind the rim of the world, darkness came on very quickly. Slowing her pace, she observed that the two men had stopped for the night and were moving about in one spot. Dusk enclosed them. To keep them in sight, she had to approach very close. Eventually, she again heard their voices and saw that they were eating. They allowed themselves no fire, and she was relieved at that. The stars appeared, and only the faintest sliver of a crescent moon with them, so there was no light on the desert. Knowing that she was as invisible to them as they were to her, she crept closer, using the sounds of their voices as a beacon, until she could make out their conversation.

By now, she knew a good deal about them. Before the light had completely faded, she had seen clearly what she had only glimpsed when they had walked away that morning—that they wore hitched-up tent-dresses, as she did, and carried packs and walking sticks like hers. After they had eaten, she had seen them stake out the hems of their two dresses with pegs and shove the walking sticks inside for center poles. As she listened to their voices in the dark, she was sure that one of them belonged to the man called "Nome," who had been on the sheep wagon; but the voice and manner of the other, who had been driving the wagon, seemed to have changed completely. Was this the same person?

When the morning sun once more looked up over the edge, it discovered that Ravenna had not raised her tent all night but had found a craggy slate pile behind which to lie out of view, but within earshot. She had awakened first and could peek from hiding to see that they and she had camped near a stele marker indicating a sharp turning toward the right, across more flatlands, and away from upthrusting hills on their left.

As she lay on her back, waiting for the men to awake, she was filled with yearning and apprehension. She remembered the kindliness of this man on the wagon, who had a scar across his cheek and chin. She thought of how he had spoken in her defense against the other man and of how he had suddenly clutched her and whispered for her to flee. How she had been dumbfounded by that sudden movement! No matter how often she had gone over those moments in her mind, she had never known what to make of it. But here this man had once again appeared, and he was on her trail. What could he be after? And the other one, the stupid one, was certainly to be feared. All she could do now, she decided, was to watch them, watch them all way to Gazi, so they could do her no harm. Then, when they all came once more to a place of trees and houses and people, she would watch where they went and go the opposite way.

The first fragments of grumbled conversation from the two waking men told her little about them; but she was strongly suspecting that the second man, the shorter one, was not the one who had been on the wagon with this "Nome." As they ate breakfast, their conversation became more coherent; but it went like this:

"What do you mean you weren't born in any country? Wasoo, everyone's born somewhere."

"Oh, yes, I was born somewhere. I didn't say I wasn't born, did I? Yes, I was born, my daddy told me I was."

"Well, that's what I asked."

"Oh, I thought you were asking what country I was from."

"Right."

"Well, I wasn't born in no country. None at all. My daddy says I was born on a barge in Lake Bukka, and that lake doesn't belong to any country. Has countries around three sides of it, but none of them owns it. It's on its own. On a barge in Lake Bukka, that's where I come from. And my mama says daddy's telling the truth about that, too, because she was there when it happened."

"I'm not surprised. But are you sure *you* are telling the truth about it."

"Nome! I wouldn't lie to you!"

"Yes, you would."

"Well...I might, but my daddy, at least, wouldn't lie to you. I don't remember that happening on the barge in Lake Bukka, although I should, because I was nine years old at the time."

"Wait a minute, what are we talking about here?"

"We're talking about me being nine years old. I was nine years old when I was born."

"Muffaw!"

"Yes, I *was,* Nome. Nine when I was born. I was, too. My daddy told me, and he even showed me it on the record."

"Muffaw, Wasoo! What are you giving me?"

"It's the truth, Nome. Daddy says the old clerk at the town hall in Clikkerty, which is where my birth was recorded after the barge got to shore...this old badger was so shaky and confused he put down in the official record that I was born in '78 instead of '87, which is the year it was then. No one noticed it till years later, and there it stands written to this day. So I am one of the few people you are likely to meet who was officially nine years old when he was born."

Ravenna listened to a good deal more of this, and somehow it put her at ease.

....

Each of these three travelers had instinctively brought into this place a protection as help to withstand the strangeness of The Plains. Ravenna continued to touch and pat the earth and to murmur that this was not her enemy but her mother. And all through the previous day, she had been sustained by what she fancifully called "holy laughter." This man, Wasoo, carried a light and amenable disposition, which looked for humor everywhere and concocted it. when it was not at hand. This was his protection off the The Plains as well as on them. Nome, himself, knew no tricks of the spirit; but he had brought along Wasoo, who kept him laughing. And, from the moment he had fearfully stepped onto The Plains of Wildness, Nome had been looking all about, in hopes of seeing, once again, the strange, little stony owls. He had seen none; although, in the beginning, he had often mistaken this rock or that for them.

That first day, when he was beginning to lose heart and thinking of turning back—for he was feeling already the presence of spirits and the weirdness of the place, and they had left the green land and had not yet found the first stele—a huge bird soared just over their heads, shooting past like an arrow from behind, unsuspected, flying straight ahead. It had startled them, with its shadowed suddenness; and Nome had cried out, "What is that! Eagle? Hawk? No, too low." And Wasoo had answered, "Owl, I think." The bird had flown on at just a little more than the height of a man's head above the ground until it became very small in the distance, then sharply veered to the left and was gone. They found the first stele, with the shorter stack sitting off to the left, telling them to turn that way, near the spot where the bird had turned and disappeared. After that, Nome went on with a feeling of lightness and excitement.

It was Aunie, of course, who had equipped and instructed them and sent them on their way. After getting out of jail in Gree am Slome, Wasoo had taken Nome to The Huts, which was well enough known in The Fields of Khorvan. They had inquired about the hut of a woman named, Aunie; and, by the time they stood knocking at her door, every woman at The Huts knew of their arrival. Aunie had not answered from within, but surprised them from behind, accompanied by two scowling companions. She had been warned that two men had been asking for her; and she was determined to meet them, not enclosed in the house, and not alone. At once, she had recognized Nome from the story Ravenna had told her. She already knew him by name, and the scar on his cheek and jaw left no doubt. But she assumed that this other fellow was Jude, who had greedily argued with Nome in favor of hunting down the starwoman.

It was some time before the confusion was cleared up and Nome could make believable his intentions toward Aunie's niece. He did this, as they stood in the yard, by telling the whole story of his stay at Dumpy's Farm, his observation of the fugitive woman, the trip to market, the fight at Tove's Keg, and jail in Gree, where he had met Wasoo.

The suspicion of the women who stood around listening to this tale was keen; but, eventually, Aunie dismissed them and invited the two men into her kitchen and offered them something to eat. She spent the morning studying them, speaking little, only asking pointed questions, listening, watching. She had allowed them to stay the night at her hut; and she had taken Wasoo to meet Oba, who said to Aunie afterword, in private: "I sense nothing of the wythies about him...although he has some weakness."

She had asked Nome to sit under the stars and talk to her, telling Wasoo to wait inside. When Nome had asked why people called her niece a "starwoman," Aunie had answered, "Do you see her anywhere in the stars? Look up. Where would be her figure?" That began a long, emotional conversation, in which Nome spoke of things he did not know he had within him. Damp with dew, they had walked back into the hut, and Aunie was reassured about this tall, thin man; but she was still unquiet about the other—until they discovered him not in the kitchen, but in Yuna Urlinda's room, seated by the bed and talking in his easy, lively manner. Aunie's sister was sitting up against the pillows laughing—the first laughter that had come from her in years. At that moment, Aunie decided that, although she had found no companion for Ravenna from among The Women, these two had been sent for this purpose from the outside. She would help them.

....

Ravenna was beginning her seventh day on The Plains. The previous one had been uneventful, as she had trailed the two men from considerable distance. They had stopped at sundown to camp near a stele-marker, just beyond a ridge formation, which appeared to snake out from canyon lands far to their left. This ridge was actually a natural esker, a long narrow deposit of sand and gravel, left by an ancient river which had carved the canyon eons before humans or wythies had ever been here. This esker provided Ravenna perfect cover from which to camp and observe the men during the evening and next morning. She could stay hidden on the side from which they had come. At dark, she could creep up to the crest of this low hill and look down the far side to where they were camping. She also had a good view of the stele-marker, the tall pivot stone cairn and the two short pointer stacks angling from it.

After she had eaten, she had spent about an hour watching and listening in darkness until they had both gone to sleep. In the morning, she had remained on her side of the esker, waiting for sounds that would indicate that they were preparing to break camp; but she began to think that they were lingering at their breakfast too long, as the sun rose higher. She decided to risk creeping back up to the crest to see what they were up to. At first, she dared not raise her head to look down, and just listened. She could hear them talking, but could only catch fragments of words and phrases. The tone of it seemed to suggest they were deliberating, uncertain and occupied with some task. When she did edge forward enough to bring them into view, she was surprised to see Nome on the far side of the stele-marker, squatting beyond the short pointer stack, which indicated a turn to the right. He was sighting backwards from that position, over the tall pivot stack, and looking directly along the esker toward the canyon opening on the left. Then he stood and pointed, and Wasoo turned and looked in the direction of the canyon.

"What are they doing?" she whispered to herself. "They've got it backwards." Indeed, there was even something about their manner that appeared confused. Wasoo wandered, looking about, scratching his head. Nome moved more slowly than usual toward his gear, stopping, then starting again. He spoke more loudly to Wasoo, who had moved off a bit, away from his own gear; and Ravenna could hear more of what he was saying.

"So what'd your daddy say in your dream?"

"He said, 'follow your fortune,'" answered Wasoo flatly, not facing Nome, but looking toward the canyon door.

"Not '*seek* your fortune'? What fortune?"

"I don't know...it was a dream. Fortune. I thought it meant follow *you*."

"Well, I don't understand...." Nome had stopped again. "I have to keep following. Maybe we're off the track, Wasoo. What are we doing out here? I had a dream, too, but I don't remember...all I remember is Chindit was in it...running, tongue hanging out. Running to Brighthome, I guess. I don't know."

"We came to follow this woman...." Wasoo started to say.

"That's right," said Nome, "that's why we're here. No fortune here.

I remember what you said to me in jail. 'There's no chance,' you said. Maybe you were right. No sign of her out here...she could be anywhere...or nowhere. We'd better go that way." And he pointed toward the canyon door.

Ravenna's eyes widened. They had not acted like this or talked like this before. They were getting ready to go the wrong way. To leave the trail. It is the wythies, she thought, confusing them, making them mistake how to read the markers and making them forget why they have come here.

She had a sudden memory of her trance, when a woman carrying no walking gear had appeared to her sitting on a rock. The first thing the woman had told her was where she would find water. And she *had* found water right there. The second thing she had said was: Whatever you do, don't go off toward the canyon on the left, be sure you turn to the right. The woman must have been telling her the truth! But, almost at once, a memory of Aunie came to her. Aunie used to say, "The wythies sometimes tell the truth in order to lie." How could she know truth from lies out here, where the wythies are at home?

Ravenna knew these men were going wrong, and her impulse was to jump up and warn them. She was afraid they were walking right into one of the forbidden power centers. Then she said to herself, no, I must not be discovered. I think they mean to hurt me...their talk about getting a fortune was alarming. Perhaps they tricked or robbed Aunie. She watched them listlessly gather their scant gear and begin setting off along the esker toward the canyon entrance.

Let them go their way, she thought. I will go mine. As she watched them grow smaller, Ravenna felt *fear* growing, instead of relief. Suddenly, she stood up and scurried back down her side of the esker to go after them. She left her pack bag, water, food, and walking stick at the foot of the slope where they were. She would certainly have to come back here for these things again, in order to take up the trail at this stelemarker, which clearly pointed a turn toward the right. Otherwise, she, too, would be lost. Girding up her skirts between her legs and tucking them into her belt, she began to run after them, without any clear plan, other than to keep out of view by staying on her side of the esker.

She ran unencumbered, in the rising heat of the morning. The men were only walking, carrying gear. She would surely overtake and pass them, with the esker in-between, keeping her hidden. Her only thought was to get far enough ahead so that she could safely cross over to their side before they arrived and to keep them from reaching a narrow opening between two cliffs, the doorway to the canyon. That was her goal, to leave them some kind of warning at that narrows, before the long, sinuous esker funneled them into the canyon. She would not wait to meet them, for they were far too unpredictable. But perhaps she could leave them some kind of sign.

When she was nearing the cliff face, she decided that she might be far enough ahead of them to venture climbing to the crest of the esker. From there, she hoped to see if it would be safe to descend to the other side. At the top, she squatted and scanned the desert floor and could see no sign of them coming yet. She stood up and waited to regain breath. In a short while, they would have to pass right below where she was standing.

Hurriedly, she slipped down from the crest onto the flat of the desert. She took a pointed piece of rock and, shuffling backward with quick, dusty steps, scratched a wavy line across their estimated path. Then she repeated a snaky line next to this one. Stepping back, she saw this would not be enough and repeated the warning a few paces farther on with two more braided, wavy lines. Still not enough. She had thought of leaving something on the ground here, an article of clothing or something, but had brought nothing. In any case, she was reluctant to personalize the warning too much and draw attention to herself. She stood and studied the lines, glancing up to be sure the men were not yet in sight. Then she stooped between the sets of lines and wrote in large letters into the dust: "You two men are going wrong!" She repeated the message at several points farther on...then stood back again. She needed to sign the message somehow, to give them an indication that it could be trusted. Should it be "starwoman" or "Aunie's friend" or something like that? They would trust that, but she abhorred the thought of revealing herself to them.

At last, she decided on an arbitrary human marking on a rock. Probably on several rocks, to indicate that they should turn around and go back the way they came. Otherwise, they would not know what to do. Again she stooped and, next to one of her warnings, wrote: "Follow the marked stones!" and drew an arrow to an upright knee-high rock standing nearby. Now, how to mark it? Something simple, easy to scratch on it with a chunk of chalky rock. A face. Two circles, side-by-side, with dots at the centers. A sharp V below for a nose. A line for a mouth. Quickly she moved toward the direction from which they would be coming and repeated the face on two other rocks, and then, for emphasis, drew an arrow from them to point the way back.

Ravenna then clambered back up to the top of the esker, lay on her stomach, and watched.

It seemed a long wait; but then they appeared, far off, approaching. She flattened herself as much as possible and lay still while they passed below, no longer appearing aimless and confused, only doggedly weary, eyes on the ground, occasionally glancing up at the canyon they headed toward. They did not look right or left. They passed over the first set of wavy lines without notice. At the second, they were about to do the same, when suddenly Wasoo stopped short and said, "Nome!"

Wasoo was frowning, glancing around at the ground. Nome saw it, too, then began looking about; and the writing in the dust caught his eye. He walked forward cautiously: "You two men are going wrong!"

"I don't like it, Nome," said Wasoo grimly. He glanced up at the spur of hill on their left, scanned the cliff face ahead, some fallen boulders on their right. "Somebody watching us."

"Maybe wythies?" said Nome, walking slowly along the wavy lines. Look, here it is again: "You two men...."

"Why wythies?" asked Wasoo.

"I don't know. First we are hearing things, then getting mixed up about how read the stele-markers, now seeing things. Aunie warned us about the powers out here."

"Look here, Nome. Something else," said Wasoo suspiciously. "'Follow the marked stones,' it says. Look, here's an arrow pointing to this rock over here, and there's some scratching on it."

Nome walked to him and looked down at the message, then at the rock. Wasoo began moving away, past the wavy lines saying, "I don't think we ought to...."

But Nome gave a sharp cry and clutched his sleeve, holding him back.

"It's them!" he shouted in a voice of elation. "Here, look at them!"

"Nome!..."

But Nome had rushed on to the next stone. "Come on, come on!"

"What is it?" cried Wasoo.

"Owlstones! Don't you see them? The signs of them! Owlstones!"

"What?"
"Come on!...come on!"

....

Hours later, long thin shadows were stretching across the rosy dust from the three stele-marker stacks as though to greet the two men wearily approaching them once again. They dropped their packs. In bewildered recognition, they saw, for the first time, how they had abandoned course in the morning and wandered mindlessly in peril until something recalled them. Then the soft-edged shadows of the stele faded before their eyes, and dusk enclosed them. The sun was gone. They camped on this spot for a second night.

Ravenna Rosalice also camped for a second night—just over the hill.

....

The next day, and in days that followed, Wasoo tried to get Nome to tell him what he had seen in the rock scratching, what he had called them, and how he knew to follow them. Nome tried, but always got lost in his words and his thoughts. He himself did not understand it, and he could not explain. Each time they spoke of it, Nome grew more reluctant and would end by pondering, not speaking. Wasoo let him alone, and they walked on in quiet.

They walked on through the heat of days, camping in the cold of nights, passing safely through the haunt of wythies and the awesome place from which had once come the sacred flame of the Greatsada. Hovering behind them, Ravenna Rosealice kept her watch and kept her distance, following Nome Ogrodni and Wasoo, who were following her. In this way, by gradual stages, the three of them moved onward toward the Endicot Mountains and to the land of Gazi.

SIXTEEN

Meeting

Their boots were worn out. Their food packs weighed nothing. But Nome and Wasoo trudged forward with new eagerness, quickened by the filmy-blue line of mountains which lay like piping on the western horizon from one end to the other. They were looking at Gazi, or, at least, at a stretch of the Endicot Range, just to the south of it. There would be a river soon, if they were still on course, if Oba had remembered it right, a river blocking the way. This would be the end of The Plains of Wildness and the beginning of hill country. They could expect to see trees and grass and birds again. Turning to the right and continuing on, they would enter the southernmost regions of Gazi. There would be houses, barns, animals, people. Their ordeal on these haunted barrens was nearly over.

 The mountains looked to be tricking them, drifting away before them. Their first sight of the thin, wavy line of peaks had come the evening before, against the setting sun; but now, after half a day's walk, they scarcely seemed closer. Perhaps it was another illusion of the desert. Neither of them had ever seen mountains before; and they had no sense of how massive they are, from what a distance they can be seen, and how long it takes to reach them. They shuffled forward, side by side, doggedly tossing one foot in front of the other.

 They had become good friends. Not much grew on this desert; but their friendship, a hardy variety, had grown there. In less than two weeks, they had been in jail together, gone tramping together, and had fasted, thirsted, faced the burning glare, the frigid dark, and the weird spirits together. There had been empty hours to fill with talk. Each had gradually brought out the stories of his life, in bits and fragments, and showed them to the other. Wasoo did most of the talking. The hardest part for Nome was to decide how much of it was confabulation. But he trusted the man, even though he wondered, more than once, why he had agreed to go with him across this searing desert into an unknown country. Wasoo had no reason, other than that he wasn't doing anything else at the moment. He was like that. He had lived a playfully aimless life, drifting about the world from adventure to adventure, getting into trouble and slipping out of it like a minnow.

But there was more to it than that. Wasoo needed grounding. His mischievous ways disguised his restlessness and uncertainty. He presented himself as a lighter-than-air balloon; but something deep wanted to feel the tug of the string. His daddy was gone. Loyalty was what he really wanted these days, more than adventure. Someone, something to which he could feel bound. And Nome needed him, too. Nome needed companionship; but, more than that, he needed someone to lighten him. He took things too seriously.

These mountains of Gazi in the distance, for example, were filling him with anxiety. Wasoo had been silent for a long time, while Nome was worrying: Now what? Now that they were about to survive the desert, where were they going? And what would they do when they got there? Look around. Look for a woman he had seen. There had been no sign of her on the desert; and he could not clearly remember why he wanted to follow her. Anyway, she had vanished into the wide world now. At this thought, Nome tasted despair like the taste of brass. He would see her no more. But hadn't he also gone to Gazi to find Korcha's army? To be taken back, forgiven for not returning? To get money—and to go into war with them for money? Overcome with weariness, he wanted to weep; but he was dry as the white powder he kicked up with every slogging step.

There they were again! Off to his right, their jiggling movement had just caught the corner of his eye. His heavy heart jumped painfully, like that of a sleeper burst in upon. Two owlstones hobbled along with their awkward, quick motions, seeming to struggle to keep abreast of the two men, and slightly ahead, twenty paces to the side. He watched them, fascinated. He could not see if they had little feet or how they moved.

They seemed to stumble and bump along, but they must have been paddling little feet. Every now and then, he thought wings would flap from their sides to balance a sudden lurch; and, once or twice, they seemed to twist their stiff bodies in a three-quarters turn to look at him, as though to see if he were still coming. He wanted to see if Wasoo had noticed them; but he dreaded looking away, afraid they would be gone when he looked back. It occurred to him to nudge Wasoo and whisper for him to look, never letting the little fellows from his sight; but, at once, this seemed something private, something just for him. Nome gratefully followed the owlstones with his eyes. When they strained about to glance at him, he chuckled. Care slid from him like a cloak, and he thought no more of Brighthome or Korcha or Gazi or the losing of the woman. All he thought was: We are no longer on The Plains of Wildness. They have come to an end. No river yet, but I know that these are no longer The Plains!

Toward sundown, they reached the river, a wide, shallow stream that ran down from the mountains and lost energy here on the flatlands. It listlessly groped its way among boulders and pebbly bars, seeking something in the south. Nome and Wasoo wasted the last hours of the afternoon walking up-river and down, looking, in vain, for a bridge or a narrow ford. The waters were icy, and wading across would be their last resort. The temperature had been dropping as they left The Plains. By the time they were at the river, they could see their breaths as vanishing ghosts before their faces. There was no other way. Into the water they walked, sucking air with sharp, painful gasps. The lazy current washed no higher than their ribs, so the men were able to hold their nearly empty pack-bags up and dry. On the other side, they drank from the river. It was clear and clean, not like the tepid pools they had found on The Plains. They filled their water bags.

Now they were very cold and had to move quickly, in hopes of drying out a little before the sun was gone, swishing onward through knee-high grass. The mountains had shed their blue cast and appeared caped in shadowy white, far down into the valleys. The men kept an eye out for dry wood, for they would have a fire this evening, their first since entering The Plains. There was, however, no deadfall on this grassland, only a few shrubs.

They suddenly forgot that concern, as their attention was taken by a broad, flat patch of gray in the distance that moved over the rising ground in the gathering dusk like a fallen cloud. They stopped and squinted, asking each other, in worried, broken sentences, what it could possibly be. For a moment they wondered if they had not escaped the weird desert, after all, but had met some floating specter waiting to haunt them. Cautiously, they moved ahead, straining to make sense of the shifting patch of gray that hugged the ground. Then Nome laughed aloud.

"Sheep!" he cried.

That was it, a huge flock of sheep driven along before a number of shepherds, scarcely visible in the failing light. Nome and Wasoo hurried toward them, in hopes of finding lodging wherever the shepherds were heading that evening. When they reached the edge of the flock and hailed the nearest one, they found it difficult to make contact. The shepherds, not much more than boys, turned and fled.

At last, four or five of them huddled together and waited for the approach of the strangers. Wide-eyed with fear and surprise, they did not respond to Nome's and Wasoo's greetings and questions. They stood dumb, with mouths open and eyes shifting nervously from one man to the other, ready to run. Nome and Wasoo could not have known that these boys had never seen any living thing approach from the direction of the evil desert. They also did not realize how strange they looked, their top half powdered white with desert chalk, their bottom half dark and damp from the river crossing.

It was a long time before the boys would talk and answer questions. They were obviously eager to follow their sheep and get them in. They showed no inclination to invite these two apparitions to join them. Finally, Nome and Wasoo squeezed out enough conversation to learn that they were people of Gazi. In the poor light, Nome recognized the Mommick brand on their cheeks, two down-strokes splayed apart and crossed by a bar. He had seen these on a few of the late-coming refugees who had joined Korcha at 'n Burning Graute.

"Where are you from?" he asked the boys. "Aren't your homes around here?"

"Fealard," one replied sullenly.

"What? What's that?"

They looked at one another, none daring to answer.

"Where are you taking the sheep?" asked Wasoo.

No answer. One of them pointed vaguely with his stick in the direction the flock was swimming.

"But aren't there some farms or towns around here? We need help. Where do you live?"

"Fealard."

"You mean a village? A town?" asked Nome.

"Ain't no village. It's a fealard," the boy answered emphatically.

"Any work there?" asked Wasoo. "We need work to be able to get food and a place to stay for a while. We just crossed the desert here, and we're all worn out. Any work around here?"

"Fences," said the boy, who was becoming the spokesman. The others watched him with timid, approving eyes. "Need help putting up fences."

"Where?"

"Over there. At the fealard." He swung his stick in an arc toward the rising ground. The knot of shepherds turned abruptly and followed the sheep, several of them trotting forward to bring in the sides. They threw nervous glances over their shoulders as they went.

It was nearly dark. They decided to gather whatever wood they could find and make camp where they were.

....

They awoke before dawn. A fine layer of snow covered the ground. Shivering, they agreed to skip breakfast and get moving. They pulled the pegs of their tent-dresses, girded themselves for the hike, and moved off in the direction of the fealard, whatever that was.

The fealard was a kind of communal village built in a series of concentric circles of houses and barnyards around an open central circle (what would be called "the village square" in a place less decidedly round). Nome and Wasoo would learn later that all the farmlands and grazing lands were worked by the people together by common plan. Most of the people who lived here were related to one another. In fact, the fealard was, to some extent, a large extended family. Fealards were common on the grassy lowlands in the southern part of Gazi.

When Nome and Wasoo walked among the buildings and entered the circle at the middle of the fealard, they saw no one about. It was still very early, even for a farming community, and the cold weather was keeping people indoors longer. Here and there, threads of smoke were beginning to rise from chimneys.

Nome lowered himself heavily onto a bench. He scanned the faces of the sturdy, sleeping storefronts ringing the circle, their eyes still shuttered. The sky was growing light, but the sun had not yet risen. He pulled his pack onto his lap and wearily rummaged about for food. Very little left, all squashed or in crumbs. He let his hands go slack. Let them lay helpless in the rumpled pack. He glanced up at Wasoo who stood before him, slowly looking about with his eyes narrowed, working something out. A wave of sorrow swept over Nome, and he began to tremble. He slumped and let his head drop forward over the pack.

"What now?" he whispered.

Wasoo maintained his stance, ignoring Nome's mood. Then he said, "You wait here, Nome. I'm going off for a while to look around and figure out how we make our way here."

Nome tilted his head up without straightening to look at him. He did not understand.

"It's something I'm used to doing. I do it best alone. You just wait here for a while and get warm when the sun comes up. I've got to poke around and find a way for us. It'll probably take me a while, depending on what I find or who I meet. I'll be back, just sit here and rest."

For a long time, Nome just stared at the spot where his friend had disappeared around the corner of a building. Then he let his eyes drop to the thick pad of snow on the ground. Footprints pressed there, those they had made coming to this bench, Wasoo's going off in another direction. Everywhere else, flat, white, unbroken snow. He wondered where Wasoo had gone...but left off wondering. He tugged lethargically at the folds of the food pack, reached a hand inside and filtered the crumbs between his thumb and fingers, counting coins, but he did not eat. He withdrew his hand and let it lie in his lap. How long he sat, round-shouldered, regarding the grime-filled streaks and cracks of his fingers, he did not know.

The low squeak of crushed snow that footsteps make sounded in front of him, a way off. Someone had entered the circle, walking. Reluctantly, he listened to the crunching tread without looking up. He knew someone was moving toward him. He did not want to lift his eyes, did not want to greet anyone, answer questions, explain himself. He continued to sit, downcast, not moving, hoping he might be ignored and left alone. But he knew he was being approached...how long could he...?

He looked up. A woman walked toward him slowly, evenly. Straight toward him. Her tracks lay in the snow overlying those he and Wasoo had made coming in. The sky was yellow-rich behind her, between the buildings; for the sun was about to break open the horizon...but it did not back-light her so much that he did not see!

He started to his feet, stiff and uncertain, and the pack-bag rolled to the ground. His mouth formed a helpless oval...an effort to speak an "Oh!" slashed by the rubbery whiteness of the scar which ran across his beard stubble. His matted eyes came to life with wide, brown astonishment, and he did not finish unwinding from his crouch on the bench but froze, half-standing, knees bent.

Ravenna Rosealice stopped beside him, stooped over and swept another spot on the bench clear of snow with the flat of her hand. She sat down and looked up at him. He had followed her movement with an arthritic half-turn and held this position for a moment. Slowly, the springs of his body, which had raised him, relaxed and carefully lowered him to the bench.

They looked at one another.

Her face was long, sunburned, and drawn tight as though with fasting. Lips stretched into a tense, withholding line, showing no expression. Her hair reminded him of the first time he had seen her, long, straight, dry with ash or dust. But her eyes danced. They were liquid blue and her eyelashes were like a splash. He did not look away and was scarcely aware of the rest—the bleached hood thrown carelessly back, the ample tent-dress that fell to her lap and draped her legs to the knees. Her shins were bare, scraped and scratched, scorched red. Pitiful reed shoes on her feet were falling apart where they pressed the softly melting snow. Nearby lay a pack-bag and a walking stick, where she had let them fall as she swept the bench to sit down.

He was dressed the same way, but his tent-dress fell freely to the ground, protecting his legs from cold, and covered his boots. His brown hair was tousled and gritty with dust. His cheeks, jaw, and throat were marbled with dirty swirls of whiskers. The long face-scar stood out and grew no hair. His look of sagging exhaustion had vanished, and he gazed at her in wonderment and joy.

She folded her hands politely in her lap. "Hello, Nome Ogrodni," she said.

He was startled. Then said, "Hello, Ravenna...Rosealice." He forgot to nod and bow and smile as he had been taught to do when meeting someone for the first time. He just looked at her. Her tight mouth loosened a bit and lifted into a smile. Then he said, "You know me? How...how do you know who I am?"

"Well, you gave me a ride once, remember? I heard them call you Nome Ogrodni."

"Ohh," he sighed, as though a great mystery had been unveiled. "But how did you come here? I mean, where...?"

"I followed you," she said simply.

"*You* followed? You...followed...*us*?"

"Yes."

He felt like trying to walk after twirling.

"But...we were following you. At least, we started to, but we didn't see any sign of you. How...? Did you know we were trying to catch up with you? I mean... *You* were following *us*? Why? Why?"

Her smile became a grin. She was enjoying this and held back a moment, deciding whether to tell him or not.

"All right. Like this. I didn't really expect that anyone from The Fields would try to follow me out onto The Plains of Wildness. But, ever since I went into hiding, I've been looking over my shoulder every step. It got to be a habit, looking around to see if anyone's following. So I spotted you two men coming along behind me, and I figured that you were on my trail. So I just stepped aside and let you pass. Then I followed behind and kept my eye on you. And let you lead the way."

"When? When did you...?"

"Right at the beginning. A day or two into the crossing."

"You followed us all the way? All the way across? Then it was you who made the owlstones for us?"

She lifted her head, wrinkled her nose. "The what?"

His eyes wavered in confusion, as he realized he had said the wrong thing. "You wrote that warning on the ground...and...wasn't that you?"

"Oh, yes," she laughed, "I did that. You two were wandering off into the hills, completely off the track! I was told you don't do that, unless you really know what you are doing. And you two didn't look like you knew up from down at that point! What was the matter with you?"

"I don't know, we both just got sort of crazy. I don't know what was going on, but...well...so you marked the rocks, too, didn't you?"

"Right. I marked them."

"Why did you put that kind of a mark on them? I mean, why did you make them look like...well, like....?

"Like what? I just marked them with any old mark so you'd be able to follow the trail back. I almost didn't, too. I almost left you go off your own way. I don't know why I wanted anything to do with you, since I thought you were after me and maybe were sent out by Mintor Ghan or something. Next thing I knew I was going after you to warn you that you were going the wrong direction. I really don't know why. Even after that, I was planning to watch where you were heading, once you got to Gazi, and then to go off a different way myself. I still don't know if I can trust you."

"Why didn't you?" asked Nome.

"I don't know that either. Well, for one thing, I'm pretty cold and tired. I've got to get some rest. And find some food in this village. I don't think I could push on today, looking for some other place. Next town could be a long way off. And I knew you two would probably have the same thing in mind, and you'd probably see me sooner or later. Maybe it's that. Anyway, I am as surprised as you are that I am sitting here talking to you. Because I was just going to get away from you men as soon as we got off the desert. But I was standing over there," she pointed toward the buildings; the sun had risen and it was warming them as they talked; a door had opened in one of the buildings; and several people were moving about their business, "watching you...and when that other one went off, suddenly I knew I wanted to talk to you, so I came over. Did I make a mistake?"

"Mistake?" Nome drew back. "Oh, no, no. You have nothing to fear from us. I can't tell you how happy I am to see you and to talk to you!"

"What about that other one? Who is he?"

"Wasoo? He's my friend. He's a good man. You don't have to worry about him. I met him in jail."

"You've been in jail?"

"Well, yes. You know...oh, no, you wouldn't know, would you. Remember when we were hauling the sheep to Gree am Slome, and I told you I would start a fight and you should run for it...?" Ravenna suddenly felt a rush of warmth at the back of her neck. "...well, I did start a fight and we landed in jail. My good fortune to meet Wasoo there. He's a jokester, don't worry about him. Nothing mean about him,

Ravenna. I wonder where he went off to...." Nome craned his neck about, searching the quiet buildings, then returned to Ravenna.

They sat now in silence, embarrassed at the admissions that they had been together and aware of each other for nearly a month. Nome looked down at his hands. Ravenna looked past his shoulder at the circle of buildings. A few people were moving about the edges. A man had led a horse and cart around the corner of a building to stand before a front door. Ravenna turned to look at the sun and let her eyes fall shut to feel the warmth.

At length Nome said quietly, "What are you going to do here?"

She quickly opened her eyes and shyly glanced down at her own hands.

"Uhm, yes, I am going to find my family. My father's family, whatever I can find of them. He came from here. I can't go back to The Fields of Khorvan for a while, so I hope to settle down here." She looked back up over his shoulder into the distance, as though she were picturing it. "He came from Mhaveen, which is the main city here. So I'll go there first and ask around until I find someone I belong to. I don't really know anybody here, but I'm sure there are aunts and uncles and cousins or something."

"Mhaveen!" said Nome in a ghostly whisper. "Oh, no." Disbelief and sadness had washed across his face.

"Yes," she said, "what's wrong?"

"What do you know about this place?" he asked quietly. "What have you heard?"

She looked at him in surprise and a bit of irritation. "A great deal. I have heard of Gazi ever since I was a child. My father died when I was a girl, but my mother told me a lot about it. And Oba did. A neighbor of mine. She was often over here. She was a guide on The Plains. Why?" She tilted her face and looked at him perplexed. "What's the matter?"

"But," Nome went on in a labored manner, "what have you heard recently? About Gazi and the Gazine people? I mean politically?"

"Politically?" her tone grew sharp. "What are you talking about? I haven't heard anything recently. What are you getting at?"

Nome dropped his head heavily forward so that his face was over his lap and he gave a low groan. Then he sighed, "Oh, Holy!"

"Tell me!" she said, alarmed. "What are you talking about!"

He lifted his head and, with mournful eyes, told her. She listened to all he had to say without interrupting, sitting stiffly on the bench, now leaning slightly forward. Once again her lips were drawn into a thin line; and her eyes did not leave his face as he talked. He told her the whole story, as he had learned it in Korcha's camp. There no longer was a Mhaveen. Hadn't been for years. The country was at war, occupied, the people scattered, branded, crushed. He told about Korcha and Ila and Mira Shannan, probably in Gazi at this very moment somewhere, and, in the process, briefly told some of his own story. No Mhaveen, in any case; and, probably, she had no family here. Or, if she did, finding them might be impossible, judging from what he had heard about the Mommicks.

When he was done, they both were silent. She was looking past him again with a pained expression.

"This place is not what you had hoped for," said Nome softly. She did not respond. "You probably would not have come, if you had known all this."

Her eyes and forehead drew into a frown, and she tightly nibbled her lower lip. Barely, she shook her head.

Nome looked away, squinting at the sun. When he looked back, he saw that her eyelashes were trapping glistening tears; and one long stream had escaped and run down along her chin. Her shoulders were shaking in little, tight jerks. A sting sprang into Nome's own eyes; and, without thinking about it, his hand shot out and took hers. She did not pull back, but slowly tipped her head forward over her chest and silently shook.

Nome watched her for a moment, then spoke gently, "Ravenna. You're exhausted, aren't you?"

He saw the top of her head slowly nod up...and...down.

It seemed half an hour like this. Finally, Ravenna straightened up, withdrew her hand, and pushed tears away from her eyes with the heels of both hands. She looked back directly at him and said with controlled poise:

"And you, Nome. What are you doing here, and where are you going from here?"

"I don't know," he said. "I don't really know why I am here. I was just following you, I think." He glanced away quickly, feeling awkward, and took a sharp breath. "I have been trying to figure this out. Ever since I left Korcha's army...I was sent out to deliver a message...I didn't tell you about that...and I got lost and lost track of the army and have been wandering ever since. I didn't know what I was doing in The Fields of Khorvan or why I was leaving there or why I was going to Gazi. I don't know anyone in Gazi! And, now that I am here, I suppose I should look for Korcha's army and try to join up with them. Except...."

"Except what?"

"Well,..." he was thoughtful..."except a lot. Except that I am afraid of what kind of reception I'll get. Korcha Rabon is a dangerous man. I would guess that, in his mind, Nome Ogrodni is either dead in the woods or a deserter. I can't be sure he would wait for an explanation. Yet, I have to risk it, because, as I told you, the very reason I left home last summer was to find money enough to ransom our home. Without that, we lose Brighthome. Korcha told us...me and my two friends from home...that money for our holdings would not be a problem as long as we were with him. And here I am, but not with him...but there is one other thing...as important as any of it, maybe...." Nome stopped.

"What, Nome?" She was listening carefully.

"One other thing. Going with Korcha means going to war for him. Or for the money he can give. I just can't...I don't know...I just can't.... Ever since...I don't know if I should say it...but I have had some help from a guide that makes me think that going to war for Korcha is not what I should be doing."

"What guide? You mean this other man you're with?"

"No, not Wasoo. I can't say exactly what they are. Maybe I'd better not talk about it just now. I'll tell you some other time; but I have been seeing some things that kind of warn me off. And I have the feeling that maybe they are warning me off of Korcha."

He was studying the ground, shaking his head. When he glanced up, she was also shaking her head, not understanding.

"But that's silly," he said. "What choice do I have? Not unless I want to turn around now and go back onto that desert. Now that I am here, it seems like the only reasonable thing to do is to go looking for Korcha and his people. As carefully as I can. That is where my friends are, my two friends from home. I think I have to join up with them and hope for the best."

She was studying him seriously, her head listing to one side. She seemed to have forgotten her grief for the moment.

"But listen, Ravenna, your situation now is not much different from mine. You probably should not have come to Gazi; but, now that you are here, you surely don't want to turn around and go back onto the desert. These mountains are too high to climb; going south is wild, unpopulated territory. Looks like we are in Gazi and have to make the best of it. I would like it if we would stick together. Will you stay with us?"

Without a pause, she said, "Yes, I will. That is, depending on what I think of your friend. I haven't met him yet, and I am not sure I will trust him. But we can find out pretty soon," she smiled, "because I think that is him over there gawking at us."

Wasoo had come jauntily striding around the corner of a shop, heading back to tell Nome what he had learned, when he was stopped by the sight of Nome sitting and talking with a woman, as though they were old friends. Nome waved him forward, and Wasoo advanced hesitantly. When Nome introduced them, Wasoo bowed more formally than necessary.

"So you are the starlady."

"Bad taste, Wasoo, bad taste!" Nome scolded before she could respond. "I'm sure she doesn't need a reminder about being 'the starwoman' first thing."

"Nome! You shock me!" said Wasoo feigning shock. "When I said star *lady,* I was referring to her pretty eyes that reminded me of stars. I don't know what *you* were thinking of!"

"Well, yes," admitted Nome. "I did notice her eyes. And I did think of stars."

SEVENTEEN

Kgopuk by the Fire

The next days were the most pleasant and restful that the three of them had spent in several months. After two days of nothing but sleep and food and conversation in a tidy warm farmhouse, they were set to work putting up snow fences along the western edge of the fealard and along the upper side of the narrow road that rambled off toward the north, linking it with the rest of Gazi. It was a work that involved most of the able-bodied people of the fealard, including children. Every winter, angry blizzards swept down from the mountain flanks and drifted deep mounds of snow across the flatlands before stopping at The Plains of Wildness. Snow fences were the only thing that would break up the drifts and keep the fealard from being buried, endlessly long rows of skinny poles, strung upright, a hand-span apart, on two lines of rope.

Ravenna and Nome and Wasoo were assigned to work as a team with their host couple and their three children. Ravenna and the other woman ran the wagon back and forth to supply the fence builders with poles. They lined up behind other wagons at an enormous stack of poles that was the central depot on the upper side of the fealard. At their turn, they loaded the wagon and returned along their fence line, ahead of the builders, to drop small piles at intervals. The father and oldest daughter worked together driving stouter posts into the ground as anchor points for each section of fencing. Behind them grew the fence, tied up one pole at a time. Nome and Wasoo leaned their weight into the ropes, one near the top, the other near the bottom, to keep the section taut. The two youngest children threaded each pole onto these lines by slip-knots with deft little flicks of the ropes as they were slackened for a few seconds, alternately, by the rope-pullers. It was cheerful work, brisk and unhurried, with plenty of rests along the way. The workers would stop and straighten, panting white breath, and look about the hillsides above their homes, where the other fences were crawling forward like caterpillars, while carts, empty and full, scurried back and forth to feed them. The fences stretched out in parallel rows, usually two or three deep, sometimes even four, in dips and valleys, where the winds would gully down fastest and drift snow the worst.

The three newcomers had been given sheepskin clothes and boots. They were warm, well-fed, and delighted with this essential, friendly work. "I'm not exactly making my fortune here," Nome had said to Wasoo as they tugged at their ropes, "but I would not mind living here for a good long time."

At first they had not been welcome. The shepherd boys had not been the only ones afraid of them. Wasoo had found it difficult to make contact with anyone that first morning. Not only did he look ragged and bizarre in his tent-dress, but he was missing one thing that would have made him a little familiar to the local people. He had no brand mark on his left cheek. Everyone he approached avoided him, answered curtly or not at all, and walked away with distrustful looks. However, by charm and trickery, he managed to find the chief of the fealard. This man wanted nothing to do with the strangers, either, but felt duty-bound to look into the matter and agreed to meet Nome. When Wasoo brought not only Nome but a woman, too, who had not been mentioned, the chief was all the more put off. He would scarcely speak to them, would not listen to their story; and it looked as though no doors would be opened to them. At the last moment, as they were being ushered away, Nome had suddenly said to the man, "The fire burns!" The chief appeared stunned. A moment later, he was listening.

By noon that same day, the three of them were sitting in front of a cheery fireplace, clad in sheepskin, cradling mugs of hot kgopuk. The chief had asked his cousin to take them in. She was married to a farmer who had a large sheepyard on the most remote edge of the fealard. With two grown sons already gone off into the wide world, they had a second family growing up behind, ages ten, eleven and twelve. The recent departure of the older sons had left room in the farmhouse for the new visitors. These sons had left the fealard, not to find employment elsewhere, which would have been uncommon in this community, but to fight on the side of the resistance forces which had entered Gazi a month earlier.

There was another new arrival in the house, an uncle of the farmer, a widower of about his same age, who had been with the refugees at 'n Burning Graute and had recently re-entered the homeland with Ila's southern column. He was one of the original resisters of the Mommicks and had fought under the leadership of Rilda Rabon, alongside Korcha, Mehtor, and Ila, and then had fled to the east when the rebellion failed. An accident in the miskworks had destroyed his hip socket and left him crippled and of no use as a warrior. His role in The Return was to ride, among the families and old people, with the heavily laden wagons on the easy High Road to the West. He and Nome had not known each other at 'n Burning Graute, for the quarry accident had happened over a year before Nome had arrived. However, this man remembered hearing of three strangers, who had been trapped in the caves by the Gaffling River and taken prisoner, only a few months before The Day of the March. It was from Uncle (this is what everyone in the household, including the new guests, called him) that Nome and Ravenna and Wasoo learned what had been happening in Gazi in recent days.

Uncle loved to talk in the evenings, as they all sat around the fire after supper. They were tired from work on the fences; but for him the day was just starting. He was home alone all day, and it took him nearly all afternoon to drag his leg around the kitchen to cook the evening meal for the family. After supper, he had a large kettle of kgopuk on the stove; and the chattering of the lid would be the signal for Uncle to begin his stories. The family had heard them several times already, but Uncle gladly started over for the new house guests.

He would lean forward with his elbow heavily on the knee of his good leg and carefully place his kgopuk on the brickwork by the grate, so his hands, as well as his mouth, would be free to tell it. He would begin by roughly tugging at the ropes of red-and-gray mustache that waggled on both sides of his chin and glancing intensely about at each face.

"Korcha Rabon is a genius, no doubt about that! There were plenty of them back there that argued with him on his plan, and some came right out and started agitating against him. But he beat 'em all down, every one of 'em, in time. I didn't have no part in it either way. What did I know about it? I just watched it all fall out, and we sure saw Korcha was right. There's not a man or woman now that wouldn't follow him anywhere after what happened at Kul Sama.

"Well, let me tell you about it. I was there. His plan was bold, but seemed too complicated to work. It worked perfect. He divided us all up on The March into three armies. We were strung out about a day's hike apart from one another and moving toward Gazi like this." He held up three fingers horizontally before his eyes and moved them relentlessly toward an imagined enemy. "Ila's group here in the south, moving right out in the open along the High Road to the West...big, wide highway, lots of people coming and going on it. I was with Ila, because most of us weren't fit for fighting. Mostly families, kids, old people, and all the heavy equipment on wagons. Only three, four hundred fighters up front to make it look like a serious army. The Mommicks couldn't help but know we were coming; and we *wanted* 'em to know. Wanted them to think we were *it*. They had scouts and spies all along that road, we knew that."

Uncle brought up his three fingers again and wiggled the middle finger, then the top one.

"Now here was Korcha's army, about a day to the north of us, couple thousand strong and armed to the teeth, and Mira Shannan a day north of *him*, another couple thousand, some of our best. Korcha and Mira Shannan are plowing through the woods under cover. They are going through places no one goes, at least not in the lifetime of any of us. There were abandoned roads up there, all overgrown; and the whole woods is full of hostile people. The whole plan depended on those two columns getting through to Gazi at the same time we did, without the Mommicks even knowing they existed. So our movement had to be perfectly timed. Couldn't have one column getting ahead of the others and showing up early and tipping the Mommicks off. Lots of runners sent back and forth to keep us connected. We lost a lot of 'em in the woods, too. Picked off, we think, by the Muicmuic. The Muicmuic were afraid of the armies, and Korcha had worked out some kind of agreement with them to let the armies through. But they must have killed a lot of the runners.

"Well, anyway, it worked; and we all got to the The Plains of Wildness at the same time. This was the riskiest part of the whole plan. You have to follow the markers. Runners are of no use anymore. We are all out in the open on the desert, and Korcha and Mira Shannan aren't under cover anymore. We lose communication and have to count on following schedule for days, right down to the half-hour. We know the Mommicks are guarding the whole eastern border facing the desert. But we are counting on their expecting the attack to come at them off The Plains at the *only* place where anyone *ever* crosses: where the High Road to the West is connected by desert markers to this little village of Kul Sama up here."

Here Uncle paused to pick up his cooling kgopuk and take a few noisy slurps, before going on to describe the Mommick Eastern Fortress up north, guarding against approaches to Gazi from the desert at that point. He said it was a huge three-story stone fort, constructed with forced labor, with the two highest lookout towers facing the desert to the east. The description made Nome picture Tosar's Keep. In the Eastern Fortress were concentrated the bulk of the Mommick troops, all those positioned for the defense of the eastern border and not needed in the many garrisons scattered throughout the country to maintain the occupation.

Nome interrupted: "Wait a minute, Uncle. Why were the Mommicks so sure the attack would come directly from the east? How did they know Korcha would not swing far around and enter Gazi from the north or the south?"

"Well, they did have guards on those borders, too, and a few outposts. But nothing like the big fortress on the eastern border. An army that tried to make an enormous swing north or south, even assuming they could get across The Plains somewhere which we've never heard of...even if they could, they'd be worn out by the time they got here. You'd have to know the terrain to see what I mean. Now do you get the picture of how things were set up? The Mommicks know that, if Korcha Rabon wants to come and reclaim his country, he has to come by way of Kul Sama."

Uncle looked eagerly from face to face and leaned forward even farther on his elbow. He was about to tell the Battle of Kul Sama.

"There we were, coming off The Plains of Wildness, ready for the worst. We knew the Mommick army would be waiting for us any time after we got to the grasslands. We also knew that, if anything had gone wrong with Korcha's plans, and the other columns were not where they were supposed to be, we would be finished off in half a day. Our fighters were fanned out in front of us like a shield. Behind, were the wagons, protected as best we could, mattresses stuck up on end all along the rails, children and old people tucked down in the midst of them. We came to the river and forded it without much trouble, but we knew that the time had come. Still, we didn't see any sight of them, and we began to get worried that they knew what was up and were leaving us alone and going after the real attack farther north.

"The thing was, it was quiet everywhere, deathly still. We saw Kul Sama there off to our left, but couldn't see anyone moving, no cows, no sheep, nothing moving there. It was like they hadn't gotten up yet. A quiet village, you know, like before the roosters start. Well, we went forward, slower now, wondering where the Mommicks were, why they were not there to meet us. Off to the north of Kul Sama, to the right of the road, there is that hill, you know, that rises up like a bump on the grasslands? We were keeping our eyes on that, because that was the only place we thought they could be. So we halted, and a few scouts went on up ahead. Then, suddenly, we saw the scouts stop and turn back at a run. They were too far away for us to hear what they were yelling, but we could guess.

"Right away, the wagons maneuvered into position. It was beautiful to see; we had practiced it over and over on the march; and everyone knew what to do. Like a dance, those wagons, nearly a hundred of them, wove in and out amongst each other, turned this way and that. And what had been a long, stretched-out caravan...it curled up into circles within circles like nesting baskets. The babies and little ones, and the old ones, and lots of the mothers got down underneath the wagons in the middle. Those of us who could do something, like me, were up on the outer rim of the wagons with the fighters. Some of the fighters stayed out front, waiting, but most used the forward arc of wagons, where the mattresses were packed thickest, as a shield. And there, coming out from behind that hill, were the Mommick. A thick, gathering swarm of them, like a black cloud rolling in out of the west, getting bigger and bigger, no end to them.

"They came forward slow, like there was no hurry to this thing. They just sort of walked down on us. Whole sections of them were on horse. It was obvious what they planned to do, no question about how they were going to take us. Here we were, out in the open, all curled up tight in a ball. All they had to do was fan out around us and surround, keep their distance, then start striking in, wherever they wanted, on whatever side was weakest at the moment. We had made ourselves a little fort and would be able to hold out for quite a while; but, eventually, they would wear us down with their superior numbers and freedom of movement. I wish I could have heard what those sloggers were saying at that moment. They must have been astounded at the hopelessness of our situation and laughing themselves weak. Some attack to regain the homeland!

"Well, they took their time all right and circled around us just like I said, and kept spread out wide, far out of shot, just sort of looking us over. Then they started, surging in on us, with screams and yells, first on one side, then retreating, then on another and retreating. It was all arrows and some firedarts. But they weren't using any tubes and balls, which was a good thing, because that's what could have done some damage. We were afraid of balls skittering and ricocheting under the wagons. But it was all arrows. They were saving their firedust, figuring they would not need it for this one.

"We were holding out just fine, and they were not hurting us much at all, as long as we stayed behind the cover of the wagons. They were dropping a few of theirs all around the circle from our arrows. So they saw that they had to engage us, and sent in some fierce attacks right up to the wagons. It was terrible hand-to-hand fighting; and our fighters had to get out there, in the open with them, to keep the wagons from being overrun. And they kept up this strike and withdraw tactic on *this* side of our circle, then on *that*, then on *that* side!"

Uncle was acting the battle out with his hands and arms. His voice was climbing and his breath coming faster. The children sitting before him were holding theirs; and their eyes were wide. The farmwife and her husband, Nome and Wasoo, also sat still, watching Uncle tensely. Ravenna glanced around at the faces and shifted nervously in her spot.

"It was turning out worse than any of us thought. They were hitting hard with each attack, and our people didn't have time to recover for a sortie anymore. It wouldn't take much more for them to roll over us; and it looked like it would be all over soon.

"Suddenly, the attacks stopped, and we looked out over the mattresses and saw that there was a disturbance out there among their lines. It's hard to describe it...but, somehow, even at the great distance...because, you know, their lines were spread out in a wide, undisciplined circle all around us out of our range...even so, we could see or hear or feel some kind of disturbance among them. And all at once we saw them start to break and scatter; and then we heard explosions, hundreds of tubes barking and spitting.

"And there it *was*, what we had been waiting for, the army of Korcha Rabon wheeling out from around that same hill where the Mommick had just come from, sending fire and ball into their scattered ranks, then rushing into the midst of them from the rear, cutting and clubbing their way home to Gazi. Well, the Mommick were in disorder and panic; and our handfuls of fighters then poured out after them from behind the wagon barricades. And the field was like a kicked anthill.

"It took all afternoon to finish; but, when we did, it was finished. Between Ila's anvil and Korcha's hammer, almost the whole Mommick host guarding the east was destroyed. Some of them escaped out of the squeeze, slipping off to the sides and running for it back toward their Eastern Fortress from which they had come. We let them go, because so far, I've only told you *part* of Korcha's brilliant plan.

"When those Mommicks who fled the battle got back to their fortress, they found it occupied by Gazines! You see, when we showed up, coming off The Plains at Kul Sama, the Mommicks sent out nearly their entire guard from the Eastern Fortress to engage us. Korcha wheeled about and descended on their rear from the north and Mira Shannan moved in on the unprotected fortress at the same moment. He took it with hardly a fight, I hear. Gazines will never forget the name of Kul Sama. Or of Korcha Rabon. In that single battle, nearly a third of all the Mommick forces in Gazi were destroyed."

Uncle leaned back exultantly, as though he had just accomplished a great feat. The farmwife got up to re-heat the kgopuk.

"So the Gazines now still have control of that Eastern Fortress?" asked Wasoo.

"No!" shouted Uncle with a laugh, leaping forward. "Listen to this! We cleaned it out and abandoned it. Let the Mommicks have it back! Korcha again. Of course our people wanted to hang onto it and use it, but Korcha said no. He said it would tie us down and make us fight the way the Mommick do, from strong positions. He said that was never our way. 'I trust the caves and the mountains of Gazi,' Korcha says. Stay moving, camp among our own people, hit and run, move quick and surprise them. That's the Gazine way! Let them have their empty fortress. It did them no good in guarding the eastern border."

The Battle of Kul Sama

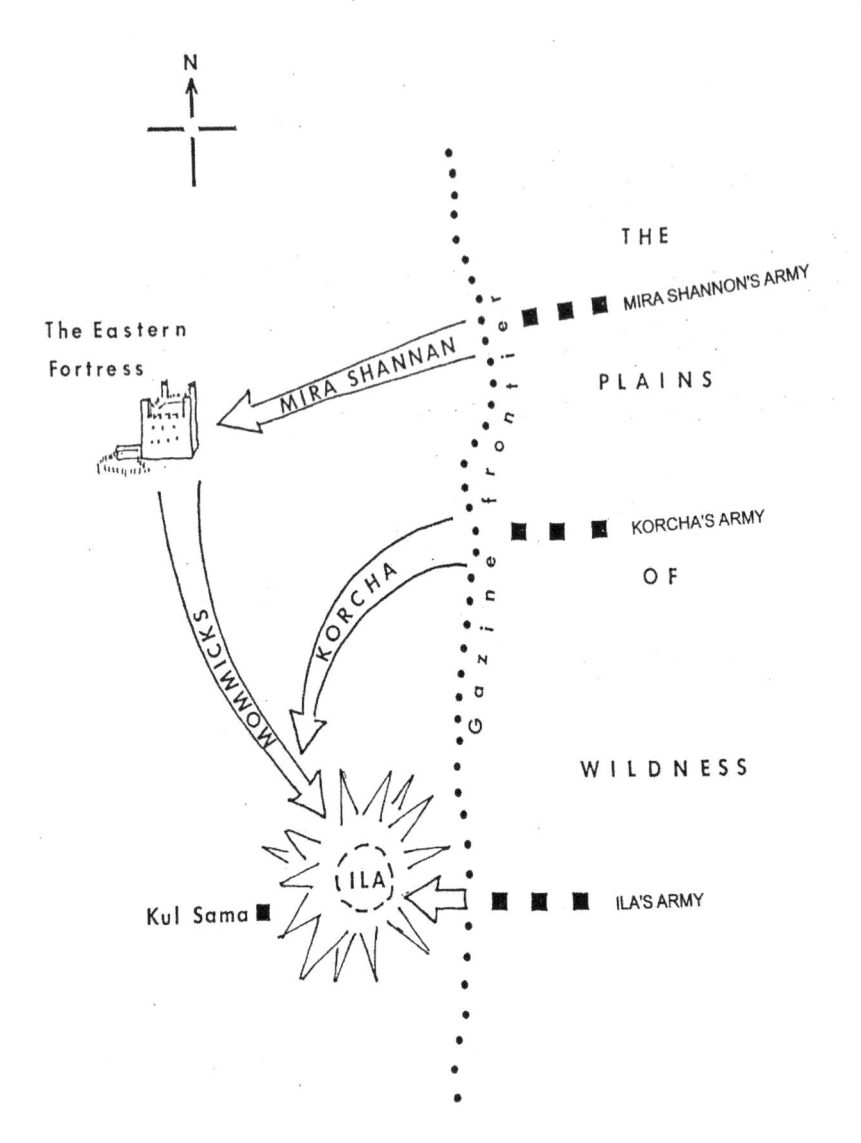

Uncle fell back, once more, into his chair, having delivered the final word on the matter, and graciously accepted a fresh, steaming mug. Nome noticed Ravenna's troubled look. He leaned close and whispered, "What's the matter?" She continued looking over the side of her chair at the floor and discretely shook her head.

....

There was even more to Korcha's strategy than what Uncle told that evening. Within a day, word of the Battle of Kul Sama had spread throughout a waiting Gazi; and a long-prepared insurrection took place. There was little open fighting, but people who had been instructed and secretly trained for years rose up with a campaign of widespread disruption. As they fled to the mountains, they left behind destroyed occupiers' records, ruined machines, burning warehouses, and poisoned animals. In their absence, other Gazines, families, the disabled, the elderly who had returned with Ila, filtered inland and blended with the population. They had all been cheek-branded ahead of time and carried with them fresh inspiration and instructions about the next phase of the rebellion. Uncle was one of these.

All this had happened almost a month ago, and the Mommick forces were just beginning to recover from their surprise. Squads of danes and fohtars were everywhere: on the roads and in the towns and villages, making searches, extracting information. It would be only a matter of time before they reached this fealard. The presence of Ravenna and Nome and Wasoo was a cause for concern. The great fear of any of the settled population was to be found harboring Korcha's fighters. Here were three strong young people, wearing no Mommick brand. How to explain to the danes, when they stormed through the fealard, that these were three guests who just dropped in off the desert...no friends of Korcha Rabon at all. Pressure on the chief of the fealard was building. Most thought that the three visitors should be fed and sent on their way. Nearly everyone agreed that, if they were to stay even a few days longer, they should be branded.

Ravenna, Nome, and Wasoo talked it over among themselves one evening after supper. They agreed that they would have been content to winter over in this place, but they knew that would not be allowed. The chief had stopped by to see them twice and had been asking when they planned to move on. They were reluctant to take to the road again, especially with the talk about early-winter blizzards. Travel for the unbranded would be especially precarious now in Gazi Yet they scarcely even considered returning to the desert. It was likely that they would be allowed to stay at the fealard no more than a few days.

"Then maybe we should leave tomorrow or the next day," said Ravenna. "They have been good to us here, and I don't want to cause them any trouble. I think we should go looking for your two friends, Nome. Hopefully they are still with Korcha."

"You're right, Ravenna; but I don't know how we are going to do that. The Mommicks want to find them as much as we do; and they have troops combing the whole country looking for Korcha. Where would we begin?"

"Look here," said Wasoo. "I'm going off for a few days to have a snoop around. Alone. I won't be gone long, and I agree we only have three, four days... five at most... left here."

"What?" Ravenna was dumbfounded. "You're going *where*?"

"I'm getting to know this one," said Nome. "It's a talent of his. He loves this sort of thing. Let him talk."

"Oh, no need to do much talking," burbled Wasoo. "No, I am a man of few words, as you know, as you'll always find me, no doubt about that. I'm a man of deeds, and I just want to let you two friends of mine know that I am about to do a deed. Yes, I just thought I'd slip out and sniff around a bit and maybe find a Mommick or two. Never seen a Mommick before. Like to see what one looks like. I won't be gone long. Don't leave without me. You don't mind filling in at my post at the fence-work, do you Nome? You're a much better worker than I am, anyway. You can pull on two fence ropes to my one, any day. Just take hold of your rope in one hand and mine in the other and pull away! Why, you've got two arms, two hands. Just the man for the job!"

Nome and Ravenna were looking at each other, heads shaking.

Wasoo was gone the next morning. He had left without telling the farmer or his wife or Uncle, also leaving that job to Nome. When they explained it, there was serious head-shaking; and they were not amused. The farmer said it was a foolish thing and he hoped Wasoo would not be coming back. Work on the fences continued and neared completion. A strained silence had settled upon the household.

Three days passed. The following morning there was a knock at the door as the family and guests sat sullenly at breakfast. At the sound, everyone started. Frightened glances flickered from face to face. A knock at the door at this hour was uncommon. Heavily, the farmer rose and went to the door.

There stood Wasoo, grinning broadly, as though he hadn't been gone. On his left cheek, puckering the skin, was the two down-strokes and crossbar of the Mommick brand.

"You alone?" bellowed the farmer.

"Yes," he answered, surprised. "Who would be with me?"

Nome jumped to his feet and came forward. "Wasoo! You're branded!"

"Oh, just a bit," he said strolling to the breakfast table where the others sat looking up, open-mouthed. He pinched at the brand and peeled it slowly away from his cheek, emitting a stiffled "Ah!" He tossed the brand intact, like a button, onto the table. They all stared at it. "Made of this," he said, plunking a small, tied bag onto the table next to it.

Nome pinched the bag gingerly, fumbled at the strings, and opened it. Cautiously he poured a bit of white powder onto his palm. He sniffed, then looked up slowly at Wasoo. "This is misk! Where on earth...?"

"Good," said Wasoo cheerily. "I thought it probably was, from what you told me about it on The Plains. You said almost anything could be made out of it. So I thought I would see if I could make a Mommick brand. There it is."

"Wasoo...why...you're amazing! Wasoo! Where did you get this? How did you make this little thing? And where is the solution...the liquid you need to....?"

"Here," he said, putting his water pouch on the table. "I brought some along with me. It wasn't very hard really. Just took up a chunk of dried mud and carved a little mold out of it, shape of a brand, like that. Then mixed up some of this powder and the solution into a paste, sort of like what you told me about. Not sure I got the proportions just right. Then I put it in the mold; and before it hardened up, I clapped the whole thing to my cheek and held it there. Waited a while, then washed the mud away, and the thing stuck. Comes off harder than it goes on, though," he added, rubbing the raw pink mark where the brand had been.

"But where did you *get* this stuff?" Nome insisted.

"It's twice-captured misk," said Wasoo. "I found it in with some Mommick gear. I don't think they knew what it was or how to use it, because it was just sitting there with a lot of other stuff they had collected in a raid on Korcha's fighters. I just took away a little bit of it. They had lots more but weren't doing anything with it."

"So you saw your Mommicks, Wasoo," said Ravenna.

"I did," he chirped. "Lots of them. I wasn't so impressed. They ain't as big as a barn or as mean as a boar. They're a lot like us...like Nome here. Two arms, two hands. They talk a little funny and carry around a lot of fighting gear, but otherwise...."

"Then," said Ravenna to their hosts, "I think we'd better be on our way today. Soon as Wasoo can fix us up with some brands like this and we get our things together...."

"Oh, do you have to be leaving so soon?" urged the farmwife lightly. The relief on her face was evident. "You know, you're welcome...."

"Hate to be leaving you with the fence-work not quite finished," Ravenna had turned to the farmer.

"We can manage," he said quickly.

"Sure you have to be leaving?" the farmwife asked uncertainly.

Ravenna smiled and nodded. "We sure thank you....," she began.

EIGHTEEN

Looking for Trouble

When the three companions left the fealard, they did not know where to go. Their only idea was to move inland toward the mountains, where most of the population of Gazi lived. Ravenna wanted to look for the ruins of Mhaveen in hopes that someone in neighboring towns or villages could give her information about her father's relatives. Nome wanted to look for anyone who would give him news of Korcha Rabon. Days of rest and comfort had enabled him to begin thinking once again beyond his own desperate needs. He was remembering Brighthome and thinking often of Mo and Fa. He had new hope of seeing his old friends, Curry and Beland. The thought that they were in this very country, probably no more than several hours away, filled him with eager anticipation. The only way to find them would be to find Korcha.

He shook his head with a little smile, not missing the irony. Here he was, setting out again with two companions to look for "the dangerous man." Only, they were not the same two companions he had started with. He had lost the other two and found these two along his road. Wasoo trotted beside him like a happy dog, taking side-trips and long-ways-about, sniffing close to the ground, returning again. Ravenna walked quietly beside him, thinking her thoughts. When she glanced sideways, she often found him looking at her.

Looking for Korcha Rabon meant looking for trouble. Nome was fearful at the thought of it. Once again, he had taken to wearing from a cord around his neck the leather envelope with a message for Ila Rabon.

Until he entered Gazi, he had been carrying it in his pack. He had often been curious, but not tempted, to open the packet. Now he felt it daily against his skin; and, as he walked, he found himself rehearsing that meeting, hoping he would have opportunity to explain, to account for himself, dreading the possibility that Korcha would have his life.

Yet he walked with an abiding mood of elation, and death did not seem possible. He was in love with this woman. She walked beside him and spoke to him and was content to be with him. He had been falling in love with her for a long time now.

They had wandered from one fealard to the next at first, but no one was willing to take them in or give them work. The word had passed. They were given food and scant information and wished well along their road. As the land began to rise, they came to villages and then towns. In these they fared better. One or the other of them found work for a day or two; sometimes all three of them together. However, it was never for long, because the people everywhere were nervous, guarded, uncertain.

They encountered Mommick squads wherever they went or stayed, on the roads, at lodging houses, in the village squares, along the narrow streets of towns. Twice they were detained by Mommick fohtars, who separated them and interrogated them through interpreters. The fohtars could speak little of the language common throughout the lands east of the Endicot Range and relied on the hireling danes to speak for them. But the fohtars had much on their minds and were hurried and impatient with their inquiries. They tossed these three bedraggled travelers aside and went their way, scanning for more believable rebels. Wasoo had skillfully coached Ravenna and Nome in their stories, and they had often practiced for such confrontations. With crusty Mommick brands pinching their cheeks, their fealard clothing, and their stuttering imitations of the Gazine accent, they passed as natives.

The weather turned very cold; then snow came swirling down the mountainside. The roadways drifted. Walking became difficult. One night they reached a lodging house just in time to be snowbound for four days. Ravenna dug payment for their stay from the depth of her pack in the form of a tiny coin, which the lodge keeper was glad to accept. He even gave back to her a considerable amount of Gazine coinage in change and giggled happily over the business.

During the protracted blizzard outside, they stayed warm and companionable with other travelers and the lodge keeper's family; and they all got to know each other quite well, chatting before a great fireplace in the front room, playing many games of dokkers, eating heartily and often, and drinking much kgopuk. They told each other stories and lies and jokes, gossiped and snoozed off and on. Eventually Ravenna, Nome, and Wasoo told their own true stories. In return, they heard the news of the day:

The forces of Korcha Rabon had been overwhelming the Mommicks in nearly every engagement. The Battle of Kul Sama was told over and over again, even though it had taken place six weeks earlier. Since then, Korcha and Ila and Mira Shannan had withdrawn to mountain hideaways, in three separate areas of the country. From these, they mounted swift strikes against moving Mommick squads and surprise raids on their camps and outposts. Heavily defended positions they left alone.

The fortress on the eastern border, taken then abandoned by Mira Shannan, had been reoccupied by Mommicks, who sat there guarded and isolated. The same with the heavy fortifications at Old Mhaveen and the one on the northern border. While the Mommicks stayed in their towers and forts, they were safe. However, when they came out in numbers large or small to administer the occupation of Gazi, they were struck.

The Rabon fighters seemed to have an unlimited supply of weapons, fashioned out of some new kind of material: white as chalk but hard as steel. This was misk, of course, quarried at 'n Burning Graute, unknown to the Mommicks. The Gazines used it for armor, shields, even for tubes and balls. They left behind temporary bridges and ramps made of the stuff. Sometimes they abandoned it in their makeshift encampments, rather than carry it; for they always moved away quickly after a strike. Later, the Mommicks would cautiously search these camps and find a good amount of misk fabrication—shelter poles, furniture, cooking utensils—but they did not know what to make of it, for they found no way of cutting or re-using the material.

As Nome and Ravenna and Wasoo heard these tales of the many uses of misk, they put their fingertips to the brown-painted brands on their own cheeks, thinking of yet another use for misk that neither Mommicks nor Gazines had discovered.

At times, during the snowstorm, the fellow lodgers fell to talking about the fire of the Greatsada and wondering whether it still burned somewhere in the mountains. Could there still be any caves that the

Rabon forces had not explored and used for hiding? Could it be, perhaps, that in one of these they had found the old guardians of the fire? And could they hope, after all these years, that the guardians were still alive and faithful, keeping the fire alive?

When the blizzard ended and tracks and pathways began to creep out from all dwellings, Ravenna, Nome, and Wasoo set out once again for Old Mhaveen. Now they had clearer directions and a better idea of what to expect. Their plan was to go to the town of Burbaki, not far from where Mhaveen had once stood. Burbaki, famous as the home of the Rabon family, site of the first uprising, held their best hope of finding residents who remembered the father of Ravenna Rosealice.

They were halfway there, only a day or so beyond the lodging house where they had been snowbound, when they witnessed a drastic change in the mood of the country. Plummeting temperatures were making life harder for everyone. However, an even more chilling climate of shock and dread settled upon the inhabitants of Gazi; for the Mommicks had gone on the offensive with a systematic campaign of reprisals.

Each day, several citizens were taken from their houses, led outside the town, and executed. They were left alongside the roadways tied upright to stakes. The three travelers began coming upon these frozen corpses, standing stiff as fence posts, at the approach to every village and town. Each day, the line of fence posts grew longer. Men and women of all ages. Some of the frozen posts were shorter. Children. The Mommicks had found a way to communicate with Korcha Rabon and to strike back.

All doors were shut to the three travelers. Faces of the people they met among the way were stricken and averted. No one gave them work. No one offered them food any longer. They scarcely were allowed to pay their way with the money Ravenna had left over from the lodging house. People were in shock, waiting.

The weather had turned bitterly cold, with cloudless days and nights. The sun hung pale and low in the sky and gave no warmth. Their white breath rolled on the air like puffs of smoke, and dry snow crunched under their feet as they trudged. Up to this point, the sheepskin coats and leggings and caps, given them in the fealard, were protection enough. Now, however, they needed to find more protection from the cold and were very glad, one day, to be given shelter in a barn. There was a little iron stove at one end, which they kept fired so hot that the pipes creaked and popped. Around this, the three of them huddled, for the barn was large and drafty. The steaming bodies of the cattle gave off warmth; and, at night, the three companions slept under blankets of hay, between the hulks of these animals, rather than near the stove.

Wasoo's windy snoring blended with the soughing sounds of slumbering cattle, but Ravenna and Nome were wide awake. They sat with hay swathed about their laps and legs, leaning against the hairy back of a huge dairy cow. At first, the animal had been skittish about this intimacy, but gradually she settled and allowed it. They moved with the slow heaving and falling of the good cow as it slept.

Nome had been talking about home, telling about his little house, his parents, all that was dear to him. He had talked on with a readiness she had not heard from him before; and she listened closely, encouraging him with quiet questions about the details. Eventually, he fell silent, like his father, and for a long time stared into the darkness of the barn, as though he had gone away. She studied his profile, traced with her eyes once again the scar that ran from his cheek to his jaw. She sought his brown eyes, but he was somewhere else.

"And now what will happen to Brighthome?" she asked.

He did not change his expression; but, after a long pause, he answered, "I don't know. That is all past. All I was telling you. I don't see how we can hang onto Brighthome anymore. It takes a lot of money to pay off the Tosars. I have nothing to send home. I wonder how Curry and Beland are doing. At least, they are still with Korcha, who will probably give them enough to pay for another hundred-day on their places. I wonder how they would get it back, though."

"How much time do you have?" she asked.

"A month. Almost exactly a month till the next hundred-day."

"I have money I can give you, Nome," she said.

He turned his head sharply.

"What?"

"Yes, I have money. I am not sure how much it is, but I would guess I have enough for you to make a payment. You can have it."

He looked at her in disbelief for a moment. Then he said, "What money? What money do you have?"

"The money I took from Mintor Ghan's house when I ran away. I told you about that. Remember? I took some coins from a cabinet in the corner of the room. How do you think I paid at that lodging house back there?"

"You paid at the lodging house with that?" he asked, still trying to take in what she was saying.

"I used just one of the coins. One of the smallest, and the man was happy to give me all that Gazine money in change. I don't know what it was worth. I just had to trust him. But I have more, Nome, and I think they are worth something, because they were locked up behind glass."

He only looked at her, not knowing what to say.

"Now you need the money, Nome. Here, I'll show you...."

"No, wait...." He caught her by the arm and held her back. "Ravenna...." He could say no more, and his eyes stung.

She let herself be stopped for a moment and looked at him through the half-light, then pulled away and said, "No, here, I'll show you." She kicked away the hay from her legs and crawled around Wasoo to her pack bag. The old cow, their backrest, started and jerked away as though to rise, but then settled back again. Ravenna returned, crawling across the hay, and nestled back into the spot where she had been. She had a heavy cloth pouch. Out came coins of silver and gold, some clean-cut, some worn. They looked dull and white on her palm, as she held them forward into a band of moonlight cutting through the wall of the barn.

"See," she said, "some of these look old. They are heavy...feel. Tomorrow we should go to Burbaki and try to change this into Gazine money. Or find out what some of these are worth and how it would compare with what you need for a payment on Brighthome. Maybe it would be better to take this back to Tosarkun just the way it is, instead of changing it here...."

"But, Ravenna...," he whispered.

"No, it's all right. You take it," she said.

But instead, he took her slender hand in his and hunched over it, pressing her palm and fingers against his eyes and let his tears run over them.

....

In the morning, the three of them sat on the hay warming their shins around the muttering iron stove. They had melted snow and cooked some cereal in a pot and now held cups of warm breakfast between their hands. Wasoo had milked one of the cows directly onto the steaming cereal. He was chewing away, looking from one to the other of his friends, turning over what they had just told him about money for Brighthome.

"Well," he said, putting his empty cup down on the ground, "changing the coins should not be hard. We are sure to find a counting house in Burbaki, from what they told us of the town the other day. They can assay these coins there, I should think, and even arrange for notes of trade to be taken back to your parents or to your Tosars, Nome. But...."

"I know: But how are we going to get it back to Tosarkun, right?"

"Right. How are you thinking of doing that?" Wasoo seemed unusually sober this morning, quieter and more thoughtful, ever since they had started discussing the problem of the next payment due date.

Nome did not answer right away. Then he said, "I am caught between two duties once again, Wasoo. The obvious thing is for me to leave Gazi and take the payment back myself. The other obvious thing is for me to stay here and rejoin Korcha in hopes of being able to make future payments. It is not a very cheerful picture. There is no end in sight, nothing I can see."

Wasoo straightened and squinted at him. He rubbed the side of his nose with a jab of his finger. He looked at Ravenna Rosealice. She stared straight ahead at the stove without expression.

"Well!" said Wasoo, as though he had just entered the room. Neither of them looked at him. "Well," again. "Well..., I wouldn't mind taking the money back there for you, Nome, if you'd like me to. Seems to me you have to stay here and keep seeking your fortune. Seems to me you can't leave just now when you are on the doorstep of Korcha Rabon, your financier. I've never seen your part of the world, Nome, and I should like to. So, if you would trust me with the money...I won't spend a grummick of it, I promise...."

Nome lifted his head quickly and looked at Wasoo as if he did not understand. Ravenna studied the man carefully, understanding him rather quickly. Nome abruptly stood and turned away. He walked the length of the barn along the ramp between the cattle, rubbing the sides of his head with both hands. Then he came back to his place and looked at Wasoo.

"Why would you?" he finally managed. "Do you know how far it is? And The Plains of Wildness! You would have to go back over them again. You can't mean what you just said, Wasoo!"

Wasoo looked at the stove, as though to consider a question he had not thought of. Suddenly, he scratched at his ribs violently, and his right hand lingered about that spot feeling and probing. "I hope we are not getting fleas," he said with a worried look. "Nome, my daddy said...what was it he said? He said a lot of things, my daddy. I listened to him, too, because he was a smart man. I'm not smart like him, but I carry him around on these shoulders of mine. And when a fellow carries a smart fellow on his shoulders the other one's smart for both of them. See what I mean?"

"No," said Nome.

"So, to answer your question...my daddy said: 'If your friend is pinned under his wagon, don't give advice. Lift the wagon.'"

Nome slowly lowered himself to a milk stool nearby.

"It's all right, Nome," Ravenna said to him in a whisper. "It's all right. He means it."

Nome sighed deeply.

"Now let's talk over how we are going to do this thing," she added aloud.

They fed the fire. Outside, the sky had clouded and the day grown less cold. Snow fell gently without a sound. Throughout the morning they made their plans.

Shortly after noon, they left the barn and trudged several hours through the new snow to Burbaki, where they asked directions to a counting house. There was only one in this town, a squat, stone building, iron gridwork over all the windows. They were unsure of procedures in such a place; but when Ravenna showed some of her coins from The House of Ghan, that did all the talking. Without difficulty, they negotiated notes of trade, payable at 'n Burning Graute, for more than the amount of the Brighthome payment due at Tosar's Keep in a month's time. Ravenna gave over three of her coins, having no choice but to trust the honesty of the mistress of the counting house.

Back in the street, they looked at the notes of trade and the new supply of Gazine currency in their hands. Now, all they had to do was buy Wasoo provisions for the journey and to part company. It had all happened too quickly, and they were all a little afraid and embarrassed.

Toward evening, the three friends ate a final meal together at an inn and spent freely. Wasoo was urged to wait until morning before setting out, but he insisted on leaving that evening. A full moon would be shining through the clouds, he argued, and his road would be illuminated. Mommick soldiers would not be scouring the roads at night; and, besides, he could not afford to delay. His plan for crossing The Plains of Wildness safely was to join a rag-tag caravan of Gazine casualties heading east. They had encountered it several days earlier, before their stay at the barn.

The three of them had spent a night with this caravan at a sheltered, out-of-the-way farmstead and had learned that they were Gazine resisters, too sick and wounded to be kept at the sick-lagers. This is what infirmaries hidden away in the mountain caves were called. The ever-moving Rabon forces had no perimeter of defense behind which to withdraw and could not maintain traveling infirmaries, so they established secret sick-lagers for their wounded up in the caves. But even these had to be moved from time to time when Mommick search expeditions drew near. This constant uncertainty and displacement was fatal for some of their more damaged people; so, at great risk, the most serious casualties were carried out of the country, eastward, across The Plains of Wildness. They were taken, not all the way back to 'n Burning Graute, for that would have been too long a journey, but to some of the settled lands beyond The Plains, to the north of The Fields of Khorvan.

Wasoo's plan was to catch up with the slow-moving caravan and to cross The Plains in their company. It was well known that The Plains were safer for large groups than for individuals, and he dared not make the crossing alone. He counted on their accepting him, for he knew that they needed assistance in caring for the sick. Once they had all crossed The Plains, Wasoo would be free to take the High Road eastward toward Tosarkun.

"It will take you all of three weeks to get there," said Nome. "More, if that sick caravan slows you down."

"Good, that gives me an extra week before the money is due," said Wasoo cheerfully.

"Don't go dining and dashing so you can see the insides of jails along the way."

"I don't go looking for food when I've just eaten supper. I don't go looking for trouble when I've just had a bellyful of it."

"And what are you going to do, Wasoo, after you have given over the notes of trade at Brighthome or Tosar's Keep?"

"Come back here and find you," he said simply.

"All the way back here?"

Wasoo looked down at the ground with a frown, rubbing his chin, pondering a problem. "Well, let's see...if I could come *part* of the way back, it would be probably be shorter...but...."

Nome took a swipe at him, but Wasoo ducked in time.

They agreed to meet at Kul Sama in about seven weeks. Nome and Ravenna would begin lingering about that village at the edge of The Plains of Wildness after forty-five days had passed. If, for any reason, they could not meet him there, they would leave a message.

They pushed back from the clutter of greasy dishes on the table and walked out of the yellow light of the inn into the pale bluish glow of the evening. The gliding clouds were back-lighted by the moon, as Wasoo had predicted; and the snow was light and fluffy under their steps.

They paused at the road in front of the inn, and one of them said, "Well...goodbye." Wasoo turned to go. Nome reached out and caught him and drew him in tight, and Ravenna wrapped her arms around the two of them. They were a strange sight on this cold and snowy landscape, in a place where people were taken out and shot every morning, the three of them standing clutched together.

"The road before you will be Holy," one of them whispered.

"The Good Mother is my mother and your mother," another one whispered.

"My...my daddy...." the third one began, but his voice tripped, and he could not finish. He pulled away and was gone.

NINETEEN

The Sick-Lagers

The next day, Ravenna and Nome set off together searching for Korcha and searching for anyone who remembered Ravenna's father. It was an aimless, unfruitful effort with no leads. They had no notion of where best to go. They simply wandered from village to town asking questions and meeting stony responses. The local people knew from their mannerisms and speech that they were not Gazines. Clearly they were not Mommick, but they might be agents and spies. The Mommick campaign of random reprisals, taken daily upon the Gazine people, had been successful in breaking the free and open spirit of rebellion among the settled inhabitants. The reprisals were aimed at terrorizing someone into betrayal of Korcha; but he had anticipated something like this and kept all his communication with the settled population one-way. No one, outside of Korcha's, Ila's, and Mira Shannan's roving bands, knew where they were or where they would appear next.

The Mommicks struck down the huddling people of the land in order to strike at their liberator. Life among them slowed to survival pace. People stayed indoors. Business all but stopped. Financial hardship settled upon them like pinching fingers. Morning after morning, new wailing broke forth in houses across the land, as members of families were taken by fohtar squads to be added to the growing lines of stakes along the roads.

Nome and Ravenna had witnessed one of the abductions. They were in a shop which faced on the town square, buying bread and cheese one morning. Suddenly, the fohtars were in the square. The shopkeeper rushed to bolt the door, shouting to them to help him draw the curtains. The three of them cowered there and peeked from behind the shades to see where the soldiers would go. They were alone in the square, roaming about, banging on doors and window shutters, getting no response. At the same time, they nervously watched the upper windows and rooftops, wary of ambush from those directions.

It was evident that the soldiers hated this duty and moved in loathing and dread. They had come into a deserted square and would not leave until they had a required victim. They were afraid to force entry into any of the shops or homes, for the people in them knew then that they had been chosen for execution and would fight like cornered animals. Many fohtars had been killed in these encounters. The soldiers nervously gathered in the center of the square and milled about, seeming uncertain. Then they withdrew, and all was silent. Before they left, two of them set fire to a house on a corner; then they, too, disappeared.

The fire hesitated, then took hold and climbed up the sides of the building. Glass shattered, but still there was no sign of life from within. Then there was movement at the upper windows, curtains drawn aside, the moving shadows of people within. All was quiet again, but the fire spread, and black smoke began to roll from the empty ground floor windows. The front door opened, and three people scurried into the street, struggling with heavy containers of water, which they threw on the flames. They wildly scooped snow in the buckets and pans and threw it, in vain, against the burning walls.

Then the fohtars were on them. In a moment, one of the people had been snatched away and the other two beaten down as they tried to cling. A soldier, in uniform different from that of the fohtars, stepped hurriedly to the center of the square and began to shout, turning to all four sides. It was a dane, one of the Mommick mercenaries who was chanting out the required formula of threat and warning to the inhabitants and to Korcha Rabon. His shouting mingled with the screams of the fallen and the dull roar of the fire. Then the soldiers went away.

This scene would not have taken place, had Nome and Ravenna been on the street instead of in the shop buying bread and cheese. One of them would have been the victim. Travel was becoming impossible for them. After witnessing this atrocity, they, too, moved in fear and distrust. Like the local people, they learned that the only safe time to be out in the open was immediately after someone had been taken away in reprisal.

Nome and Ravenna had helped fight the fire that day, alongside the shopkeeper with whom they had hidden. The terror they had shared had dispelled the natural distrust the man would normally have felt; and he allowed them to return to his shop and even to meet his family. They were all shaken and weeping and needing one another. In better days, this family had managed a modest living by taking in travelers, two or three at a time, and feeding and lodging them. There were no travelers now. Nome and Ravenna were the first they had seen in months. They would certainly have been turned away; but tragedy had thrust them in, and the family badly needed the income. Ravenna still had a good deal of Gazine currency left for the expenses she and Nome were incurring.

Ravenna was given a room at the back of the shop, and Nome was given the shop itself as his quarters. The owner decided to go out of business until these terrible days passed, and the income from the new guests allowed him this luxury. He boarded up the front of the shop from the outside, so it would appear to be an abandoned building. The counters, from which he had sold bread and pastries, kgopuk and cheese, were pushed against the wall.

At the back of the shop, just off Ravenna's room, was a small sitting room with a friendly stove, where they were invited to join the family in the evenings. The family lived upstairs; but there was a second bedroom, off the sitting room downstairs, which was being kept for their eldest son, who was away and expected home soon.

The two guests spent days and evenings of inactivity with the family. They were treated as a couple; and it was clear to Ravenna and Nome, themselves, that they had become more than just travel partners. Yet they did not speak openly to each other of this. They continued to speak, in a businesslike way, of their missions to find Korcha and to find her father's relatives. But already, with almost no discussion, she had given him a great deal of her money. All planning for the road assumed they would go together. To stay in Gazi or to leave Gazi was discussed in terms of "we." With the departure of Wasoo, their bond became more obvious.

It was even more than that. Although they wandered the wintry land without reward, and were severely suffering cold, hunger, and uncertainty, they both felt unaccountable joy. It would not be too much to say that Ravenna and Nome were happy. There was that evening, as they had been walking along a roadway at the first winking of stars, when they heard, from somewhere, the fragmentary notes of a stringed instrument. As one person, they stopped still, and breathlessly drank in what seemed to them both the most beautiful music they had ever heard. And that other evening, when she had handed him something across the campfire, and had accidentally brushed the back of his fingers with her hand. Nome had given no sign of the sting of pleasure that had rushed through his whole body; but, a long time afterward, when he casually referred to it, she knew exactly the moment he spoke of.

But now, in close quarters, they grew shy. There was always some member of the confined family about. Ravenna and Nome spoke with each other about everything but what was uppermost in their thoughts and feelings. He spent an inordinate amount of time studying maps. She appeared bored and aloof.

To relieve his restlessness, Nome had taken to going out into the snowy streets for short walks on the days after the fohtars had come and gone. Twice he saw owlstones. Once, it was only a glimpse, as he turned into the doorway at the back of the shop. When he darted back to look, they were gone. The other time, they were standing at the edge of a low, flat shed-roof, the two of them, round eyes gazing at him with the wide stare of an infant. They had swayed there slightly, much as they had that morning when he had first seen them at the cache hole, curiously regarding him as he awoke.

Both times, he had gone to Ravenna, happy and eager to tell her what he had seen. The first time, however, he could not. When he came into the room, she was turned away, interested elsewhere, not acknowledging him. His joy wilted. The second time, he told her abruptly what he had seen. As soon as he had, he regretted it, knowing he sounded foolish. Until then, he had never spoken to her openly about these experiences.

But this time, Ravenna looked at him quietly with her lovely, moist eyes; and he felt that his next breath would not come. She nodded gravely, listening, as he described to her the owlstones, told her about seeing them on the High Road, on The Plains, other places. He described the bird which had swept over his and Wasoo's heads the day they first set foot on The Plains of Wildness, and told her how it had glided toward the first stele and then veered off in the correct direction. He was talking to her then, freely and excitedly, and the formality between them was melting.

Finally, she said, "Well, remember, I was on The Plains of Wildness, too; and, after that, it is not hard at all to believe in your owlstones. I don't know what they are, Nome; but, having lived among The Women all my life, I know something about the spirit world. From what you are saying about your owlstones, how they've helped you and how you feel when you see them, I would say they sound like the opposite of wythies."

Her words were like sunrise to him. He enthusiastically told her about the owlstones on the way to Trapple Rock, when the unknown horse and rider had turned back to him and he had fled. He told her about the ride in the sutton, and his flight from there to the "pig village" of Hay. She laughed at that. It was there that he had first seen her. Together they were laughing now, tilting their heads together till they bumped. Nome snatched up her hand from her lap and kissed it. They looked up from the head-bumping, and Nome leaned forward and kissed her a quick, laughing kiss on the mouth. At that moment, one of the family members came into the room; and they both fell back in their chairs, suppressing laughter, caught, not caring.

....

The eldest son returned home that evening and settled into the second little room at the back of the shop. He was a thin, frightened young man, about seventeen or eighteen years old. His hands and head and shoulders were hard and bony. He looked like he had not eaten well and had seen horrors. His speech was nearly inaudible; and even his parents had to ask him to repeat himself. Despite his father's assurances about the two guests in their home, he acted like a child afraid of strangers when Nome and Ravenna were present. No explanations were made to them about where the young man had been. When Ravenna once made a polite conversational inquiry about it to the mother, she was met with cold silence.

"But I know where Deluke (the young man's name) has been," she said to Nome one evening when they were alone.

"You know?" he said. "Where?"

"He's been in the sick-lagers."

"How do you know that?" asked Nome. "He's not wounded or sick. He's strange, but he's not sick. I assumed he's been among the fighters, because he is of good age for that. But he looks too frail and broken to be a fighter. What makes you think he's been in the sick-lagers?"

"Didn't you smell the ammonium and camphor? It's clinging to his clothing still. Faint but unmistakable. The same smell on the people we met when we first learned about the sick-lagers, before Wasoo went off with them. I'm sure of it."

Nome pondered darkly, but the thought struck him quickly. He looked up sharply at her. "So you think he is on leave from tending the wounded up in the sick-lager caves?"

"I think so," she answered.

"Then maybe that's our answer," he said firmly.

"What?"

"Maybe that is our first step in finding Korcha Rabon."

Ravenna just looked at him.

"If you are right about his being from the sick-lagers, Ravenna," he continued slowly, weighing each word as though it were a thought, "we may be able to convince him to show us the way up there. And once we are there, we are among Korcha Rabon's people once again, and may be able to get in contact through them."

She straightened in her chair, an objection forming.

Nome hurried to continue, "I know what you're thinking. This scared rabbit would never take us there. But I am not so sure. We do not have to convince him, we have to convince the father. The boy will do what his father tells him, doesn't it look that way to you? Well, we are pretty trusted here now, and we know the one thing that will convince the father. Your money. They have no livelihood. If we announce we are leaving, their income stops."

"We bribe him to take us up there?" asked Ravenna.

"We hire a guide. We hire the man's son."

It took three days of negotiation, the three days the young man had allotted to him at home. Ravenna's guess was correct, Deluke was on leave from nursing duty in the caves, far up in the mountains. At the end of three days, he had to set out again to return to work. So desperate was the family for security, that the father commanded his son to take Ravenna and Nome with him. He convinced himself that this would not be a betrayal, even if he had misjudged them as loyal to the Gazine cause; for, once they arrived at the sick-lagers, he knew they would be allowed to leave only if the authorities there permitted it. Ravenna and Nome had to double the amount of their first offer before a bargain was struck. Ravenna made another trip to the counting house.

....

The trip to the sick-lager took two days of hard traveling. The trail followed a switch-back path far up into the mountains. At night they dug snow caves and slept in quilted sleep sacks. The snow was deeper every hour of their climb; and, at times, the three of them had to pick their way gingerly across the face of unstable drifts which threatened at any moment to become the beginnings of an avalanche. Nome asked Deluke why the Mommicks could not find the sick-lagers by following the tracks in the snow of people coming and going. He was told, "You will see." Later in the day he did. The trail in the snow branched out into several trails, which in turn branched into many more. Evidently, a number of people from those tending the sick-lagers had been employed in creating a maze of false trails leading every which way, to empty caves or to nowhere. Nevertheless, the Mommicks did have scouting parties constantly combing the mountainside, trying to find the sick-lagers with the same purpose that Nome had—of being led to Korcha Rabon. It was dangerous work for the Mommicks; for they were easily ambushed, unless they came in sufficient number. When they came in great number, their approach was easily detected, and the sick-lagers, together with all the sick and wounded, were moved higher, to more secure caves. It was this moving about on the mountainside that some of the most severely injured people could not endure, so that they had to be carried away out of Gazi on a slow, painful journey.

Toward evening of the second day they encountered a lookout and were allowed to pass when Deluke gave the word. They passed two other guard points, then approached a dark spot on the side of the mountain that fell, free of snow, like a rent in the rock face. The opening, where a handful of exhausted people on break were sitting about, chewing dried, cold food, was an ugly hole in the mountain, three times the height of a person. However, beyond the entry, the path dropped quickly at a receding angle to a small doorway punched into the stone, so low that those who came and went had to stoop. Nome and

Ravenna were told to wait at the entrance, where the eaters silently watched them, pushing tired breaths into the cold air. No one spoke.

Deluke returned in a few moments with the captain of the sick-lager, who was surprised and troubled to be presented with these newcomers. They were clearly not used to visitors here. Night fell quickly, while the captain kept Nome and Ravenna standing and answering questions. At length, he assigned a guard who led them inside the cave.

The roof space lifted, as they passed through the low doorway; and they were met with muted sounds of groaning and weeping, which continued uninflected like the murmur of a crowd. The smell of rotting flesh, carbolic, and camphor made them swoon; and Ravenna reached out to steady herself against the frost-rimed stone wall. Into a vast room with a vaulting ceiling they came; and, in flickering yellow light, they saw rows upon rows of stretchers, low to the ground, with swaddled forms upon them. Among them slowly moved the bending and straightening figures of the sick-lager tenders. Deluke, who no longer appeared, had blended back in among them.

Ravenna and Nome were carefully led to the rear of the cave, past all the sick and broken people, to an area of empty stretchers on which disheveled blankets lay. This was where the tenders slept. They were given food; and, while they ate, two stretchers were pulled away from a stack leaning against the wall and dropped down. Nome and Ravenna lay down upon their stretchers and listened to the ceaseless drone of suffering, trying to adjust to the putrid, sweet odor of the unmoving air. They felt buried in the murk of the torch light. They slept.

....

In the morning, they were allowed outside into the open air and given a small amount of food again but were kept under guard. After breakfast, they were given long aprons and put to work. This suited their plans. They hoped to work at these sick-lagers long enough to gain trust and, eventually, to be allowed to make contact with Korcha Rabon. Nome and Ravenna were separated and given duty in different areas of the caves. Their work shifts were staggered so they would have little contact, even on breaks. Ravenna's job was the more tedious. She joined several young women, not much more than girls, who continually hauled in snow to be melted in a huge miskware cauldron. Then each of them dipped smaller pans of water from it and added an acrid soap which fizzed and bubbled. On hands and knees, they mopped the entire floor of the cave, beginning at one end and slowly working their way toward the other. The floor was smooth, but uneven, and rock-hard. The women sloshed and wiped under each stretcher, reaching and sweeping and pausing to wring out their rags. The water ran out gray-pink between their fingers, for there was much blood on the floor under the stretchers. Their faces were at the level of the sick people; and Ravenna talked to them as she crab-crawled backwards along the aisles, stretching underneath, pausing to wring her rag. Some of them smiled wanly at the sight of her lovely face; some answered in brave good humor; some mumbled incomprehensibly and looked with glazed eyes; some had no eyes; and some continued to groan or cry out.

Nome was assigned to a boy a little younger than Deluke. They did a variety of jobs that required lifting and carrying: moving in firewood, taking out corpses, transferring people from one stretcher to another, moving stretchers about, hauling water.

Both Nome and Ravenna had work that frequently brought them to the mouth of the cave, she to dump the dirty water, he to gather wood or snow for melting or to deposit the dead. Once or twice that first day they met, but only briefly, to greet one another and to say as much with their eyes as a moment would allow.

Nome had just returned to the cavern from a trip to the cave entrance; and he was standing among the stretchers in one of the aisles, looking about, waiting to be told what to do next. Suddenly he heard a shout from behind:

"Nomo! Nomo!"

He whirled about, astonished, to see a man with a shaggy, black beard bearing down on him, arms thrown wide, legs high-stepping in a hurried, lumbering gait, as though he were running through a bog.

"Nomo!" he cried again.

And, in the last moment before he was seized, Nome gasped, "Beland!"

They grappled each other like wrestlers and twirled about, tipping and losing balance and nearly falling sideways on one of the stretchers, so that the poor man who lay there gave out a screech of alarm.

They laughed and pounded each other and tried to talk and squeezed each other around the neck. At length, they eased up; and Nome leaned back to study his old friend. He gently stroked the side of his head, down along his beard. Beland had always been clean-shaven. He had been stocky, firm; and his frightened, darting eyes had been set in a fleshy face. But in the embrace, Nome could feel his bones. The untended beard clung like moss to sunken cheeks. Black eyes shone with a fierceness Nome had never seen there before.

"Beland," Nome murmured tenderly.

"Oh Holy," said Beland, looking back into Nome's good face, shaking his head slowly from side to side. He looked, once again, at the long scar on Nome's face, the work of his hand, and again to Nome's glistening eyes. "Holy."

"Thank you, Beland," said Nome, "for leaving me that message at Trapple Rock. It saved me."

Beland looked puzzled, not understanding for a moment, then remembering; and his face relaxed back into his joy. He nodded. That seemed so long ago to him. He had forgotten. Lifetimes ago.

....

That evening, they sat together in the open air, beneath the armies of stars which were slowly crossing the black winter sky. Their backs leaned against the mountainside at the door of the sick-lager. The captain had given them time off together after supper. The weather was mild.

Beland learned why Nome had not met them at Trapple Rock. He and Curry had feared he was dead. He learned about Ravenna Rosealice and Wasoo. Nome wanted to know if Korcha had given them payment for the second hundred-day on Beland's Farm and Curry House. He had, but there was no way to get the money home. They both still had their money, but the holdings would be going forfeit in a few weeks. Beland did not show much interest in the matter.

There was much changed about him, most of all a sense of calm that had never been there. Nome learned that Curry was with Korcha and had been granted his wish to fight for Gazi. In fact, Curry was much in Korcha's favor and served him as an aide. Beland was one of the tenders in this sick-lager. He had started out in another lager doing the kind of work Nome and Ravenna were doing now; but he had been promoted to tender and given direct care for the sick and wounded. He had been learning a great deal about herbs and poultices and cutting and draining and setting bones. As Beland talked about this, Nome knew that his old friend was living a new life. Who would have thought it? In this dreadful, dismal place, timid, sulking, petty Beland had found something to be happy about. Nome silently wondered about this, as they talked under the stars, with blankets tugged tight about their shoulders to keep the chill away. The answer to his wondering came clear in their conversation which went like this:

"And how did you get across The Plains of Wildness, Beland?"

"Oh. It was a hard crossing. I've never known such a weird place. All desert and strange spirits about. Wythies. Have you heard of wythies, Nome? At first, I didn't believe any of that talk; but afterwards I knew what they meant. What we always thought of as meanness or sourness in the mind or hatred...things like that...you know, like people getting dark in their heart or crazy...or sometimes even sick for no reason at all. Most of that is the business of wythies, Nome. They're not just in The Plains, although there's more of 'em there than anywhere else. The Plains, they're a big wythy-farm. They are in Tosarkun, too, I've got no doubt. And I think that they are what controls the Tosars. I don't know what those whthies really are. You can't see them. But, Nome, I've had my fears...I haven't said much about it to anyone...I've had my fears that some of the wythies stuck to our group, as we were passing through, and came into this country with us. Sort of like swarms of mosquitoes, you know, when they are terribly bad in the first part of summer; and you can't help but bring a few of them with you as you go into the house, no matter how hard you try to beat them off at the door. Well, we had to zig and zag all over those Plains, looking for stele marking rocks, so we would not go into dangerous centers of power, they called them. We made it. Kept on schedule, too."

"I know what you're talking about," said Nome. "We came across The Plains of Wildness, too; and it was a harrowing two weeks. I can't imagine what it would be like for an army to go across. But, when I asked how you got across The Plains, I was asking about you, yourself. How did you keep yourself on track?"

"Well," he said thoughtfully, "it's probably easier with a big group. I would never go out there all alone. But even with our army...there were strange things...Curry got strange out there. I don't know about me."

"What did you think about? What was your attitude when you were there?"

Beland was silent for a long time. It was obviously a hard question for him. He looked up at the stars, then blew out his breath in little puffs of mist, as though cross-eyed, trying to watch his attempts at smoke rings. Then he said: "I thought about Anna a lot. And I wished I was back with her." He was silent again for a moment, then said, "I beat her, Nome. How I wish I had *never* beat her. It was wrong to her. And...and it was the breaking of my life!" Beland let his head fall forward against his arms which hugged his knees. Then, his voice muffled by the embrace, he continued, "I promised the Holy I would never hit anyone again."

Nome sat motionless. The dying coals of a little campfire in front of them cast a mild glow in a circle around itself. Beyond the fire, the two owlstones stood, also motionless. Their bodies were stone, but the eyes were alive, watching the two men. Nome smiled at them and gave only the suggestion of a nod. Then he slowly turned his face and continued to listen to Beland.

"No one to talk to out there, Nome, no one but the Holy. I talked a lot. I guess I got crazy out there on The Plains with no one to talk to but the Holy. That's how I ended up here. When we got to Gazi and the war started, I was put on the tending and burning detail. I was no good to them as a fighter. I wouldn't fight. There's been more burning than tending lately. When Gazine people die, they have to be burned. It's part of their belief. It has to do with the Holy Fire they believe in. So I was among the burners, following after the battles. It's a dangerous job, too, because, if the Mommicks are near and we have to move out of an area fast, the burners are the last to go, and the smoke lets the Mommicks know just where we are. I nearly got caught by the Mommicks more than once. One time, I ran out on the burners. We saw the Mommicks coming, and they just stayed there and kept burning. I ran. I don't believe in it as much as they do. Been raised different. The Mommicks slaughtered them all. I watched from cover. I probably did the wrong thing, abandoning my post like that. Korcha would have me shot if he knew. But I didn't want to be killed by the Mommicks. I never told this to Curry. I wouldn't put it past him to tell Korcha. Anyway, after the Mommicks moved on, I went back out there and started burning again. I had a fresh batch to do. Some of them my good friends. I nearly ran off that time, Nome. Probably would have, if I wouldn't have had to cross The Plains again. I think we're trapped here. Curry, he's changed. All along, getting to worship Korcha more and more; but he really changed on The Plains...I don't know how to say it.... I don't want to talk against him. Probably just that I'm jealous because he has no time for me anymore. He must despise me. I don't despise him. I got no right to.... No one who does what I did to Anna has a right to anything. The only hope I have is in my promise to the Holy never to hit anyone again (Nome's eye was caught by a motion of the owlstones, a sudden fluttering of wings, something he had never seen them do before)...no matter what." Beland was silent. He was looking down and showed no sign of seeing anything beyond the fire. Then he added, "It helps me to be here tending these people, Nome. I want to stay here. I don't care if I go back to the Farm. Ever again. It's hard work here and horrible. But, when I get worn out and terrified by all the burning and blood and death I see, I look into the faces of these poor, hurt people, and I tell myself, 'This is Anna. You're taking care of Anna.'"

Nome tossed his head up against the rock wall at his back and sucked in the cold air of night. Here is something as wonderful as all you stars, he thought.

"You're a good man, Beland," he said.

"No, I ain't. No one who...."

"You're a good man. What you did is past."

Nome heard in the darkness a long, slow intake of air...then a releasing of it. Then, at almost a whisper: "I won't argue with you, Nome."

TWENTY

Report to Korcha

For security reasons, the sick-lagers had no direct line of communication to the fighting troops, which were always in hiding and on the move. Messengers from Korcha, Ila, and Mira Shannan often arrived at the sick-lagers with orders and directives and, in turn, carried messages back to the nomadic headquarters. After Nome's arrival, two days passed before Beland could send out a message begging Curry to come at once. The messenger had brought alarming news that Korcha was sick and Maincaptain Streeter had assumed command for the moment. After the messenger left, Beland and Nome waited six anxious days for word from Curry. Finally Curry himself arrived.

Nome was amazed. Curry stood smartly before him, trim and fit, dressed in a brown uniform, tricked out with leather and studs. He wore a new sandy-colored mustache and no longer looked boyish. When they met, he reached out and grasped Nome's hands enthusiastically but, with stiff arms, held him away.

They talked for little over an hour. Nome told Curry that he had been able to send money back only for Brighthome and asked if he and Beland had been able to do so for their two holdings. Curry had not thought to mention home, until Nome brought it up. They had found no way to send money back. Curry then insisted that they return to Korcha together. Nome would not hear of it until he had Korcha's word that it would be safe for him to approach. He removed from around his neck the leather pouch, still unopened, containing the ill-fated letter for Ila and gave it to Curry. This pouch and letter, he said, would be a sign that he had been a loyal messenger, who, through no fault of his, had been unable to deliver the message. Give this to Korcha, Nome pleaded, and ask him to hold nothing against me. Earlier, Nome had been eager to introduce Ravenna Rosealice to his old friend; but, somewhere during the conversation, he had decided not to mention her to Curry just yet.

....

It was night. A member of the bodyguards had led Curry into this room and left him there alone to wait. Five empty chairs faced each other at untidy angles. On the floor, by the chair legs, were crumbled wads of papers and empty cups, one tipped over and staining the carpet dark. At a tilt on a table top was a large topographical map of the northern region of Gazi. It was grease-smudged and worn, boldly scarred by pencil with circles, lines, arrows.

Curry remained standing, fist cupped in hand behind his back, although he knew the wait could be a long one. At the end of it, when the door opened, he would have to be on his feet, at attention. He was familiar with the procedure. He had often waited for Korcha in this room since they had camped here. Before that, he had stood waiting in tents, in the snow in the forest, in an abandoned shepherds' hut. People were no longer brought into Korcha's presence for audience, but were placed where he could observe them for a while from hiding. Only after he was satisfied that the situation was safe, did Korcha appear. He continued this practice with painstaking caution, even with his closest associates and lieutenants, even with his brother, Ila, and with Mira Shannan, who periodically left their own commands to travel across the mountains of Gazi in order to report and confer. At times, Korcha would keep subordinates waiting a very long time, while he pondered and scrutinized them, seemingly waiting for a sign, some movement of his soul. In the past few months, Curry had exerted himself in correctness and devotion and had succeeded in winning a position as junior aide. He knew that, at this moment, Korcha's eyes were upon him from behind the door. He waited, composed and stiff.

The door jerked open. Korcha strode in as though in a hurry and took a chair, motioning Curry to do the same.

He looked even more haggard and drawn than he had on The

March. Deep lines dropped down his hollow cheeks and curved inward to the tight line of his mouth. In contrast, puffy bags hung from his lower eyelids. This was the first time Curry noticed that the sides of his hair were graying. His grooming was still fastidious, except for a spot on his neck which he had missed shaving. Curry waited to be addressed, enduring the brooding gaze.

"They tell me you've been away to see Ogrodni," he said without introduction.

"Yes, sir. A message came to me, sir, from Beland in the sicklagers, sir." Curry hesitated, striving to word it right. He felt a sudden flick of fear, realizing that he was in trouble. "I knew how strongly you felt about Nome...about Ogrodni, sir...and that his whereabouts were of concern to...."

"Why didn't you report this to me? Who gave you clearance to go to Ogrodni?"

"I tried to, sir," Curry replied hurriedly. "You were unavailable at the time. I waited several days, sir, knowing that you would want to deal with this news directly. But it was right after you saw Bima...."

Korcha's hand shot up in front of his face, and his head jerked sideways, and he screeched, "Don't!" His face was a grimace.

"I'm sorry, sir, I'm sorry!" Curry pleaded. "I'm sorry!"

But Korcha held his painful pose and, only slowly, relaxed his face and arm, then lowered his hand. But he continued staring sideways, off toward the dark corner of the room.

"I'm sorry, sir," Curry tried again, more quietly. "Sir? I had clearance from Maincaptain Streeter, sir. Since you were unavailable for a number of days there. And Maincaptain Streeter agreed that this Ogrodni matter had to be responded to right away, sir."

Korcha did not answer. He seemed to have gone elsewhere. Perhaps, for all his brilliance as a leader of people and commander in the field, Korcha Rabon was not suited to be a soldier. He took upon himself the suffering of his people and responsibility for their sacrifices in such an intensely personal way that he was being destroyed. Those closest to him had always worried about his health and wondered whether his mind could stand the strain of his agonies. They became keenly anxious when they saw him on The Plains of Wildness lose all signs of rationality from time to time.   When they finally reached Gazi and exulted in the overwhelming success of Kul Sama, they were relieved to see their commander regain his grip; but he nursed certain preoccupations. One of these was Ogrodni. He had been furious when Nome had not rejoined his army at Trapple Rock; and, for several days, he was beyond talking to when told that Ogrodni's dog had run off. There was no sense to this obsession, and his staff looked at one another mournfully and shook their heads. He was appeased, only when convinced that Ogrodni had run afoul of the Muicmuic or been killed somewhere on the road. Surely he was dead. But on The Plains of Wildness, Korcha became convinced that Ogrodni was alive. Voices had spoken to him, he said. Clear and truthful voices, he insisted, that let him know that Ogrodni was alive. He was sure...he had been warned, he swore...that Ogrodni intended to betray them all. Ogrodni was hurrying to Gazi at that very moment to warn their enemies of their approach. The entire March, the years of planning and preparation, the future of the people was all in danger if Mommicks were told that, not one, but three armies were coming at them from the east.

Korcha's anguish had been contagious on The Plains. His staff, too, were afflicted by the anguished wheezing of wythies, and they began to lose heart. Only the discipline of keeping to schedule in tandem with the northern and southern armies, and Korcha's own furious will, kept them together and moving forward from stele to stele. When Korcha and Ila had burst upon Kul Sama and destroyed the best of the Mommick forces while Mira Shannan had taken their unguarded stronghold, the fighting Gazines released all their haunted fears. But, unreasonably, Korcha Rabon continued to mutter about betrayal, to remember past breaches of discipline or security, and to fret over his certainty that Ogrodni was still alive. None of this, however, prevented him from capably leading all his coordinated forces in a series of small-scale attacks and skirmishes, maintaining the initiative and pushing the Mommicks into an increasingly defensive posture.

A turning point might have overthrown him when the Mommicks began their desperate campaign of random reprisals against the settled population of the country. But Korcha Rabon refused to be intimidated. How deeply the systematic execution of his fellow citizens affected him he never revealed to the enemy. His closest staff and associates saw that the steady count of reprisals drove Korcha to a new depth of grimness; but, outwardly, he stayed on course; and, from hideouts in the mountains, he continued to orchestrate the hit-and-run offensive on the north, central, and southern regions of Gazi. Now that the Mommicks were shooting the unresisting inhabitants of the land, the joy of victory was gone. The relentless pursuit of victory, however, was never abandoned.

Then something happened that changed the course of the war. It was the incident to which Curry had clumsily referred and which had drawn such a pained response from the commander.

Korcha's army had been moving downhill from an encampment among the caves to brief occupation of several of the higher towns which the Mommick troops had just evacuated. Whenever possible, Korcha led his fighters back among the villagers and townspeople to be warmed and fed and cared for, so they would be fresh and nimble for the next sudden move. He was personally leading a detachment of troops into one of these towns. The snow on the road was well-packed from the recent withdrawal of Mommick forces, and the midwinter day was clear and cold. As they approached the town, they were met by the usual grisly procession of motionless corpses, stone-gray and frost-rimed, tied to stakes alongside the roadway. The weary Gazine soldiers slackened their pace slightly as they approached. Some of them looked away; some stared straight ahead, as though they had seen nothing; some regarded the row of frozen bodies without reaction.

Korcha Rabon and several aides separated themselves from the sluggishly advancing line of troops and approached the upright dead. Four burners came up from the rear of the column. They knew his custom. In ordinary times, what Korcha did next had been reserved to certain men and women ordained as Servants of the Fire. Now he took to himself this funeral ritual whenever he came upon these reprisal victims. This time, as usual, he walked from the road and stood knee-deep in snow, facing the first, the most recently executed person. He looked into the blackened face, where the only sign of movement was a stiff tag of scarf blowing on the breeze. When he spoke, it was not to the dead person but to the burners: "Burn this woman with holy fire. Let her return to the Greatsada."

He then waded through the snow to the next. His retinue followed. "Burn this man with holy fire. Let him return to the Greatsada." Then on to the next: "Burn this...this child with holy fire. Let him...her...return to the Greatsada."

When he came to the fourth in line, he said nothing for a moment. The troops continued to march past in heavy silence, filing into the town.

Suddenly, Korcha let loose a shriek that cut the winter air like a blade. "Bima!" he screamed. "Bima! Bima!" and he crumpled to his knees before the stake, clutching his face and rocking forward into the snow.

For three days, Korcha Rabon languished in bed in the back room of a comfortable, well-heated house in the town. People hovered about and did all they could to tend him, but he refused food and drink and scarcely spoke. Maincaptain Streeter took over the command, and dispatches were sent out to Ila Rabon and Mira Shannan. The staunch fighters huddled in small groups, bewildered and speaking in worried voices. No one had any idea what this Bima had meant to him. All that was known about her was that she was a very old woman who had been his servant or housekeeper at 'n Burning Graute. There was nothing special about her, and no one could remember Korcha's even mentioning her. She had accompanied Ila's group on The March, riding on the wagons during the return to Gazi. After Kul Sama, she, like so many of the very young and old among the returnees, had slipped back into the interior of Gazi and blended with the settled population.

On the fourth day, Korcha emerged from his sick room, fully dressed in uniform, and asked for something to eat. He was pale as death and swaying as he stood in the doorway, but he angrily brushed away all expressions of concern. He ate, then returned to his room. For the next two days, no one saw him, except the aides and lieutenants, captains and maincaptains, whom he constantly summoned to the small room for conference. Ila and Mira Shannan arrived. They were sequestered in secrecy with Korcha for four hours without interruption. When they emerged, they left immediately for their respective commands in the south and in the north, without a word to anyone.

In the dark, suffocating closeness of the sick-room, Korcha had done battle with the wythies wrapping him, choking the hope and fight out of him, striving to leave him mindless, breathless, and without will. At last, they yielded to his furious resistance and, by a process in no way conscious on his part, agreed to release him and become his allies. In these timeless movements, a new decision was being formed about the war in Gazi. As he regained his strength and clarity of mind, Korcha announced to his senior staff that the "bandit-fighting" phase of their struggle had come to an end. They were to begin to prepare at once for a united, coordinated, sustained offensive against the Mommicks. The Gazines would no long strike and withdraw, no longer dart about from hiding to hiding. They would seize and hold territory. They would draw front lines and push them forward, driving the Mommicks in retreat until these hated invaders were out of their country. Out of Gazi, once and for all!

This little town, high up along the skirts of the great mountains, was to have been a stopover for the weary troops. Instead, it became the first permanent headquarters. In a few days, Korcha moved out of the house where he had lain sick and commandeered a building suitable to be his residence, office, and war room.

It was here that he had met with Curry at night to receive the news that Ogrodni was still alive.

"Why did you not bring Ogrodni with you?" demanded Korcha severely.

"Sir...I tried to. I asked...I *told* him to come back here with me. *Ordered* him to come. He wouldn't, sir, no matter what I said. He's come all this way looking for you, sir; but, now that he's found you, he won't come this last step, sir. He wants to know how you will receive him, sir. He's afraid. But I did bring back Beland, sir. Beland has been with Ogrodni since he showed up at the sick-lager."

"Come *looking* for me, has he?" muttered Korcha sarcastically. "Now that he's found me. Now that he's found me *out!*" he exploded, glaring at Curry. He waited for some response, a word of protest or defense. But Curry sat stiffly with his eyes wide and his pale lips parted. "The enemy," continued Korcha, "will not track me down by finding those sick-lagers. Tell Ogrodni *that*, when you see him. He has found me out too late! In three days, our wounded will be moved out of the caves, down into the hospitable houses of Gazi where they belong. No more running, no more hiding in holes. For *none* of us!"

"You want me to go back to Ogrodni, sir?" asked Curry.

"Yes, I want you to go back to Ogrodni," said Korcha, in a tone suggesting it a foolish question. "But not alone. This is an order: Get a squad of four men from Maincaptain Streeter. Take them back to the sick-lager. When you get there, leave the squad out of sight; and you go forward first, so Ogrodni won't be suspicious. When you have him located and engaged in discussion, in an enclosed area of the lager, signal to the squad to come forward and take him."

Curry nodded, "Yes, sir."

"Now get some sleep. Be on your way by daylight. That is all."

Curry rose to his feet, then uncertainly moved across the room.

"One more thing!" came a sharp command from behind him.

"Sir?" Curry turned at the door.

"Is he branded?"

"No, sir."

Korcha continued to scowl at him, waiting, as though he had been expecting a different answer. He looked at the floor, agitated, pondering, then muttered, "That doesn't mean a thing!"

Curry waited for the word, "dismissed," which never came. He decided he had been forgotten. Silently, he backed from the room and eased the door shut.

....

During the early hours of the morning, Korcha called for Beland. Warm from bed and blinking, he stood before the commander. Korcha sat in the same chair in which Curry had left him, several hours before. He regarded Beland thoughtfully the way one regards a possible purchase, yet his mind was not on Beland or on Ogrodni but on Curry. Korcha had misgivings about this fervent young aide, so recently adopted into the Gazine people. Why was he so eager? Was he really ready to hand over a lifelong friend with a simple "yes, sir"? He gazed at Beland, who stood uneasily, with beads of perspiration beginning to show on his forehead.

Curry. Korcha had been pleased with his service. More so, with his simple devotion to the cause of the Gazine people. Was it simple? Curry now wore the uniform of Gazi, the only non-Gazine to do so. Some around Korcha had been surprised when he had authorized it. Had it been wise? Perhaps too soon. Probably too soon.

He wondered what was behind Curry's readiness to hand over his friend. Some old grudge? Some old hatred unrevealed? Here before him stood someone who might answer that.

"Tell me," he said, slow and friendly, "you have known Ogrodni and Curry a long time, haven't you?"

"Oh yes, sir. Since we were kids. We were all born on neighboring holdings and grew up together."

"And were the three of you good friends? Did you get along well? Or were there problems among you?"

Beland frowned, puzzled at this talk. "We got along mostly, sir. I mean, we had fights like all kids. I've got a bad temper, sir, and maybe I had more fights than most of them. But we always made up. I'd say we were good friends." Korcha waited for more. "Just the three of us you mean, sir?" Korcha nodded gently. "Nome and Curry were real close, I'd say. Nome, especially, was always good to me; but I could never hope to be friends with Nome as good as Curry was. Always wished I could, but I just knew it wasn't that way."

"Well, what about Ogrodni's and Curry's friendship?" Korcha pressed in a detached manner, "Have you ever noticed that something went bad about it? I mean, is there any reason to think that Curry might have a grudge against Ogrodni?"

Beland looked shocked and confused. "You mean...I don't understand...."

"I mean, is there some old hurt, some bitterness, some old hatred that Curry might have against Ogrodni?"

Beland stared in disbelief. "Oh no, sir," he said slowly. "They've been pals ever since they were kids. Where did you ever get that...?"

"That's all right. Never mind, nothing to it," said Korcha briskly. "Dismissed."

Beland stood gaping a moment, then quickly got himself out of the room.

"Greatsada," murmured Korcha when he was alone, "nothing to it." His face relaxed, and he shut his eyes in peace for a moment.

Curry had been successful. He had distanced himself from the suspect Ogrodni, and now was again securely in favor with Korcha Rabon.

Outside the door, Beland leaned heavily against the wall and threw his head back to catch his breath. His heart was pounding. He understood nothing of what had just happened. Then he stumbled forward down the hallway, steadying himself lightly with one hand against the wall. Turning a corner, he heard Curry's voice down the next hallway, off in a room somewhere. He had to talk to Curry, ask him what this was all about. Beland came to a door which was slightly ajar and listened discretely. Curry's voice, no mistake. Then he hesitated and looked to see what door he was about to knock on: *Maincaptain Streeter*. He lowered his hand and did not knock but backed away and leaned against the opposite wall. He decided to wait for Curry to come out.

He could not help hearing that there were several voices in

conversation in the room. Curry. The maincaptain. Others. Then he began to listen, and the blood left his face. It was Curry who was giving the instructions. Curry was telling the soldiers what they were to do when they came near the sick-lager. Beland's eyes fell on the backpack which lay on the floor just inside the door of the room. He could see it through the narrow opening. They were preparing to leave in a very short while, it seemed, and nothing had been said to him about returning to his sick-lager with them!

As he stared at the pack, fear rose higher. There was a familiar bulge on the outer pocket of the pack, with a strip of leather thong peeking from the top pocket. He had seen it just this way on the back of Curry's pack when they had made the trip from the sick-lager to Korcha's headquarters the day before. He had watched Curry stuff Nome's leather packet, the message to Ila, into this pocket before they left. There it was still. Curry had not given it to Korcha.

When Curry came out of the room with the four other men, the hallway was empty. They stood conferring briefly at the doorway. An aide rounded the corner and approached them in a hurry. He asked if they had seen the un-Gazine, Beland, who was in this building just a short while ago. None of them had.

"Korcha has just given orders," the aide said, "to hold this Beland in town and delay his return to the sick-lager for a day. But we're having trouble finding him. If you see him anywhere...." the aide was moving off down the hall at a quick pace..."send him directly to the day-guard. Better yet, take him to the day-guard yourselves!"

"All right," they said...and returned to their final preparations for leaving.

TWENTY-ONE

Mablic Prison

Ravenna Rosealice huddled before the fire at the door of the sick-lager warming her hands around a metal cup of hot kgopuk. Around her shoulders draped a sheepskin blanket, kept near the firepit for the rotating shifts of tenders, burners, and handlers as they came exhausted to their meals. On the log bench beside her sat a young woman with tousled hair and a wistful, emaciated face. She, too, clutched a sheepskin around her bones, shivering. The two women had just eaten supper and were resting for a few minutes before returning to the cave for the evening chore of preparing bandages for the next day.

Ione was years younger than Ravenna, not much more than a girl. She had been a friend from the first day, when she had instructed Ravenna in her duties. They worked together, took breaks together, ate together, and slept side-by-side on cots at the back of the lager. Ravenna confided in this younger sister, and Ione brought her news circulating among the Gazines. She was fascinated with Ravenna's relationship with Nome and referred to him as her "honey." She loved to hear over and over the story of how they had become aware of each other, followed one another, and finally met. Ione was full of questions about the smallest detail, and would have been happy to have Ravenna make up a few more. She thought it wonderful and tragic and unfair and exciting that Ravenna and her honey were so close in this sick-lager, yet kept apart by the rules, the shifts, and the distrustful supervisors.

During the days, Ravenna and Nome saw each other across the open space of the cave as they came and went in their work; but they seldom had opportunity to speak. The captain of the lager was nervous about being responsible for un-Gazine strangers and saw to it that they were separated and watched. (First this man and woman appear at his lager, unannounced, wanting work. Then, it turns out that they know the un-Gazine, Beland, who has been here a while. On top of it, another un-Gazine shows up from Korcha's camp to visit them, this one in uniform!) If Ravenna and Nome came near enough during their work to talk, they were interrupted and told to get back to the job. Occasionally, they had a moment or two together outside the cave where Ravenna dumped dirty water and Nome wrapped the dead in gray sheets.

It was in one of these meetings, immediately after Beland had returned from Korcha's camp, that Nome had taken her by the hand and pulled her off to the side, as far out of sight as possible, and spoken to her in hurried whispers. He had begged Ione, who was also there, to go and stand watch for them near the door of the cave.

Now, hours later, Ravenna and Ione sat together in the last minutes of rest after supper, scarcely saying a word. Ravenna squeezed the cup between her hands and nibbled the lip nervously, as she stared into the dying fire. Ione hunched forward, unusually silent, glancing sorrowfully at her friend from time to time.

Nome was gone. In a few broken sentences, he had told Ravenna what Beland had said about Korcha and Curry and his impending arrest. He said that he planned to wrap himself in one of the gray sheets and lie on a litter among the corpses, because the burners were going to be taking them away in a few moments. The burning was always done far away from the sick-lager, and done slowly with ceremony, so he would have time to get away. She had broken in at that point, saying that she wanted to go with him; but Nome hushed her fiercely and said no. It would be much harder for two of them to run and hide than for one, he insisted. She was not in danger. She should stay where she was. He would come back, he promised, after the squad with Curry had come and gone, after the concern about him had died down. It would be several days, he said, but he would come back for her. She should gather food, provisions, whatever she could filch, and be ready to slip away in the night when he came. Then he was gone.

From her scrubbing position on the floor a short while later, she had seen and heard the excitement and consternation when Curry appeared, and then the squad of soldiers. Beland was summoned and interrogated and scolded and taken outside and brought back in and taken outside again. Finally Beland was left alone to cringe in the rear of the lager, as Curry and the soldiers talked to the captain of the lager and questioned Nome's co-workers. Then they all left, and the lager was quiet again. Ravenna was left with her imaginings of Nome among the dead, Nome slipping away from the litter as the burning was being prepared or jumping up at the last minute, to the horror of the burners.

But cold horror came upon her later that afternoon, long after Curry and the soldiers had gone, when she first heard the news that swept through the lager like a murmur. The burners who had set off that morning with the dead to be burned had been attacked by the enemy.

When they did not return, a tender had been sent out to look for them. She had found the gray-wrapped corpses scattered about, not far from the place of burning, and clear signs in the snow of many footprints and a struggle. There was no blood and no indication of a slaughter. She had followed the trail they left, descending the mountain for a distance, then returned to the sick-lager with the news.

After this, the occupants of the sick-lager lived in fear. The Mommicks had been very close. Why the burners were not killed was a mystery. Perhaps they were captured in order to be tortured for information. Was the location of the sick-lager already compromised? Perhaps the squad was too small for them to attack the lager. Perhaps they would be back in number.

Earlier that morning, Curry had implied to the captain that this lager was going to be moved again soon, although no orders to this effect had arrived yet from Korcha. A move was always a harrowing experience; and it would be worse now, with the number of able people depleted. Six burners were gone, and this un-Gazine, Ogrodni, had run off. Some of the tenders became burners and trudged out into the snow to finish off the business of that morning. Beland, back in his former occupation, was among them. Ravenna and Ione abandoned scrubbing and became tenders.

"We'd better be getting back in there," said Ione.

Ravenna continued to stare into the fire and did not answer.

Ione did not move, allowing her friend a little more grief. Finally, she asked, "You thinking about your honey?"

"Mm-hmm." Ravenna rocked imperceptibly on the bench.

"Of course you are. What else?" Ione pretended great experience. "He got away, Ravenna. I bet he jumped off that litter before the Mommicks ever hit. Or, probably, he just lay there waiting till it was over. Then when all was quiet and he knew they were gone, he gets up and pulls off that sheet and walks away. I bet that's how he did it."

"Thanks, Ione. I've pictured it both those ways. And a dozen other ways, too."

"Well, you just do what your honey said. You just wait here till he comes back for you. And, when he does, you just call on me, and I'll help you, Ravenna. I'll help you any way I can to get away. Though, it'll break my heart! Who am I going to talk to? Who's going to be my friend in this horrible place?"

"You won't be here much longer, Ione," said Ravenna. "You told me they're saying the lager might be moved down into the towns?"

"Yeh. I heard that these ones that came this morning to grab your honey told the captain that Commander Rabon wants to move the lagers to the towns. Can you believe it! Greatsada, I hope it's true!"

"Well...," Ravenna was thoughtful for a moment,"...if Nome is alive..." her voice broke, and she sucked in breath...Ione's little hand came out from under her blanket and groped for Ravenna's arm, "if Nome is alive...that is a prob...a problem, because he will come back here...and...and we won't *be* here."

Both were silent. Ravenna said:

"Let's go back to work. I'll wait here for Nome Ogrodni. If we have to move the lager, I'll decide then what to do."

Ravenna waited for six days. She gathered whatever provisions she could for a journey and stashed them away. The orders came from Korcha Rabon to break up the lager and move the sick and wounded down into the highest towns and villages in the neighborhood. Nome did not come for her.

She also gathered information, most of it through Ione. Whatever Ione did not know, Ravenna sent her to find out. She learned that Mommicks sometimes took prisoners. Where? Ravenna wanted to know. Does anybody know? Probably Mablic Prison, Ione had said. Mablic was attached to the big fortress that guarded the eastern border, the one Mira Shannan had seized, then abandoned, during the Battle of Kul Sama. However, there were other prisons, one attached to an outpost on the southern border, another far in the north. He could be at any one of these, if he were alive. But Mablic Prison is what one heard most about. Do the Gazine fighting forces ever attack these outposts to try to free the Gazine prisoners? Never, said Ione, because the prisoners are weak and unfit for fighting. They are captured to do forced labor. Soldiers are not taken prisoner, she had heard; they are killed. Only tenders and burners are taken prisoners.

This had sent a shudder through Ravenna. Nome was not weak or unfit. The Mommicks would see that. He had, however been among the burners. Even among the corpses, what had they made of that? That could mean he was dead. That could mean he was in Mablic Prison. Or that he had escaped but could not find his way back to the sick-lager among the maze of false trails that had been created to foil detection. It could mean anything. Many possibilities...but, for her, only two choices: she could wait, or she could go to Mablic Prison.

Through Ione, Ravenna gathered detailed information about pathways to the Eastern Fortress. She contrived a map of central Gazi and pinpointed her present location. The day came to move the sick and wounded down the mountainside into secure towns, which now fell behind a new perimeter established by Korcha. Ravenna moved with them; but, when the group to which she was assigned was settled, she kept going...out of the town, beyond the secure lines, farther down the mountainside. In the hubbub, she was not missed for several hours. No one knew what had become of her, no one but Ione, who did her work and said nothing.

....

One problem Ravenna had, as she worked her way from farmstead to village, traveling as she and Nome and Wasoo had before, was that she was no longer branded. Upon their arrival at the sick-lager, she and Nome had peeled the misk brands from their cheeks. Now she had no misk to make a new one and dared not go about unbranded in the open where the Mommicks roamed.

At first, she traveled by night and slept in haylofts during the day. At one place, she risked approaching a farmwife, who took her into the house for the night, fed her well, and helped her devise a new false brand of sawdust and glue. The result was not as convincing as Wasoo's misk brand; but, from any distance, Ravenna appeared, once more, to be a subject of Moma; and she continued her journey.

It took her five days to reach the Mommick garrison to which Mablic Prison was attached. It was near the edge of The Plains of Wildness, a half-day walk north of Kul Sama. The imposing fortress with high towers was situated far from the mountains, on open grassland, giving the guards on the battlements clear view in every direction. Ravenna had to study it from a distance. She could make out a scattering of smaller buildings around its base and surmised that one of them must be Mablic Prison...unless the prison was within the fort itself.

She could not see how she would approach this complex for a closer look; and she glanced around at the failing light, knowing she would soon need shelter for the night. It was beginning to snow heavily, and the building was blurring into an uncertain patch of blue against the milky landscape. She would see Mablic Prison no more closely this day. Time to turn back to find shelter and a place where she could build a fire.

Unless...unless she used the cover of darkness...and the falling snow...to approach. Without a moment's hesitation, she began moving down the road which led to the garrison. Whenever she drew near enough to see it clearly, she stopped and waited for the light to fail a bit more. Before long, the snow was falling in slow, thick flakes, and evening was about her, gray-black. Fortunately, the sky was a warm blanket of overcast, for she would be sleeping out in the snow that night.

Ravenna left the road and waded through the snow until she came up to the fence that hemmed the smaller buildings at the rear. She was careful about her tracks and, every two steps, turned to brush the snow smooth with her mittens. Now she could see that the fence enclosed a large yard. The buildings there were black hulks in the darkness, studded with a few dots of yellow light from windows. Above them floated the shadow of the fortress, like a great ship on water. Ravenna dug a hollow for her body, close to the fence, and carefully banked snow up along the side facing the yard. Thanking the Good Mother for the constantly falling snow, she burrowed into the hollow, pulled her sheepskin clothing tight, and slept.

She awoke to the muffled sound of voices. She lay still, eyes wide open, seeing only diffuse, white daylight. She and her little dugout were covered with a blanket of snow. The voices were speaking a language she did not understand. They came and went from the direction of the fence. Slowly, she rolled over and eased to a sitting position, careful not to raise her head enough to be able to view the towers of the fortress.

Cautiously, she scooped a slit in the dike of snow which she had built between herself and the buildings the previous evening. She piled snow atop her head for camouflage, then edged up a bit to look out.

She was no more than ten paces from the fence, and it gave her a start to see that she had camped so close. It was high and sturdy, woven of long iron rods. Scanning the area, she could see that whoever had been speaking had gone away; and the yard enclosed by the fence was now empty. Only a few tracks in the fresh snow laced from one point to another. All the outbuildings here at the rear of the fortress were wood-frame and small, except for one which was much larger and built of dark blue stone. There was heavy grill-work on its windows, and the fence of the yard converged on its only door.

Ravenna knew that she was looking at Mablic Prison. The Eastern Fortress, built of sand-colored block, stood three stories tall. It threw morning shadow over the prison yard. Along its top, she could see silhouettes of people moving. She hugged the wall of her snow cave more closely to stay out of view from the battlements and towers.

Now there was nothing for her to do but wait and watch, hoping that her hideout blended into the whiteness of the surrounding field. From time to time, she saw a few guarded prisoners led out into the yard for brief periods, watched them moving among the sheds and lower buildings, but saw no familiar form.

Shortly after noon the single door opened, and dozens of men filed slowly into the yard. She was surprised at the number of them...perhaps a hundred or so. They appeared weary, ragged, and dirty. They milled about the yard aimlessly or stood in small groups talking in low tones. Guards, armed only with long sticks, circulated among them, watching closely and listening to conversations.

Feeling a surge of panic, she leaned forward, her cheeks pressing against the snowbank, her eyes darting here and there, searching for the one figure, the tallness, the characteristic stance. It was hard to make out faces, but she was sure she would know him, even if she could not see his face. Moments passed, and she could not find him; but she strained her eyes and began the sweep of the yard again. A whistle blast cut it short. The men shambled back toward the open door where the fences converged. They were swallowed, and the yard was silent.

A short time later, the door opened again; and again Ravenna was at her post. But only women came into the yard, defeated and tattered as the men before them. There were fewer women, thirty or forty. They, too, were whistled back after a short time in the open air. That was all for the day.

Ravenna had not been certain that Nome had not been there. She could not give up yet. Besides, there was nowhere else to go. She spent another night huddled in the snowbank. She ate food from her pack, melted snow to drink between her hands, relieved herself in the far corner of the dugout when it became dark enough for her to move freely. In the darkness, she stood and stretched and stamped her feet and shuffled back and forth, the two paces available. Then she curled up, lay awake thinking a long while, and finally slept.

The next day was the same. Shortly after noon, the herd of men were let out into the yard for a short while, then recalled. After them the women. The door shut behind them, and Ravenna had not seen Nome. Perhaps he was there, standing in one of those groups or reclining on the packed snow. She could not see some of them clearly. But despair was taking her. She would watch one more day. Mercifully, the weather was staying mild. She could not stay here, once the weather turned bitter.

That afternoon, waiting for night, waiting for sleep, eager for the passing of this day, Ravenna sat slumped against the wall of snow, now packed icey-hard. She was listlessly talking and humming to the Good Mother and vaguely musing on how frustrating it was to spend so much of her relationship with Nome Ogrodni watching from a distance. She wanted to be with him. Just be with him. Oh, Mother, how she wanted to be with him now! She heard the door across the yard open again. This hadn't happened yesterday. She rolled forward to her knees and pressed her face against the watching place. A Mommick guard was coming out of the doorway. He was giving orders; it was in her language...this must be a dane, not one of the fohtars from Moma. He was saying to be careful, be careful, don't slop any of that. Two prisoners followed slowly, bent over and shuffling, as they carried a deep container by handles between them. They were struggling and moving with great care, trying to keep some liquid from spilling. Across the yard they waddled with their burden, the guard continuing to nag.

Suddenly, Ravenna's heart lept. But she did not trust her thoughts. She pressed forward, and her rapid breath was melting the ice crystals in the snow before her face. The guard and the two men had reached the fence on the far side, away from the door. The container was tipped forward against the fence and a black, lumpy liquid ran out through the fence iron onto the snow beyond. The three of them were far off, at an angle of the yard from where Ravenna watched, silhouettes against the white. One of the prisoners then straightened up and slowly brushed the back of his arm up over his forehead and across his hair.

"Nome!" she breathed.

....

She watched one more day and saw him one more time. Clearly, she saw his face. At one point, it almost seemed that he had looked at her. Could he feel her watching? But now came the time she had not thought about. She had found Nome Ogrodni but could do nothing for him. She could see no way of getting to him. Even if she went in to be with him, she had seen how the women and the men were kept apart. What could she do but wait here and watch? For the first time, she broke down and wept and wept.

That night, as she sat leaning against the hard-packed wall, she knew what she had to do. She and Nome had promised Wasoo that they would meet him or leave a message for him at Kul Sama forty-five days after they had parted. Tomorrow would be forty-seven days since they had last seen Wasoo. She would leave Nome here and go to Kul Sama to meet Wasoo or wait for him. She could no longer do this alone; her loneliness was too great. It seemed unlikely that Wasoo would be there, the journey so long, the dangers so many.

"Good Mother!" she whispered into the night, "let Wasoo be there!"

Before dawn, Ravenna Rosealice left her hiding place and dragged herself through the deep snow back to the road. She would not have been able to keep her post much longer, in any case. The clouds were drifting away into wisps across the sky, and the morning stars were twinkling. The weather was turning colder. Stiff, hungry, and frozen, she set out for Kul Sama. A bleached sun rose on her left, and then she saw them on the right-hand side of the road. Two short, statuesque figures that watched her approach; then, with a flutter, turned and waggled forward, leading the way.

TWENTY-TWO

Welcome the Dane Recruits

Ravenna Rosealice found lodging in Kul Sama with two old sisters who had been left to run the farm as best they could. The younger members of their family had gone off to join Korcha's army. The sisters moved about their yard slowly and patiently all day, in and out of the sheds, bundled in thick sheep wool against the cold, working, working, from morning till night. Morning started hours before dawn, and they worked for the first quarter of their day in darkness. They stopped often for short and skimpy meals: kgopuk, toast, perhaps a sweet roll or some cooked carrots. They both wore broad kerchiefs around their expressionless faces, tied tight under their chins; and they were never seen without them. Probably they slept in their kerchiefs. They moved with the even, heavy pace of sad-eyed horses and accomplished a great deal; but the farm was too much for them. It was falling into disrepair.

When Ravenna had arrived at Kul Sama about noon, chilled to the heart from her long watch in the snow, she had asked about for a place of lodging where she might work for her keep. She had been referred to the old sisters. They took her into their kitchen and set before her a mug of kgopuk and a plate of cake, threw sticks of wood into the crackling stove, then sat and listened to her story with large, round eyes. They reminded her of the owlstones which she had seen that very morning.

What impressed the sisters most was Ravenna's inquiry about her father's relatives. No, they had not known her father, nor his family, they had said; but then, of course, he had been from the capital, and they themselves were rough frontier folk. In their minds, however, Ravenna was Gazine; and this counted much. Devout believers that the Holy Fire would one day be restored, they had already given away their family to the cause of the Gazine struggle; and now they were ready to receive this wandering daughter of Gazi into their home. Besides, they needed help with the chores.

Ravenna was ready to begin work at once, but the first thing the old women did was put her to bed. They saw that she was chilled and feverish. While she slept, they prepared hot water for her bath and cooked a meal. They themselves were cheered by the work. It was like a holiday to spend the whole day in the house, creating warm baking smells, spicy, liquid, roasting smells, buttery aromas of honey-glaze. They knew that what this woman needed, more than anything else, was to wash clean, to sprinkle on rosewater, to pull over her head a crinkly dress that smelled of sunshine, and to sit down to a table where the place-setting was beautiful.

Next day, Ravenna set to work alongside the sisters; and she kept their schedule of long hours with meager bites of rest and food. The three of them were happy together. Ravenna went about with a tool kit and did many of the repairs that had been neglected for a long time. She learned about farm life and the care of animals. One day, in the middle of the morning, the sisters stopped work and took Ravenna out to see the site of The Battle of Kul Sama. There was nothing to see, under the blanket of snow, but the knoll which had hidden the armies, and the open fields stretching out toward The Plains of Wildness. The sisters, however, showed it proudly, commenting every now and then in their monotone voices.

Ravenna's life with them would have been peaceful, were it not for her constant anxiety about Nome and her nervous waiting for Wasoo. She frequently interrupted her tasks to go to the the end of the farmyard and scan the flattened horizon in the direction of The Plains. The sisters told her not to worry, that there were very few people coming this way off The Plains of Wildness these days; and those who did always came in groups. The whole village of Kul Sama would know, long in advance, if any group was approaching from that direction. In fact, they said, the only people coming to Kul Sama across The Plains of Wildness would be dane recruits. The danes were mercenaries from the eastern lands hired by the Mommicks to help put down the Gazine rebellion. No one else would be crossing that desert of wild spirits to come to Gazi in these sad times. The sisters had little faith that this Wasoo, of whom Ravenna spoke, would arrive.

She continued to go to the end of the yard several times a day. Wasoo was overdue. The sisters told her not to bother. When groups came to Kul Sama off The Plains, which they hardly did anymore, they always went to the lodging house to wash and rest and eat well. A call would be sent throughout the village to come and help wait on the guests. This was the regular practice, now that the lodging house was so seldom used and kept no staff. The call would come to this farm, too, for Ravenna's help would be needed. All the village knew she was there.

She had been with the sisters for a week when the call came. A group of haggard, half-starved dane recruits for the Mommick army was approaching Kul Sama from the direction of the desert. Forty or fifty of them, it was said. All able women in the village were needed at once at the lodging house to cook and serve and carry. No one dare refuse, or the Mommicks would be told of it.

Ravenna hurried to the lodging house with more eagerness than was seemly in a daughter of Gazi. She arrived moments after the travelers had poured through the gate into the courtyard. The scene was a turmoil of weary activity. The guests were all men, short-tempered and dirty. They would have been dangerous, had they not been so worn out. They were dressed for the heat and dust of the desert, not for winter. They dropped their gear in the courtyard and pushed into the sitting and dining rooms, where they flopped down and roared for food. Ravenna scurried about, searching for the face of Wasoo, but did not see him.

Suddenly her arm was seized by a stout woman with a fierce scowl who thrust a large pail into her hands and pointed to the water pump in the courtyard. She stumbled over to the pump, looking frantically at the faces of stragglers limping through the gate. Three women waited their turn in line at the pump. Ravenna took her place behind them, turning and turning about, trying to catch a glimpse of each face. She was tempted to call out "Wasoo!" but was kept from doing so by the angry activity of the place. Black smoke from new fires was rolling from the kitchen chimneys. Women and young girls hurried past, carrying food or blankets or utensils. Throughout the courtyard, and coming from the building, was a babble of shouts and questions and commands. She stopped her turning about, as the last of the recruits stomped along the wooden porch and slammed the door.

She stood there looking absently at the door. One of the women tugged a full pail away from the pump and the line moved. A dog was sniffing about her. She glanced at it, then held her pail in front of her with both hands and waited. The pump handle screeched up and down, as a woman ahead furiously leaned back and shoulders onto it. Water hammered against the inside of a pail. The dog was sniffing her legs intently. Ravenna was about to push it away with her pail; when, suddenly, it let out a yip and began to wiggle and wag its whole body, dancing back and forth and barking little high-pitched yelps. She looked at the dog with astonishment and took a step backward, but the dog reared up on hind legs and pawed at the front of her skirt. The girl in the line ahead of Ravenna glanced back; but it was her turn at the pump, and she bent forward with her pail to the water. Ravenna backed around in a circle, trying to avoid the dog, but it continued to prance and yelp and shimmy around her. Suddenly, from somewhere, there was a sharp whistle and shout. The dog hesitated, began to return to Ravenna, then turned and ran off around the end of a high fence that edged a wooden gateway at one side of the courtyard.

Ravenna stared after it, but whirled around as she heard at her ear: "Hey, you're next!" She held the pail beneath the gushing spout, then swung it away and lurched toward the porch. Resting there a moment, she set the pail down; but her eyes were on the small gateway where the dog had gone. An arm poked around the gatepost and made a beckoning motion. As though in a trance, she left the pail of water and began to move slowly toward the gate. Women came and went in a hurry, and no one stopped her.

She passed through; and there, squatting on the ground, restraining the dog, was Wasoo. His face was sunburned and dirty, but he was grinning up at her like a slice of melon. He quickly shot a foot out and kicked the gate shut behind her, then leaped up into her outstretched arms, saying "Shhh! Shhh!" as she began to cry out "Wa--!" They hugged tight and waltzed in a circle as the dog clambered up against their sides and began to yelp again. Wasoo quickly broke from the embrace to shush the dog.

"Wasoo!" whispered Ravenna deliriously, "Oh, Wasoo! Good Mother, thank you! Wasoo, why the secrecy? Why are we whispering?"

"Shhh! I am a dane recruit now," he winked. "You don't fit into the story I have been telling them. I can't be seen with you. Come on...." he jerked her by the hand away from the gate, pausing to look this way and that before they rounded any corner.

They hurried behind some outbuildings near the lodging house.

"That is to say, I *was* a dane recruit. I think I'll be a deserter next. Where's Nome? How are things going? *You* look good!"

"Oh, Wasoo! Wait!" she said urgently, putting her hand over his mouth to still the torrent of talk she knew would be pouring from him. "Don't desert yet! Not yet. We have to talk. There is so much I have to tell you...!"

....

(*Bang! Bang! Bang!*)

"Wait a m'nit! Wait a m'nit! *Ashtok!*"

(*Bang! Bang! Bang!*)

"Ashtok! Hold on, m' coming!...."

(*Bang! Bang! Bang!*)

"...There."

"Bah! Moma-bedamned! Brrrr! You're sleepin'? What?"

"Nah! Bedamned-yourself. What's th' hurry?"

"Hurry? Ashtok! 's cold out there!"

" Cold here, too. Cold everywhere."

"Ahrrrr! Stinkhole! Cursed vermin*!*"

"What you come for?"

"Come for? Vermin! You got *vermin* here, don't you? Come for one of 'em."

"What? Which one?"

"You got a smoke? I wanna smoke. Got a smoke?"

"No!...just a little bit. I don't have a lot left."

"Good. Need a smoke, cold everywhere!"

"No, wait...you're taking too much! I don't have a lot left."

"Good. That's good."

"Ashtok! you took a *lot*. Who you come for?",

"Never mind. No hurry. Le'me sit my sacks here for a bit. Ahhh.... Good."

Nome stirred in the cell and laid his head gently against the steel grating. The warm body of the man next to him also stirred and lay against him more heavily. Nome turned and looked into the gloom of the hallway, but his eyelids were heavy and wanted sleep. Tonight it was his turn to be against the bars with his left side exposed to the cold, while his mates dozed, tucked into one another like birds in a nest. He wondered if he had slept or not. The rough voices had awakened him. Or perhaps he had been awake.

"Got anything to eat?"

"Mucksucker! you come here to clean me out? No, I ain't got nothing to eat! I would have ate it if I had, what you think? You got lot's of leftovers lyin' around in your section?"

"Hah. Ate good two nights ago, though."

"Mmm. Eat cow muck here. Not much better than the prisoners."

"*We* ate good two nights ago."

"What'd y' have?"

"Good slop. Curried Beland."

"Never heard of it. Good, hey? What's in it?"

"Leeks, lentils, onions, rutabaga, curry powder. I don't know. I never said I cooked the muck, I said I ate it. Good."

Nome's eyes were wide open and glistening. He held his breath.

"I hate leeks."

"What do I care. Got any more smoke?"

"No! No more smoke!"

"Ashtok, you leek-eater. Well...let's have a look at your vermin you keep here."

"Wait, I ain't turning over no prisoners to you. Who says so? You ain't no fohtar."

"No, I ain't. But you want to know who says so? Marshall Rena and Drogofohtar Baron O say so! So, don't get in my way!"

"I never heard of this!"

"You did, too. Just now. I got orders from the Drogofohtar himself. You want me to go back up there and say you says 'no'?"

"Up where? Where you going with this prisoner? You ain't said which one you were taking yet."

"Up *where*? Up inland, of course. Up to I.C.S. You heard me say I got orders from the Drogofohtar, didn't you? Well, I got *orders!* One prisoner from here. From your block. The best one you got, I'm to pick. There's a new bunch of greasy dane recruits just come in, and I'm taking 'em up inland. You heard *that*, didn't you? Them and one of your vermin here. I'm to pick which one."

"Well...you didn't report in...I'm not sure...and what if my prisoner escapes? You'd lie, you mucksucker, and swear I'd never turned 'im over to you...."

"Escape? *Escape?* One of these worn-out weasels you keep in these cages escape from me? By Sula, I'll chindit his tosar if he even *thinks* of running from me!"

(Nome in his cell murmured under his breath, "Wasoo, you oaf! You'll go too far!")

"But you didn't report...."

"Ashtok! Moma-bedamned! All right, you're one of those! Just like they taught you in training. All right, if you insist: Dane Khirbleth Wasoo reporting *sir!* Beg permission, *sir!* to remove prisoner of my choosing, *sir!* at the direct orders of Drogofohtar Baron O, *sir!* for purpose of transfer to Inland Central Stronghold, *sir!* How's that? That hold you? Now show me where you keep your vermin!"

TWENTY-THREE

Snowstorms

"Well, here we are again," said Ravenna. "Seems like we spend a lot of time living in barns."

"Is this a barn?" asked Nome, slipping his arm around her shoulder and pressing her to himself. "After being in Mablic Prison for...what was it?..nearly a month, this is a palace."

"Well, this *is* one of the better barns we've slept in, my friend," said Wasoo. "The place has a good smell about it. A good *strong* smell. Now, jails...I've spent a lot of time living in them, too, just like you, my friend. They have a strong smell, too, wouldn't you agree, a bad strong smell? We met in one of them, if I remember it right. What I always liked about the jails was that they let you sleep most of the day and only disturb you to bring your meals. A wonderful public service. And some times the meals weren't half bad. Like at that place where we met...what was it called?...the food there was actually not so bad. That's the only thing lacking till now in these barns. The cows and chickens and sheep are always brought their food, but in most barns no one brings ours. Until now. Until now! This is the greatest barn I have ever stayed in, much better than the jails! Roomier, too. Better company. And look how they bring us our food!"

Wasoo, Ravenna, and Nome sat in the loft on sweet-smelling hay. Between them were empty porcelain plates and cups and greasy silverware from their meal just finished. This barn belonged to the two sisters at Kul Sama. Ravenna had continued to live and work openly with the old women, but Nome and Wasoo, who had arrived a week later in the dead of night, had to remain hidden during daylight. It would not do for any of the villagers to know they were there, for the Mommicks controlled this area. The sisters, however, were happy to house these refugees. Ravenna brought food to the men and usually ate with them. Nome and Wasoo slept during the day and rose after dark to begin the farm chores. When the women got up in the early morning dark to begin their workday, the men had already been cleaning stalls and mending broken places for several hours. Together, the five of them worked side-by-side until daylight, when it was no longer wise for the men to be about. At first, Nome had been too weak to be of much help, but he regained strength quickly on a diet of good food and love.

When Ravenna had found Wasoo with Chindit at the lodging house, she quickly told him that Nome was in prison nearby; but there was not enough time to make a plan. Ravenna had returned to the work of serving the dane recruits, and Wasoo had rejoined them in the dining area. The recruits were to stay there for two days of rest before moving on to the Eastern Fortress, to which Mablic Prison was attached. During that time, Ravenna and Wasoo were able to slip away several times to meet in some hidden corner for short periods. Wasoo had been observed in this by his companions, and they leered and laughed at his trysts with the serving woman. At one point, he nearly had to fight another recruit who wanted to join him. When the contingent finally re-grouped and shambled out the doors to complete the last leg of their journey, Wasoo was with them. Chindit remained behind, lying quietly by the outbuildings in back. Ravenna joined the other women in cleaning up the disorder at the lodging house.

Wasoo had then remained in drill and training at the Eastern Fortress for six days, watching for an opportunity. By this time, he had learned in which block Nome was being held and how he could gain access to the prison from within the compound. When orders were given that the newly trained danes were to march to the Inland Central Stronghold, where the old capital of Mhaveen had once stood, he went to the prison in the early hours of the morning and fetched Nome. Ostentatiously holding him under guard, he marched him through the halls of the fortress to an area near the front gate, where sleepy soldiers were gathering in the chilly gloom. Only twice was he questioned about his prisoner, but both times it was by fellow soldiers. He managed to steer Nome away from officers. Minutes before the squadron was ordered into rank, he and Nome edged their way into the shadows of the early morning and moved off down the road to Kul Sama. The squadron of danes formed and turned westward, moving inland. It was the last they saw of the Mommicks.

When they arrived at the farm of the two sisters that night, the joy of meeting was beyond all speaking. Chindit yipped and yodeled and gamboled around the single figure of Nome and Ravenna wrapped in each others' arms, as they cried and kissed each other on the cheeks, on the mouths, on the eyes. Then Wasoo was drawn into the embrace; and Chindit sprang up against their sides; and they began to totter and move in a stumbling shuffle; and, finally, the two stiff sisters were pulled into the dancing group, laughing and looking about bewildered.

That first night, they all stayed in the farmhouse. Eating a late supper by low candlelight, they told their stories far into the night. Nome was particularly eager for news from Brighthome.

"Your father and mother are well," said Wasoo. "Not as rich as they were when you left home, but eating every day and apparently content. Except for their anxiety about you. I was treated like Nome Ogrodni himself while I was there. I almost didn't come back, they treated me so good. But your mother, Nome, insisted I take her dog and go find you...so I *had* to leave."

"Yes, I know about her insisting," laughed Nome.

"A beautiful woman she is. Beautiful," said Wasoo. "And your father. A fine, good man if ever I saw one. With his white hair blowing all over the place like a blizzard in Gazi. I didn't get down to see your little house in the woods, Nome, because they have secretly rented it out to a young fellow from somewhere nearby. I forget his name...sorry."

"Rented it out?"

"Mm-hmm. Had to. The farm not producing at this season and them not allowed to slaughter or sell livestock or sell or trade farm equipment. About all that's allowed them is milk and eggs from the cows and goats and chickens. Can't use up anything the Tosars claim are assets."

"I know, I know. But is that all they are living on?"

"That and the rent. And some secret barter. There was food in the cupboard, don't worry. Oh, they're not poor. No one with a place like Brighthome is poor. But, you know, they have no income other than what you have sent home. And most of that has gone to the Tosars. Your father took it right up to them the day after I got there."

"But, are they...?

"I don't know if they have money...they didn't tell me that. Now, don't get so worried. They are doing all right, I tell you. Better than *you* have been doing by a bow-shot, I should say. No, if you could see the way they fed me, you wouldn't worry about them not having enough. They are talking about letting the fields lie fallow next summer, since they are not allowed to sell produce. Unless they can find a way to rent them out, but they don't think the Tosars will allow it. You know...," Wasoo reached out to scratch dozing Chindit behind the ear, "...I didn't think they were much worried about their future. They were mostly fretting about Curry House and Beland's Farm."

"What about them?"

"They're going forfeit, Nome. What you sent back was enough for the hundred-day on Brighthome, but not much left for the other two. Your Mo and Fa wanted to put the balance of what was left on their payment on those holdings and hoped that the neighbors could raise enough to give Curry House and Beland's Farm another hundred days. But that was just wishful. There was *no* way your folks and the neighbors could raise enough to save them. The neighbors had to talk hard to convince Baron and Rena to hang onto the extra from what you and Ravenna sent. They do need it."

Nome looked down into the hay and pressed his lips together. He said nothing. Ravenna slid her hand over and groped for his fingers.

"What did they do?" Nome asked quietly without looking up. "Curry's mother. And Beland's family."

"I don't know. They were talking about it and trying to work out plans and arrangements, but nothing had been decided before I had to start back. I'm sure they'll be taken care of."

Nome tilted his head back and breathed deep. He nodded. "Right," he said. After a moment: "This paying ransom on the holdings can't go on too much longer. We knew that from the start. It's only a matter of time. Beland and Curry didn't send money back...how could they? Even though they are still with Korcha. I don't know...." He did not finish. Then he brought his head down and looked directly into his friend's eyes: "And *you*, Wasoo. I thank you once again. From the bottom of my heart."

Wasoo waved his hand, "It's all right. T'was worth it. Now, one other thing, all the holdings south of Brighthome are vacant. There is some coming and going on them...all Tosarmen...no one knows why. Brighthome and Curry House and Beland's Farm are the only three left along the Sula River all the way to Tamrasset Lake. Probably, by now, it is only Brighthome. No one knows what the Tosars are up to, but they are closing in on your place, that is certain."

Wasoo was uncharacteristically silent for a long moment. Then he said, "Speaking of 'closing in'...Ravenna, I have a bit of news for you...that you won't like. I have been keeping it to myself until the three of us had enough time to talk like this. Druska Paba is in Gazi."

"What?" she cried. "No!"

"Yes. She is here."

"Wasoo! You're joking. Don't *joke* about this!"

"I'd like to say that I never joke about serious things, Ravenna," he replied evenly, "but you know me too well for that. All I can tell you is that, this time, I am not joking. She is here, not far away."

"Then you're mistaken! What makes you think she is here?"

"I saw her with my own eyes."

Ravenna sat stiff upright on the hay staring at Wasoo with a hurt air of incomprehension. She turned and searched Nome's face. He returned her look mournfully and slowly nodded. Obviously, Wasoo had confided in him earlier, and the two had waited till the right moment to tell her. She tried to form a word of protest, but no sound came from her moving lips.

"I saw her in the Mommick fortress," continued Wasoo quietly. "Not once, but three times."

"No," whispered Ravenna, pleading for him to change what he was saying. "You must be mistaken. It was someone else."

"It was she," he insisted.

"How do you know it was?" Ravenna now sounded angry. "You're not joking with me now, are you? Because, if you are...! How do you know it was Druska Paba? You don't know her! You've only heard me describe...."

"You're forgetting," Wasoo interrupted forcefully, "that I told you I know her well! Better than you, actually. Remember that I told you that I had often been in the House of Ghan, in various disguises? I've told you what I thought of that treacherous hag. It was she, Ravenna. I didn't want to believe what I was seeing in the Eastern Fortress, but it was she."

Ravenna put her face in her hands and stayed motionless for a few moments. They all were silent.

"Perhaps," said Nome eventually, "if it is she, it has nothing to do with you, Ravenna."

"It does," her voice came muffled, between her fingers. "It does. I don't know how or why...but it does."

"But she can't hurt you," he urged. "What can she do to you here? An old woman who hobbles about on a stick, not able to stand up straight? She can't drag you back to Mintor Ghan herself. And why would she want to? It's obvious you won't go to him, and would not stay if you were forced."

"What you don't understand, Nome," said Wasoo, "is that Mintor Ghan considers Ravenna his woman. Already. Because he decided, and because he sent for her. She is his starwoman, who has run away. I know that, because I have observed what kind of man he is. And Ravenna knows this, too, even though she has never laid eyes on him. As for Druska Paba...I can only guess that her position in the House of Ghan is in jeopardy because of this runaway starwoman. I can only guess that Druska Paba is ruined unless she brings Ravenna back. The woman is mad, Nome, but not pitiful. Without this starwoman, she is the oily hag she appears to be. With her, she herself *is* the House of Ghan."

"She is with the wythies," Ravenna added, lifting up her head from her hands, "and the wythies are with her. That is why she is with the Mommicks. And I doubt if she is alone. I don't think she is harmless."

"What do you want to do about her?" Nome asked.

"*Do* about her?" She seemed annoyed by the question. "What *can* I do, but what I *have* been doing. Get away. Get *away* from her!"

"There's nothing more for us here in Gazi," Nome said solemnly. "There never has been. We have been chasing dreams. Smoke, rainbows. You have asked everywhere, Ravenna, if anyone remembers your father's family. No one has...no one but that couple near Burbaki. No other information. Gone up in the smoke of Mhaveen, most likely, they said. And I came to find Korcha Rabon. I found him, and now I am running from 'the dangerous man,' just as you are running from Druska Paba. And all three of us are running from the Mommicks. Wasoo! What are *you* doing here? You're with us, that's all! You've no business here."

Wasoo looked away from Nome briefly at these words, but Nome did not notice. He continued:

"What are any of us doing in...in *Gazi*? He looked from one to the other as though awaiting an answer. Chindit, with muzzle on paws, opened his eyes, sensitive to the change of tone. Like a conspirator, Nome whispered: "Let's leave."

Still, neither of them spoke. They both seemed lost in thought. Finally, Ravenna shifted her weight on the hay and cleared her throat.

"I've had these same thoughts for quite a while. Even before what Wasoo just said about Druska Paba." She paused for a long moment. It seemed she had said all she wanted to, but then she went on. "There *is* nothing here for us but hunger and prison and probably death. Or, for me, abduction. But, Nome, how? How do we leave? We are boxed in. Mountains to the west. Mommicks to the north. To the south, thick, trackless lands with no population. And to the east...The Plains of Wildness. Where do we go?"

They talked this over for a long while. Wasoo was strangely silent. Finally, Ravenna said:

"We can't stay in Gazi any longer. And, although it seems as though we can't get out either, we did get in, didn't we? We will have to go out the way we came in."

"Plains of Wildness," said Nome in a flat voice.

She nodded.

"Wythies, powers, voices, heat, wind, hunger, dust."

She nodded, then added, "But this time from Kul Sama. Back across the way you came, Wasoo."

At that, he came alive. "I wouldn't recommend it! Not out here from Kul Sama across those Plains. Not the three of us. *Four* of us, excuse me, Chindit."

"Why not?" the two of them spoke together.

"It was far weirder, far more dangerous than the way the three of us used down south to come into Gazi. I would not go back over *this* way again. There were forty-seven of us crossing, and that was some protection; but the kind of people who have been crossing The Plains at this point seems to have drawn in all sorts of rasping wythies and dark spirits. It has become a road for war, my friends. Not for three innocents like us. Four innocents...sorry, Chindit.

"Then there is no way out for us?' asked Nome.

"Not this way," answered Wasoo with certainty.

"Then we go back south to go out by the way we came in," said Ravenna.

"Back to the fealards," said Nome. "It probably would be better in any case. The fealards are still far from the battlefront that Korcha is forming now. Let's hope that our old hosts will take us back for a few days while we get rest and food and equipment to prepare for the crossing. And we left the tent-dresses your Aunt Aunie made there in the fealard. Maybe they still have them. That would be very important for a safe crossing."

"But where would it be taking us?" Ravenna pointed out. "We would come off The Plains at the edge of The Fields of Khorvan. Doing Druska Paba's work for her. Her being here in Gazi is a clear sign that it is not safe for me to return to The Fields."

"No," said Nome, "we wouldn't go there. We would come off The Plains at the edge of The Fields of Khorvan, of course, but turn sharp north and hike a couple of days to the High Road to the West. Then we follow it back home to Tosarkun. The same way Wasoo went. I make the next payment on Brighthome in person. I'm ready to go home. Over-ready. And I want you, my friends, to come with me!"

"Sounds right to me," said Ravenna. "Only, if we are on the edge of The Fields, I would be slipping in by night to see my mother and my Aunie again. I couldn't go by without seeing them. I want to go home, too, but I know I can't stay there."

"You would risk it?"

"I would risk it. I'm getting excited!"

"Wasoo? You're not saying anything. What about you?"

"Oh...," he hesitated. "I'm just thinking. Sure.... Let's go down to the fealards. Sounds like a good plan."

....

The next evening after sundown, the three companions said goodbye to the two old sisters, received their blessing, and, with the dog, slipped away from Kul Sama into the oncoming night. They traveled south for two nights and a day, keeping to back-roads, where possible, and at length came to the first of many settlements where the houses and barns were drawn together into concentric circles. On they went, another day, until they came to the last of these fealards, where Ravenna and Nome had first met. They went directly to the farmhouse where the three of them had lived those first weeks.

Nome knocked at the door. There was a long wait. Another knocking. Some shuffling from within, then the door was opened by Uncle. "The fire burns!" said Nome with a broad smile, peeling away the made-of-misk brand from his cheek.

"Ho, ho!" roared Uncle, supporting his broken body with a firm grip on the door frame. He swooped out and snatched Nome into a one-armed embrace.

The rest of the family welcomed them also, and neighbors greeted them warmly and stopped to talk when they met on the roads the next day. Gone was the constant tension and abiding dread which had forced them to depart months earlier. The campaign of Mommick reprisals had never reached into this remote corner of Gazi. Ravenna, Nome, and Wasoo were eagerly welcomed as bringers of news of the struggle. In the evenings, with kgopuk by the fire, they had the storytellers' chairs of honor, which Uncle yielded to them.

They had roamed freely through Gazi. They had been as far as Burbaki, home of the Rabon family and the place where the resistance was born. They had been in the sick-lagers. Talked with people who were in communication with Korcha himself. Nome had spent a month in Mablic Prison and had escaped (Oh, tell that one again!). They were in awe of Wasoo, inventor of the removable Mommick brand, who had entered the bowels of the Mommick fortress and seized his friend from the hands of the enemy. They had been in Kul Sama, seen the battlefield.

The three of them were the first to bring detailed information on how the Gazine struggle had moved into a new phase, a final phase, with drawn battle lines and concerted holding of territory. The people of the fealards kept asking, "Are we now in Free Gazi?" Their guests could not answer truly, for they did not know enough about what areas Korcha, Ila, and Mira Shannan held; but they assured them that the Mommicks were being held at bay, far to the north.

The tent-dresses were brought out. Food and equipment was gathered for the crossing. Their hosts urged them to be in no hurry to leave; and the three travelers, feeling safe and welcome, were glad to prolong the days before they faced more impersonal enemies on the searing desert. The countryside was enjoying a thaw; and it seemed that winter would be passing early this year. It took a long time to prepare their food; for everything had to be slowly dried over low heat, shrunken to small, disfigured, waterless lumps for the long trek across the wasteland. A time of peace and anticipation.

But Wasoo was moody and quiet. Ravenna and Nome gave one another worried looks and shook their heads. Didn't he feel well? they asked him. Was he dreading The Plains? Had one of them hurt his feelings? Was he worried about something?

Finally, Ravenna said to Wasoo, "You don't want to leave, do you?"

He looked at her with fearful eyes, began to shrug...then slowly shook his head.

"Come on," she said; and, taking him by the hand, led him outside on the road for a walk.

They were gone for nearly three hours that afternoon. Nome stayed in the house and helped Uncle prepare supper. When they came back, Wasoo lay down for a short nap before supper; but he fell into a deep, exhausted sleep, and they could not wake him for the meal. Nome was eager to know what Ravenna had found out, but she would only say that Wasoo was going through an inner struggle and would be telling him about it as best he could that evening.

The rest of the family had gone off to bed when Wasoo apologetically stumbled from the bedroom rubbing his swollen eyes. His two friends sat with him by lantern light at the kitchen table and watched him eat warmed leftovers without much interest. Gradually, he began to explain that his heart was not in leaving Gazi.

"I'll do it, of course," he insisted, "no question of my backing out on you. 'Stick by your friends,' my daddy used to say, 'Stick by your friends.' I don't really know what is the matter with me. Maybe I got too used to the peaceful life when I was with your folks, Nome, and with the old sisters, and now here at this fealard. Maybe I'm tired of traveling. Probably it is easier for me to think of staying in Gazi than it is for you two. It's less risky for me because I am a man of disguises and can get around easy. And I don't have any Druska Paba or Korcha Rabon hounding me to get raped or killed. For me, this is just another interesting place...although more dangerous than most because of the war. I don't know. It'll pass. I'll be back telling lies and foolishness in a few days, don't worry about me."

He paused, looking absently at the dirty dishes on the table between his elbows. "Maybe I am just tired of being on The Plains. That last crossing was worse than the first one, I told you that. But...I don't think it's really that. It's just that when I think of packing to leave Gazi, my insides sort of shrink up inside me, like. You know? And I lose my joy. Lose my joy. And.... Well, know what I think I feel worst about in all this? I told you this already, Ravenna. Nome, you and I have been through a lot together...and when I met you in that jail in Gree am Slome, something inside me said, 'stick with this man; be loyal to him; he is what you need.' And I did. And that feeling was right...even though it might have been nice if that feeling had stuck me to someone who wouldn't of drug me around to so many places where I could get killed. But I've been sticking to you, and to your Ravenna Rosealice, too, and I've been happy.

"I'm like Chindit. I know my duty. Or thought I did, till the past few days....'my duty'...huh, that's a word I never used much before.... I don't know what's come over me. I'm sticking with you two, 'long as you are willing. But there's something sticking to me, too, like a stone in my shoe."

He was silent for a long while. Ravenna stirred. Nome looked at her, expecting her to say something, but she did not. Nome, said, "I understand, Wasoo."

"Do you? Explain it to me."

Nome gave a thin smile and absently stroked the scar that ran along his face.

Ravenna stirred again, then said, "Wasoo, you have a stone in your shoe."

He looked up at her, then laughed. "Yes. Or in my head, more likely."

"Or in your heart, more likely," she said. "Come out with me under the stars."

"What?"

"The stars. It is a beautiful clear night."

He looked fearful. He looked at Nome. "Should I?"

"Yes," said Nome quickly.

"Why for?"

"She's a starwoman. Go ahead. Don't be afraid."

The evening was warm enough to continue the early thaw. The black velvet sky was awash with drifting clouds of stars and flittering points of light. Ravenna and Wasoo sat in the open yard on the tumble-down, free-of-snow end of the firewood pile and tilted back their heads.

She guided him among some of the patterns, pointing out The Table, The Sailing Ship, The Queen's House, The Wagon, The Fish. He lingered in his questions on a shape that most people could not make out, even with someone's careful pointing. "It is called The Green Branch," she told him. Wasoo saw it at once. She cautiously probed and led in other directions, listening carefully to the sound of his voice as he talked in a subdued tone. She let him drift with the current, fell silent for a few moments, played him like a nibbling fish, then heard him move back toward The Green Branch. Then she took in slack and began to speak...very quietly.

Wasoo also began to speak, halting at first, uncertain, then more clearly. He began to talk about the branch in the sky, how he could see its pattern plainly, even though the stars of it were faint and swamped on all sides by swarms of others. In the next moment he was speaking of trees, full trees, flowering trees, bent trees, broken trees, blasted, wasted, dead trees...with no transition he was among the sick and wounded of Gazi; his voice changed and filled with tears.

For the first time since he had returned, he spoke of the crossing of The Plains—not the return trip among the dane recruits—but the outward trip, when he had tended the sick and dying casualties of the war. He spoke of warding off wythies like flies day and night. He cared for them, washed them with precious drinking water, carried some of their corpses for days because it was not safe to burn them on The Plains. When they reached the world of winter on the other side with the survivors, after many days, he wanted nothing more than to stick with them. This was his duty, he felt. But, in his pouch, strapped tight to his waist, he felt another duty: the money entrusted to him for Brighthome. So, wearily, caught between two loyalties, he tore away from the sick-caravans and hurried on along the High Road.

"There were little creatures following me, too," he whispered, "little bird-things with big eyes popping up along the way, in the snowdrifts by the roadside. Wythies, I was afraid. I saw them...unless I was crazy by that time. I ran from them, ran, and tried to get away."

"Oh, Wasoo!" she sucked in her breath.

He continued, as though she had said nothing. Told of feeling relief from his guilt as he came nearer to Brighthome, but how it returned when he made the return trip to Gazi and neared the places where he had left the sick.

It was all he could do, he said, to take up with the dane recruits and play the soldier. Since he had been back in Gazi, he had felt displaced, uneasy, even though he was overjoyed to be back with her and with Nome.

When he heard them tell of the sick-lagers, he wanted to go there, not go out of Gazi. It almost felt like a physical pulling in his body, he said. He didn't know what it meant. He had been in jail, beaten, hungry, thirsty before, and often very lonely. But he had never known misery like the feeling of this pulling.

Wasoo had stopped speaking.

Ravenna said quietly, "You have taken your eyes off The Green Branch. Look, find it again. See it? It has moved a little to the west while you have been talking.

"Nome told me, Wasoo, how Aunie came to trust you, when you and he came to her house looking for me, after you got out of jail in Gree am Slome. Do you remember? She found you talking to Yuna Urlinda. She found the two of you laughing. Wasoo, my mother has not laughed for years. I have carried that in my heart, that picture of her laughing with you, ever since I heard it.

"You have what we among The Women call a 'goodcharm.' It means you have a skill or a talent for something good that has to be used in a certain way. You're meant to be a tender, Wasoo, that's all. A tender of the sick and the hurt and the dying. That is all. I think you dread leaving Gazi because this is where they are. It's your heart that is pulling at you to follow your goodcharm.

"No, don't look at me, keep your eyes on The Green Branch. And listen. Your duty is no longer to Nome Ogrodni. Or to me. You are a tender. Go where you are needed. Your joy and your outrageous humor will return. They are part of your goodcharm."

She quietly got up and went into the farmhouse. Wasoo remained sitting on the lumpy woodpile looking up into the sky.

....

During the next two days, Nome began keeping a sharp lookout for owlstones. His anxiety about crossing The Plains without Wasoo was keen. He saw none. Wasoo had told him that the presence of Chindit, when he had crossed with the danes, seemed to provide some protection or comfort in the midst of the spirits. Perhaps this would be true for Ravenna and himself this time. They filled their pack bags tight with dried food and tied them shut. Two walking sticks leaned by the door. A grand supper was planned by Uncle on the eve of their departure. Then a final gathering by the fire, some stories, some songs, the beginning of goodbyes.

It had begun to snow. During the night the wind began to howl and gnaw at the corners of the house. No one slept soundly through the night, for sharp gusts rattled the windows and doors. The farmwife was first to crawl from bed in morning's dull light. Ashes from the grate had blown back out onto the floor; and, just inside the front door, was a delicately sculptured knife-edge pile of snow. The house was chilled, and a great fire was needed at once.

Throughout the day, the wind blew and the snow swirled. The barn across the yard could be seen from the windows only as a faint, brown hulk, which came and went on the edge of visibility. With difficulty, the men floundered through the snow to see to the animals. All night and the next day, the storm continued and, finally, on the third day, began to ease. Only on the fourth was the wind down enough to make it worthwhile to begin shoveling paths. There was no question of opening roads yet; and it was six days after the farewell supper that Nome and Ravenna began planning once again to set out. They waited two more days at the fealard to be sure that there would be clear enough passage along the roads to bring them to the open fields leading to The Plains. In that delay, the second snowstorm swept down from the mountains. It was less violent than the first, but it quickly erased all shoveled paths and cleared roadways. The fealard was snowbound for another five days.

"Well, that's the end of winter," said the wise old people of the fealard. "We knew it seemed to be thawing too early. The mountains just tricking us." But they were wrong. A third storm came upon them, drifted snow past the ground-floor windows and left long, swooping runways up the sides of barns to the eaves. When the skies were pale blue again, and the air still, the people of the fealard valiantly dug themselves out once more. Pathways they cut through the snow walled higher than their heads in places. No one alive remembered blizzards like these. This winter would be talked of before the evening fires to grandchildren yet unborn.

There was no longer any possibility of Ravenna's and Nome's leaving before the spring thaw. Even when the roads were eventually cleared, the fields through which they would have to trudge to reach the edge of the desert would be drifted deep.

"We can wait," said Ravenna, "but what about getting money back for Brighthome. I have coin enough for one more payment; but is there enough time left?"

"It is due at Tosar's Keep in a month, if I have figured it correctly," said Nome.

"We can't make it."

"We can't," he said. He looked down at Chindit.

The mountains were spent. Day after day, the sun rose higher in the sky and turned the glistening, wet countryside warm. Men in shirtsleeves were out in the yards, scraping trenches in the dirt and ground-ice with shovels to drain away pooling water. The roads were open, but muddy, and nearly impassable for carts and wagons. Nome wrote a long letter to Mo and Fa and rolled it tight into a slender tube to be attached to Chindit's collar. He took the last of Ravenna's coins, which she had stolen from The House of Ghan, and prepared for a long, sloppy trek to the nearest town where there would be a counting house, in order to purchase a note of trade.

Before he could leave, however, an excitement spread through the fealard, news brought by runner from the neighboring fealard, that left Nome standing in the doorway, looking out at the beautiful blue-and-white mountains, pondering. Word was being passed throughout Gazi that a final battle with the forces of Moma was planned. Every able-bodied resident of the land, men, women, youth, were under call to begin moving northward as soon as the roads were passable. All were to be enlisted in the final struggle. "The Fire burns!" was being shouted everywhere.

Along with the call to arms, came the incredible news that the Fire, the original Fire from the shrine of the Greatsada in old Mhaveen, was still burning. The flame, it was reported, had indeed been carried high into the mountains by a few survivors of the destruction of Mhaveen. They had lived for years in a remote cave, descending to the upper settlements for food and provisions, always careful to guard the secret until the signaled moment would arrive. To hear the wild rejoicing on all sides of him, Nome would have thought that victory over the Mommicks had already arrived.

But these people...he found himself thinking...these people are going into war. Surprisingly, he found himself thinking of Beland at that moment. Then he was aware that he was half-whistling a little tune. He whistled it again more clearly and recognized the refrain of "Ride Again, Woldman, Ride." He stopped. Two faces had come to memory, Mardek and Burton. Burton then took the pipe from his mouth and solemnly said, "The song is about your father."

Nome shuddered; and again, from the open doorway of the house, he was seeing the beautiful blue mountains in the distance with their snowy tops wrapped in light wisps of white cloud like the head of Baron Ogrodni.

"Every able-bodied resident of the land," he said aloud, "called to the final struggle. I suppose that includes us."

TWENTY-FOUR

At the Front

Spring came quickly, and quickly the drifts and snowbanks shriveled under the sun. Standing water and gurgling rivulets drained away, and the mire turned to firm ground. During this time, the fealard was in fevered preparation for mobilization. Within a few weeks, the entire population was on the road, moving northward, blending with other moving crowds from other fealards.

Chindit had preceded them, scampering purposefully along the still-muddy road which would lead to Kul Sama on that chilly spring morning. Nome had stood alone, watching him go with the future of Brighthome wired into a tight wad on his collar, hoping that he would find his way safely across Gazine lines into Mommick-held territory and across The Plains of Wildness and onto the long High Road leading homeward. Chindit had been calm and seemed to know what to do when Nome had wired the collar and told him simply, "Go home, Chindit! Home to Rena!" Down the road he had trotted, not looking back.

Soon afterward, all the roads in southern Gazi were filled with grinding wagons and people marching, slowing to a shuffle as their numbers swelled. In the villages, fealards, and towns only the oldest and youngest were left with a few caretakers to maintain a semblance of home, as the Southern Army of the People took shape along the way. Buried troves of weapons, hidden for years, were brought out. Men, women, and youth were trained for combat as they went. Even children moved with the army; but they were given tasks of hauling and feeding, cleaning and packing. With great difficulty, Ravenna, Nome, and Wasoo pleaded that they themselves not be armed to fight but be assigned to the tenders once they reached the front lines. The captain of their unit insisted that they were fit for combat and would not be excused simply because they were unGazine; but he finally relented when they argued that, at the sick-lagers, they had not been allowed to join Korcha's forces but were given only the most menial jobs among the tenders and burners. They were then assigned to organize and train some of the older children in the caravan as assistants to tenders.

Living farthest from the front, the people of the fealards were last to gather behind the camps forming the perimeter of Gazine lines. The Southern Army of the People now mustered in the thousands under Maincaptain Streeter's command and was stretched out in a chain of separated camps, each within sight of the other, but not so close as to tumble into panic and rout, should the Mommicks swarm over any one of them. This line of camps was positioned just south of Kul Sama and dotted the greening countryside toward the west near the towns of Bobaken, Whimler, and Mhir Koven. Beyond them stood the army of Ila Rabon, and beyond that, the army of Korcha Rabon. On Korcha's left, tucked under the mountains of the Endicot Range along the far west, were the skillful troops of Mira Shannan. Now expanded from three to four armies, the Gazine forces poised in a semi-circle, hemming the entire Mommick force along the south and far up into the west. In fact, Mira Shannan's position actually stood somewhat to the northwest of the Mommick stronghold at the site of old Mhaveen. The Mommicks were not adept in mountain terrain and avoided contact with Mira Shannan in those regions. While blizzards had been raging in southern Gazi, and inhabitants of the fealards had found themselves snowbound, Korcha's and Ila's soldiers had been driving the scattered occupation forces out of the south in a series of hard and bloody engagements and pushing them back to their two strongholds, the Eastern Fortress, where Nome had been imprisoned, and the Inland Central Stronghold.

The Gazines now regretted that the Eastern Fortress, captured by Mira Shannan during the Battle of Kul Sama, had not been destroyed; for it offered the Mommicks a second strong position of defense and spread out the focus of the Gazine attack. Now Korcha had to revise his strategy and move, first, to neutralize the Eastern Fortress, before concentrating the press of all four armies on the Inland Central

Stronghold. There were other Mommick forts in the northern regions of Gazi; but these, he believed, would not stand, once the Inland Stronghold fell.

Nome, Ravenna, and Wasoo found themselves at the outermost encampment of the Southern Army of the People. They could stroll up along the grassy hills in front of them and look across at the village of Kul Sama. They could almost see the farm of the two old sisters, with whom they had stayed, and wondered if these dear women, living just inside Mommick territory, were safe. Because of their experience in the sick-lagers, they were given primary responsibility for setting up a sick-camp at the rear and gathering bandages, medicines, herbs, supplies of water, blankets, and cots. Then they were separated from one another and sent along the lines to set up other sick-camps, farther inland.

Wasoo was happier now. There were no casualties in the camps, but he had a sense of purpose. Nome was content with his duties, and even felt a vague sense of relief, he couldn't imagine why. He had not understood his own tangled feelings. Perhaps there had been a sense of failure in giving up on Brighthome, in his eagerness to go home to Brighthome. Perhaps his initial elation at the prospect of getting away from Gazi had left him with unease about something unfinished. Korcha again. He wanted Korcha to know he was wrong about Nome Ogrodni. Perhaps he understood Curry a little in this: a need for the great man's approval. The commander's florid hostility persisted; and, although Nome knew it was best to get away from this man and his bleeding country, he was feeling an irrational comfort with the delay.

Ravenna, too, was conflicted. She did not know why she was still here, going in the opposite direction from where she had resolved to go. Several times a day she would stop, mid-action, while wrapping bandages or checking through a list, with a feeling of unreality, as though asking herself: Are *you* still here? What made it more baffling was that she was moving, with this great band of people, right back toward where she had heard Druska Paba had been seen, only a half-day's journey away. What foolishness!

Yet, she wanted to go where Nome went. After the snowstorms and the sending away of Chindit, he seemed to take it for granted that they should respond to the general call-up. She was also yielding to the insistence of their hosts in the fealard. Moreover, she had especially dreaded crossing The Plains, and feared what she might find on the other side; for, if she went alone, where could she go but back to The Fields of Khorvan? Tending the sick was not her goodcharm, as it was for Wasoo...and for Beland. Nor was it Nome's. But here they were, on the edge of someone else's war, preparing cots and bandages for the healthy, eager people about them, who would be crippled and bleeding to death tomorrow.

The evening before the attack on the Eastern Fortress, Ravenna, Nome, and Wasoo were back together again. Their field infirmaries were ready and waiting. In the morning, they would be moving out at the rear of the troops, prepared to spring forward into the thick of the battle to pick up the wounded.

Nome was having grave misgivings now. He had imagined that this would be like the sick-lagers, slow, heavy suffering, remote from the killing. Tending the sick and dying had seemed like a good and decent service to the people of Gazi; but he had not known it would include going into combat. Now, on the eve of battle, he felt thick, swollen fear in his belly, as he visualized the death of Ravenna Rosealice. He had brought her here, he knew; and now he seriously thought of taking her and running away. If he could do it over, he might have.

But now they were compromised. They had set up the sick-camps. They were in charge. To run now would be despicable, leaving the dying at their time of need. And they would probably be caught and shot for desertion.

That evening, Wasoo was cheerful and talkative. Ravenna was calm and resolute. Nome was near panic. He felt this was a nightmare, and each moment he suffered a pang at the realization that he could not wake up. He remembered his night of terror in Korcha's camp at the cache hole, before setting out with a message for Ila. He thought their present situation was now the fulfillment of that dread foreboding. How had he come to this? How had he brought Ravenna into it? Wasoo had come willingly enough; but what did this trap, this cage of death, have to do with seeking his fortune, with saving Brighthome, with Ravenna's flight to safety? What a mistake!

....

At dawn, the Southern Army of the People moved out with speed, past Kul Sama, along the road to the Eastern Fortress, across the fresh fields. Three thousand men and women, armed and ready, swept across peaceful countryside, stampeding flocks of sheep out of the way as they went. They encountered no resistance and, by early afternoon, were closing on the Fortress itself. At that point, they paused briefly; then half the division separated and moved eastward to approach the Fortress from the direction of The Plains. The remaining half slowly moved up from the south.

At that moment, far away, the armies of Korcha Rabon and Mira Shannan were engaged in diversionary combat with the more heavily defended Inland Central Stronghold. They were attacking and retreating, thrusting and withdrawing, staying out of harm's way. They had no intention of engaging the Inland Stronghold seriously at this time; but the Mommicks did not know that. All the Mommick scouts had reported was that the three trained armies of the Gazines were hovering about the Stronghold, sure to attack in concert soon, while a fourth ragtag group of civilians, poorly trained and armed, appeared to be intending to run at the Eastern Fortress. The Mommicks felt sure that the troops of the Eastern Fortress could sally out in disciplined formation and tear their way through this mob. They expected the real battle at the Inland Central Stronghold.

But, as the maneuvers went into motion, the army of Ila Rabon feinted toward the Inland Stronghold, already harassed by Korcha and Mira Shannan, then, suddenly, wheeled away. In a lightning march, Ila descended on the Eastern Fortress from the west. That Fortress had been built by the Mommicks, in their early days of conquest, to defend against attacks on the country coming from the east. It had stood guard, facing The Plains of Wildness, with the high mountains at its back, adamantine and forbidding. But now, the real attack came from *within* the country, from the rear; and the stony giant could not turn around to meet it.

Ila's screaming soldiers surged across the flatlands, easily tearing down the fences, clambering over barricades, hammering their way into the fortress through the unprotected doors and window gratings of Mablic Prison, at the very moment its Mommick troops were surging out the front gate to tear apart the citizen army approaching in clear view.

It was the Battle of Kul Sama all over again: the weaker force approaching in the open from the front, drawing out the Mommick forces to be struck, in surprise, from the rear by the strong army. Their tight ranks outside the front gate were thrown into confusion by the noise of battle at the back of the fortress. Some, perceiving the trap, tried to retreat quickly back inside the gate, while others continued to face the attackers at their front and on their right flank. The Southern Army came on with surprising organization and fierceness, holding up light-weight misk shields overhead against sharp and steely missiles raining down on them from the battlements.

Within moments, they were grappling hand-to-hand with the Mommick defenders; and the shower from the battlements ceased; for both sides were mixed in a rolling welter of confusion.

Ila's fighters were now within the fortress. They had been expecting to free their fellow citizens as they broke through Mablic Prison, but they found that whole area empty. The Mommicks had foolishly pulled all the prisoners into the inner rooms of the fortress and put them to work erecting obstacles and moving firedust barrels along the battlements. Prisoners had been considered too weak and beaten to be a risk during the battle, and they were kept under guard and separated from one another. But, as the roar of the fighting sounded within the fortress itself and at the front gates—which had just been shut, cutting off a large number of the Mommick from retreat—the prisoners found strength and will to turn on their masters and use against them the blades and sharp points that were near at hand. Their guards wheeled upon them in rage and cut them down; but some prisoners were near open casks of firedust. A series of deafening, suicidal explosions ripped open the entire north wall of the fortress at the second story, so that the battlements on that side crumbled into the courtyard, darkening the sun with rolling smoke and dust.

Beset from the front, the rear, and within, the Mommicks could not hold out. Their fohtars and danes were cut off from their officers and ran wild, at contrary purposes, through the fortress, at times killing their own in confusion. The end came, inevitably but slowly: there was no longer a shred of discipline among them allowing a surrender order to be given.

Only when the firing and explosions and shouting died away, leaving the cries and moans of the wounded, interrupted now and again by the slow tearing of a timber, the rattle of masonry, and the terrible crashing of a wall or a ceiling—only then, did the soldiers of Ila Rabon move cautiously from room to room flushing out the last resisters.

And only then, did Nome, Ravenna, and Wasoo advance, with the corp of tenders, to extract the wounded. The battle had been too close and confused for them to do it sooner. They crawled through the ruins, scraping their legs and bloodying their hands, as they tore beams away and rolled stone and plaster to get at trapped and mangled bodies. Those fallen in combat in the open were easiest to get at. They were carted away on stretchers and laid out in wavering rows on the green grass of the fields across which the Southern Army had recently come. There was no telling Mommick from Gazine. More than half of the Gazines wore the Mommick brand on their cheeks, received during the years of occupation, as did the Mommicks themselves. Which were the enemy did not matter to the tenders anymore. All they saw was blood and soot and limp intestine and wet, white bone sticking through tissue; all they heard were moans and babbling and liquid gurgling in broken throats. All they smelled was the metallic stench of gore and sulfur. They dragged and ferried all the fallen indiscriminately, staggering drunkenly in their numbed hurry, lengthening the rows at a distance on the green grass.

Nome looked for people he knew, fellow inmates of Mablic Prison. He recognized a few in the rubble, but they were all beyond need of his help. Ravenna feverishly glanced here and there, expecting at any moment to see Druska Paba; but she saw only the broken bodies of soldiers.

They worked through the afternoon, clearing the ruined fortress area; and, toward evening, they were able to begin tending the wounded. The equipment and supplies of the sick-camp, which had been prepared the day before, were brought forward to this grassy field. The damaged people were eased onto cots, in place where they lay, one-by-one. The Mommick wounded were moved off to an area separate from the Gazines, but both groups were tended with care. There was no shortage of attendants now, for the Southern Army of the People had not yet moved off, and many of the warriors lingered about the field to help tend the sick. They stretched tent-like sheets on upright poles over much of the area, protecting those most seriously hurt who could not be moved, if the weather turned bad.

The open field, burdened with moans, ranting cries, and a constant drone of murmuring, sounded like the sick-lagers; only the sounds were not contained in echo but blew away on the spring breeze. Dozens of tenders slowly moved among the cots, bending over, squatting down, kneeling to bandage or wash or to spoon a numbing concoction into delirious mouths. Ravenna, Nome, and Wasoo did not speak to one another, occupied as they were, and separated in different parts of the camp; but, if they could have shared their grieving hearts, they would have said the same thing: "All this! All this was not here this morning. They have *done* this to one another!"

....

Night eased over the camp. Fires were kindled about the edges, and more blankets were dragged from the pony carts. Lanterns were hung from the poles which supported the open-sided tent. The numbing potions had taken effect on most of the seriously hurt, and merciful sleep had come to many. Still, there were a few who screamed out suddenly and tried to sit up or who wept noisily. Ravenna moved quickly to the section where the Mommick wounded lay to quiet a young man who had begun to wail and beg for mercy with such clamor that he was beginning to wake the others. As she neared his cot, he let out a watery, blubbering cry in what sounded like gibberish; but it stopped her in her tracks.

"Madaba...mo-mo...kilipaa!" the writhing figure shrilled. "Mo-mo-na...!"

"Shh!" she quickly knelt at his side and bent close to his face. "Matuuni?"

The clenched eyelids of the man suddenly opened wide in astonishment and pain, and he stared up into her face. His own face glistened with sweat. He swiftly reached up and clutched on both sides of her head her long hair, which hung down above her shoulders. "Matuuni," he whispered, then with explosive force: "Matuuni! Mo-mo noa guruapu moamoa niki baatanupua...."

"No, no, I don't understand your language," she interrupted, "but you are from the Fields of Khorvan!"

In his delirium the man had been crying out in the language of his childhood, a dialect still used by a small population group settled in a corner of The Fields of Khorvan. They were the Matuuni, and Ravenna had heard some of the old women in the market speaking its melodic rhythms to one another. She had never heard one so young as this man speak Matuuni.

He stared up into her eyes with wild intensity, still clasping her hair in both fists as though afraid she would vanish. His chest heaved with panting. Ravenna evenly repeated:

"You are from The Fields?"

He nodded slowly, still staring. Then his lips formed,

"You...you...?"

She nodded. "Yes. I am from The Fields of Khorvan."

He breathed heavily, then grimaced and arched his body, as a wave of pain took him. He clutched tighter to her hair, so that Ravenna had to grasp his fists and hold them to the sides of her head to keep him from pulling. She tilted her head down to see if his writhing was doing damage to any bandages and saw that his body, under the blanket, stopped half-way down the cot. She continued to hold his fists in her grip, until she felt the wave of pain in him subside through the relaxing of his fingers. Gently, she pried his hands loose from her hair and lowered them to his chest. He lay there almost peacefully for a moment, then slowly opened his eyes again. For a long time they were both silent. Then he said, "Who are you?"

"My name is Ravenna Rosealice. I am from The...."

But, at this, his face contorted and rolled sideways into the pillow, and his fingers dug into his shirt and began to tear it apart. From his mouth dribbled a pitiful groan, and he began to rock his head from side to side. She looked down at him, astonished, unable to tell if she was watching pain or grief.

"What is it?" she whispered. "What is the matter?"

But he continued to babble and to cry and reverted to his childhood language. At length, he croaked in the most forlorn of voices: "Not die this way. Not this way. An evil man. Ohhh, no-o--o!"

"What *is* it?" she insisted.

"I know who you are!" he said, suddenly more quiet. "I came here to get you. Ohhh, no-o-o!" and his face puckered like a child's about to cry.

"Get me? What do you mean '*get* me?'"

"Dru...Drus...."

Ravenna sucked in her breath sharply and straightened suddenly away from him. With wide eyes, she stared down at the sweating man. He lay quiet for the first time and gazed up at her helplessly.

"How?" she said gently. "Tell me. Tell me about it."

Pain flickered across his face like heat lightning; but he began to speak, laboriously but steadily.

"Four of us...three others and me...all Matuuni. She came to us...and, and said for us to go, to go with her...to bring you...back. Bring back the starwoman...for her...across...all the way across the Evil

Desert...she said we w...wouldn't regret...."

"For a reward?" asked Ravenna softly, now bending closer.

He nodded.

"For three thousand kurakhs?"

He frowned, shook his head. "Not three...not enough...she said...she said when we bring the star...woman back home, she would give us...high places...in The House...of Ghan. She said join soldiers to fight here...she would come, too, but not...not with soldiers. So we signed on...danes...you know what danes is?"

Ravenna nodded.

"Danes. To fight...here. And it was a bad...a *bad* thing to do!" His face crinkled, and the young man began to sob and shake. Ravenna instinctively reached out and stroked his forehead, which promptly produced heavier shaking. At length, the sobbing drained away; and he sighed deeply, as though relieved. He opened wet eyes and said simply, "I am sorry."

She smiled sadly and said, "It's all right." They were both quiet for a moment. Then she asked, "Where are the other three who came with you?"

"Gone," he said simply. "They were along the wall. In there. We had just been told to start shooting the prisoners...one was there by the barrel...they were nearby to him, all Matuuni,...and he had flint and steel...and the firedust...and...." He looked away.

Ravenna closed her eyes. Then slowly opened them and looked down at where the man's body ended under the blanket.

"And Druska Paba," she spoke in the slightest whisper, "where is she?"

He shook his head slowly, still looking away. "I don't know. I did not see her when the fighting began." He lay still for a moment, then added, "She is a liar."

Ravenna nodded, then stroked his forehead again. She took a cloth tucked into the belt at her waist, rose and went to a bucket at a camp table at the end of the row of cots. Returning, she knelt again and sponged the man's face. He looked at her and slowly asked, "Are you...the starwoman?"

She nodded.

"I am sorry," he said.

She nodded. "Now I will send somebody with a drink that will help with the pain. Try to sleep." She rose and walked out of the tent area, looking for Wasoo.

When she had found him and sent him in to the man, Ravenna walked out away from the cots and the brash glare of the lanterns into the coolness of the spring nighttime. Out of habit, she tilted her head back, drew in a deep breath, and let her eyes drift across the sea of stars. She paced back and forth for a while, thinking and not thinking, deeply stirred by what the suffering man had just said. Aimlessly, she circled the area of the sick-camp in a slow gait, enjoying the stretching of her aching muscles.

Then she began to move back in to make one last round among the cots, before finding an empty one on which to lay herself for a few hours. She looked across for Nome and, across a dozen rows, saw that he and another tender were busy in calming another agitated person. There were only a few tenders up now, slowly moving up and down the rows, pausing and bending, straightening, and continuing on. One of them caught her eye, someone that moved haltingly from cot to cot, hoisting a lantern at each, bending stiffly to peer. Ravenna watched. There was something strange about the movement. Something missing. This tender never stopped, seemed to be searching for someone. Limping forward.

Suddenly, Ravenna Rosalice felt a chill slide over her body. She stood rigid and watched the bent, shuffling shape for a moment, to be sure. She looked across at Nome, who was still kneeling beside a cot. Then, feeling very calm and very sure, Ravenna walked down that row of cots and stood before the advancing figure with the lantern. It moved forward, at first unaware, bending and peering into each face. Suddenly it stopped, tense, and arched slightly, like a cat. Taut silence. Ravenna spoke.

"Druska Paba."

The lantern jerked up to illumine the speaker and, with the same movement, threw a harsh light on the terrified face of the old woman. Her dribbling lips fell loose and began to shake. Her eyes squinted and twitched. At the instant of recognition, she recoiled, as though burned by fire, and dropped the lantern to the ground, letting out a screeching noise that dissolved into a fit of crying, and scrambled to get away. The lantern cracked, as it struck ground; and oil spilled across the trodden grass of the aisle, throwing up a sudden dangerous flare. Ravenna immediately seized a blanket from the nearest cot, threw it on the flames and stomped. But, in the moment before the glow was extinguished, the panicky form of Druska Paba was seen climbing across cots of wounded bodies and disappearing into the night, at a crooked, waddling run.

....

That night, a sentry, coming off duty, awoke the Maincaptain and reported that he had spotted a squatting shadow, moving quickly, off away from the camp, inland toward the Mommicks. It could have been an animal, he said; there was no response to his challenge. It was out of range, too, and just slipped away into the darkness.

TWENTY-FIVE

The Final Struggle

At dawn, the Southern Army of the People was finishing breakfast and breaking camp, preparing to follow Ila's army, which had moved out in the dark an hour earlier. There was little time to rest: strategy called for the cinch around the Inland Central Stronghold to be kept tight, now that the Eastern Fortress had been eliminated. At the sick-camp, preparations were underway to transfer the wounded back southward beyond Kul Sama, away from the front. However, this task was left to the youngest and most dispensable of the tenders. Nome, Ravenna, and Wasoo were among those moving out with the army, getting ready for the next battle. They stayed at the rear again, walking alongside swaying supply wagons, roped high with blankets and bundles of bandages and stacked with crates of medicines, potions, and herbal mixtures. They left the burners behind to their work of returning the dead to the Greatsada, those killed in battle, amputated parts of bodies, and those who had expired on cots during the night.

The advance of Ila's army and the Southern Army of the People now hemmed the enemy at the Inland Central Stronghold in a half-circle of threat. Ila camped to the east. The Southern Army was between him and Korcha on the south. Mira Shannan hovered on the west. In the coming battle, the Mommicks would hold the advantage of the defending posture, with tight internal lines of communication and a strong concentration of professional soldiers. They were in danger, however, of being surrounded, with a quick turning movement by Ila on the east or

Mira Shannan on the west, and were obliged to position their strongest forces on those two flanks. This left their southern front weaker and vulnerable to Korcha. The one thing the Mommicks could not afford was to be encircled. Their external lines of communication ran only one way—to the north, where they had reserve troops and outposts. This, too, was the avenue of contact with their homeland, Moma, far in the west beyond the mountains.

Contact with Moma was very much on the minds of the Mommicks at this point, for they were feeling very hard pressed by this Gazine rebellion. It was an hour of humiliation for these great invaders, no matter what the outcome of the battle might be. A dozen years earlier, they had proudly marched into the land with the air of rightful masters and claimed this parcel for Moma, as they had done to so many of the other lands across which they had come. They would have gone farther, had it not been for The Plains of Wildness and the fact that the high peaks of the Endicot Mountains behind them were stretching communication with Moma to the breaking point. This made occupied-Gazi the remotest province of the Mommick Empire, and the most difficult to secure. It was not a choice assignment for officers of the army in Moma. As a result, the military leadership which faced this rebellion was uncertain and incompetent. They avoided the mountains; they randomly hunted down the rebels; they relied on mercenaries for intelligence; they developed no strategy for repressing the uprising other than the campaign of reprisals, substituting brutality for planning.

As the armies of Korcha Rabon had them in rout out of the whole southern part of the country and holed up into two strong positions (one of them now overthrown), the Mommicks had sent back to Moma desperate requests for reinforcements. But the way to Moma was long. Messengers had to ride far to the north, along the Endicot Range, until they came to a low pass, then cross westward with difficulty; for the snows of winter had not yet left the heights. Once across, they must ride on still farther to the capital.

Korcha Rabon knew all this. He knew it from fighting them, and he knew it from his spies. A few of the dane mercenaries under orders of the fohtars were actually Gazine loyalists. In the same way that Wasoo had entered the Eastern Fortress, these spies had found quiet positions within the Inland Stronghold itself. They reported that the harsh end of winter had delayed the Mommick request for reinforcements. They had smuggled out word that Moma itself was said to be in a state of political upheaval, with factions of the army threatening one another. It was likely that the Mommick contingents in faraway Gazi would not receive prompt attention from Moma.

Korcha had all his troops poised for a final initiative. Although they were in the weaker attack position, spread thin in a wide arc around the Stronghold, they were, in a more basic sense, the defenders. Their single objective was not to destroy the Mommick force, but to drive it from their land: either northward, from where it had come, or upward into the mountains, where it would break down, or outward onto The Plains of Wildness, where it would dissolve. In this defense of the homeland, Korcha had always maintained the offensive; and his skirmishes and battles were studies in simplicity. They had worked because he had maneuvered and maintained mobility and skillfully used the element of surprise.

Now, all along the line, the seasoned fighters of Korcha, Ila, Mira Shannan and the farmers, villagers, and townspeople of the Southern Army looked across the sweet fields toward rising land where their capital city once had stood. Sacred Mhaveen was no more. In its place was the Inland Stronghold, not an arrogant, high, stone fortress, like the one brought to rubble in the east, but a veritable city of war, a low-lying, sprawling encampment, bristling with a defending perimeter of waist-high, needle-sharp stakes, embedded in the ground and leaning outward. Behind the stakes were rows upon rows of low stone pedestals, close together and staggered in a pattern to interrupt a frontal assault. These provided shielded positions from which the front-line defenders could fire. Behind them was a wall, ringing the entire stronghold like a city wall. It stood no more than the height of the tallest man, but there was no break or gate at any point. All traffic in and out passed over movable wooden ramps, which were controlled by those within. Far back from the encircling wall, out of range from incoming missiles and firedarts, stood nearly fifty high, spindly, wooden towers, scattered throughout the entire stronghold area. These were the lookouts, which could view any movement or approach in all directions among the fields, which sloped gently away from the well-defended bluff. A curious system of wires and pulleys connected each shed atop a tower with the ground for the speedy passing of messages during the noise of battle. Within the stronghold walls were fifteen thousand Mommicks, nearly all men, well

The Final Struggle

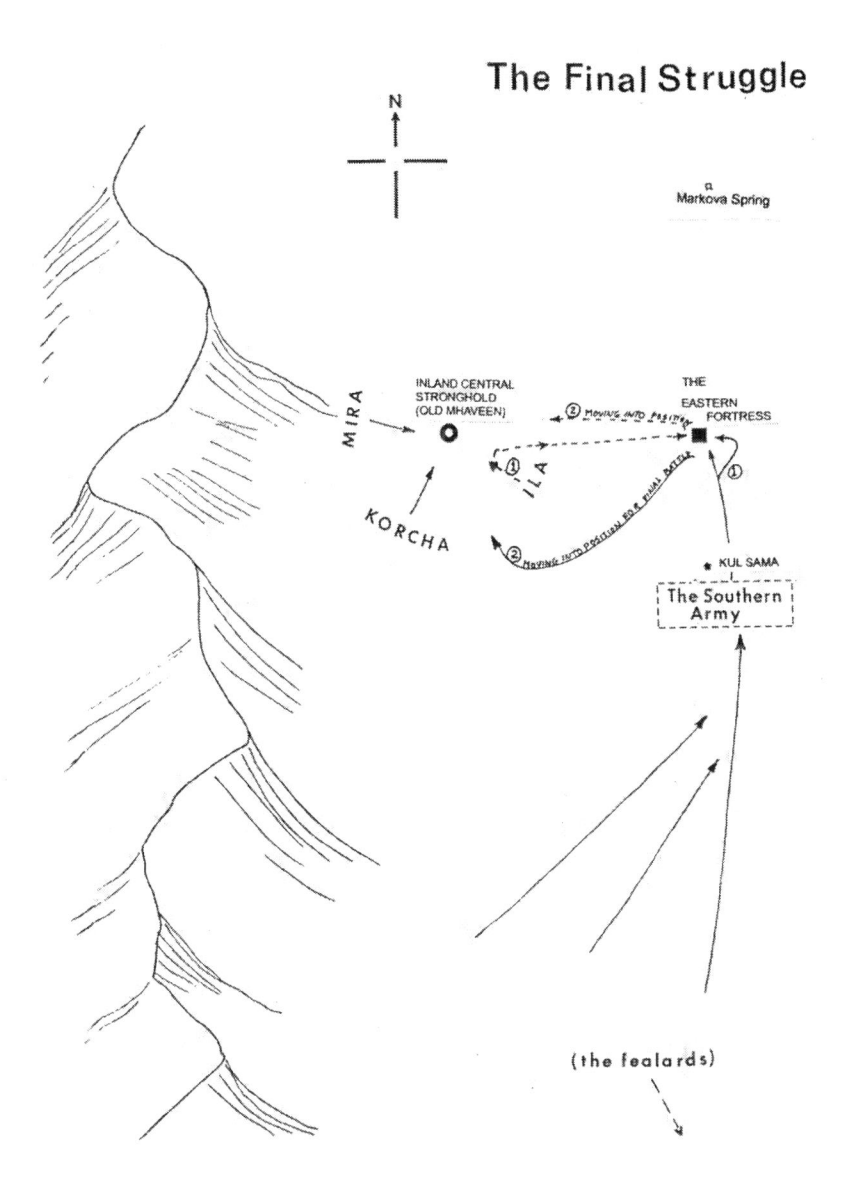

Markova Spring

INLAND CENTRAL STRONGHOLD (OLD MHAVEEN)

THE EASTERN FORTRESS

② Moving into position

MIRA

KORCHA

ILA

①

② Moving into position to a final battle

①

* KUL SAMA

The Southern Army

(the fealards)

provisioned and armed with a variety of tubes, cannon, and launchers, along with a seemingly inexhaustible supply of firedust.

The diversionary strikes which Korcha and Mira Shannan had made on the stronghold, while Ila and the Southern Army had been attacking the Eastern Fortress, had given the Gazine commanders a feel for the way the Mommicks would fight. One of their alarming discoveries was that, although the Gazines relied on bows and hand-thrown spears and spiny-disks, supported by firetubes and some small canon, the Mommicks held back from close contact and raged out with tubes and canon. Casualties had been light in those first encounters because Korcha and Mira Shannan had not been making a serious attempt to breach the perimeter; but it was clear that the final battle would be very bloody.

That was evident to Nome and Ravenna simply by looking toward the bluff. In melancholy silence, they rolled bandages and waited. Wasoo had been transferred to the waiting sick-camp area to the rear of Ila's army. Smoke from those campfires could be seen far off on the right. On the left, to the west, a haze of smoke lingering above a line of trees indicated the position of Korcha's army.

"Beland is probably over there," Nome said to Ravenna pointing in that direction. "Over there behind Korcha."

"We may see him...later," she answered. "When we have to move forward."

"And Curry," he added.

Ravenna looked at him thoughtfully. "How would you feel about seeing Curry again?"

Frowning, he stared out across the clean fields toward the smoldering Mommick sprawl. She watched his eyes flick back and forth. He said simply, "I don't know."

The armies were all in place by early evening of the day after the Battle of the Eastern Fortress. The people ate their suppers, unrolled their sleepsacks, checked over their weapons, and sat around campfires in a subdued mood. Word had been passed that they would rise before dawn, kindle no breakfast fires, and be in position to attack before the sun broke the horizon.

....

The next morning, as faint light appeared in the east, a white, low-lying mist blanketed the fields around the bluff, which poked like a mountain cap through clouds. Silently, the Gazine troops crept forward, converging from four directions under perfect cover. The mist, however, made the lookouts atop the towers in the Mommick stronghold intensely alert; for they could not see far afield, and they were anticipating attack at any moment. Slowly, the eastern horizon unfolded like a golden flower; then sun-glare broke through. As the mist lifted, the ranks of two thousand white-shielded figures came into view, gliding stealthily toward the pincushion perimeter of sharpened stakes. The front of every rank was led by dozens of strange, white, V-shaped shields, improvised plows, worked by two men together to push furrows through the clusters of deadly stakes, to clear pathways for the attacking troops behind. Like the body-shield, which each soldier carried, these plows were fashioned of thin plates of lightweight, hardened misk. The secret material had been freighted in powder form all the way from 'n Burning Graute during The March. It had given the Gazines great flexibility during their first stage, the hit-and-run campaign against the Mommicks. Once again, it was playing a crucial role in the stand-and-fight frontal engagement.

As soon as the fog thinned under the first warmth of sunlight, the wires and pulleys from the towers to the ground throughout the stronghold began to whir and squeak with little message canisters sliding down and up. A moment later, a single canon report came from the wall. The swarms of advancing Gazine troops broke into a jiggling trot, closing on the perimeter of stakes. At once, a sputtering of muffled explosions erupted from the wall; and hundreds of tiny white puffs appeared and were lifted away by the morning breeze. So quick and undetected had been the attack through the fog, that the Mommick defenders had not had time to position troops beyond the wall at the firing pedestals. The misk plows hit the stakes, and those who carried them threw their weight forward. The stakes gave way, twisted aside; and, from the rear, it looked like a comb being pushed through hair.

Ravenna and Nome were at the rear of the attack, also protected by misk body-shields, running along with the other tenders behind the last of the advancing soldiers. They heard the swelling shout of attack, which was joined by the awful sounds of battle: barking canon fire, explosions, clash of metal on metal, screams of rage and agony, the rattle of grapeshot on shields. The forward movement of the attackers slowed and wavered, as their onslaught hit the wall of the stronghold. Canon fire and longtube fire died away; for the attack was at close range, and fighting on the wall was hand-to-hand.

The tenders in the rear stopped and dropped to their knees, cowering behind the misk shields from which stray pellets ricocheted with fearful whacks. Nome and Ravenna huddled close together, overlapping their shields, breathing hard, looking into one-another's scared eyes, saying nothing. Nome ventured a peek around the edge of the shield, but his head snapped back when a whining whizzed close to his face. There were shouts from their fellow tenders a short distance to their side, and they saw themselves beckoned forward. Reluctantly, Nome and Ravenna separated a bit and rose to a trotting crouch, inching their way forward along with their comrades toward the places near the sharp stakes where the first attackers had fallen. They came upon a man lying on his back, writhing and moaning a little. His eyes were open but glazed, and he was breathing in sputtering gasps. A large dark stain, just below his collar, was spreading down the front of his coat. Ravenna held Nome's shield alongside hers while he detached and unfolded a light stretcher, which had been strapped to his back. He snapped the locking latches of the poles and lay the stretcher on the ground alongside the man. Then they strapped their shields to their backs as quickly as possible, for they were in the open and unprotected for a few moments. They straightened the man's arms and legs, speaking to him soothingly and constantly through their grunts and panting, then hoisted him by ankles and armpits over onto the stretcher. When they bent to lift the stretcher, Nome, who was in the front, found that the shield across his back prevented him from grasping the stretcher poles. He desperately hurried to twist the shield this way and that across his back, then furiously wrenched the shield off and threw it aside. Ravenna cried out in protest, but Nome was already squatting down and lifting his end of the stretcher, so she could do nothing but take up her end. They ran from the field in a new panic, with little attention to how they were jostling the bleeding man.

Back at the rear, out of canon range, they turned their invalid over to others. Nome folded the stretcher, reattached it to his back, was issued another shield and practiced strapping it cross-wise on his back to cover only his upper back and head, then swung it around again to protect the full front of his body...and they were sent back out onto the field.

Seven more times the two of them rushed back and forth to the edge of the fighting to extricate slashed or pierced people from underfoot. They moved right up among the rows that had been plowed through the thicket of sharpened stakes, to the midst of the empty firing pedestals, almost to the turmoil of the fighting. Each time, they executed a rescue a little more smoothly. Each time their paralyzing fear gave way to numbness, sweat, gasping panting.

On one return trip away from the battle, they had to stop and lower their freight to the ground and throw themselves alongside to shield him. They were both totally out of breath and could run and carry no farther without a rest. Ravenna twisted her head around back to Nome and shouted between heaving gulps of air:

"He's dead!"

"What?"

"Dead."

"Sure?"

She threw her head down between her elbows where she sprawled on the grass and nodded fiercely, as though to save breath while she tried to suck air from the earth.

Nome said nothing, but squinted up into the sun and shoved the back of his hand and arm up to his elbow across his mouth. Gradually his panting slowed. He crawled over Ravenna to the man on the stretcher, leaned an ear against the open mouth for a moment, then grasped the edge of the stretcher and rolled the man free onto the grass. They stayed there for a while longer, drinking in a few more moments of rest. The noise of the fighting continued at their backs, and they began to drag themselves up to enter the fray once more.

Suddenly a man came running up to them and slid to his knees alongside them, positioning his shield against the fight.

"Houda! Holy!" he cried.

"Beland!"

They could not embrace, so encumbered they were in their squatting, kneeling, sprawling positions with shields and stretchers; but the three of them clutched at one-another's hands and arms, eyes shining, faces stained with sweat and dirt, lungs pumping bursts of words and phrases.

There was nothing to say and everything to say. No time to speak, and yet their joyful faces said everything all at once. Clutching, squeezing hands: "Korcha's lines...over there!" "Thought...you were dead!" "You all right?"

Then Beland gasped, "Got to go!" and, still out of breath, he was back on his feet and disappearing in the direction of the fighting. Ravenna and Nome dragged themselves up, arranged the empty stretcher and their shields and turned back toward where the fighting was thickest. Nome did not have time to ponder it; but, as Beland left them, a flash of awe passed through him at the thought that this was the same man who had left home with him fearful, surly, dark, cowardly.

A short time later, a signal for retreat was sounded; and the Gazines at once dropped back from the walls of the stronghold and withdrew to their lines at the forest edge. They had probed the stronghold and harried the enemy. Not many had passed over the walls to gain a foothold inside, and those who had were overrun. Casualties on both sides were high.

As the attack ended, the work of the tenders began in earnest; for now the field was clear for gathering up the wounded and dying. It was still dangerous work; for the Mommicks randomly fired at the scurrying tenders with longtubes; but most of their attention was taken in gathering their own dead and wounded. Nome and Ravenna, like the dozens of other tenders who swarmed over the field, not daring to go close enough to the wall to retrieve many of the most seriously hurt, had to keep their shields up; and, from time to time, a high-pitched singing whack! against the plates of misk reminded them to go carefully.

At length, the fields in the open were fairly cleared of the fallen; and, while the tenders lay exhausted at the rear, their leaders talked worriedly about how they could get close enough to the wall to bring in those still lying there. Then the unbelievable word passed that the Gazines were preparing for another assault.

From Nome's and Ravenna's vantage point, this battle had looked like a defeat for the Gazines. They had seen swarms of soldiers advance under good cover in the early morning and then thrown against the wall of the stronghold. There they had been stopped and driven off. Surely, they thought, the troops would rest, regroup, spend at least the night, perhaps a whole day, before attacking again with a more promising tactic. This is what most others thought, too. It was certainly what the Mommick thought. This is what Korcha wanted them to think.

That evening, an hour before sundown, while a thousand Mommick soldiers were scattered outside their stronghold wall, scarcely armed, painstakingly repairing the scattered stakes and collecting their dead, hordes of screaming Gazines rushed at them across the open fields. So swift and wild was the second attack that some of the Mommick, fleeing to the safety of their walls, impaled themselves on the stakes. Few of the canon and longtube were manned when the first cries of attack were given, and the Gazines once again reached the perimeter before firing from the stronghold began in earnest.

As Korcha had intended, the first attack in the morning had been a test and a trick. Now he had the forces of Ila and Mira Shannan on the eastern and western sides of the stronghold feint a turning movement, threatening to surround the Mommick position entirely and cut it off from forces in the north. Anticipating this movement, the Mommick threw the the bulk of their forces against these two side attacks; and thousands of the best-trained fohtars surged out of their stronghold, beyond the walls, to head off Ila and Mira Shannan. This left the southern wall facing Korcha weak; and, against this, he threw the strongest force of the entire Gazine resistance. Within minutes, the army of Korcha Rabon had plowed through the rows of stakes, hacked down the panicky Mommick work crews, thrown up misk gangplanks against the low walls, and surged over into the stronghold itself.

As at the Eastern Fortress, the battle was suddenly being fought within the stronghold; and the fohtars, who had sallied out to engage the attackers on the east and the west, now found the strongest point of the Gazine attack at their backs. The Mommicks were desperately fighting for survival, and only their great superiority in numbers and the contact-fighting skill of the fohtars kept them from collapsing in confusion. They pulled back all their forces to fight within the walls, and the battle surged back and forth for nearly an hour as the sun hovered on the horizon.

....

But something was happening on the field, far short of the southern wall, which was to turn the tide of this battle. A tight cluster of shields had been propped up around one spot, and a group of people were huddling there into an anxious knot. Around these, a guard of soldiers had been hurriedly placed, facing outward toward the stronghold; but they were not advancing or taking part in the attack. At the center of this group, a number of people knelt over a figure on the ground. The rumor slipped out and quickly passed among the troops, up the bluff, and over the walls, spreading even among those locked in deadly combat. Korcha has been killed.

The onslaught took on new fury at this news, but their blows flailed wild and off the mark. More of them threw themselves at the Mommick in white rage, and more of them died.

Whispers passed back behind the lines and reached the sick-camps and, from there, spread among the tenders, who ran back and forth stretchering the wounded from the field. In this way, Nome and Ravenna heard that Korcha Rabon was not dead, but lay on the field seriously wounded from canon fire.

Nome was stunned by the news. He stood at the edge of the sick-camp, leaning heavily on the poles of a stretcher, which he held like a staff, breathing hard. Ravenna stood beside him, slumped and limp. Nome looked out through tree branches toward the top of the bluff where the battle was raging. Then he squinted off to his left, across the fields, trying to see where Korcha might have fallen. He chewed his lip, laboring with a decision. He looked at Ravenna, who looked back with tired, sad eyes, waiting for whatever he had to say. Her long hair, tied back behind her head, was gray with dust. Her face was streaked with sweat-washed dirt, and her liquid eyes were heavy, half-lidded. Her clothes were dirty and torn, and her arms dangled at her sides. Her hands were brown with dried blood.

"Stay here," said Nome, at last, in a voice full of weariness. "Stay here and help at the camp. It is time for us to be relieved for a while, anyway. Don't go back out there until I get back. Please! Don't go back out there without me."

She looked at him with a hint of question forming. But then she only nodded.

He gathered up the stretcher, buckled the poles at the middle, and strapped them once more to his back. He reached for his shield leaning against a tree; but, she intercepted his hand and held it tight for a moment. She bowed down over what she held between her palms and placed her dry lips there. She then let his hand continue its movement toward the shield. Nome pushed through the bushes and was out on the field again.

He did not trot forward toward the battle, as they had before, but angled off toward the left, straining his eyes. All across the field, he could see white and brown figures scurrying back and forth like ants, heading toward the bluff and returning from it with heavy burdens between them. Far off he saw one spot of white, not moving, a gathering of shields planted in the ground. He headed for it.

It took nearly ten minutes for Nome to cross the field; and, when he drew near to the crowd of people huddling behind a line of guards and a bank of shields, he could sense their mournful solemnity. The clamor of the battle above them seemed to die away. Because he wore the markings of a tender, no one hindered him as he approached. He stood on tip-toes and stretched to look over the shoulders and heads, but he could not see the object of attention on the ground. He could hear one voice of command over all the others which gave alarmed, urgent, contradictory orders; and he shrank back, incredulous. It was Curry's voice, calling for this one or that to get back and give more room, sending someone back to the rear lines for more medicines and splints, commanding the tenders to be more careful and to hurry.

Fascinated, Nome began to edge forward through the crowd, drawing mutterings, fierce looks, shoves from those about him. Careless of this, he worked his way forward until he stood in front. He could see Curry standing there, bent forward with anxiety. It was not the same Curry he had known. This one was a soldier, uniformed, armed, mustached, barking orders with heavy curses. Suddenly, Curry turned on the gawking crowd gathered around and reeled off a stream of abuse, commanding all but the tenders to get out and get to their duties. He furiously called them cowards and told them their place was in the battle. He pushed forward at the crowd, using the barrel of his longtube in both hands as a rod. Some of the other aides followed his lead and roughly dispersed the crowd, leaving only the tenders. Nome now stood among a small group of tenders looking down at the broken body of Korcha Rabon.

His left side was mangled from the ribs downward. The shape of his left leg was hard to discern. His eyes were open and fixed, and his mouth formed an expression of surprise. No sound came from him, but he was conscious or half-conscious. The tenders who crouched over him and hurried to tie off the bleeding and to restore shape to his form with splints and bandages had done nearly all they could do. One of them looked up at Curry, mumbled something, and gave a quick jerk of his head in the direction of the camps. Immediately, Curry shouted for stretcher bearers, and Nome felt himself roughly pulled forward by the shoulder. He was on his knees at what was left of Korcha's feet, working with another tender at Korcha's head to hold stretcher shafts steady, while a row of others painstakingly hoisted him sideways onto the canvas. Curry was terrified, keeping his eyes now only on his dying hero. His eyes did not see Nome.

The stretcher bearers hefted and struggled to their feet, then began to trot away toward the camps, surrounded by shields and an entourage of lieutenants, stricken with helplessness.

Korcha was carried into a large, dark tent in the sick-camp attached to his army. He was laid on cushions on a high, long table; and a number of tenders and healers surrounded him. The front-most stretcher bearer left the tent, but Nome discretely withdrew to a corner among some baggage and hunched down on the ground.

Hours passed. Lamps were lighted, and tenders worked. Korcha began to murmur and then to moan. He was given numbing concoctions, but he refused to drink and shook his head, sputtering away the stuff they tried to pour between his lips. Curry came and went, checking on progress, then withdrawing, overcome with frustration. Tenders silently slipped in and out, bringing supplies to those at the bedside. On one occasion, Beland entered the tent, carrying a pitcher of something that had been ordered. As he moved toward the tent-flap to withdraw, Nome edged over to catch him by the arm and draw him into the shadows. He begged his astonished friend to get word to Ravenna in the next sick-camp that he was all right. He told Beland he had to stay here for now and that he should tell her he would come to her as soon as he could.

Before Beland withdrew, Nome asked him, in hushed whispers, about the outcome of the battle. The Gazines had given up, Beland said. They had abandoned the stronghold and retreated back to their lines.

As the night wore on, Korcha began to speak in broken sentences. At times, his voice rose to a ranting hoarseness; at times, it dropped away, weak and listless. There were moments when he became lucid and spoke to those at his side, asking about the battle. More often, he slid into a delirium and mumbled about things no one there understood, calling out names no one knew. He was clearly growing weaker.

Nome wiggled among the baggage in the dark corner of the tent, trying to find a more comfortable position. The ground under him felt damp; but he was exhausted and was finding it difficult to resist sleep.

He struggled to stay awake. He drifted...drifted....

Suddenly, he was wide-eyed awake. He had heard his name called loudly, sharply.

"Ogrodni! Where is Ogrodni?"

Nome held his breath. He lay motionless against a bag of clothing. Korcha was calling out in delirium. Nome expected all eyes in the tent to look about and turn on him; but he only saw through the gloom a weary tender rise from a stool near the bed, go to a stand and pour some liquid in a cup, and approach Korcha with it. Where he lay, Nome could watch the whole action without lifting his head from the pillow of clothing onto which he had slumped. The tender tried to offer the cup to Korcha's lips; but the sick man's undamaged right arm raised up and listlessly pushed it away. Then Korcha turned his face directly toward the tender standing over him and looked up at him with clear eyes.

"Where is Ogrodni?" he whispered. "I want to see him."

The tender was uncertain. He tried to make another motion to offer the cup, saying, "Sir...."

"Please!" whispered Korcha.

"Sir," pleaded the tender, "I don't understand...."

Another man rose from the shadows and approached. "Sir," he said softly, "Ogrodni is long gone. Don't think of him, sir. He had nothing to do with...."

"I want to see Ogrodni," Korcha insisted in a hushed voice. "See if you can find him. I want to talk to him."

"Yes, sir," the second attendant said in utter fatigue. "I will have somebody sent to look for him. But first, sir, if you would take a little drink of this...."

Both attendants turned suddenly at the motion behind them. Nome Ogrodni was emerging stiffly from the shadows, moving toward the side of the table on which Korcha Rabon lay. They tensed, as though to intervene, but stayed frozen with surprise as this man, appearing from nowhere, stopped quietly at the side of the table within the ring of lantern glow.

"I am Ogrodni," he said. "I am very sorry to find you like this, sir."

Korcha's glistening eyes had fallen down to meet the approaching figure. They stayed there, fixed on him, without expression. His hair was matted with sweat. The skin on his face seemed stretched tight over a skull. But his eyes were alive and piercing.

"Is it Ogrodni?" he asked at length, showing no surprise.

"Yes, sir. Nome Ogrodni from Tosarkun. Are you in much pain, sir?"

"Nome Ogrodni," he said quietly.

"Sir, I know you have been thinking I betrayed you when I did not meet Ila and did not return...."

Korcha cut him off with a slow rolling of his head from side to side on the pillow, his eyes closing. He opened his eyes wide and clear and looked up at Nome. Nome did not know what to say. He simply returned the gaze of the dying man, feeling the sting of wetness coming into his own eyes. Then Korcha dropped his glance toward the shadows and looked off to the side for a moment.

"What are those?" he asked.

Nome frowned a bit and leaned forward, "Sir?"

"What are those things?" Korcha repeated in a fading voice.

Nome looked at him keenly, then followed the direction of his look over his shoulder. He startled and gripped the edge of the table!

At the edge of the lantern light, toward the corner from which he had come, stood two low, rounded figures looking like smooth rocks; but on each, above a beak-like feature, were a pair of eyes glinting and unmistakably alive.

Nome trembled. "You see them, sir?"

"I see them. What are they?"

"Owlstones, sir."

"What are they doing here? How did they get here?"

Nome swallowed hard. "I don't know, sir. I've seen them often enough. I don't know what they are or where they come from. But I think they are good."

"Funny looking things," said Korcha quietly. He closed his eyes and was still for a long time. Nome thought he had fallen asleep. But then he said, "I feel quieter now." His breathing deepened, and Nome knew he was asleep.

The tenders in the tent cautiously approached Nome and tried to draw him away and began asking who he was and what he was doing there, but he waved them away and pulled over one of their stools alongside the table and sat on it. He closed his eyes, rested both hands on the sick-table, and motionlessly refused to respond to any of them.

How much time passed, much or little, none of them could say; but, suddenly, all were awake at the rasping, rattling sound that came from the throat of the sick man. The attendants hurried round the table and shoved Nome away. There was little they could do and were sure it was nearly over, but Korcha's chopped breathing eased and leveled out. He began muttering aimlessly and tried to raise himself up. The attendants tried to restrain him; and he gave up easily, allowing himself to be lowered back to the pillow. He lay quietly, breathing once again with effort.

"O...Ogrodni," he forced out.

Nome stepped forward. Korcha raised his eyes to him, and his lips rounded and quivered, straining for a word.

"Uh...buh...buh...."

They all leaned forward to catch it.

"Buh...book. Book!"

"Book, sir?" said Nome.

He gave a slight nod, more with his eyes than his head.

"What book, sir? You want a book?"

He looked at Nome with strange intensity, then twisted his head sideways to the right and heaved his right arm from the table with a wretched effort to point toward the side of the tent. His eyes and a quivering finger drove all eyes in that direction.

"There's a book over there you want, sir?" asked one of the attendants.

He continued pointing, wavering, and the effort was causing him great fatigue. Then: "Under...th'box...under...no, bottom of th'box...."

An attendant suddenly broke away and went into the darkness, and the sound of his rummaging through clothing and papers could be heard. The shuffling stopped; and he stepped back holding a large, blue, cloth-bound book. Uncertainly, he approached the side of the table; and the others made way for him. Korcha relaxed back onto the cushions and exhaled, keeping his eyes on the book.

"This it, sir?" the attendant asked, not knowing what to do with it now; for Korcha's hand, still hovering in a vague gesture, was too flaccid to grasp it.

Korcha murmured, then moved his hand toward Nome.

"You want me to give this book to him, sir?" asked the attendant.

Korcha gave a sound somewhere between a murmur and a moan and waved his hand again.

"To him, sir?" the man asked timidly.

"Ogrodni!" his voice grated.

The attendant slowly slid the blue book into Nome's hands. Korcha lay back looking up at Nome's face. His eyes flickered and glistened. Then he struggled to form words again.

"Ogrod...Ogrodni. You...you finish it." Nome leaned forward, striving to catch the meaning. "My journal...about Gazi...you finish it."

He held Nome's stare until he was satisfied that he had been understood. Then Korcha Rabon relaxed and let his eyes slide shut again and breathed quietly. It appeared he was sleeping once more.

Nome hugged the book and did not dare to open it in the moments or hours that followed. He found his stool at the table-side, once again, and remained quietly hunched over, waiting. The attendants returned to their places and also waited. The lantern sputtered, the shadows danced on the ceiling of the tent. All was still.

Again the rasping and rattle, deep in the throat, came suddenly. All around him lurched forward, alert. His body shuddered and was still.

TWENTY-SIX

The Battle of Cloverfield

The camps of the Gazines were quiet all the next day, and there were no more stealthy preparations for battle. A melancholy air of mourning lay upon them like a shroud, and everywhere there was bewilderment and misgiving about the struggle. Korcha had died in the gray hours of the morning. His body was washed, dressed, and laid out on the ground in an open field behind the front lines. Throughout the day, Gazines gathered around it and sat on the grass in silence, forming an ever growing circle of people, until the shape of the crowd around the fallen leader resembled that of the exultant crowd that had gathered around him at 'n Burning Graute, nine months earlier, on the Day of the March. Now, however, there was no fire in their midst, no speeches, no songs. Only silence, weeping, and fasting under the gentle sun of springtime. No fires were lighted anywhere in the camps; no food was served.

At sunset, dry wood was carried in among the people, and a pyre was built at the center alongside the still body of Korcha Rabon. When the rack of wood was high enough, and had been tested for sturdiness, six men came forward and carefully lifted the stiff corpse onto it. As they were in the midst of this motion, however, a noisy disturbance began to ripple in from the outer edge of the crowd. Those at the center, near the pyre, twisted about and craned their necks, in indignation and astonishment at this sacrilegious outburst; but the disturbance continued and spread; and the tidy weave of the circle began to unravel. People in the back were on their feet. There was shouting, and many were leaving and running away. A movement of panic suddenly seized the crowd at the expectation that they were under attack; but they were astounded by the shouts that violated the silence, shouts leaping like bursts of flame through dry grass: "The stronghold is burning! The Mommick stronghold is burning!"

With cries of "Greatsada!" and "The Holy Fire burns!" the tight circle became shapeless; and, leaving the funeral pyre and its unmoving sacrifice, the people surged out of the field toward the thickets, where they encamped, and beyond to the open meadows, which looked up toward the Inland Central Stronghold. The clamor of voices rose to a unified, sustained cheering, as thousands of them spilled out toward what had been the field of battle. In the soft twilight, they danced, jiggled, and jumped, clutching at one another, and threw their arms into the air; for the stronghold upon which they had thrown themselves in bloody conflict was ablaze from one side to the other. The wooden lookout towers were spears of flame, some of them tottering and crumbling into clouds of sparks. All the houses, buildings, and shacks which the Mommick had built up over the years to make this their administrative center were engulfed. The low, stone, defending wall encompassed the great fire like the rim of a burning cup. There was no silhouette of a human figure moving anywhere against the flames.

The evening grew dark; and jubilation among the Gazines continued until, out of their hubub and babble, emerged a swelling chant: "Korcha! Korcha! Korcha!" Spontaneously, the thousands moved back through the thickets, back to the grassy meadow from which they had come, chanting "Korcha!" in an even, pounding rhythm. They teemed about the funeral pyre and continued their dancing and tumult. A flame sprang up at the base of the pyre and quickly climbed among the dry branches; and, with it, a great shout of exultation arose. The flame crackled up and reached, like a great open hand, to grasp the still body of Korcha Rabon. The people wept and cheered and gave themselves over to frenzy.

....

Nome Ogrodni watched the burning of the stronghold from the window of a little stone hut, to which he had withdrawn after Korcha had expired. When the deathwatch was over, he had silently withdrawn from the tent in the dark hours of the morning and groped his way to the sick-camp at the rear of The Southern Army of the People. He had awakened Ravenna Rosealice and whispered to her his plans and begged her under no conditions to go back into battle with the stretcher-bearers. Then he had taken writing materials and a lantern and gone off across the fields toward the first light of dawn.

This abandoned shepherd's shelter he had noticed when he had come with The Southern Army after the overthrow of the Eastern Fortress. It was situated on the slope of a hill, within sight of the Inland Central Stronghold, but far to the side of where the Gazine armies had taken up positions. Once there had been a wooden door and a casement in the gaping hole of the window. Now the stone house was open to the wind. There were black ashes on the dirt floor, where children had made fires, and the corners smelled faintly of urine. There was no furniture, except for several slats of wood built into the wall below the window to make a bed. Nome sat on the boards with his feet tucked up under himself and watched the burning of the stronghold. Beside him was the cold lantern, Korcha's blue journal book, and three pens with a bottle of ink.

Faint in the distance sounded the thrilled celebrations of the Gazines, like the noisy chattering and chirp of intoxicated flocks in trees. But Nome knew that this was not yet their hour of victory. All afternoon, from his neutral vantage point, he had watched the Mommick forces across the valley forming an orderly withdrawal away from the stronghold. He could see that they were not in hasty retreat, but were bent on some strategy. They had disappeared over the rolling hills toward the north; but, after a while, he noticed the smoke of their cook-fires stretching out in a long line across the northern horizon; and he correctly guessed that they had abandoned the constraints of the stronghold to arraign themselves in a more expanded position, a short distance away. As the last of them had left the stronghold, the fires had sprung up there.

Gazine scouts would discover all this in the morning. It was likely that some of them had already observed what Nome had and were on their way back to the Gazine lines with news that the Mommick had not fled but had simply retreated to a fanned-out position along a ridge of hills that ran down from the spurs of the Endicot Mountains. The Mommick had been stunned by the ferocity of the Gazine assaults on their stronghold and now were in desperate fear of being surrounded in their fortress. Leaving nothing to the enemy, they had put their entire encampment to the torch, while they moved into the open, where they could maneuver.

The stone hut was dark, but the glow of the fire threw a faint, dancing square of light through the window onto the opposite wall. Nome turned his face away and tried not to hear the sounds of rejoicing. A burden of responsibility was on him. He felt in his pocket for flint, steel, and tinder, then kindled a light and carefully turned up the wick. Taking up the blue book, he opened randomly and let his eyes be led by Korcha's precise, angular handwriting. He paged about and re-read passages of what he had been reading all afternoon, ever since he had awakened from a stiff and cramping sleep. Then he came to the last entry, and the blank page confronted him.

The journal had been started during the early days of the first uprising against the Mommicks, shortly after the branding laws were promulgated. At first, it was a factual description of the campaign under the leadership of Korcha's sister, Rilda, a chronicle of raids and battles and strategies. But after the betrayal of the resistance and the treacherous deaths of Rilda and their brother, Mehtor, the tone of the journal changed. This was the period of the flight from Gazi, the wandering on The Plains of Wildness, the gathering of refugees in exile at 'n Burning Graute. Korcha's writing became much more personal, thoughtful, even visionary.

Up to this point, he had often called himself "the tailor," a reference to his former occupation; but, soon after the sojourn at 'n Burning Graute began, he ceased referring to himself at all. Instead, he developed an idealized picture of the suffering people of Gazi, an image which became the preoccupying theme for the rest of the journal. Korcha wrote as much about developing the quality of his nation's character as he did about developing the people as a fighting force. There were drafts of some of his speeches, masterpieces of dignity, eloquence, and clarity. There were anecdotes about many of the personalities involved in the struggle. His older brother, Ila, for instance, so unlike himself, he loved; but Ila was repeatedly passed over for promotion to the key positions of authority in favor of Mira Shannan and others. Had Ila not been a member of the famous Rabon family, he would have remained in obscurity. Korcha made it plain that, in "Gazi restored," no member of the Rabon family would have a place in government. He enjoined that, in Gazi restored, no monuments be built, no statues erected in honor of anyone who had taken part in the resistance. Later, a strange passage toward the end of the journal modified this with the request that, in Gazi restored, one single monument to the suffering, victorious people of Gazi be built: the likeness of the old woman, Bima.

Nome was curious to see if he or his friends were mentioned, but there was only a passing comment about "three men found in the cave behind the waterfall" during the time of the floods at 'n Burning Graute. The name "Ogrodni" did appear one time in an entry written while Korcha's army was on The Plains of Wildness. At this stage, the writing became confused, and even the handwriting changed. The philosophical and idealistic tone of the journal became a tone of fury. The glorious victory at Kul Sama was described in cold, factual detail. The focus shifted to military strategy and tactics. The personality of the writer dropped away, except for occasional trite, raging rhetoric against "the demons of Moma." The final entry, a dry comment about positioning the Gazine armies and supply lines, abruptly ended a long series which suggested Korcha was embattled with demons other than those from Moma. It was a sad ending to a noble and stormy account.

Nome slowly took up a pen, examined the tip in the light of the lantern, dipped it carefully in ink, and dated his entry. Then he wrote: "The finishing of this journal must be done by a hand other than the one which began it. At the moment of this writing, Korcha Rabon is returning to the Greatsada on holy fire. He fell in battle in the service of the people of Gazi yesterday evening. In his final moments, he entrusted me with his writing about the struggle of his people for freedom, and asked that I finish it. I am unGazine...."

Nome continued to write far into the night. He did not give his own name, nor any clue to his identity. Returning to the style of meditative description which Korcha had used in the earlier entries, he speculated on why the patriot would entrust this task to someone who was not of his own people. He sought the answer in his description of the manner of Korcha's death. During his dying hours, Nome wrote, Korcha Rabon had experienced a profound personal reconciliation, and an obvious sense of peace. He had been a man of great and loyal spirit who, nevertheless, found himself more and more beset by wythies, as he committed himself and his people to this war. Wythies hovered about him and plagued him, certainly as early as the 'n Burning Graute period. He appeared joyless and driven, racked with headaches and physically frail. He was compassionate, just, and selfless; yet the opening to wythies was that he had pledged what remained of his life to war. He battled them daily as much as he did battle with the flesh and blood occupiers of his homeland. When he led his people onto The Plains of Wildness, he was no match for the overwhelming power of the wythies, and his spirit was crushed and driven to the edge. When he and his people emerged from The Plains, they regained themselves, but the wythies clung to them and assisted them in the works of death. They had taken up the weapons and the ways of their enemy; and now, increasingly, they were taking on their spirit. Perhaps he had chosen someone not caught in the passions of his nation's struggle to finish the journal. "It is not my place, unGazine as I am," Nome wrote in a moment of hesitation, "to say more about this. Perhaps I have gone too far already. But I have seen much. I have witnessed the life and the dying of Korcha Rabon; and I have seen that, at the last moment, he was delivered."

With that, Nome put the pen down and the cap back on the bottle. He paused, staring at the loose, ambling gait of his own script, then flipped back the pages to compare it to Korcha's. He experienced a feeling of unreality...that he should be sitting here finishing Korcha's life, passing judgment on it. He closed the book, laid it aside, turned off the lamp. He slid down on the bench and, open-eyed, waited for sleep.

....

The next morning, all was still, except for the whistle and trill of bird song and the light hiss of breeze through the infant leaves of trees. He slipped the journal up onto the rafter of the hut and wedged it against the ceiling in the shadows, then walked out the door. Hunger pulled at his insides, for he had not eaten for a day and a half. The beauty of the morning refreshed him, however. The sun was just about to rise; there was a slight breeze; and the moist smell of springtime was rising from the earth. Nome drew in the air with several long, deep breaths. He slowly looked about in all directions, up at the clear sky, down at the new grass at his feet, then began walking down the slope toward the valley. His mind stayed empty, his senses alive and delighted. Coming down onto the level ground, he looked ahead and upward toward where the stronghold had stood. The entire crown of the hill was blackened, and wavering columns of pale smoke lingered there. He strolled off to the right, crossed the valley in an aimless direction and came to the crest of another low hill, north of the stronghold. Here the grass was pressed flat and the earth gouged and cut from the passing of the Mommick army in retreat. Standing there, Nome let his eyes follow the broad swath of track they had made, straight down the slope, across a wide valley, matted with green and purple clover, and directly up the next rise to the ridge where they could still be seen, arrayed and dug-in behind earthworks, all along the northern horizon.

"This is where it will happen," he said aloud.

Then he slowly walked forward, down the hill, veering away from the path the army had left, and straying amid the new clover in the valley. He sat on the ground and continued to look about, taking in the warmth of the rising sun, the flitting of songbirds, the buzzing of flies, and the fresh puffs of air wafting from the direction of the mountains, massive, misty, purple.

This moment, thought Nome, has come to this place day after day, year after year, for thousands of years. Forever. And it will come, again and again, long after we are gone. After this day has passed.

"This is where it will happen," he said again, meaning the final, bloody battle.

He looked north at the line of horizon cut against the sky by the long ridge, and watched the busy ant-like preparations. He could sense the gathering of another horde, massing behind him from the south, and ready for death, behind the low hill at his back.

Then the breeze stirred again, and the fragrance of the blossoming clover and sweetgrass drifted through him; and Nome suddenly knelt up straight and cried: "The perfume of the Holy! The touch of her hand!" He knew, without thinking it, that this cloverfield, this air, and this sunlight would belong to the warriors of neither army, when the fight was over, but that they, like he were passing through, like the swooping birds, the humming bees, the scuttering bugs, the breeze.

....

The sun was nearly overhead when Nome arrived at the sick-camp and found Ravenna. He took her away from that place, telling her that their time among the tenders was over.

"Let the Gazine people care for their own," he said firmly. "It is no longer our duty."

There was something strange and certain in his manner, and she did as he said. They gathered some food, looked for Wasoo briefly, without success, then withdrew to the stone house where Nome had been staying.

As the armies of the Gazines mobilized once more and began to move forward, past the burned-out stronghold, down the next valley and up to the top of the low hill facing the Mommick host, Ravenna asked only once: "Shouldn't we be there to help them carry away the wounded?"

Nome simply answered, "No." Nothing more was said about it.

The battle raged all that day in the valley between the two camps. Most of the time, Ravenna and Nome remained in the stone house; but, toward the end, when the noise began to die away in the distance, and the Gazines appeared to have advanced well beyond the hill from which they had originally taken up position, they went out of the shelter and climbed up on high ground to see the outcome.

Not many of the soldiers of either side were in sight, except those dead and wounded in the valley. The Mommick forces had broken rank along their entire defended ridge and were in headlong flight. The Gazines were in pursuit, and both forces had passed beyond the rolling hills to the north.

Ravenna went down to the moaning quiet of the valley and began to help with the gathering of people from the blood-soaked clover and sweetgrass. Nome returned to the stone hut, took down Korcha's journal, and lighted the lantern.

....

In the days that followed, Nome wrote as detailed an account as he could about what he named The Battle of Cloverfield. The name became official when Korcha's journal later became a cherished national treasure. Nome remained in the stone hut alone until the work was finished. Ravenna brought him meals and news. He had a few other visitors, including Wasoo and Beland. Beland had a rather serious leg wound, but he was able to get about with some help.

The journal entry describing The Battle of Cloverfield ended this way: "As the tide of the battle turned against the Mommicks, they did not simply retreat northward and withdraw from the country, as had been expected. The entire force attempted to make a strategic retreat by hooking eastward, in hopes of regrouping, perhaps even with the intention of circling southward to re-attack below the Gazine advances. Evidently, they were determined to break out of the narrow corridor which this country forms between high mountains and The Plains of Wildness. But the Mommicks did not appreciate how severe a constraint The Plains are. Perhaps because they had never explored The Plains themselves, and relied only on danes and hirelings to go there, they did not understand the vast and deep power of that place which cannot be entered casually, even by great armies.

"Throughout the sixteenth and seventeenth of the month, the Mommick force charged out past the grasslands and entered The Plains of Wildness, just to the north of Markova Spring. The army of Mira Shannan pursued them to the edge of The Plains and stopped. Ila Rabon led his forces in a fanning movement south of Markova Spring to preempt any effort of the enemy to swing back and re-enter Gazi. But the Mommick forces disappeared into the great cloud of dust they made as they fled, and were seen no more. It was as though the desert had swallowed them. In the days that have followed their disappearance, several isolated Mommick soldiers have reappeared, desperate and dazed, as though washed up on our shore.

"The day for which Korcha Rabon lived and died has come," Nome wrote further. "Recall now the words which he put down here while he and his people were still exiles at 'n Burning Graute:

I have one desire—
to rescue my people from the tyranny of strangers
who have disgraced and dishonored them,
to restore freedom and peace to the mountains and valleys.

"All of this Korcha did. He fell in the final hour, but his spirit rose from the flames and enabled the people to finish the work. There was even more that he wanted to do, but he was not allowed life to do it. For he also wrote of his people:

With my own hands I want to bind their wounds, wash the blood
from their clothing,
rebuild their houses, sweep the rubble from their streets.
I want to see the holy fire once more in the house of The Greatsada.
Then I can go. Gazi restored will not need another tailor.

"Korcha Rabon, the warrior, could not do this. He could not even finish his journal, and has asked an unGazine to do it for him. I have done it; and now I, too, must go away. It is for the living people of Gazi to bind the wounds, wash the blood, rebuild the houses, sweep the streets and bring back the holy fire. And, if any of those who were once your enemy survive The Plains of Wildness and are washed up alive from the desert onto the shores of your beautiful country, show them mercy, and help to heal them. It is what Korcha would have done."

Nome put down the pen and closed the book.

TWENTY-SEVEN

Journey to the Sea

A day or two later, Nome and Ravenna invited Beland and Wasoo to a picnic on the grassy slope, just below the stone hut. It was their farewell meal.

Sheep browsed nearby, nibbling and jerking at the new grass while their spring lambs danced and kicked spindly legs. The sun was warm, the sky clear blue; and cottony clouds billowed high, as though it were already summer. The four friends sprawled, half on the grass, half on the four sides of the blanket on which was set the picnic fare: boiled eggs, slabs of cheese, ragged chunks of rip-bread, sour-dip pickeldy sauce, a jug of uppledok hayfield, and a small mound of victory cakes. Uppledok hayfield was a sweet drink made from the juice of sour fruit, honey, and water, as popular in Gazi in summertime as kgopuk was in winter. Its strange name was given because this thirst-quencher was downed in the pitcher-fulls by farmhands working the fields on sweltering days in the Uppledok grain-growing region of Gazi. Victory cakes were something new. These airy-light, sweet, white mouthfuls had been created recently in a kitchen, not far away, by a housewife—even as the Battles of the Stronghold and of Cloverfield raged. They were an instant patriotic success, and the recipe spread throughout the land with the speed of gossip. Everyone had tried them by now, and the jubilant people of Gazi could not get enough of them.

"You're feeling better now, aren't you, Nome?" said Ravenna, smiling at him across the feast.

"Yes, a lot better. Relieved. Relieved to have that book out of my hands."

"You do look relieved," said Wasoo. "For a while there, when you were working away at Korcha's diary, you were starting to look like him. All stony-faced and tight and wrinkly around the eyes. I almost took to saluting you and saying 'yessir!' and 'no,sir!' when my one-legged friend and I was up here to see how your literary efforts were coming."

"One-legged!" Beland rolled over on his elbow and squinted. "Who's one-legged? I got *three* good legs here. Well...truth is, I got one good leg and one bad leg and one stout wooden leg!" He picked up his walking cane and brandished it across the blanket at Wasoo.

"*Four*-legged!" shouted Wasoo back at him. "You don't get far without leaning on *me*. Shuffling around like an old duffer. I'm your fourth leg, don't forget about *me*!"

"All right, four!" cried Beland. "Four-legged animals are the best kind. Look at them good sheep over there, four legged every one of 'em, just like me. And four-legged animals is the kind we have on our farms, ain't it? Horses, cows, pigs, asses...just like me. Four-legged all of 'em."

"Wait!" cried Wasoo sitting upright. "What about chickens? What about ducks? What about geese? *Two*-legged, all of 'em. Just like the rest of us here at this picnic. Why are you leaving them out...and *us* out? They're on the farms, too, so are *we*. Why are you trying to make out that you're better than the rest of us two-footed animals? Beland, of Beland's Farm!"

Beland rose up on one elbow and was gesturing fiercely with a chunk of rip-bread, when he began sniggering and then coughing and collapsed back onto the blanket.

"Stop, stop!" said Nome, holding aloft his mug of juice and honey. "We just got one war over with. Let's not start another one so soon! Wasoo, this Beland used to be a sober and sensible fellow when I knew him in Tosarkun. Look at him now, giggling and choking on his bread. You're a *bad influence* on him, Wasoo!"

"Yessir! Thank you, sir," snapping crisply to salute. "I done my best, sir."

Nome gave up. Ravenna was giggling.

"So you two are staying for sure then, are you?" she asked, when they all had relaxed and were once again paying attention to the picnic food.

"Yes, we're staying," said Wasoo. "We talked it over, Beland and I, and agreed that, since he wanted to stay in Gazi, I had to stay with him...because, if I left, that would make him a three-legged animal, and we don't got none of those on any farms...."

"Oh, no, don't start again....!" Ravenna pleaded. "Really now, *you* tell me, Beland. Quit laughing...Nome says you were once a sensible fellow. *You* tell me. Now, Wasoo, you be quiet!"

"All right." Beland was winding down from jiggling laughter, which made his leg hurt. "All right. Yes, we're staying here. We agreed. To help out the sick and wounded in the lagers. Seems like that is where we can do some good."

"I see that," said Ravenna. "I think you're right. Did Wasoo tell you what I told him about his goodcharm?"

"Yes, he told me about that, Ravenna."

"And I think it is your goodcharm, too, Beland. You look to me like a man doing the right thing."

He grinned and looked away, a boy complimented.

"And what about the Farm...?" asked Nome after a pause, "Oh, no, I shouldn't have said that. I'll get you two going again about legged animals. What about Beland's Farm? In Tosarkun?"

Beland suddenly looked crestfallen. He stammered when he began to answer. "It ain't that I haven't been thinking about it, Nome. Fact, been thinking about it all along. But I just can't manage doing anything about it the way you can. I mean sending money back there...and I know I haven't been doing my part."

Nome started to interrupt, but Beland went on, "No, I ain't saying you're blaming me, Nome. But I blame myself...but not a lot, but I just don't see how I could...I think I just see things for what they are. For one thing, I'm more cheerful now. More than I have ever been, I don't know why. Doesn't make sense with a war going on and people suffering all around me. I feel a lot of sadness, too, don't get me wrong. And another thing, it's different with me and the Farm than it is for you. And even for Curry. I mean, I don't have no wife there anymore and no old parents like you have and no old mother like Curry got, trying to hang onto the holdings. I got brothers and sisters and cousins and one old uncle. But they'll have to do the best they can. I can't save them, I haven't got it in me. Maybe they should have sent someone else out to raise money to save Beland's Farm. Anyway, it's probably gone by now...."

"I understand, Beland, I understand," said Nome. "But what about the money Korcha promised? Didn't you get any of that?"

"Well...funny thing...things changed after we got to Gazi. That's when I started being a burner, and then a tender. Seems like I was out of the picture, out of Korcha's mind. I got pay from the quartermaster like everyone else, but it was nothing like what he gave us back there on the march. Remember that, Nome? We almost fell over when that fellow pushed all that money across the table at us. Remember that? I don't know what Curry got paid by the quartermaster here. I haven't seen much of Curry. He was always with Korcha. When I did see him, we didn't talk much, never about money, for sure. So I don't know if Curry has been sending money back, I don't see how he could. Far as I know, Nome, you're the only one that has been coming through for the folks on the holdings back home."

"I don't see how I can keep it up, either, Beland. I don't have anything for the next time. Let's see, the next hundred-day is due in about...well, in about two months, maybe a little more. We should be good at Brighthome for now, if Chindit made it back. 'Course, we don't know if he did. If not, it's all over, and we might as well be talking about something else."

"See what I mean? It all rides on a dog making it back, weeks of trotting through wild territory, not getting lost and getting there on time."

"He did it once before," said Nome.

"I know. And I think Chindit will make it through...has *already* made it through this time, too. That's because he's a *four*-legged animal, and everyone knows that they're the best kind."

Nome snorted a laugh and shook his head, grinning. "I like you best cheerful, Beland. And I think it's right that you're staying here where you became cheerful. Stay here and help heal these people. The Farm is just a farm. I am really glad for you, Beland; but the Holy knows my heart and knows that I will miss you sweetly."

Beland looked down shyly.

"I say the same to you, Wasoo," said Nome. "You've been a fine traveling companion."

"Oh, you don't need another traveling companion, Nome. You got one, and she's prettier than I am."

"Well, you're right there. So we are setting off this afternoon,

Ravenna and I.

"Why are you going up north to cross The Plains? I still don't understand why you don't go back to the fealards and cross down there, like we were first planning to go."

"A number of reasons," said Ravenna. "First of all, Nome and I are as eager to get out of Gazi as you are to stay. I guess we are just sick at heart, the war and everything. At what happened to Korcha, at Nome's finishing the journal..."

"At what happened to Curry," Nome added.

"What do you mean?"

"Oh...," he searched for words, "...*you* know, Beland, what I mean. He was our good friend. Like family, him and me...more than you and him. But...I don't know...somehow he needed to push us away so he could be more acceptable to his hero."

"He did more than that, Nome," Beland said in wrath. "He betrayed you!"

"Well, now let's not say more about that," said Nome. "We don't know what has been going on with Curry, because, as you say, we haven't had a chance to talk to him."

"Haven't you seen him at all?" asked Wasoo. "Not even when you went to hand over Korcha's journal?"

Nome shook his head. "I asked for him. Was told he was not available. I went to Mira Shannan's headquarters and asked, because that is where they say Curry is now. He's first aide to Mira Shannan."

"And Mira Shannan is in charge of the country," said Wasoo. "So that puts your old friend right up there."

"It is not what Korcha wanted," said Nome. "It's very clear from his journal that he intended to step back from all public leadership as soon as the war was over. He didn't want Mira Shannan or Ila or any of the military leadership running the country in 'Gazi restored.' He wrote about that several times in very strong language."

"But Mira Shannan is definitely running the country."

"I know. And when Korcha's journal is published, that's going to be an embarrassment for him. And for Curry, and a number of others."

"Do you think Mira Shannan will let those parts of the journal out?"

"It won't be up to him," Nome answered.

"Why not?"

"Because I didn't give the journal to Mira Shannan. I gave it to Ila

Rabon."

All three looked at him in surprise.

"I did not feel right about Mira Shannan. The very thing we are talking about. I took it to Ila because he was Korcha's brother. He was an adequate commander in the rebellion, not one of the greatest. But he was Korcha's brother, and now he has his journal. I am done with it all. Then I went to Mira Shannan's headquarters, not to see him, but to look for Curry. To say goodbye, at least. I waited a long time. I didn't see him."

They were all silent in their own thoughts for a time. Then Nome added, "Beland, you will probably be seeing Curry sometime or other. This is his home now. He has become a successful man in ways neither you nor I have become successful. I am sure he will be staying here. Tell him for me, please, that I wish him well. Tell him what we say in Tosarkun: 'The Holy be your home.' Tell him those were Nome's words to him."

"I will," said Beland quietly.

"Well," said Wasoo lightly, "now what? Korcha's gone. No ransom money cash from the quartermaster. You say you're nearly out of money. You are on your way back to Brighthome. And?"

"Right. I went to the quartermaster, but he had no orders concerning me—or us—from Korcha or from Mira Shannan."

"That's what I started telling you about a moment ago," broke in Ravenna. "We got off on another track. I started telling you why Nome and I plan to cross The Plains up north here where we have never been before. There are two things foremost in Nome's mind. He needs to try to raise enough money for the next payment on Brighthome. And he needs to get it back on time. We have a bit over two months to do that, and going the length of Gazi to the fealards again is too roundabout. We need to begin crossing The Plains now. Maybe two of us can find work along the way to get...."

"But how...?"

"Listen. While Nome has been up here finishing the journal, I have been talking to a lot of people in the camps. And do you know who one of them was? One of the very scouts Korcha sent out from 'n Burning Graute to plan The March. She has been everywhere, and has knowledge of all kinds of places. She was one of those who actually made contact with the forest people and helped work out a safe passage truce with them and helped plan the route for the armies. When I told her about Nome's being with Korcha when he died and about the journal, she just opened up to me. She knows all the roads and drew me maps. I'll show them to you before we leave; they're in my pack. And she showed me a way across The Plains that is straighter than the other ways and is almost never used. The only risk is that some of the stele markers are reported to have been moved or destroyed. But she says that it still can be crossed there, if we are careful about some directions she gave me. Most important, is that this northern crossing will put us on the road to the sea!"

"The what?"

"To the sea! We are going to the sea! Nome has been wanting to ever since he was on a road called 'Sea Road North.' I never thought much about it; but, since we have been talking about it, I can't wait to get to the sea. They say it is water, water, out as far as you can see! Like the fields back home...only water!"

"But what are you going to do there?"

"Wait now!" She was excited. "This same woman told me that the road she marked will take us to a string of towns along the seacoast. She says, if we leave here right away and hurry, there is a chance we can get there in time for 'the spad run.' Spad are a kind of silvery-gold fish, she says, that swim up along the coast in big flocks. They go past these towns for days, at a certain time every spring, and the people go out in crowds of boats and work day and night and catch all they can until the fish are gone. I don't know what they do with all of it; but she says you can make a lot of money very quickly during those days, if you can get a job with the fishing boats and work till the fish are gone. I told her what we needed for the next payment on Brighthome; and she said the two of us might get somewhere close to that if we could get hired right away. They need extra help during that time, too, so there is a good chance we could do it, if we get there in time."

Ravenna's face was flushed, and her eyes shone. Nome thought: How lovely she is. They had reached the victory cakes now at the end of their picnic and were drinking the last of the uppledok hayfield.

"That's why we have to leave today, without delay," said Nome, "to take this northern route. Hate to leave these behind," looking at the last piece of cake between thumb and fingers before pushing it into his mouth. "The Gazines sure know how to make war and cake."

"I have the recipe," said Ravenna. "I will make you some when we arrive at a house with a real stove and no longer have to cook over campfires."

Wasoo caught Beland's eye at this and smiled, but they said nothing. The four friends lingered a while longer and talked about the coming trip, about adventures passed, about many things. As the sun moved past noon, they got up and stood awkwardly about with one another, embraced, separated with halting words and promises. Wasoo stood still beside Beland, who leaned on his cane. They watched Nome and Ravenna shoulder their packs, wave, and move away. They watched for a long time until the two trudging figures became small on the horizon, moving northeast toward The Plains, until they became one dot, until they disappeared.

....

Ravenna and Nome walked as far as Markova Spring by nightfall, the frontier town near which the Mommick army had passed onto The Plains of Wildness. They were readily welcomed into one of the homes the first time they stopped to ask for information. Gazines were in an ebullient mood, expansive in their hospitality, especially here in the north, free of occupation for the first time. They were fed and housed and kept up late, far past sleepiness. Their hosts could not hear enough about the war, especially when they learned that Nome had known Korcha Rabon personally.

Nome and Ravenna had roamed about this country so long in wariness, seeking shelter from distrustful citizens, that this new mood lifted their spirits; and they thought they might have carried away warm, fond memories of Gazi, if they had only visited it in peacetime. It was too late for that, and they graciously resisted the urging of the family at Markova Spring to stay a few days longer and rest for their journey.

They were eager to be gone; and, by mid-morning, they were hurrying farther north and angling to the right in search of the edge of The Plains, where the first scattered remains of a stele marker was to be found.

The farther east they went, the more the green beauty of the countryside dropped away. Mountains still rose behind their backs, dusty-blue and draped with snow; but, only now, did they fully appreciate how beautiful the hill country of Gazi had been. As they went on, the earth became barren and yellow, and puffs of dust rose with every step. Ravenna had found a bolt of material and hastily sewn two tent-dresses, but these were much heavier than the ones Aunie had made. Everything they carried was heavier. There had been no time to dry food and make light packs. Ravenna now wore Gazi boots, not reed sandals. The sun was very hot, and they perspired constantly, losing body-water more quickly than was good.

They were worried and spoke to each other in hushed voices as they walked. They did not know if their water would hold out or if they would find fresh pools along the way. They had not yet found the first stele marker. Most of all, they were anticipating with dread the whispering spirits. Nome had been looking all around, to the sides, even toward the rear.

"What are you looking for," she asked.

"Ohh...I don't know. I...suppose I was just hoping...."

"What? The stele marker would be up ahead somewhere."

"Well, I just thought that maybe...."

"Maybe...?"

"...that maybe there might be a sign...or something...that we are doing the right thing...or going the right way."

"A sign? You don't mean a stele marker?"

"No, I mean....well, Ravenna, I have been looking for the owlstones. I have been looking for them for days."

"You haven't seen anything?"

"No."

"I haven't been looking, but I haven't either. I saw them only that one time last winter I told you about. Why are you expecting to see them now?"

"I don't know how to answer that. Except to say that, the closer we get to The Plains of Wildness, the more I wonder if we are doing the right thing. We are very vulnerable out here. I have never figured out what those little owlstones are or why they appear. But they are a comfort."

"I see," she said, beginning to look around herself.

"Or a warning," he added.

They shuffled along in silence, both of them now looking around. They found the first stele marker at about the place where the map showed it should be. The map, drawn for Ravenna by the scout, would be of little use for a while after this point. The Plains had few dependable landmarks. There was a blank space on the map until the road leading to the sea began. This marker had been knocked down and strewn about, but there was enough of it left to see how it had once been laid out. Who had dared do this? And would it be the same, or worse, with the markers on the flat, trackless waste ahead of them?

Ravenna and Nome stood looking at the flat stones scattered on the ground. They hesitated, uncertain about going forward, although now they knew the correct direction.

Something was happening around them. They both sensed it in some hidden place of awareness, long before consciously knowing that something was changing. The air. Was there something about the air that was changing? The color of things? What was it? The light? That was it, the light. Something about the quality of daylight was changing...they felt it, sensed it, while their thoughts were busy elsewhere, rambling over the scattered stones and out across the flatlands and back to the greenlands in indecision.

Suddenly, Ravenna tensed and looked up...overhead.

"Nome," she whispered. "Look."

"What?" He looked into her face anxiously, then immediately followed her gaze toward the sky.

"Nome, look!" she repeated more loudly.

He was looking. His mouth hung slack. They both were looking. A thin film of cloud cover was muting the sun. More than that, the gauzy cloud was bunching slowly into ripples, long, sweeping, evenly-spaced ribbing that stroked the entire sky. In their many days on these Plains of Wildness, they had never once seen clouds that blocked the merciless glare of the sun. Yet this band of cloud was slowly creeping across the whole dome of the sky, from one horizon to the other, in a rhythm of wavelets taking clearer shape by the moment. The sun was still visible behind it, muffled and pale; and the features of the desert softened. Then the vast pattern became an image, whose enormity overwhelmed them. It was the image of a wing, a feathered wing, whose majestic greatness rose out of the distant horizon and arched slowly across the vault of the heavens. It was, no doubt, a mighty, outstretched wing, hovering, limned with soft, sweeping feathers.

"Ahhh, Nome."

"Hohhh...Holy..."

They stood and stared and swept their eyes over the arch of the sky. She reached out sideways, searching for his hand.

"Nome," Ravenna said, "there are no wythies here!"

He could not speak. He only shook his upturned head slightly from side to side.

....

They traveled across The Plains of Wildness by day and by night, resting when they were tired, sleeping when they needed, eating and drinking what they carried without concern. By day, the sun warmed but did not scorch them. By night, the white moon glowed through the vapor like a ghost ship slowly sailing toward the mountains of Gazi, which they had left behind. The desert was silent, no lisping spirit-murmurs, no plaintive keening to chill their souls. By day and by night, the overarching wing of cloud remained. The stele markers failed them, disturbed and scattered beyond recognition; but Ravenna and Nome had let fear slip away like a heavy pack to the ground and continued to walk toward the east in a straight line. And so it happened that, long before they expected, the green lands appeared once more, coming forward gladly to meet them.

Only then did the wing of cloud begin to drift and mingle into itself, casually blown by some high breeze, and lift away like a dream. They were walking forward again through weeds and shin-high grasses, past shrubs, bushes, and approaching trees. Perhaps somewhere here, to the right or to the left, would be the beginning of a road, pathways at least, leading to a road, the right road to take them to the sea.

They found the shabby ruin of a roadway, lumpy, overgrown, and choked with spiky saplings. It seemed to strike eastward, so they followed it; and, before long, they were led to a narrow dirt road that burrowed through an ever-thickening forest. This way had seen some traffic recently, human and animal. Before long, it led them to a proper high road; and then Ravenna's hand-drawn map began to become useful once again. There were towns and villages ahead, if she were reading it right. They had come off The Plains too far south but apparently had groped their way up to the right path.

That night they camped in the woods, just out of sight of the road. Over a small fire, while they ate, Nome said this reminded him of his lonely travels from the cache hole to the High Road and up to Trapple

Rock and back down again and onward to Hay, where he had given up all hope of saving Brighthome. All those nights he had slept out in the open like this, rain or clear, in the woods beside the road. Except for Trapple Rock where he had lodging. He remembered Imber Troutman who had been so kind and Troutman's daughter, with whom he had fallen in love for a few days.

"It would be nice if we could find a friendly inn like that in one of these towns coming up," he said.

"We don't have enough money left for an inn," she said. "Only a little left for food."

"You concerned about the money? Or about the inkeepers' daughters?"

She looked about the ground for a stone to throw at him, but settled for a stick.

The next afternoon, they came to the first settlement, no more than a cluster of houses around a widening in the road. There were no shops; but the people there sold them food, as they often did to travelers. The following day, they began to meet others, coming and going, some on foot, some on horseback or driving carts. Then the villages and towns began to appear more frequently, strangely named places: Wells, Cold Beer, Fetching, Pot 'o Soup, Michael's Love.

At Michael's Love it was market day, and the square and side streets were bustling. Nome was sitting on a stone doorstep, barefoot, studying the rotted seams of his flapping boots, trying to decide if they were worth repairing or if he would have to spend the last of their money on a new pair. He ignored the people who jostled and squeezed between the stands and piles of goods for sale, milling past him in the narrow alleyway.

Ravena had gone off to buy fruit and bread and some kind of juice with which to fill their flattened waterskin. She got to talking to a woman, who was waiting beside two odd-looking carts. They were high, enclosed structures that looked as though they would teeter and sway as they rolled on their skinny-spoke wheels. At the front, just above the shafts, was a long plank for the driver's seat; and, at the rear, a door. The shafts drooped sadly to the ground, for there were no horses hitched between them. Perhaps it was the strangeness of the carts which had drawn Ravenna into conversation with the woman, for she had never seen anything like them and was asking what they were used for. In any case, she hurried excitedly back to Nome telling him to quick! come with her! she might have a ride for them to the sea!

In this way they met Ruby and Finn, who were to become good friends. While she waited for her husband to return, Ruby stood by the carts and chatted with Ravenna and Nome. She was a small woman, but she stood in her blue coarsecloth trousers with legs apart and hands on hips as though she were inspecting troops and about to give orders. Her white hair was carelessly tied up in a frayed plaid scarf. She cocked her head like a bird listening, and her aging face was creased leather; but her lively eyes pranced about, darting from one to the other.

And here came Finn, striding through the market crowd, forearms held high on either side, leading two horses by their bits, as though he were carrying them over his shoulders. When he saw the three of them, he stopped where he was on the street and studied. Who has she taken up with now? was on his face. His old face, scowling now, was baggy and ringed with mutton-chop whiskers and bushy white eyebrows. Onto his head had been tugged a blue cap with a short bill. He stood bow-legged, not much taller than his wife and dressed in the same dirty blue coarsecloth.

"These here say they want to go to the sea, hey?" said Ruby in a lively, clipped speech as her husband approached.

He moved past them, hauling the horses, casting only a quick side-glance at the strangers. "They do, hey?" he said without interest.

She winked at Ravenna. "Seem nice. What do you think?"

Finn said nothing, but pulled and shoved one horse into place between the shafts. Nome started forward to hold the other steady by the bit. Finn glanced up at him sharply. His eyes seemed to linger on the scar that ran down Nome's cheek. Then his eyes dropped to Nome's hands and studied them, then returned to his own work of strapping the horse. Still he said nothing. He moved to put the second horse in place on the other cart and accepted Nome's help of holding up the shafts, but did not look at him again. Finally, he stepped back and surveyed the two carts and horses in slow, careful manner. Nome stood beside him surveying them, too, as though the two of them had just completed a great work.

Finn turned, squinted at both Nome and Ravenna, and said, "You drink beer?"

They were stunned, uncertain as to whether drinking beer were a requirement or an obstacle. Nome looked nervously at the others, shrugged slightly, and said, "Uh...if it's good."

"C'mon, hey?" Finn beckoned with a toss of his arm and led the three of them through a set of doors beneath a wooden sign reading "Mug and Flagon."

It turned out that Finn was capable of far livelier talk than he had displayed outside. It was not the pint or two of beer that loosened him up, but the decision he had come to that these two were "all right." He prided himself on being "no fool"; and "being in the trade as I am, hey?" he knew he couldn't trust many a man or woman on the road away from home, even when they "seemed nice" at first glance.

An hour later, the four of them clattered out the Mug and Flagon more noisily than they had entered, laughing and talking and eager to climb up on the highhouse carts, as they were called.

"Me and Ravenna on this here one, hey?" shouted Ruby to her mate. "We can swap off at Fiddle Switch. I want to ride with you after that, Love! We never get a chance to ride together, hey?"

It was true, with two carts to drive, Ruby and Finn had to ride separately hour after hour, day after day, these long trips. It was lonely time, and it passed too quietly; for one of them loved to talk as much as the other. They were glad to have these riders along, not only for good company on the long road back to the sea, but because they could take over driving one of the carts and let Ruby and Finn have some time together.

They were from a fishing town called Quiet Waters. It was tucked in a bay along the seacoast, and they made a living processing fish and selling them inland. They were on the road as many days as they were at home. They packed these highhouse carts to the ceiling with fish, crab, lobster, or clams and rolled from town to town, selling, until the load was gone and the ice melted. Their best customers were the inns and lodging houses along the roads, in places like Pot 'o Soup and Michael's Love. With some of their earnings from the sale of fish each trip, they bought supplies in the market towns for resale to the people of Quiet Waters and other towns up the seacoast. Right now, the fish had all been sold; and, into its place inside the carts, were packed coils of rope, netting, wicker baskets, bolts of blue coarsecloth, crates of fresh fruit, boxes of rutabagas, axes, shovels, spikes, and buckets of paint.

Spad? Did they know about the spad run in early summer? Ruby and Finn laughed loud at that question. Didn't everyone know about spad? It would be their next haul, and the one after that. Spad were the best fish they sold and brought the highest prices. Yes, it was likely Ravenna and Nome could find work on the spad boats, if they got there on time. But getting there on time was doubtful. The run could be starting any day now. Finn thought it would be early this year. And they still had several days travel before they reached the coast.

At night, the four of them did not stay in the lodging houses along the way, but atop the carts. Finn and Ruby did not want to spend their new earnings in those expensive places, and Nome and Ravenna had almost no money to spend. They would stop at the edge of a village or town well known to the old trading couple, or sometimes in the yard of a farmer they had visited for years on their trips. They would kindle a campfire, cook up a hot meal, and watch the stars pop out of the indigo sky, drifting in tired conversation, telling stories. There were no end to the stories. When the fire died to coals, and the story teller of the moment was interrupting the adventure too frequently with yawns, it was time for Ravenna and Ruby to climb to the top of one cart and roll out the sleepsacks. Finn and Nome checked on the horses, one more time, and climbed wearily to the roof of their cart. When it rained, they simply reached down and pulled over themselves a covering of seacloth, wound on a spool attached to the roof. During the days, they took turns driving and riding, switching places whenever they came to a rest stop. But, most frequently, Ruby and Finn rode together; Nome and Ravenna followed along behind.

Spring was now right at the edge of summer. They drove late into the evenings; and still they had daylight, for the days were longer. Nome and Ravenna grew weary of riding and driving; but it was better than walking all this way and faster. How could they ever have hoped to reach the sea on time for the spad run without this ride? The two carts rolled through long stretches of dark forest, past open fields and farmsteads, through settlements and towns. They passed Meeting, Fiddlehead, Two Rivers, Steamer, Getcho, Famous Bridge, and Hilltop. Ravenna consulted the smudged and wrinkled map the scout had made for her. It had been remarkably accurate, and the sea was not far off now.

Up ahead, Finn and Ruby talked about the spad run. Their heaviest season of work waited for them at the end of this trip. Following behind,

Nome and Ravenna did not talk much about spad. They talked about Ruby and Finn and how it was that they loved to be together after so many years. They talked about other things. Even as they continued to travel, they were finding rest and healing in the constant grinding squeak of the wheels, the rhythmic clopping of the horses, the warmth of the sunshine, the hospitality of these two sprightly gentlefolk. Druska Paba, Mintor Ghan, Korcha Rabon, Mommicks, the sick-lagers, wythies on The Plains, Mablic Prison, the terror of running the battlefields with shields and stretchers...all these seemed like a dream, strangely unreal memories, which came alive only at the evening storytelling. This time of peace and rest was just beginning to let them feel how deeply tired they were.

And, as they rolled along one afternoon, they noticed that there was something different in the smell of the air, something tangy and unfamiliar. Finn leaned around the side of his cart and shouted back to them, pointing. But they could not hear. Then they came to the top of a rise, and their cart stopped. Ravenna and Nome sat side by side on the board and looked out from a height at what their imaginations had not prepared them for. The white sky dropped down from far out in the distance but found no horizon and seemed to go on and on. If that was still the world, it was vast, endless. It was the sea. Ravenna Rosealice and Nome Ogrodni had come at last to Quiet Waters.

TWENTY-EIGHT

Quiet Waters

The town was built on a steep hill going down to the sea. It wrapped around the bay like an amphitheater, and its quaint houses sat like spectators looking out at a flat stage, waiting for something to happen. One play performed daily on Quiet Bay was the rising of the sun. It was always popular, sometimes sensational.

Each house had a good view of the bay, at least from its second story. From these upper windows, wives and little children would look out anxiously, especially after there had been gale weather, to watch for the first moving dots along the horizon that meant that the men were returning with the boats and were safe. During busy times, like the spad run, younger women sometimes went out with the fleets; but fishing was physically hard men's work; and young mothers were never allowed to go. There were many widows in the town.

The houses were all packed together like fish in a crate, painted white but trimmed around their edges and window frames with gray, weathered wood. Across their front walls, nets hung on wooden pegs, and long wooden oars leaned like emblems against the door frames. The streets twisted back and forth between the houses, following the contour of the hill, paved with cobblestones, so that horses straining at wagons could get a grip with their hooves. Wagons and carts going downhill depended on sturdy brakes, against which drivers leaned hard, lest the conveyance break loose and run over the animals. Before Ruby and Finn's two highhouse carts had eased their way over the brink of the hill and begun their slow, steel-rimmed, clattering descent, Ruby had replaced Ravenna as driver of the rear cart. Riding the brake was not for a novice.

A salty breeze blew up from the sea, carrying the pungent stink of fish. To Ruby and Finn it was the welcome smell of home, familiar as a good manured field to a farmer. At first, Nome and Ravenna, with squinting eyes and wrinkled noses, tried not to breathe too deeply. In time, they gave up and adjusted.

Ruby and Finn's house was about halfway down the hill. The carts were rolled into their yard and the wheels blocked. While Finn unhitched the horses and led them to the shed for feeding, Ruby went to a neighbor to hear the news. She returned a short time later, shaking her head and looking solemnly at Nome and Ravenna.

"They're gone, hey?"

"Gone?" said Ravenna. "You mean the spad fleet? They're gone?"

Ruby nodded, jerking her thumb in the direction of the neighbor's house. "Gone day before yesterday, she says, hey? You missed 'em, loves."

Finn ambled up scratching his jaw. "What's this? Spad runners out already, hey?"

"Day before yesterday, love."

"Huh!" He looked down at the ground, still scratching. "Thought'd be early this year. Well...c'mon in the house. We'll clean out them carts later."

Nome sat hunched over the kitchen table, forlornly rotating the mug of tea that Ruby had just brewed. Ravenna sat and watched him, sipping hers. For the third time, Nome asked:

"You're sure there's no way for us to get hired out on the spad fleet? No way for us to take a boat out to where they are and ask?"

Ruby, facing the stove into which she was poking another stick of kindling, shook her head. Finn strode across the room to the table, wiping his hands on his pants, and stiffly lowered himself into a chair and poured himself some tea. He, too, was shaking his head.

"No," he said, "they'll have all they need out there now. Once they're out, they won't be hiring on anymore. You can ask, when the runners come in, if you like; but I think you'll find I'm right, hey?" He took a noisy slurp of tea and smacked his lips. "The runners, they're the smaller boats that bring the spad in from the fisherboats every evening, hey? If the run is good, the first ones should be in tonight. You can ask then, but I don't think it's any use. They'd take you out to the fishers if there was need of any more hands out there, but they'll probably tell you no. Don't worry, though. You can work with us. We'll have plenty to do here when the runners start dumping."

"Can we make as much here as we would out on the boats?" Nome asked hopefully.

"Ah, no, that you cannot," said Finn. "No, you'll not get rich quick packing spad. But it'll be a good enough living, hey? Good enough for me and Ruby."

"But Brighthome...," Nome objected.

"I know, man, I know," said Finn shaking his head. "No, you'll not make that kind of money packing fish, hey? I don't know what else to tell you."

....

That evening the four of them were on the wharf with a crowd, waiting for the first spad runners to come in. There was a festive atmosphere: women and men standing about in small groups, talking and gesturing and children careening among them noisily and bumping into people and having to be jerked up sharply by the arm and crossly shaken. Finn and Ruby were welcomed home and asked how they did on their trip and what news there was from inland. They took the occasion to introduce Ravenna and Nome to all their neighbors.

"They're staying with us for a time!" told Ruby. "Going to be giving a hand with cleaning and packing, hey?"

"Welcome! Welcome!" said the neighbors. "Can always use more hands cleaning and packing, hey? Ever done it before? How're y' liking Quiet Waters? Good little town, this, hey? Where'd you say you were from?"

Twilight was gathering. A shout rang out over the socializing, and then a cheer went up. The lights of the first spad runner had been sighted far out to sea. In a few moments, more pinpoints of light were seen, then the horizon was dotted with them. The crowd gave way, and flatbed carts were rolled and rumbled into place on the wharf. By the time the runners rounded the jetty and slid, one after the other, alongside the pilings, it was dark; and lanterns had been lighted everywhere. The townspeople swarmed about the wagons; some of them jumped down into the boats; and there was an eager flurry of hauling and shifting and slithery dumping. The first boats, now emptied, slipped away and gave their places to others, waiting out on the water. Wagons lurched away and were replaced by waiting wagons. Ravenna and Nome went with the first wagons, hauling the fish to a huge, low, wooden building called "the muckage." Inside, it was a long, open hall with a dirt floor strewn with sawdust. Rows of long board tabletops on trestles ran the length; and, in the middle, amid the tables, was a raised, square platform.

At the end of an hour, the muckage was filled with all the people who had stood on the wharf earlier. The spad runners had glided away into the night. The tables were covered with glistening spad, and around them stood the people wielding sharp, short knives, slitting and ripping with quick, expert strokes. The hall was noisy with talking and shouting, the scraping of fish guts into boxes and the shifting and chopping of ice blocks.

When the bustle had been going on for quite a while and a kind of rhythm among the workers had been found, an old man hopped up on the center platform and proudly raised aloft his squeezebox. There were whistles, catcalls, cheers; and the grinning old whiskers began to bob and press out a tune. He played a good number of lively pieces, then took a break when the steaming tea and breaddogs were served.

It was the middle of the night. The slimy work went on, and the people grew quiet and looked tired. A woman got up on the platform and, in a loud voice, told a comic story about the mayor and his pig. She followed with a few others, was cheered and laughed at; then her voice gave out, and she climbed down and returned to her table. There was one other entertainment in the early hours of the morning, a young girl who sang; but she was somewhat limp with fatigue, as were most of the people now finishing the cleaning.

When the sun rose, the people of Quiet Waters were back in their houses, pulling shut the shades and climbing into their beds.

Nights became days and days nights. The routine was the same, meeting the runners, the long night in the muckage, moving the cleaned fish to cold storage in "the pack house." After a few nights the people had adjusted to night work, and the entertainments in the muckage became livelier. There were joke tellers, a small band, dancing, sweet choral singing, even a wrestling match. Hot tea was kept brewing on a stove in the corner, and all kinds of sweetbreads were served.

Then, about the fifth night, not long after the runners had left and the joyful work in the muckage had just begun, Ruby and Finn leaped onto the platform and raised their hands shouting for silence.

"Listen here, hey! Listen here!" bellowed Ruby into the noise, cupping her hands around her mouth, while Finn strolled round the edge of the platform, grinning and nodding to the crowd and pointing to her. The catcalls died down, and there was a final, isolated hoot. She waited, looking out smugly. Then said: "In a couple of weeks the spad run'll be over, and we'll be done here, hey? You know what we'll be doing then, hey?"

A cheer went up, for they all knew she was talking about the great celebration in The Cove House, their town hall, at the end of the spad run. It was an annual welcome-home to their heroes, who had been out on the boats all this time. Then the singing and dancing and joking and storytelling and even some wrestling would continue without the interruption of work. It would no long be tea and sweetbreads but high feasting, and would go on for three days.

Ruby and Finn raised their arms high and restored order. Ruby went on: "Well, this year we got something new for The Cove House, hey? Something we never had before! This year we got...a wedding!"

There was puzzled silence. Then Ruby and Finn reached down over the edge of the platform and tugged up Ravenna Rosealice and Nome Ogrodni, stood them in the middle, stepped back, and gestured. The hall went wild. It was a long time before the applause and whistling and cheering died away. Ravenna and Nome were not allowed to do any more work that night. They were kept busy thanking one person after another for congratulations and protesting that, no, please, they couldn't eat another bite of sweetbread or drink any more tea!

....

They did return to work the next night, however, and worked every night as long as the spad kept coming in. In the meanwhile, they had to find time to prepare for their wedding. This meant finding suitable clothes, planning the ceremony, and, a day ahead of time, gathering flowers.

Finally, one afternoon, the spad runners returned early; and, in their wake, came the large fishing boats. The schools of spad, those untold number that had escaped the nets, had now passed and gone farther up the coast, out of reach. The run was over. None too soon, for the pack house was filled nearly to the high rafters; and, in the windowless ice house, where blocks of winter ice had been preserved in beds of sawdust, there was less than one layer left. There were two days of cleaning up and organizing fishing gear on the boats and cooking and baking for the feast. Then The Cove House celebration began.

    It began slowly with a light meal of roasted spad on a half-dozen outdoor grills. Nome and Ravenna had introduced the town to the lemony-sweet drink of uppledok hayfield from Gazi, and this was the featured drink at this meal. Everyone approached the three-day festivities carefully, for experience had taught them to resist the temptation to get it all in the first day. Every other year a music recital followed by a dance began late in the afternoon. This year, however, a wedding was to come first.

    Ravenna and Nome joined in the feast of roasted spad at mid-day, then withdrew from the celebration, and went off in separate directions. Ravenna spent the afternoon alone on the brow of the hill above the town looking out at the sea. Nome wandered farther away into a forest. Before sunset, they came down; but they did not meet. Nome put on a suit of fine clothes, the like of which he had never worn in his life, and walked with Finn to The Cove House. He saw no sign of Ravenna as they approached the hall in the soft evening light, where the grownups were sitting about the yard talking and the children playing. The bell on The Cove House roof had begun to ring. The people began to mill about and move into the hall. When all were inside, Nome and Finn stood nervously outside the open front door. They heard the strains of string music and squeezebox rising from within, and then the swelling voices of people joining in "This day, this day...." the traditional wedding song.

    Finn took Nome's hand and said, "This is it, hey? Let's go."

    They walked through the door, and the voices rose over them like a wave. Passing down a narrow aisle through the standing crowd, they saw old wrinkled faces, weathered faces, young, flawless, clear-eyed faces, bearded faces, milk-white baby faces, all with mouths open wide singing "This day, this day...!" Nome felt a shudder rising up within himself. Then he saw his bride.

    She was walking in from a side-door, through a tight aisle between the people, holding Ruby's hand. She wore a plain, white dress from her neck to her ankles; and a wreath of blue and yellow flowers crowned her head and spilled down in streamers all about her shoulders and back, stippling her chestnut hair, which hung loose in soft waves to her waist. From her neck, on a fine thread like a necklace, hung a simple golden ring against her chest. Her movement forward was slow and grave. She held her head high, and her blue eyes glistened.

They came together at the center of the room, as the circle of people around them sang the last words of the song. The strains of the fiddles and squeezebox died. Ruby and Finn let go of the hands, and took a step back. Finn cleared his throat nervously and made his speech:

"Friends, this day we bring before you Nome Ogrodni and Ravenna Rosealice who have chosen to marry. Join us as their witnesses."

There was an uncertain silence. Then a whispered "Go 'head" from Ruby.

Nome and Ravenna each took a breath, then, in clear voices began to speak to one another, taking turns, words they had earlier written down and learned by heart:

"Ravenna Rosealice, this day I marry you."

"Nome Ogrodni, this day I marry you."

Nome slipped a shiny golden ring out of a waist pocket, took her hand in his, and slipped the ring on her finger. He said: "I marry you with a ring...a ring of quiet water that ripples in growing circles where my love drops."

Ravenna reached both her hands to the thread around her neck and, with a sharp jerk, snapped it. Letting the thread fall to the floor, she took the ring and placed it on Nome's finger. She said, "I marry you with a ring...a ring of firelight that casts its glow all about the flame of my love and drives back the darkness."

There was a pause, then she continued, "I marry you with the moon's circle, the sun's circle, the circling dance of the stars."

He replied, "I marry you with all the directions of the earth...north, east, south, west...and all their ways in between. With all overhead and all underneath."

Her voice began to quaver: "May the Good Mother bless us. Us and our children."

"The Holy be your home," he said.

"You are my home," she replied.

Together they recited: "This day forward...as long as we may live!"

Ravenna's shoulders began to shake, her mouth to quiver; and her eyes pressed tight together. Nome reached out and pulled her to himself. The people clapped and cheered and then, once more, broke into the chorus of "This day! This day!" not waiting for the fiddles and the squeezebox to catch up.

....

The wedding dance lasted far into the night. Gifts were heaped on Nome and Ravenna, odds and ends, household items, handmade things. They laughed and looked around at all their possessions and at each other and at the people who kept bringing them presents and wondered where they would keep all this. They had no home, and certainly no way to carry all this with them. But it did not matter. They were happy with an overflowing happiness. Finn and Ruby told them they could stay at their house while they went back on the road with the load of spad. They would be leaving a day or so after the celebration...as soon as they could pack their highhouse carts. After that, well, no need to think about that now, hey? Not tonight!

But those concerns were taken care of for them by an unusual gift. A burly, whiskered seaman sauntered over to them as they sat amid their fry pans, blankets, pot holders, kettles, and jars of preserves. He looked at them thoughtfully for a moment, then said:

"Where you going to keep all this, hey?"

They grinned up at him and shook their heads.

He pulled at his beard for a moment, seeming to mull something over. Then he said, "Didn't bring you a gift along. Wish I had something for you two. But I'd like to offer this: I got a little house down the coast a bit. Place I call Seaside House. Empty now in the summer. I use it come winter when I don't have to be in town so much for the fishing. You can use it for a while, if you need a place. You can use it all summer, if you want, hey?"

They were overwhelmed. Yes, they did want! A place of their own for a while...something they only dreamed of. They thanked him profusely. He said he would give them directions and instructions after things quieted down at the celebration. He seemed momentarily shy. He hesitated. Then he said again:

"Didn't bring a gift along. Wish I had something to give you." He shoved his big fist into his coat pocket and paused, seeming uncertain about something. Then he pulled it out quickly and pushed something suddenly into Nome's hand saying, "Well, here's something. Just something I whittled on the boat, hey?" He turned and sauntered away.

Ravenna and Nome bent over the object that rested on Nome's palm. It was a little roundish ball of softstone carefully carved with a penknife into the shape of a saucer-eyed owl.

....

Several days later, Nome and Ravenna went down to Seaside House and settled in. It was a small, one-story, stone house with a steep-pitched slate roof. The shape of fireplace and chimney formed one wall, and wood-frame glass windows looked out at the sea. Inside, the furniture was handmade, well designed, and sturdy. There was a small kitchen, pantry, bedroom and a sitting area by the fireplace. On the mantle over the hearth stood a neat row of books. Old mariners' charts with pen markings and years of dirty finger smudges at certain points were tacked to the walls. On every space of shelf and windowsill were small figurines of fish, birds and animals hand-carved from wood or softstone.

A path led from the stone door sill down to the beach, where a broad strand of tawny sand ran along the water's edge to the south as far as one could see. The entire length sloped down from a sandy bank, tied together and held in place against the wind by beachgrass, saltgrass, and cordgrass.

Here Ravenna and Nome spent timeless days in peaceful, instinctive ways that were new to both of them. Often and long they were in one-another's arms. They walked barefoot, hand-in-hand, along the damp edge of the sand, sat side-by-side looking outward, lay on their backs in the breeze and the warm sun, dozing. They walked up the beach to where the sand gave way to cobble. They gingerly picked their way among the rounded rocks, pausing to stoop and examine driftwood or the rusted cleat from some ancient shipwreck, still firmly attached to a bleached and sanded timber.

"Here is where the paving for the streets of Quiet Waters came from," said Ravenna of the endless stretch of smooth cobble.

But there was no sign of life from the town, no other drifters roaming up and down the beach. They had the land, the house, the strand, the sky, the entire sea to themselves. They watched the slow flapping of herons across the dunes, the gliding and swooping of gulls, the bobbing of cormorants and pelicans on the water. They watched seabirds disappear beneath the waves and pop up somewhere else. They squatted and playfully hounded the tortuous, scuttling crabs, searched at low tide for sea stars and sea urchins on wet boulders, goose barnacles on tumbling, black timbers, periwinkles and clam shells and channeled whelk rolled up onto the draining sand. When, on windy days, their ears tired of the ceaseless rush and hiss of rollers, they retreated above the dunes, strolled among the goldenrod and beach heather and sought the more familiar sound of the wind in the pines. At times, they romped in the cold water, laughing at the surprising taste of salt and at the alarming undertow tugging at their feet. At times, they returned, chilled and naked, to the Seaside House and lighted a fire and two lamps and curled up in separate chairs to read the books from the mantelpiece.

One morning, they lay in bed, looking up at the rafters, studying the grain of the wood, following the cracks in the plaster walls aimlessly with their eyes, half-talking in sleepy voices. The sun, already high, shone in through the kitchen windows, across the table and the floor, searching for the open bedroom door of the late-sleepers.

Nome had his fingers locked behind his head. "I could go on living like this forever, couldn't you?"

"No," she said.

He turned his head and looked at her. She smiled slightly, but did not pause in tracing the zigzag pattern the roof boards where they came together.

"No?"

"Neither could you." She smiled frankly, turning to him and sliding her hand back onto him beneath the covers.

He studied her eyes...and for a moment forgot what they were talking about. Then he said, "No, huh? Couldn't live like this forever?"

"Let's talk about it," she said, rolling fully over onto her side to face him. "You've been thinking about Brighthome the past few days, haven't you."

He nodded silently, letting his eyes wander over her hair and around her face.

"How much time left till the next payment, Nome?"

"I don't know. I have some idea...but I have really lost track of how many days we have been here. Do you know?"

She shook her head. "About two weeks, I would guess. I haven't been counting. It doesn't really matter."

"Matter?"

"About the payment. About getting there on time, does it?" She adjusted her head on the pillow and moved her face closer to his. "We could get there by payment day, but you have nothing to pay with."

"I could give the Tosars all our fish money and all our wedding presents."

She laughed, they laughed together.

"But I want to go home, Ravenna. I want to take you home to Mo and Fa."

"I want that, too. And I wish I could someday take you to my mother and my Aunie."

"You will, Ravenna. Someday we will go back to The Fields of Khorvan. Soon. When we know it is safe for you. I would love to see your mother and your Aunie again. As your husband."

"Oh, Nome. But first, Brighthome."

"Yes, first, Brighthome. We are not far away now, only a few days. *Listen* to how we are talking, Ravenna! We are planning a future. We know we are going to lose Brighthome; I can't do anything more to save it. It's not the end...not for me, not for Mo and Fa. Our hopes are changing, and we are starting to get used to them."

"They've been changing all along," she said, looking back up at the ceiling. "Who would have thought...all that...and then this joy!"

"This love. Sure, I could start all over again, seeking my fortune...not recognizing that I have *found* it...again...and again. *Let's* go home to Brighthome, my love, even if it is to say goodbye. Let's go today...or tomorrow."

"Let's!"

TWENTY-NINE

The Fall of Brighthome

For a long time the road followed the shore like a lingering goodbye, and they could look out to sea for many a "last time" on the rises. Slate-gray clouds were building on the horizon. There was a strong breeze, and the gulls hovered, holding their positions. At last, the long arm of beach curved out seaward, and their road took a definite plunge opposite, away from the sand and tufts of grass, into a pine forest. The numbing rumble of the rollers breaking on the beach suddenly died away; and, once again, they were hearing the crunch of their boots on the gravel of the road. They both had good, new walking boots and fresh clothes and ample provisions in their packs.

Even when the sky turned dull in the afternoon and a fine drizzle started, their spirits remained high. At a rest stop, they tugged yellow seacloth sheets from their packs to drape over their shoulders and hold tight at their necks, letting the rain drip off as they walked. Toward evening, the road wanted to turn sharply left to search out the seacoast again; but this was their sign to watch for a much narrower way, not much more than a forest path, going straight ahead. They found the sidetrack, clearly marked by a felled tree, and entered the darkening forest. The sky was heavy and wet, and rain fell steadily now. Evening came early. They stopped and camped, nearly on the path itself, and managed to get a fire going. That night they snuggled together happily and listened to the drumming of rain that filtered through the pine boughs onto the seacloth, which covered them completely.

The next day continued cold and wet. Neither seacloth nor good, oiled boots kept them dry. They ate their rations plain, without fire; and conversation was meager. Nome grew pensive, and twice missed sudden turnings in the path, leading them into bushy dead-ends. Ravenna took the lead after that, and Nome plodded along thinking and walking, thinking and walking. At suppertime they were both miserable, and Ravenna complained that he was gloomy and wouldn't talk to her. This offended him; and they began the second cold, damp night sleeping under the seacloth back to back.

The third day out began with blue sky overhead and the sun stabbing through the dripping branches. Under some deadfall they managed to find enough dry kindling for a merry breakfast fire, and fed it with the dead lower branches snapped from the pines. They were friends again. By mid-morning, they came out of the forest and looked down on the town of Kezzlhjem. Nome became lively at the sight; for, although he had never been here, this place had been marked on the first map he had ever used, the one sketched for him by Burton and Mardek the day he had left home. He was now full of memories, as he felt himself approaching Brighthome. The past two rainy days in the woods reminded him of the way he and Curry and Beland had started out. Kezzlhjem. There was supposed to be a prince here, he remembered. This is where Beland had wanted to go when he heard that there was "a dangerous man" at 'n Burning Graute. How their lives all would have been different today, if they had done what Beland wanted!

Kezzlhjem was a pleasant, prosperous town; and they found out that there was, indeed, a prince ruling there. Nome and Ravenna were detained by a police guard and interrogated for an hour or so as they approached the town. They were treated severely but respectfully and eventually allowed to go their way. They found an inn, had a warm lunch in the dining room, then, after inquiring the way to 'n Burning Graute, took to the road again.

At nightfall, they came to 'n Burning Graute and took a room at a lodging house. After a late supper, they joined the other guests and the landlord in the back yard; for it was a lovely, warm evening. As always at inns like this, there was a good deal of smoking of pipes and sipping at mugs and trading of stories and news. Nome and Ravenna soon became the center of attention for their ability to tell eyewitness tales about the recent war in Gazi. The people of 'n Burning Graute were very interested in what became of "those Gazi folk" who had lived as refugees among them for so many years.

In the morning, they walked about the town. Nome eagerly pointed out the sights, reliving the days he had spent here. Ravenna would have liked to have seen the misk quarries. She had seen how skillfully the Gazines had used it in their war. She herself had worn misk on her cheek. This is where it had come from. But the quarries were off a good distance in the wrong direction, and Nome was getting eager to set out on the last stretch of road.

They soon crossed the Gaffling River bridge; and, several hours later, Nome pointed out a shabby, rutted road which broke away on their right. He told her it was the beginning of the High Road to the West, believe it or not, that well-tended highway leading all the way to the Fields of Khorvan and the Plains of Wildness. The open lands about them then disappeared, and they found themselves crowded on both sides by dark, spiny woods of black spruce.

"We are not far from Tosarkun now," said Nome. "I don't remember just how far we came through this spruce bog, but I think we can make it yet today if we hurry. We have to get there by sundown, or they won't let us in."

They picked up their pace, and Ravenna was uncomplaining. She had observed his worry over the past days, understood he was troubled at returning empty-handed, despite his brave words, anxious about crossing the border, uncertain about what lay ahead. There was still an hour left before sundown when they saw the border station down the road, longed-for and dreaded. Gray-coat guards were moving into position as they approached. Nome had earlier discussed with her the possibility of skirting the guard station by thrashing a long way roundabout through the spruce bog. In the end, he had decided there was really no legal reason he knew of under which they could keep him out. It was just a deep-seated fear of all Tosarmen, which had been with him since childhood, which made him want to avoid the confrontation.

"We'll try the front door," he had said to Ravenna, thinking to himself that this sounded like something Wasoo might have said. "If they don't let us in, then we'll go around and find a side-door."

They were stopped at the guardhouse and treated rudely, then separated and interrogated. At first, Nome had been told he could not enter because he had no written entry permit. He insisted the Tosars were expecting him at the Keep and he had payment due there in a few days. When they were not impressed, he showed a much folded document from Judges' Rooms that he had carried out a year earlier. Then he was told he could enter, but the woman could not, for she was Outlander. Nome produced a document from the town clark of Quiet Waters proving that they were married. All at once, the guards, squinting at the setting sun, lost interest and brusquely waved them both through the border.

They spent the night at Hite's Farm. Wilman Hite's beard was even longer and more matted than it was when Nome had last seen him on his way to the Outlands. He still gaped with the screwed-up face of a madman and screeched instead of talking. But his self-effacing service and his kindness was humbling. At one point he said something to Nome about "those two weasly fellows you had with you last year," and then, roughly pointing at Ravenna, added, "but you done smart trading 'em in on this one!"

The next morning they hurried up the Grandmaison Road. Only once did they encounter a Tosarman on horseback, riding hard from behind them. It could only have been one of the guards from the border station; and, at first, they feared they were being pursued. Nome pulled Ravenna off to the side of the road, and together they stood deferentially in the grass, as all citizens had learned to do whenever a Tosar guard was near. But the horse thundered past, and the rider only turned and looked in their direction for a moment. Horse and rider disappeared up the road in the direction of The City.

Shortly after noon, they passed what had been Curry House and Beland's Farm, then turned into the little road leading to Brighthome. Across the river bridge, the big house stood stately and aged beyond a ring of orchard.

Heart pounding, Nome entered the yard, leading Ravenna by the hand. His father was the first to see them. He stood by an apple tree, slightly stooped, wearing his red leather work apron. In one hand he held a pair of pruning shears, in the other some tender branches just clipped. He stared for a moment, then dropped both and lifted his arms wide toward his son. They came together and held each other tight for a long time, the two men, groaning softly. Then Nome pulled back and, through tears, attempted to introduce his wife. But the old man grinned and bowed formally, his eyes tight with tears, and winked at Ravenna, and could only chuckle, gesturing back to the apple tree: "I'm not su-supposed to be doing even that, you know...'gainst the law for me...." Suddenly, he stepped back, wide-eyed, and looked at his son, moving his mouth, and pointed at him and then at Ravenna with an enormous questioning look. Nome nodded vigorously. The old man lunged forward and swept them both into his arms and shook. Then he marched them toward the house to find his own wife.

They got only as far as the porch, when Rena Ogrodni burst from the front door upon the three of them with crying, incoherent words. Ravenna tried to step back at the last moment to make room for Nome to greet his mother, but she was not quick enough. The mother, understanding what had not been spoken, went to her first. She grasped Ravenna's head between her hands and kissed her hard on each cheek, then held her away and gazed into her eyes. She relaxed her hold and slowly stroked the side of Ravenna's face and her long hair before she even said a word. Only then did she turn and throw herself upon her son.

In all her anxious mental preparations for this meeting, Ravenna had never dared to dream such a fierce and wordless welcome. At that moment, her heart bonded to her husband's.

The welcome-home had to continue in Brighthome's large, sunny kitchen that afternoon; for Mo insisted on preparing a great feast for supper and would not allow the other three to go off somewhere while she worked. She refused Ravenna's repeated offers to help, since Ravenna was the special guest.

"Just this once," Mo pleaded, "just this once. After today, you can help whenever you want."

Fa wanted to go to tell the neighbors that Nome was home, but the others convinced him to wait and keep these first few hours to themselves. Nome said that he and Fa could start tomorrow morning with a visit to Curry's mother and Beland's family.

"But a wedding celebration at the Croft!" Fa had insisted. "We will want that soon! Soon!"

Of course! they all agreed, of course! The annual Croft Midsummer Day celebration would be happening exactly a week from today, the twenty-first. Wouldn't *that* be a great time to have it! They would need time to prepare and to let everyone know Nome was back...and married!

....

The next morning, after breakfast, Baron Ogrodni and his son set out on foot to visit Magda, Curry's mother. Since the Tosars had claimed her property for default on payment, she had been living with her sister's family on their holding, two miles west. Nome was able to tell her that Curry was alive and well and prospering in high office in Gazi. He was able to say he had truly become a man, a brave soldier, and the personal aide to that country's national hero. He could not tell her when Curry would be back to visit her in Tosarkun; for he now had many new responsibilities in that country's transition to peacetime; but her son loved her and would not neglect that love. He told her many other things about Curry, all of them true and honorable. They left Magda weeping, proud, and deeply grateful.

As they walked back along the road, Nome spoke more openly to his father about Curry. In fact, he opened that place of sadness in his heart and did not hold back. Baron said little, only nodded from time to time, and then placed his large hand on his son's shoulder and let it ride there for a long time as they walked.

They came to the Grandmaison Road and turned north, passing beyond Brighthome, to what had once been Beland's Farm. They need not hurry, Baron said, for the Farm was still being run by Beland's brothers and sisters, as hirelings, not owners. The Tosars needed experienced hands there and kept them on when they seized the holding after its hundred-day default. Nome and Baron would probably be able to talk to them during their lunch break. Baron surprised Nome by returning to the topic of Curry.

"I too, Nome, was in war. And I, too, was betrayed and gravely disappointed once during that time. I understand what you are telling me. Only Rena...only your mother knows this. I have not talked to you about those days...it has not been safe here in Tosarkun to talk. Your mother and I have agreed on that. But, after listening to you and Ravenna...I know I must involve you...you both. Nome, let's tell each other old war stories some other day, when times are better. Right now there is trouble; and I have to ask you to do something."

Nome stopped walking. Baron also stopped and turned to him. The two men looked at each other for a moment. His father had never spoken to him like this. "What is it, Fa?"

"I want to put you in touch with Danny Surd. I want you to go talk to him."

"What about, Fa? What is this all about? This trouble. Can't you tell me?"

"Danny will explain...."

"No! I want *you* to explain! Fa, talk to me. I *need* you to talk to me. There is 'trouble'...I have had my *fill* of trouble this past year in the Outlands. I don't want to go blindly into more!"

Baron was taken aback, and seemed embarrassed. "All right," he said quietly. "I'm sorry. You're right, Nome. Well, here is something you need to know about, that your mother and I have never talked about. Something you need to know now, before you go to talk to Danny Surd."

His father told him that, for a long time, there had been a secret underground network in Tosarkun. This group referred to itself only as "Holderhope." When he and the other original freeholders of this region were bandit-fighting the Tosars—before Nome was born—they had referred to themselves simply as "the holder," meaning the whole bunch of them, the original settlers. Everyday use of that word died out when Bau Shahn suppressed the Tosars and the Obratch, and created a new *kun,* Tosarkun. But the hope never died out that this cruel arrangement might be temporary—that the peaceful, decent people of the land might one day live freely in this *kun* of Bau Shahn. Holderhope was the secret network working to help Bau Shahn to see things their way. It had to be secret; the Tosars would never tolerate it. This is what Nome's father wanted him to talk to Danny about.

"Fa, are you and Mo...?"

"No, Nome. Your mother and I are not members of this network. There's no actual members; it's not a club. There are some people more connected with the...the planning and investigations than others. And there is a leadership...because there's...well, organization...but *even I* don't know who they are. Better that I *don't*. And for sure, better that the name of Ogrodni does not get associated with it. That would attract the attention of the Tosars. That is why your mother and I are not active with this network, even though it carries our own hopes...and we privately support it. That is also why we have never talked to you about this before. You are an Ogrodni, too; and, for this reason, you have never been contacted or recruited before. But, for certain reasons, that has changed now. I have been contacted by someone...never mind who...and asked that I put you in touch with Danny Surd."

"But, Fa, I don't know Danny. I mean, I know who he is and have seen him at Croft gatherings, but..."

"Please, Nome, don't ask me for more just now. I know it's not fair for me to drop this on you like this, and not answer what must be a cartload of questions you have. I am sorry. But, for your own good and ours, please accept that this is important, or I would not ask it of you. And there is a fine balance of trust and distrust that must be kept. For now, I cannot tell you more. In fact, I don't *know* much more; I would not be able to answer most of your questions. I am only a 'resource' to Holderhope because of my so-called experience and prestige. And I am now a conduit. But I am not on the inside, and have never been in leadership. That's all. That's all. Talk to Danny at The Golden Crumpet, will you?"

"Well sure, Fa, if you want me to. At the Golden...?"

"That little bakery shop up there on the Grandmaison. That little hot-meal place there just beyond where Surd used to be. Danny works there...actually has worked there since before the Tosars took the Surd holding last year."

"Oh, yeh, I know the place. Houda, this is strange! What about Ravenna...what do I say...?"

"That is up to you, Nome. That's between the two of you. But be very careful. This business is an *awful* dance of trust and distrust. I trust you, Nome. I am *very* proud of you."

After that, Nome could say no more. His heart was suddenly so full it hurt.

....

At noon, Nome and his father arrived at The Farm and were allowed to talk to Beland's brothers and sisters while they were eating lunch outside at a table near the house. It was a much easier conversation to have than the one with Magda. Beland would not be back, they came to understand; but they found it hard to imagine him the way Nome told it: a transformed man, joyful, open-hearted, courageous. No longer dark and fearful. And not alone. He had an excellent friend in Wasoo, and the two of them were doing wonderful work in the healing of Gazi.

However, Nome did *not* tell them that Brighthome, too, would soon be forfeit to the Tosars...that he had brought back no money for another payment. When Nome and Ravenna had arrived home the day before and spent it secluded in the kitchen with Mo and Fa, they did more than tell their adventures and the details of their courtship and marriage in Quiet Waters. They also let it be known that they had brought no money for the payment, due in three weeks. The four of them talked into the evening about the inevitable loss of Brighthome and began to make plans about where they would go to live, how they would make a living, how they would manage.

Nome had insisted, and they all agreed, that they should not let word out that he had not come to make another payment, but to move his family out of Brighthome. They agreed that they would keep Brighthome till the hundredth-day, and not let the Tosars have it early. The public impression would have to be maintained that Nome had returned home briefly to make payment and celebrate his marriage before going back into the Outlands to make more money.

Nome had wanted to keep all options open as long as possible. The past year had taught him that almost anything can happen. Moreover, he simply wanted a few more days of normal life at home, at beloved Brighthome, celebrating with friends and neighbors, enjoying life as he and his parents had known it, before it would be forever taken from them. He just wanted a bit of comfort, a bit more time, pretending to the neighbors that there was still hope for Brighthome.

It did not seem this would be allowed. Going to see Danny Surd would not be life as normal.

....

Nome had not paid any attention to this place the few times he had ridden up to The City. Two days had passed since Fa had talked to him. Now he sat on Chalky and looked at the sign over the door, smirking at the pun. Painted there: *The Golden Crumpet*, on either side of which were triplets of yellow trumpets appearing to be blaring. He swung his leg over the saddle and down to the ground, led his horse forward, tied the reins, and stepped through the door of the bakery. It was empty, but a young man came out of the kitchen and stopped behind the counter.

"Danny Surd here?"

"I'm Danny."

"Oh, sure...sorry. I didn't recognize you right away. It's been a long time."

"Nome. Right? 't's all right. Nome Ogrodni, yeh, it's been a while."

"Uh, Danny...."

"Your dad sent you, right, Nome?"

"Yeh...yes, he asked me to stop by and talk to you." Nome was relieved it was so direct, that he would not have to explain why he was here.

"Let's sit over there. No one else around right now. We can talk. Mug of khavla? Crumpet or two?"

"Oh. Oh, sure, why not? Sure."

Danny brought it to the table and sat down opposite Nome. He was quiet for a while, as though he had something to say but was not sure how to start.

"What'd your dad tell you?"

"Well, not a lot. Something about a network and what he called Holderhope...and, let's see...he said he wasn't really involved, just a conduit, but it was important...and...and he said there was trouble. Pretty vague. He said I should talk to you."

Danny nodded slightly, appearing satisfied. Nome watched him. He was probably five or six years younger than Nome, probably the reason they had not known each other well, although they must have gone to school at the Croft at the same time in the past. He sat with his floured hands folded on the table in front of his flour-dusted white apron. Nome had expected someone older, more assertive. Danny, eyes down, seemed shy.

To break the mood, Nome said, "Sorry about Surd, Danny. About you and your folks losing it last year, I mean."

"Yeh, well it's been hard. And that's how I got involved in this. After they took Surd, I mean. The Tosars pushed a lot of us toward Holderhope when they did that...I mean up at Filtown and Gamgame, and up by you, at Beland...although, I'm not saying who they are," he interrupted suddenly, as though he had maybe said too much."

"No, that's okay," said Nome. "Why don't you just start telling me what you are supposed to tell me. My Fa said I should talk to you and I could ask you questions instead of him."

Danny started talking more freely then. He repeated much of what Fa had told him, elaborating on the one-way lines of communication within the network, because trust could not be taken for granted. He, himself, was on the very outside edge, with very little access to information, names, plans. Nome would be even one step removed, should he accept involvement. There were small cells, where individuals knew each other; but these cells did not communicate without vetted conduits. It reminded Nome a good deal of the setup among the Gazines in their bandit-fighting phase. The great difference, according to what Danny was saying, was that Holderhope was an information and evidence gathering operation, with no plans to rebel against the Tosars. The "hope" in Holderhope was that Bau Shahn might one day intervene directly to replace them. This might come about if a campaign of subtle disruption and interference in Tosar-Judges activities could provoke the Tosars into overreaching, once again. The hope was also that evidence of covert Tosar operations, behind their strange designs on the holdings, for example, might influence remote Bau Shahn in the direction of redesigning rule in this *kun* by replacing a Tosarkun with a Holderkun, a settled, peace-loving body politic under governance by the original settlers of this land. It was visionary; and it was, indeed, more of an aspiration than a strategy. Holderhope was, in short, a network of long-suffering individuals who were willing to run risks and wait patiently for opportunities that they could not directly control.

"We do not plan to fight the Tosars," Danny said. "We do not want to bring down war upon our people. The network, I am sure, does not tolerate any hotheads who try to call for an uprising to overthrow the Tosars. A moment's clear-headed thought tells us that would only bring Lop ge Dol's Green Troops down out of Bau Shahn upon us all. If you agree to do a little work for Holderhope, Nome, you have to agree to be ready, like all of us, to live in peace here...even though they take away our homes...to live in peace here, even into the next generation, until the right time comes. Which we do not know how to bring about. Which we will know only if it comes."

Nome was impressed by this young man and by how eloquently he spoke once he got going. "We know, Nome, you are back here in Tosarkun only for a few weeks. Until you make the payment on Brighthome and then have to leave again to go back to the Outlands. I have been instructed to contact you because you will be in the Keep for a short time to pay. Someone higher up sees that as an opportunity to learn a few things. Anyway, that's why I offered to recruit you; and your dad said all right. Normally, an Ogrodni would be kept out of this, but you will just be here for a couple of days and then gone, right? So someone decided we should jump on the opportunity."

"So, what next, Danny?"

"So...are you interested?"

"Interested, yes, but I have to know more what else is in the box."

"Sure, that's it for now. I have to report back. Sleep on it. Talk to Baron. Let's get together again. Give me a few days."

"After Saturday sometime, Danny. Midsummer Day at the Croft. My wedding celebration that day. You could meet my wife."

"Would love to, Nome, but I think I'd better not. Not right now. We have to talk more. Come by here, would you, a couple of days after the party. This is as good a place as any...."

The door of the bakery suddenly scraped open and a large man came into the room and shut it behind him.

"So, anyway, Nome! I gotta get back to work." Danny's manner was suddenly jovial. "Be right with you, Dorwen!" he loudly spoke to the man. "Great to see you again, Nome, been a long time. And congratulations on your marriage!" Danny turned away and went behind the counter saying, "What'll it be, Dorwen?"

....

Midsummer Day at the Croft, including wedding reception, was a great success. Weather was perfect. Food was great. Neighbors left their work at home and came together. Children had noisy fun. The big news was that Nome Ogrodni was back, but not Curry or Beland. And Nome had brought home a lovely wife. Everyone said what a remarkable fellow Baron's and Rena's son turned out to be, sending back enough money every hundred days to keep Brighthome away from the Tosars. How did he do it? Must have gotten rich out there in the Outlands. He and his wife could only stay a short while, folks said, because they would going back out there to keep the payments coming.

Nome and Ravenna attracted crowds with their stories of places few had ever seen or heard of: 'n Burning Graute, the Muicmuic forests, The Fields of Khorvan, The Plains of Wildness. And their stories about the victorious Gazine rebellion! They were there when it happened! Almost none of the guests had ever seen the sea. "Quiet Waters? Sounds like a nice name. And that's where you got married?"

So, it was a wonderful day for Nome and his family. Yet, they were tired at the end and glad to get back to quiet Brighthome-on-the-Sula.

....

Three days later, Nome dropped in at the Golden Crumpet to see if Danny was around. He was, but so were a number of customers, sitting and munching and slurping at tables in the bakery. Nome hung around till closing time. Danny and he went for a walk along the pathways behind The Crumpet away from the Grandmaison Road.

Nome had talked the whole situation over, first with Ravenna, then with his Fa and Mo. Since he and Ravenna would not be going back into the Outlands, Tosarkun would be their home for the future. Nome was ready to risk something for that future, even if the Holderhope vision seemed to offer a prospect more wishful than hopeful. They agreed he should take the next step.

He told Danny he was on board; but he did not yet tell him that he had brought home no money for the next payment. So Danny began by saying:

"My instructions are to recruit you now, Nome, before you go back into the Outlands. Everyone knows you will be going to Tosar's Keep in a few days to make your next payment. Holderhope has very few opportunities to get anyone anywhere near the Keep, let alone actually in the Keep. We don't expect a lot, and you will probably be in there for a very short time. There is no risk to you, and all you have to do is keep your eyes and ears open and bring back to us anything you learn. That is all. We want information. That doesn't seem like much, Nome; but there have been a lot of strange things going on with the Tosars, new things; and anything might be helpful. For example, the seizing of the holdings last year, and the three of you northernmost holdings being treated differently...what is that about? And the increase of foreign workers from other nearby *kun* going in and out of the Keep. Why them? Why not Tosarkun workers? There seems to be some increased coming and going up there. Why is it secret?"

"So, what could I possibly find out during a few minutes inside Tosar's Keep that would help?" Nome asked. "Fa has made the payments up there in the past; and it has only been in-the-door, money-down, out-the-door. They're not very friendly."

"I can't answer that," Danny said simply as they strolled. "I am only passing on what is told me. But, as long as you ask, I could guess that you might observe some of the workmen from the other *kun* coming and going. You might overhear talk...although they have funny accents. You might get a glimpse inside the building at how the Keep is laid out. Stuff like that."

"Doesn't sound so hard," said Nome.

"Have you ever heard of Dramen Bonder?"

"What?"

"I didn't think so. I was told to ask you that and then tell you this: If you hear the name, Bonder, or Dramen Bonder, pay attention, take note. That is information. I can't tell you why because I don't really know. I am just told it is important. All I have heard is that this is a dark character from one of the other *kun*. An engineer...doesn't sound so bad...but someone with a dark reputation, arms-dealer or something, I don't know. Anyway...."

"Anyway?"

"That's it for now, Nome. Let's meet one more time before you go up to make that payment. After I report back on our talk this evening, I will have some important instructions you will need. Then you can go there, pay up, let us know whatever you have seen and heard, and you are on your way back home. All done."

....

Nome met with Danny Surd for the third time a week later. The due date for the hundred-day payment at Tosar's Keep was on the sixth of the new month, two weeks after midsummer day. Despite his resolution to wait till the last moment to default on payment, he had decided to go to the Keep on the fourth, two days early, to plead for an extension. Failing that—and he certainly expected to fail—he planned to ride home by nightfall and return two days later, payment day, to Judges' Rooms to make a final appeal there for an extension of terms. It was all futile, he knew, but not impossible; and the two long trips to The City would be his last, desperate effort to save Brighthome. He had endured harder things for this.

The third discussion with Danny took place, like the second, on the pathways behind The Golden Crumpet, shortly before sundown. Nome told him he was going into the Keep two days early, on the fourth. Danny repeated the previous instructions, told him to keep an ear cocked for the name, "Draman Bonder," keep an eye out for foreign workmen, where they were coming from, where they were going, any movement of supplies or material in or out of the Keep. Nome had a question for him:

"I've been wondering what Holderhope will do with incriminating information about the Tosars. I mean, how would you ever get it to Bau Shahn? How would they ever believe you? And why do you think you could manipulate Lop ge Dol and Great Bau Shahn into acting on our behalf?"

"Nome, answering that is way beyond my level of being trusted within the network. I don't know things like that. They are for others to know. But I can tell you what I think...it is only my guess, remember. It is everybody's assumption that Bau Shahn maintains spies throughout Tosarkun. Has *always* had informers here; they would be foolish not to. I would also guess that they are aware of Holderhope, and it would not be unreasonable to think that some in our network are sources of intelligence for Lop ge Dol. It would be part of his mechanisms for maintaining stability among the ten *kun* of Bau Shahn. No one has ever told me this. It is not what I know about how the network operates. It just makes sense to me that something like this must be the case. If you know our history, Nome, the early freeholders who lived at the time of your great grandfather, Toohy, were actually recruited by the Nur of Bau Shahn of that time...I forget his name...recruited as lookouts watching the Tosar nomads who were plundering and raping in those days. Maybe the network is something like that now. Trust and distrust again. I have to trust that some wiser heads in Holderhope would know what to do with important information that would help our cause...I mean, our hopes."

"All right, Danny."

"Now for the last thing, Nome. And the most important: what you do with any information, any notes, any objects you bring out of the Keep when you get there and get out. You don't bring them to me. You don't bring them to anybody. I am going to show you a place where you leave whatever you've got.

"Come on, let's go. I am not going to tell you, I am going to *take* you there. It will take a good half-hour walking the back-roads now, and it's going to be nearly dark when we get there. But memorize the way. This is the last time you and I are meeting."

The way to the bin alongside a cowshed on someone's farm was not complicated. As they walked, Danny had one more thing to say.

"I almost forgot to tell you this, Nome: a code word you are to use when you have done your job. It is only used for *this* drop-box and not for any other. Drops are always changed after they are used. Anyway, when you leave your notes or drawings or whatever in this bin I'm going to show you, you must get a message out in code by saying something out loud, very clearly, at a Croft meeting...any gathering where most of the folks are there, like Midweek or something. There is no hurry, and no special time for you to do this; but do it before you leave for the Outlands. Maybe at your good-bye gathering. Here are the words you are to say: 'A safe place. A *very* safe place.' You got that?"

"Yes, Danny. 'A safe place, a *very* safe place.'"

"Those exact words. Don't change them. Someone will know what they mean and what to do. Not your problem. Remember, 'A safe place. A *very* safe place.' Put it into one of your travel stories or in a joke or make a speech. Something everyone can hear. You'll think of how to do it. But don't forget."

"Got it."

Danny showed him the bin, a weathered, empty feed box with a hinged lid, no clasp.

....

It was the fourth of the month, two days before the due date. Nome had ridden on Chalky at slow pace up to The City and had stabled him at a keeper's place for the day. From the stable, it was only a ten minute walk to Tosar's Keep. Now he stood there in the open space before the main entrance, looking at the massive five-story building. It reminded him of the Eastern Fortress in Gazi. Only, this place was no fortress for defense against assault. It was surrounded by houses and shops of The City, making an intimidating declaration of authority and control. It was not heavily defended. This was a grim palace in which The Tosar and his family lived on the top floor. On the floor below lived the adjunct ruling families and officials. The third and second levels housed Tosarmen, the security and police apparatus; and the first floor, at street level, was for administrative offices.

This was the building which Holderhope wanted Nome to get into to have a look-around. He had never seen it up close before. He knew he would not be going up that imposing, wide, main staircase through those tall, heavy, closed double doors. That was a relief. Fa, who had delivered the earlier payments, had instructed him on where to go: a plain, ordinary door, down at street level, well to the left of the main entrance. That was where "Payments" was. However, Nome could see that door was blocked off, with wooden crates pushed in front of it and long boards nailed together across it. On the boards there was a hand-painted black arrow pointing left.

It seemed he was the only person in the square before the Keep, no one to ask. He sauntered in the direction indicated by the arrow, along the stone wall, glancing up several times at the five stories looming above. At the eastern end, he peeked around the corner and looked along the seemingly endless eastern wall. However, not far from where he stood, there was an open door. There was a good deal of dried mud in front of it; and, even inside, there were muddy footprints and iron-wheel tracks. As he approached, a man came out, not a Tosarman, but a workman in long apron, holding a sheaf of papers. He stopped when he saw Nome.

"What!" said the man.

"Good day," said Nome, approaching carefully, "Excuse me. I am trying to find the 'Payments' office. The other door is closed...."

"What business here?" said the man. The way he said it sounded funny.

At that moment, a Tosarman came out the same door, in full, gray uniform, visored hat on his head, sheathed falx in a holster at his belt. He stopped abruptly alongside the workman and stared at Nome.

"Excuse me, please," Nome said quickly. "I was just asking...I am looking for the "Payments" office? I am Nome Ogrodni from Brighthome holding...and I need to ask about hundred-day payment..."

He did not finish, confused by the reaction of the two. They were silent, and the workman's eyes opened wide, his mouth opened a bit, but he did not speak. The Tosarman gave the other man a nervous glance. They continued to stare at Nome. Then:

"Name!" from the workman.

"Ogrodni. Nome Ogrodni, from...."

The workman turned suddenly to the Tosarman and gave an order in a strange, clipped accent. The workman then turned and quickly entered the building through the open door. The Tosarman remained, clearly standing guard.

They stood outside the door for a half-hour, Nome not daring to speak, the guard not looking at him, not moving. Eventually the workman, still carrying his sheaf of papers, returned, dismissed the guard and said to Nome:

"Follow!"

He led Nome into the Keep, down a long hallway with poor light, around a corner, past a heavy, four-ply wooden door, and stopped at an office door with no marking. "Wait!" he ordered Nome.

The man was inside the office for only a minute; then he came out and held the door for Nome to enter. As Nome stepped in, he saw the room was nearly empty, except for a long, high service counter dividing the room. Without a word, the workman left. There was no sign of files or papers or records, anything one might expect in "Payments." Only a closed door on the side of the room behind the counter. That door suddenly swung open, and a clerk came in quickly and stood behind the counter. He looked angry or frightened or harried...or something. Impatient, for sure, waiting for Nome to say something.

"Excuse me, sir," Nome began. "I am Nome Ogrodni from the Brighthome holding? I...I am here to ask about the payment due here? The hundred-day..."

"Too early!" the man insisted. "You are here too early..."

"I'm sorry, sir, I know it is not due until the sixth, but I just wanted to ask about an extension...."

"You cannot pay now," the clerk interrupted. "You cannot pay early. There is no judge here. There must be a minor judge here from Judges' Rooms when you pay. Read the rescript from Judges' Rooms you were given. We cannot accept payment without a judge here to witness."

"Oh. I am sorry, sir. I did not know. When I come back two days from now, can I ask for an extension here, or must I go to Judges' R..."

"Do *not* come back in two days. There will be no judge available then. Come back in *five* days! There is no judge that can come here until then. Pay at that time!"

"Oh...I see, yes, sir....but could I ask..."

"I am *not* here to answer questions. I am here to tell you what to do! Now get out! Get out!"

The clerk turned, marched out the door he had come in and slammed it behind him.

Nome stood there for a long moment looking at nothing. He had come to plead for an extension, had not been heard; but an extension had been forced upon him. Five days, it could be of no use. There had been nothing in the rescript about Judges being present when payments were delivered. He and his parents, as well as Burton and Mardek, had studied that document a dozen times, no mention of Judges witnessing payments. Fa had said nothing about that in his instructions this morning. Apparently Nome's appearance here this afternoon was unexpected and unsettling for these people. But all he could do now was do what he was told. He left the room and stepped into the hall.

Then he stopped. He was inside Tosar's Keep. He was not under guard. No one was about. He walked past the heavy four-ply door to the hallway by which he had come and looked around the corner, out to the still-open door framing the golden light of late afternoon in the city. This was an unexpected opportunity to do what Holderhope was asking him to do. He could go deeper into the building, have a more thorough look-around. When he was stopped, apprehended, as he surely would be, he would say he had taken a wrong turn coming out of "Payments" and was lost in the maze of hallways, trying to find the exit.

He turned back and continued past the office door he had just closed behind him. Little oil lamps in wall brackets provided just enough light along the dim hallway to see by. He came to an open door on his right and looked in. It was some kind of large storeroom, and a bracket-lamp on the hallway wall opposite the door threw enough of a glow for him to see many shovels, muddy from wet use, muddy pails and buckets, and some sturdy, low, rectangular carts with steel wheels, also caked with dried mud. He was surprised to find such things here; he would never have pictured it. He was even more surprised when a shadow slid across the space where he was standing and light disappeared entirely from the storeroom. Someone had pulled the door shut.

Panic. There were people in the hall. How could he say he was lost and trying to find the exit if he was discovered in a storeroom? He moved in the dark to the door as carefully as he could and listened. Someone, or more than one, walking. He would have to wait until they went away, until he could pretend, once again, to be lost. Noises and a few muffled voices, just beyond his door, continued for a long while. Then came a terrible sound he could *see* as an image: the scraping swing of the four-ply massive door along the stone floor, a dull, wooden thud, and the scrape of sliding metal being pushed into place. The Keep was being shut down for the night.

More than panic, cold fear. 'I am caught' passed through his head, 'I am in prison from now on.' Almost at once came the image of Ravenna watching for him outside Mablic Prison. 'I have let her down.' He lowered himself to the floor, hunched against the door, hugged his knees, and gave himself over to remorse and self-pity.

How long he stayed like this, there is no way to say. All sounds from the hall had gone away. He began to think. He would be discovered during the night or in the morning. He would be apprehended, held prisoner, if not killed. Perhaps the Tosars risked too much in killing an Ogrodni outright. Held on charges of attempting to assassinate The Tosar, more likely. Judges' Rooms would be involved in his fate, most likely, not to save him but to complicate procedures. Perhaps exile. Exile of all Ogrodnis could be negotiated.

As he ran through the options during the night, something like hope began to rise. He had been in a hopeless situation before, when the Mommicks had him; but here there were big differences in his favor. He had lived among the Tosars since birth and had some understanding of their behavior, attitudes, limitations. He knew that, despotic as they may be, this *kun* was a diarchy, where they do not have absolute power. With the Mommicks there was no common language, no claim to rights; and here, at least, he had allies nearby who would rally, once he went missing.

Far into the night of total darkness, he followed this thinking; and it allowed him some calm; and he began to plan. First of all, he must do all he could to escape. Get out of here somehow. Escape would probably have to wait until daylight, for he expected all ways out were now closed for the night. He would have to look into that. Looking into anything would be safest if he moved about only on this floor, the office areas, probably not staffed at night. Better yet, a basement...there must be one to service this enormous place. If he could find a basement, he might be able to move about without running into anyone. On the other hand, that would be an unlikely place to find a way out. However, if he could find a way down one level, he would start there. One more thing: If he were to flee in daylight, he would have to have some disguise. He thought of Wasoo. Two possibilities, a Tosar uniform or a workman's appearance. Even then....

He left off planning and opened the storeroom door. The hall was in complete darkness. The first thing he needed was light. He had steel and flint in his money pouch...a habit kept ever since he had been in

Gazi...and he found some burnable wick material tucked into the wall brackets for the lamps. Shortly, he had a tiny torch of light, enough to see that the massive door blocking the way out was, indeed, barred shut from the inside; but the heavy bar was also chained in place with a keyed padlock. Wasoo had said that, whenever he snooped about buildings in disguise, he always checked every door with an exterior lock to make sure it could be readily opened without key from the inside. Nome told himself to remember this and do likewise.

It was not long before the muddy footprints and wheel tracks he had noticed in the afternoon led him to a wide door nearby that opened to a set of stone steps going down. It was unlocked, but Nome examined the latch to make sure. As he thought, a basement area, completely dark. He took more wick material from several brackets, then began to descend. It led him to more hallways, more doors, another maze one level down.

None of the rooms were locked, some even without doors. Here were the laundry area, the tool rooms, the paint room, the food storage areas. In a tool room he found what he most needed: a lantern. He then found his way to some black paint with which he covered the lantern chimney, leaving a narrow vertical strip untouched. He now had a directional light to carry about without throwing a glow all about a room or hall. He could only hope that the acrid smell of burning, drying paint on the lamp globe would not give him away, if anyone should be up and about. But he could see no light, wherever he moved through the hallways; and he gradually relaxed, becoming increasingly confident that he was alone down here.

At first, he tried to memorize the path he was taking; but he soon realized he would get lost without taking notes. In a room of shelving, floor to ceiling, there was paper and folders and writing materials and all things needed for the upstairs administrative areas. He took a pencil and a blank notebook, and began very carefully drawing a map of the hallway network he was walking. He stopped and recorded, shone his lamp all about to make sure it was accurate, did this every twenty steps or so. He would need this to find his way back. He would also have something to bring out for Holderhope, if he should ever get out; although he was not concentrating on that for now.

Nome spent many hours during the night creeping about this way, repeatedly retracing his steps to the stairs by which he had come down to the basement to make sure he could find his way back. Eventually, he found other stairs going up to the street level by other doors, as he groped his way ever farther in. And he found other things. Full sets of Tosar uniforms, including boots, caps, belts and empty falx holsters, in a large space adjacent to the laundry room. Room after room full of digging and hauling materials, dirty and recently used. Vast, open spaces, held up by once-white pillars of some kind, filled with lumber and massive timber, cross-hatched squares of planks nailed together, the height of a man, stacked against walls, other stacks the same size of pallets, nailed together like grates.

Then he came to one set of doors different from any other. They were wide, double doors, visibly heavy, on very large hinges bolted into an upright door frame of thick timber, which, in turn, was bolted above, on both sides, and into the floor of the stone inner structure of the keep. An ordinary door, enough for a person to pass through, stood to the right side of the double doors. When he opened it, he shone his lamp light into empty space. Tipping the lamp light down, he could still see only stairs going down. He was about to explore a sub-basement.

Carefully stepping down, shining the light this way and that, his right hand keeping contact with a dirt wall on his right, he could see, on his left, a double system of ropes and pulleys upon pulleys that seemed to operate a wooden platform below, a lift that could be hoisted from the sub-basement floor up to the wide double doors. There was every indication that all of this was recent construction, a project still in process.

Nome reached the lower floor and shone his light about. This space seemed to swallow light, it was so vast, so open. It felt cold down here. A sudden memory seized him: a sense that he had been here before. It came to him that he had stood with Curry and Beland in such a place, in that cave behind the waterfall. This underground hall, too, was stacked along one wall with shelving and crates in orderly rows. Along the other walls were rows upon rows of barrels. The white-painted barrels were stacked three-high. The red-painted barrels not stacked at all. There were more red barrels than white, and they occupied much of the open space. But in the middle of the hall, on open racks, were axes, bows, lances, shields, maces, and longtubes. The longtubes were white. The pillars supporting the ceiling were white. He moved slowly forward holding high his lantern. He had a sudden suspicion. He moved to a pillar, rapped it with his knuckle, scratched with his thumbnail.

"This is misk!" he said aloud. He looked across at the white barrels and thought he knew what they contained. He looked then at the red barrels...and stepped back quickly! holding the lantern away! He moved, as carefully as he could, to the stone steps and hurried back up.

Nome closed the door very quietly. He felt utterly weary. Yet, there was one more discovery he would have to endure that night.

He decided to continue to map the basement maze, mark the location of the sub-basement entrance, and explore a bit farther before returning to the eastern side of the keep, where he had started, in order to find a place to hide and sleep.

On he went, fairly certain he was moving toward the western side. As he had hoped, he came to another set of stairs ascending to the first floor. He went up. Instead of administrative offices, he found, on this side of the building, the mess hall for the guard, the kitchens, and food supply pantries. Not surprisingly, there were also signs of a service door, now blocked by a barred and padlocked four-ply door, like the one on the other side of the building. Beyond *this* heavy door there would have to be a short passage through the keep wall, where food and supplies would be delivered. This could be an alternative way out, in case of emergency.

As he came back down to the basement, he read a wall sign he had not noticed earlier. It stopped him: "Bonder's Area–No Entrance." He entered, walked slowly down a long hallway, passing door after door, testing each of them gingerly. All locked, every one. The "No Entrance" sign was repeated often along the way. He came to the end of the hall. It went nowhere, ended at a wall of rough stone, the foundation of the western wall of the keep, apparently. He returned to the foot of the steps, which led up to the first-floor mess and kitchen area. He sat on the bottom step and made his map sketches and notations in the notebook. He had crossed the whole width of the keep on its north side underground. That was something, he thought.

He made his way back to where he had started; and his map-sketch did not let him down. He found some food in a storeroom, carefully selected a complete Tosar uniform, chose a place to sleep behind crates in an out-of-the-way storeroom for cleaning supplies, piled in some unwashed laundry to make a bed, crawled onto it, ate and drank a bit, curled up, and slept. He had no way of knowing; but, outside, dawn was just breaking.

....

He awoke in the early afternoon. He lay on his bed of laundry for a long time, thinking and just listening. Ravenna and Fa and Mo had expected him home last night. By now they would be very worried. He thought, this may just be the first of many days of worry and fear for them. I should not have done this to them.

He was distracted from this whenever he heard voices. They came often, men's voices, women's voices. He made no effort to do anything except lie there and listen, to see what he could learn that might be of help. He learned that some women were quarreling about missing laundry. He learned that workmen were about, and they frequently were in the company of Tosar guards, and that the oddest thing was that the workmen seemed to be in authority, and the Tosars were trainees. And that Tosarmen did not all know each other, which seemed strange, since Nome assumed they all lived in quarters upstairs. He could only surmise this might have to do with their rank.

Eventually, Nome decided that, if he were going to try to get out this day, he would have to try the disguise. There was nothing about the workmen that offered disguise, and he could never manage the accent. He put on the Tosar uniform, which was clean and pressed; he had handled it carefully the night before. He noticed now that it had scarlet piping around the stiff collar and about the shoulders of the sleeves. He had not noticed this red on other uniforms when he had pawed through the rack, making his selections. He hoped this would not call attention to him. Dropping the notebook down inside his shirt against his skin, he stood and took a step out of hiding. It was now late afternoon, but that could not be seen from the basement.

He had thought he might try the nearby basement steps to return to street level and take a chance on the door by which he had entered the keep yesterday. However, after more thought, he feared being recognized by the workman, the guard, or the clerk, who had all seen him, and would remember his scarred face if they saw him. Moreover, if he had to run for it, where would he run? He was on the opposite side of the keep from where he had stabled his horse, and the space around the keep was broad and open.

He decided to test his disguise more slowly, crossing the basement to the western side where he was last night, trying the stairs to the street level, lingering casually near the mess hall and kitchen area, trying to see if the deliveries entrance might be an option.

He emerged from the cleaning supplies storeroom slowly, looked about, then marched purposefully along the hallway, acting the part. He followed hallways and turned corners, recognizing what he had done by the aid of a lantern, now made easier by the lighted oil lamps in wall brackets. He was nearly half-way across, when, turning a corner, he suddenly saw two Tosarmen marching directly toward him filling the hall space, looking straight at him. 'This is it,' thought Nome, 'This may be how it ends.' No way to run. He would have to edge aside and yield, or be stopped and spoken to. Yet, Nome simply walked straight at them, looking directly back. At the last moment, the two men halted, separated, faced each other, eyes to the floor, pressed their backs to the walls. Nome passed between them without a pause and kept marching. 'It's the red piping on the collar! I outrank them!'

He came to the stone stairway near "Bonder's Area–No Entrance" and briskly skipped up the steps, opened the door, and walked into the hall near the double doors to the mess hall. As he had thought, daylight poured in from a tunnel leading to the square around Tosar's Keep. That was his way out. But six Tosarmen stood silhouetted at the entrance, looking outward.

"That's too many," he muttered to himself, and abruptly turned and went back down the basement. He stood there alone for a moment, gathering himself, waiting for his thumping heart to slow. "Bonder's Area." He looked down the unlighted no-entrance hall and noticed a spill of lantern light on the right, about the sixth door down. An open door.

"I should not do this," whispered Nome to himself, as he slowly walked toward that unmoving blade of light falling across the hallway floor and part-way up the opposite wall. He slowed almost to a stop as he came to the edge of the open doorway. Listened. Tried to sense whether anyone was in there...he had the sense there was not. If he startled someone working there, or if someone suddenly came out, he would bravely say he saw the light and was checking that the door had not been left open by mistake. To say that, he could not be seen creeping along. Casually, he stepped into the light and looked in. Took a step forward. The room was indeed empty. He went in.

Charts and maps and mechanical drawings were pinned to softboard mounted on two walls of the room. At the center of the room was a high drafting table with a number of large sheets of architectural plans lying on it at various angles. The first thing Nome did was check the latch on the door, thanking Wasoo, and noted that it could be key-locked from the hallway but could be opened from within by a spring-bolt, to prevent anyone from being locked in. He then looked about for a place to hide, if he should be taken by surprise here; and there was a stack of five or six tall, wide drafting boards leaning against the far wall. He went to inspect the space behind them, squatting down and reaching into the angle the leaning boards made with the wall. He decided he could squeeze in there if he were trapped here.

All the while he did this, he was thinking, 'So this is what Bonder's Area is about. This room...and how many others along this hallway...the man Danny was talking about, arms dealer or something. Engineer, or architect, whatever. Designing the sub-basement arsenal. Tosars brought him in, some kind of expert...from one of the other *kun,* or even more likely from outside Great Bau Shahn. Otherwise, where would all the misk be coming from?...and firedust, so many barrels of it! What are they planning? We are in way over our heads...me, Danny, whoever else is in this holder network. And where did they get misk? 'n Burning Graute, of course, or maybe there are deposits elsewhere...but they obviously know how to work it...and that is a secret process...obviously no longer a secret.'

Nome stood up from inspecting the hiding place and walked about the room, studying the pinned-up floor plans and schematic side-views of large buildings on sheets the size of table-tops. He could not read them, had no experience with such things. They were very detailed, meticulously ruled and angled and annotated. He was thinking he should leave, now that he was beginning to make sense of what he had seen elsewhere in the basement last night; and he passed by the drafting table where these plans had been made, brushing his hand absently across the top sheet lying there, glancing down.

He stopped, and reeled. The room spun, and he could not catch his breath. At the tips of his fingers, where his hand lay, he read his name. Surely a mistake, a mirage from his fatigue and anxiety, but no...he steadied himself against the table.... There in the lower corner of the sheet, in large, fine, block letters, exquisitely penned was "*OGRODNI.*" Below that, smaller, was "*Erector: Toohy.*" There were dates, specifications, property description numbers in smaller print. It was all enclosed in a neatly ruled box. Nome looked up at the rest of the sheet and recognized the top-view analytical drawing of Brighthome. He quickly slid it aside and looked at the sheet below, a side-view drawing of Brighthome. He paged to the next sheet, but it was something different, the top-view of a large, rectangular, complicated structure. So he went back to the top view and studied.

Something was wrong with it. Nome knew nothing about reading such drawings, but he could sense at once that something was not right. It showed not only the big house but included the yard around the house, a part of the Sula River, even the footbridge. There was a complicated network of lines cutting away from the river toward the house and out the other side. He flipped back to the side-view. It showed the house, not only at ground level, but something that looked like a partial basement under the front part of the house, and this was drawn in greater detail than all the rest. That was not right. There was no basement under Brighthome. Unless...unless...could old Toohy have planned a basement? Put it on old drawings, but never executed...and that transferred to these new schematics....?

The vacant sound of footsteps and voices sounded in the hall, coming closer. Nome arranged the sheets as he had found them, took off his Tosar's dress cap, and pulled it after himself as he lay on the floor and wiggled behind the stack of drafting boards. He lay still, suppressing his breath. The voices were now entering the room:

"...something you don't want to do every day of the week, that's for sure. Come here, look now, let me show you." Silence. "Look here, see, we have taken care of what you're worried about. See these supports...? And these drivers here...these buckle and wash, right away before the cave comes...here and here. See?"

"Wait a minute. Let me look...where's that other one? Where is it now? Show me on this one...."

"Right here. See? Here's the drivers, the supports, the knuckles mid-point...here, here, here...and here. The wash hits here, then this goes, then this, all in order, see? The cover drops, the slide. See? Nothing left behind above a hundred and a half. You'd have to dig for it to find it, and this far down wash at that. No one's going to do that."

A long silence. Some absent-minded humming.

"Well..., you're right. Looks good. Looks like that would cover it, all right. You say you've tried it and it works like this?"

"We did it on open land, no structure over it, on section thirty-six and section thirty-seven. Right here, upstream from this holding, here...soon to be 'section forty,' after tonight." (Laughter.) "No sign of debris sighted anywhere along thirty-nine."

"Well, all right, it looks like you've got it figured. Because you know, if anyone even suspects that we are behind this or that The Tosar has anything to do with this...."

"Of course they are going to *suspect,* we can't do anything about *that.* What we want is to be sure there is no *evidence* of the undermine. And that is what this design does, washes away the evidence with the cave-in."

"All right, no evidence. That's what I meant."

"And another thing you've got to remember is that the whole front part of the house is going to be falling right on top of all this and covering. So we've got cover over the cover."

"And what about Judges' Rooms, when we finally get to that? That is a lot more spread out than this Ogrodni building. How are you going to bring down something like that without it looking like an obvious undermine?"

"Didn't they explain that to you? Here, let me show you, we've got that figured in. Here, just under these sheets is Judges' Rooms...."

"No, no, I don't want to go into that one! One at a time. I just want to be sure this one tonight comes off right. Your Gamgame and Filtown tests were safe enough, being on Tosar land with no one around, but this Brighthome is the real event. Everyone is going to know about it by tomorrow morning."

"Well, Bonder knows that. And The Tosar knows that. And The Tosar said, 'Do it!' So, we are going to do it. Tonight, at last."

"What's the hurry on this? I mean, we can't be too careful...."

"Look, you know what the hurry is. You wait another few weeks, a month, and the current is too feeble to do this. That means wait till next spring, when the river is in spate again. Ogrodni comes in with another payment. You want to wait another hundred days? The Tosar doesn't. That means waiting till next spring, for sure."

"Well, now...."

"No, listen! Ogrodni crossed the border the other day, did you know that? The son, not the old man. He's the one coming up with the money for the holdings and now he's here again, just when the payment is due. You heard, didn't you? He showed up yesterday wanting to pay early. They had to put him off, so he left; but he'll be back in a few days with money. The Tosar knows this. And Bonder knows this. And then....well, that's not going to happen. We've been working on this for a long time. No more letting the Judges or the Ogrodnis set the timetable for the bigger things to come. It's been set forward to *immediate!*"

"Calm down...."

"I'll calm down. I'll calm down when we pull the plug tonight. This is tied into all Bonder's other projects; this is actually small. I don't know what he has in mind, but, when it all goes into the open, I don't want to be around here."

"All right, all right. Enough of that. I didn't come down here for that. I've seen what I want to see. Let's go back upstairs. You want to take these?"

"No, leave them there. Get the light, will you?"

The room went dark. The door shut and the lock snapped into place.

Nome lay stunned, caring nothing about the big house. He had just listened to a casual discussion about the murder of his family. He did not lie still to see if it was safe to come out. He squirmed and wrested himself from behind the boards and groped toward the drafting table, knocking the lantern to the floor with a crash. He tapped about on the table top till his fingers had the drawings, four of them. He rolled them into a tube, flattened it against his chest, then folded it over and then again into a bulky square which he thrust under his buttoned coat and beneath his belt, against his belly. He crawled to the floor and felt about for his visored cap, found it, and placed it on his head. Then he crawled to the door, felt for the spring-loaded bolt and yanked it. He stood and stalked from the room, down the hall to the steps, bounded up them two at a time, yanked open the door into the first floor hallway and moved toward the open service door. A Tosar guard stood there, looking out; but he turned toward Nome who brushed past him glaring with a face of fury which bore a vicious cheek-to-chin scar as though from a saber cut.

It was sundown! The city gates! Beyond the square, he broke into a run. People in The City had never seen a Tosarman run through the streets like this, and they scattered and clung to doorways and the sides of buildings. He found the stable where he had left Chalky and burst in upon the keeper and two groomers doing evening chores with the horses.

Nome saw old Chalky standing in the crib; but across the shed were three fine horses, and over the crib gate rested a fine saddle with two empty falx holsters attached to the pommel.

Nome pointed at the saddle and the nearest horse and roared at the frightened keeper, "Saddle this horse! Now! Now! Hurry!"

The keeper winced and scrambled to act, ordering the two terrified boys to help him. Nome continued to shout at them. Meekly, they led the saddled horse out into the open, but not fast enough. Nome seized the reins, shoved the keeper aside and sprang up. He raced out of the stable into the street, wheeled left and raced toward the gates. It was gray evening now, with only dull stripes of rose on the western sky beyond the city walls. With a roar, he wickedly kicked his heels into the sides of the horse and lunged forward through the streets at full gallop. People fled, and a few Tosar guards on patrol simply turned and stared after him. He came to the gates, and they were shut fast. A guard came out of a little house at the side. Nome rode up hard at the gates, reined back, shouting "Open up! Open the gates!" Then he wheeled and rode the horse around and around in circles in the open street, shouting, "Open the gates, hurry!"

The guard on the ground looked panicky and uncertain. He needed a written pass to do this; but the Tosar rider did not offer one and seemed ready to trample him. He scurried to the gate and pulled back the bars which levered back the massive iron tongues binding the double gates shut. He rushed forward and tugged on the right gate, urging it ajar. Nome steered the nervous, tapping horse to the opening, slipped through, and raced off into the purpling darkness.

It had taken a half-day to ride from Brighthome up to The City. Now he drove the Tosar horse cruelly to get home in two hours to warn Ravenna, Mo, and Fa to get out of the house. He did not care if the horse's heart burst, as long as it did not do so before it carried him to Brighthome. His mind was only there, not to save it, but to separate his loved ones from it in time; and he cried out "Holy! Oh, Holy!" as he thundered along the great Grandmaison Road.

The night closed around Nome, and the stars appeared, increasing his anguish. He rode fiercely, leaning forward, his cheek brushing the neck of the horse. After the first hour, he came to familiar surroundings and dashed past darkened Surd, Gamgame, and Filtown. He thought he would have to stop to rest the horse opposite Surlico, at the top of the hill near the Croft. He was afraid the heaving, foaming horse would die under him if he pressed it further. Yet these moments of delay might be just what he needed to warn his family in time. But, if the horse collapsed, he would not get there at all.

As he debated, the Croft came into view, its windows alive with light! Midweek! Of course, he had not remembered, Midweek, when people from the holdings gathered for a social evening. Ravenna and Mo and Fa would be there! He rode into the yard and jumped from the horse, not bothering to tether it to the rail. Nome burst through the door and squinted around the room. There was a stricken silence among the people gathered, some standing, some seated, men, women, children playing on the floor. Some of them rose from their chairs and moved back; some standing pressed themselves toward the walls. Not a sound, except chairs scraping.

He stared at them wildly. "Mo and Fa...are they here?" he shouted. "It's me! Nome Ogrodni! Where are they? Where is Ravenna? It's me, Nome Ogrodni! You *know* me!"

The face and voice was known to them, but it was a Tosar guard who had rushed in upon them. They were terror-stricken.

"By the Holy Mercy!" screamed Nome, "where are they? Did they not come tonight? Where are Baron and Rena Ogrodni?"

Still, there was paralyzed silence. Then a child's voice: "They stayed home."

"Home?" Nome screeched. "Houda, not at home! Ohhh.... Follow me," he called out to them. "Please come with me. I'm Nome Ogrodni, see?" and he swept off the uniform cap. "Come with me, please, I'm in trouble!" He turned and ran to the door, but paused, and called back into the room, "Branny Lamanson! I'm taking your horse!"

And he was gone.

....

Baron Ogrodni was pacing slowly in the front yard. Rena Ogrodni sat on the porch steps beside her daughter-in-law. Both women had their eyes closed. They sat pressed close together, but each gripped her own hands in her lap. They felt the earth shake under them suddenly, and both opened their eyes. Baron stopped pacing and looked at them. But there was silence, and he returned to his numbness.

From far out on the road they heard an unfamiliar sound...not utterly unfamiliar; Baron and Rena had heard the driving sound of hoof-beats approaching on another night not long ago. All three had eyes wide open now, tense and watching the entrance onto the road. The sound of rapid hooves hammering the earth louder and louder, then the unmistakable clatter of hooves on the river footbridge, and then the black shape of horse and Tosar rider plunging into the yard. The horse was jerked sharply to one side to avoid overrunning Baron, and it reared and neighed shrill and painfully. Rena screamed and seized Ravenna, pulling her up the porch and into the house. She was screaming, "Baron! Baron, run, get away!" But Baron simply stood where he had been pacing. The rider rolled from the horse, lost his footing and sprawled to the ground. The cap rolled from his head. Frantically he clambered to his feet and ran toward the house.

"No, no!" he screamed, "don't go in there! Mo! Ravenna! Come out of there! It's me, Nome!" And he tore the coat from himself and flung it away as he ran.

His father recognized him, and the old man's face lighted with joy. "Nomo!" he cried, and he reached out for his son with both arms. But Nome brushed past him, spinning him around and leaving him bewildered with his arms still extended, facing the house.

Nome bounded up the porch steps and through the front door, shouting, "Ravenna! Mo! Come out of here!" A moment later he reappeared, dragging the two delirious women with him and pulling them forcefully down the steps into the yard. He swept Fa up in their forward movement and pushed the three of them, stumbling, toward the footbridge. They were all weeping and exclaiming and questioning; but he was grim and determined as he pushed them over the bridge and far back from the river bank.

"The horse!" he said and shook himself free of them, ran back into the yard to pull it away from the house toward which it had strolled. "Chindit!" he shouted. "Chindit!" And the dog came trotting out of the house, down the steps, and into the yard. He led horse and dog across the bridge to where his bewildered family huddled.

"Nome! You are alive!"
"Good Mother!"
"Holy! Oh, Holy!"
"Nome, what is it? What's happening?"
"Are you being chased? Are you in trouble?"

He was heaving and gasping for air and throwing his arms around their necks and kissing them and nodding and gasping and pulling all three of them to him in embrace. His mouth worked but he could not speak, and he began to sob.

"Nome, what is it? What on earth is happening?"

"Look!" he gasped, casting his eyes toward the house. He straightened his arm, which rested heavily on Ravenna's shoulder, and pointed. "Watch."

They all looked at the house but saw only the good house with it downstairs front window casting a friendly glow across the yard like a carpet. Suddenly, there was a disturbance behind them, the sound of more horses and people out by the road, now crowding in toward them.

"What?" growled Baron, turning to face whatever was coming.

"No," said Nome, still breathing heavily. "The people. From the Croft. I told them to come...they have to see...this. Just watch. We can't go in there to save anything. Not now."

Ravenna and Rena were hanging onto Nome, searching his sweat-streaked face with imploring looks, but Baron kept his eyes toward the dark road, where he could see the bobbing forms of people approaching from the shadows. Nome's eyes were fixed on the house.

"There!" he whispered. "Now!"

They all turned to follow his gaze, just as the first of their neighbors came cautiously around them asking if they were all right. The carpet of light on the lawn began to dance and quiver. Nothing more happened for a moment. Then a sound of rushing water was heard. Suddenly, there was a sharp, prolonged creaking noise that seemed to tear the air itself and the front porch began to twist and sag like a grimace. It dropped and fell into the ground, and there came a high-pitched screeching and tearing. Windows popped, then a tremendous roar went up, as the entire front wall tore loose from the roof and sides, slid forward, halted momentarily, and dropped from sight. With a greater roar and splintering, the main bulk leaned slowly forward and toppled into a heap. It lasted only moments. The yard was in total darkness; and, except for the sound of flowing water, all was still.

THIRTY

Hite's Dogs

At daybreak, the sun rose upon dozens of people picking around the edge of the ruins of what had been the magnificent house at Brighthome. Many just stood on a new section of river bank looking on in bewilderment.

"I've never seen anything like it."

"No, nor I, but rivers have a mind of their own, I guess. They don't stay put."

"Yes, but the Sula never even flooded! Such a quiet river."

"This house stood here a hundred year. No one knew."

"And it seems the river must have been chewing against this cutting for maybe *hundreds* of years. You'd have thought Baron's dad would have noticed it and not built here."

"No, it was Baron's granddad, Toohy, what built it. They didn't have proper engineers to prospect it in those days. Just saw a beautiful place for a house and built there."

There were timbers lying across the new stream like trees tumbled. The water continued to swirl gently and push debris down toward Tamrasset Lake as though it had done no harm. There was wreckage everywhere about the yard, where the face of the front wall had fallen flat, and on the other side of the new channel, where remnants of fireplace, bedroom, and back pantry still stood exposed to the day from what had been the inside of the home. This part stood precariously on what was now a small island; and the Sula split around it and rejoined, where pieces of the house flooring and furniture continued to break free from time to time to float languidly away north.

....

Soon after midnight, the stricken Ogrodni family had been taken to stay with Willi and Marlis Patoftok at Redapple down near the Croft. Oldman Patoftok, Baron's friend, who had lost his Gamgame holding a year earlier and had been take in by his son, Willi, gave up his own two rooms to them and said he would sleep on the couch that night and as many nights as they needed until better times. After Nome had given the shortest version of what had happened at Tosar's Keep the past two days, everyone agreed that there had to be an emergency meeting of all nearby neighbors at the Croft in the morning.

"*Very* early in the morning," Nome had insisted. "Someone needs to start calling in the people right after sun-up, maybe even before that. We don't have much time."

When his family had been moved to Redapple, someone wondered what should be done with the Tosar's horse, a fine, valuable animal. No one wanted to be found in possession of it. The horse was led up the Grandmaison a short way and turned loose to wander. The Tosars will be up here looking for it, someone had said. Nome had disagreed:

"They will not be up here looking for a horse. I think they will not come here right away, because they do not want to be seen having anything to do with the wrecking of our house. But, once they discover certain things...and it will be very soon...they will come up here in a desperate fury. And all Ogrodnis had better be far away. I think we have a little time, not much. No more than the morning. Then your dad, Willi, can have his rooms and his bed back. We will need them only for the night."

"But, Nome...." Willi and Marlis had objected.

"No, no. We cannot stay. I don't have time to explain. I will say it at the Croft in the morning. But I am not done yet tonight. I have to ask you, Willi, to borrow your horse."

"When, Nome?"

" Now. Tonight. I have to go out again...for an hour or so. There's something I have to do. I have to do it tonight, it won't wait."

"You're not *serious!*" Marlis exclaimed.

"I *have to.* I can't say more. Please, just trust me. I need something from you. I need an hour by myself away from everybody, someplace quiet here in the house. And I need four or five...no, ten...sheets of paper and ink and pen. I have to write some messages...please don't say a word to *anyone* about this...you can tell Ravenna and Baron and Rena, if they are not asleep. Let them know *after* I have gone out with your horse. They will make a fuss, but tell them I will be back soon for a few hours of sleep. If they are sleeping, let them sleep. I will explain it at the Croft in the morning. I *really* need your help and your trust. Willi? Marlis?"

It took Nome nearly two hours to write two letters and another hour to ride back up the road to place them, along with the Tosar uniform and Draman Bonder's draft drawings, in the dropbox. He wrote to the anonymous leaders of the Holderhope network a description of what he had seen and heard inside Tosar's Keep, and asked them to put his second report, together with the evidence that he was leaving in the bin, into the hands of those who would deliver it to Bau Shahn.

The second report he addressed directly to Lop ge Dol, the Nur of Bau Shahn. After a respectful preface stating who Nome Ogrodni was and summarizing his background and experiences in the Outlands, he wrote in much greater detail how he had entered Tosar's Keep, what he had seen and heard in the twenty-four hours he was there, how he had escaped in time to directly witness the fall of Brighthome ordered by The Tosar. He added that the confirming evidence of this would be delivered to him: the Tosar uniform and, most important, the four pages of architectural schematics detailing the plot to destroy the house at Brighthome and documenting a similar further plot against Judges' Rooms. He dated and signed the report: Nome Ogrodni, son of Baron and Rena Ogrodni of Brighthome Holding in Tosarkun.

....

Nome was sleeping soundly at Redapple as people were beginning to gather at the Croft, while Rena and Ravenna were helping Marlis make breakfast for the household. Baron and Oldman Patoftok sat talking on the couch where Oldman had slept during the night. They were discussing the Ogrodnis' plans to flee into the Outlands. While Nome had been writing during the night and then away with the horse to his mystery destination, Marlis and Willi had stayed up pulling clothes and provisions into four backpacks. They slipped in some money, too, since nearly all Nome's and Ravenna's savings from fish packing at Quiet Waters were now floating away to Tamrasset Lake. No doubt, folks at the Croft would be pressing more into their hands that morning.

An hour or so later, the Ogrodni family and the Redapple folks entered the Croft, encountering a larger crowd than they had seen there for years. The place had been buzzing about the night ride of young Ogrodni and the collapse into the river of that wonderful old house and word that the Ogrodnis were going away. Baron and Rena, Nome and Ravenna fended off all the agitated questions and said that all would be told by Nome in a few minutes. They had to get started right away, if people would quiet down and get orderly and get the chairs into a circle, a big circle. Most would have to stand around, there were so many of the neighbors there. The Ogrodni family took four chairs, just inside the front door, while people pulled as many chairs as they could find into rows around them. The older folk were offered these, and the younger sat or stood, filling the hall all the way to the kitchen in the back.

There was no ceremony to the meeting. Nome stood and waited for silence. Without drama, he simply told what had happened to him in the past two days. He said nothing about Holderhope or his meetings with Danny, but began with his going to the Keep two days early to ask for an extension on payment and being put off for five days. He told that he had been locked in, was afraid of being caught and held there and, so, had gone into hiding, planning to find a way to escape. He then described, in general terms, his nighttime exploration of the basement, discovery of many signs of plots and preparation for war. He said he would not give the details publicly, but would entrust the details to proper authority. He declared that what he had seen and heard in the Keep would break open the Tosars' most guarded secrets; and, when they discovered that breach...today, certainly, perhaps even at this very hour...they would turn desperately dangerous. What he had seen and heard in the Keep, he insisted, proved that it was The Tosar who had destroyed Brighthome. This was the first of their secrets, now betrayed; and it would lead to a cascade of other revelations that would change the fate and future of this country. At this point, Nome paused, looked about to weigh the effect of his words, then continued with great urgency

"I *beg* you, now, to be very careful! This is *not* a time for action! It is extremely important that we people of the holdings do not react to the fall of Brighthome or to this dark news that I am telling you. The Tosars have not been around these parts in recent days, for they have been distancing themselves from what they knew would be happening here. And they did not want to be associated with my family's tragedy. But they will soon know...probably know it already up there at The City...that they have *lost* control. That *all* will know they are, not only associated with, but directly responsible for our tragedy, and that they have been planning more of the same elsewhere. So, *please,* my friends, do not provoke them in any way. Do nothing to oppose them. Protect yourselves and your families by obedience and submissiveness, as we have learned to do for years. Watch, wait, remain calm, and do not be afraid. There is great hope afoot, things you do not know. My family and I must leave this morning, within minutes now. We are not safe; our lives would be worth nothing if we stayed. We will go elsewhere into Outlands and make our way. But your lives are safe if you stay quiet. You have reason for *great hope.*

"I cannot say more," Nome added after another pause, "but I have brought something out of the Keep. I had thought to hide it at home for a while and watch for a better moment; but it is a good thing I did not, for home is gone. *It is in a safe place! A very safe place!*"

They were absolutely silent, staring at him. Nome waited tensely, holding his breath, as silent as the folk looking at him. It seemed they wanted him to say more. Then he sensed a small movement at the back, across the room, ever so small. But...but...yes, someone was edging to the side and backward...gliding rather than walking...approaching the kitchen. The kitchen, where there was a back door. He saw her slip out of sight, and he drew a breath like a sob. ('Oh Holy!' he whispered only to himself. 'It's Murchew's daughter!')

"Now we must go, my friends!" he fairly shouted. "It is not safe for us any longer!"

Someone started *The Song of the Croft;* and, as the traditional closing music rose, shakily at first, then rising, the people came forward, all around the four of them with embraces, blessings, thanks, pleas that they be careful. With the crowd pushing them, stumbling toward the door, they all came out into the yard. But Nome broke free and ran out onto the road, looking about to be certain, suddenly elated at what he did *not* see. Murchew's horse was gone.

He could not help himself. Calling up the Grandmaison Road he shouted: "Go, darling, go! *Ride Again, Wold-woman. Ride!*"

....

Willi Patoftok had the wagon waiting for them. He would take them half-way to the border, perhaps a two-hour ride. Farther would not be advisable, neither for them nor for Willi. The Ogrodni family with Chindit would have to proceed from there on foot. They dared not attempt the Tosar guard station at the border and knew they would have to circumvent it.

"This is the time when we are going to have to take the long way around through the spruce bog," Nome said to Ravenna. "It will be rough going, and it looks like we may be doing some of it in the dark. Hopefully, not camping there. Wet and scratchy and mucky walking in there, Mo. Are you up to it?"

"Yes."

Baron said: "We'll stop at Farmer Hite's and ask if he can put us on the best way around the border station. There might even be paths."

"That's pretty close to the border," said Ravenna. "Do we have to worry about the guards coming there?"

"We have to keep watch for it anytime after Willi drops us off." Baron said. "Have to be ready to duck into the woods fast if we have any sighting of Tosars. Get far deep into the woods where they can't go with their horses."

They rode on in silence for a long while. They wanted to continue an earlier discussion they had been having, in interrupted fragments during the night, about where they would go. However, they did not want Willi to hear it now, not because they did not trust him, but because they did not want anyone from back home to know how to find them in case the Tosars should be determined to track them down.

In fact, they themselves did not know where they were going. To 'n Burning Graute, almost certainly, for their first short stay; because, in the Outlands, it was closest to Tosarkun. But they would not likely stay there; too close, probably. They talked about Quiet Waters. Nome and Ravenna had good friends there, and the Seaside House would probably still be available, at least through summer. "And," laughed Ravenna, "we have a lot of pots and pans and other fancy wedding gifts stored in a shed up there!" But the most appealing possibility that they returned to again and again, was The Fields of Khorvan. It was a long way off, a daunting trip for aging Mo and Fa; but family. And, maybe, safety now for Ravenna, returning there with a husband and his parents; and hopefully Druska Paba having perished with the Mommicks on The Plains, and hopefully Mintor Ghan tired of waiting and having moved on to choose a different starwoman. Hopes and dream, of course, but why not? And why not all three places, 'n Burning Graute, which Nome knew well, for a short rest in safety, a longer rest at Quiet Waters, and then the long trek back west along the Sea Road, then down past Trapple Rock to the High Road to the West, and onward to The Fields of Khorvan. To Yuna Urlinda, Ravenna's mother, and dearest Aunie.

Each of them was ruminating on these fantasies, savoring the possibilities, as Willi's wagon rolled along with only the sound of the clopping horses in front and the grating of steel wheels under them. They all came back to attention as the sounds slowed and stopped. Willi was pulling to the side saying, "Well, I think this is it." Almost the first thing he had said since they started.

They all climbed down and pulled out their packs. Chindit jumped down. Willi got down and held out his hands, and they all four took hold, pressing and squeezing, nodding and smiling. Then Willi turned and faced Nome. Nome started to thank him for all his help....

"Thank *you*, Nome. Thank...you, all," insisted Willi. He looked at the others, then, soberly added, "Think you'll ever be back, Nome? Think we'll ever see you back in Tosarkun?"

"I hope, so, Willi. I think so. I think I'll be be seeing you again in Holderkun."

Willi grinned at him broadly, then looked down at the ground shyly. When he looked up again into Nome's eyes, he was still grinning. He turned, climbed onto his wagon, turned the team around, and, waving without looking at them, clopped back the way they had come.

As they walked along, they noticed that the last holdings and farmlands appeared more poorly tended and scattered, and the tamarack and spruce bog took on a wild and overgrown look. Finally the weathered buildings of Hite's Farm came into view on their left, looking ancient and abandoned under noonday sun.

They turned in at the rutted farm road. Baron took the lead, thumping along with his walking stick. Rena, struggling under her pack, hurried to keep up with him. Chindit, ears back, trotted along beside her. Nome and Ravenna, side-by-side, followed behind.

Two large dogs rushed out from Hite's Farm bellering and lunging forward with murderous yowling. The travelers stopped. Wilman Hite, squinting and scowling, ran into the open, holding an axe. His tangled beard, down to his belt, wagged and twitched as he ducked his head down and thrust it forward trying to be ready for whoever was attacking his farm.

Baron Ogrodni took a step forward. "Call off your dogs, Hite!" he shouted. "We need your help!" Not waiting for an answer, he turned and beckoned his family to follow.

Rena looked fearfully at the dogs, then followed her husband. Ravenna and Nome also stepped forward, first looking ahead to where Hite was standing, then glancing sideways apprehensively toward the dogs. But they could see no dogs. They only saw two small, feathered, stony shapes that stood staring at them, unblinking. These turned suddenly and began hobbling and tripping forward beside them to Hite's Farm.

Made in the USA
Middletown, DE
24 May 2015